Praise for *Decider* and Dick Francis . . .

"ONE OF THE MOST RELIABLE MYSTERY WRITERS WORKING TODAY IS DICK FRANCIS, whose prodigious talents are once again on display in *Decider*. Francis's secret weapons are his protagonists. They are the kind of people you want for friends—resourceful, smart, full of integrity, with just enough flaws to be human."
—*Detroit News and Free Press*

"UTTERLY GRIPPING AND DEEPLY THOUGHTFUL, *Decider* is in every way a thoroughbred out of the Dick Francis stable." —*Mostly Murder*

"ANOTHER WINNER . . . Francis's plotting, pacing, and characterization are first-rate, and *Decider* breezes along to a breathless conclusion." —*The Orlando Sentinel*

"TOP-NOTCH." —*Seattle Post-Intelligencer*

"AFTER WRITING DOZENS OF THRILLERS, DICK FRANCIS ALWAYS RETAINS A FIRST-NOVEL FRESHNESS." —*The Indianapolis Star*

"WITH *DECIDER*, DICK FRANCIS HAS DONE IT AGAIN. If you are a Francis fan, you will enjoy his latest. If you have not read any of his books, you have a lot of good reading ahead of you." —*Bookpage*

"A RARE AND MAGICAL TALENT . . . A master of suspense who never writes the same story twice."
—*San Diego Union-Tribune*

"THIS IS NOT A BOOK CONDUCIVE TO A NICE NAP." —*The Houston Post*

continued on next page . . .

"*DECIDER* MOVES AT A QUICK PACE, full of plot twists and likable heroes."   **—*Ft. Lauderdale Sun Sentinel***

"FRANCIS WRITES RACING SCENES THAT EXCEL and his plot moves as fast as the races themselves."
—*Tulsa World*

"THE CHARACTERS ARE GREAT . . . a satisfying conclusion. Hip hip hooray for Dick Francis."
—*Rainbow Electronic Reviews*

"DICK FRANCIS IS BACK doing what he does best . . . good reading."   **—*Newark Star-Ledger***

"*DECIDER* IS PURE FRANCIS: quietly compelling, morally on target and with characters both bent and wonderful. And always, always, the sure knowledge that you're in the hands of a real pro and when you turn the last page, you will regret that you did."   **—*The Detroit News***

"FRANCIS ONCE SAID ALL HE TRIED TO DO was write in a way that kept readers wanting to turn the page. In *Decider*, he succeeds brilliantly."   **—*Chicago Sun-Times***

"DEEPLY SATISFYING . . . Francis's deft plotting and sharp characterization are, as usual, on the mark."
—*Publishers Weekly*

"THE MOST ELABORATE AND SATISFYING OF HIS RECENT BOOKS."   **—*Kirkus Reviews***

DECIDER

DICK FRANCIS

JOVE BOOKS, NEW YORK

This Jove Book contains the complete text of the original hardcover edition. It has been completely reset in a typeface designed for easy reading and was printed from new film.

DECIDER

A Jove Book / published by arrangement with the author

PRINTING HISTORY
G. P. Putnam's Sons edition published October 1993
Jove edition / April 1995

ISBN: 0-515-11617-3

A JOVE BOOK®
Jove Books are published by The Berkley Publishing Group, 200 Madison Avenue, New York, New York 10016. JOVE and the "J" design are trademarks belonging to Jove Publications, Inc.

PRINTED IN THE UNITED STATES OF AMERICA

10 9 8 7 6 5 4 3 2 1

My thanks to my godson

ANDREW HANSON
Dip Arch (Edin) RIBA

and love to my grandchildren

Jocelyn
Matthew
Bianca
Timothy
William

1

O K, SO here I am, Lee Morris, opening doors and windows to gusts of life and early death.

They looked pretty harmless on my doorstep: two middle-aged civil Englishmen in country-gent tweeds and flat caps, their eyebrows in unison raised inquiringly, their shared expression one of embarrassed anxiety.

"Lee Morris?" one of them said, his diction clipped, secure, expensive. "Could we speak to him?"

"Selling insurance?" I asked dryly.

Their embarrassment deepened.

"No, actually . . ."

Late March evening, sun low and strong, gold light falling sideways onto their benign faces, their eyes achingly narrowed against the glare. They stood a pace or two from me, careful not to crowd. Good manners all around.

I realized that I knew one of them by sight, and I spent a few extended seconds wondering why on earth he'd sought me out on a Sunday a long way from his normal habitat.

1

During this pause three small boys padded up the flag-stoned passage from the depths of the house behind me, concentratedly threaded a way around me and out through the pair beyond and silently climbed like cats up into the fuzzy bursting-leaf-bud embrace of an ancient spreading oak nearby on the lawn. There the three figures rested, becoming immobile, lying on their stomachs along the old boughs, half seen, intent, secretive, deep in an espionage game.

The visitors watched in bemusement.

"You'd better come in," I said. "They're expecting pirates."

The man I'd recognized smiled suddenly with delight, then stepped forward as if in decision and held out his hand.

"Roger Gardner," he said, "and this is Oliver Wells. We're from Stratton Park racecourse."

"Yes," I said, and made a gesture for them to follow me into the shadowy passage, which they did, slowly, tentatively, halfblinded by the slanting sun outside.

I led them along the flagstones and into the cavernous room I'd spent six months converting from a rotting barn into a comfortable house. The revitalizing of such ruins was my chief livelihood, but recently the inevitable had finally happened and my family were currently rebelling against moving to yet another building site and were tel-ling me that this house, *this one* was where they wanted to live.

The sunlight fell through tall west-facing windows onto the sheen of universal slate-gray flagstones which were softened here and there by rugs from Turkey. Round the north, south and east sides of the barn now ran a railed gallery bearing a row of bedrooms, with a staircase giving access at either end.

Under the gallery a series of rooms stood open-fronted to the great room, though one could close each off with folding doors for privacy. They offered a book-lined room for watching television, an office, a playroom, a sewing room and a long capacious dining room. A breakfast room in the south-east corner led into a big half-visible kitchen with utilities and a workshop wholly out of sight beyond. The partition walls between the open-fronted rooms, partitions which looked merely like space dividers, were in fact the extremely strong load-bearers of the gallery above.

Furniture in the central atrium consisted chiefly of squashy armchairs scattered in informal groups, with many small tables handy. A fireplace in the western wall glowed red with logs.

The effect I'd aimed for, a dwelling built like a small roofed market square, had come out even better than I'd imagined, and in my own mind (though I hadn't told the family), I had intended all along to keep it, if it was a success.

Roger Gardner and Oliver Wells, as was usual with visitors, came to a halt and looked around in frank surprise, though they seemed too inhibited to comment.

A naked baby appeared, crawling across the flagstones, pausing when he reached a rug, wobbling onto his bottom and looking around, considering things.

"Is that yours?" Roger asked faintly, watching him.

"Very probably," I said.

A young woman in jeans and sweater, fair hair flying, came jogging out of the far part of the kitchen in business-like running shoes.

"Have you seen Jamie?" she demanded from a distance.
I pointed.

She swooped on the baby and gathered him up unceremoniously. "I take my eyes off him for *two seconds . . .*"

She bore him away, delivering a fleeting glance to the visitors, but not stopping, vanishing again from our view.

"Sit down," I invited. "What can I do for you?"

They tentatively sat where I indicated and visibly wondered how to begin.

"Lord Stratton recently died," Roger said eventually. "A month ago."

"Yes, I noticed," I said.

"You sent flowers to the funeral."

"It seemed merely decent," I agreed, nodding.

The two men glanced at each other. Roger spoke.

"Someone told us he was your grandfather."

I said patiently, "No. They got it wrong. My mother was once married to his son. They divorced. My mother then married again, and had me. I'm not actually related to the Strattons."

It was unwelcome news, it seemed. Roger tried again.

"But you do own shares in the racecourse, don't you?"

Ah, I thought. The feud. Since the old man had died, his heirs, reportedly, had been arguing to a point not far from murder.

"I'm not getting involved," I said.

"Look," Roger said with growing desperation. "The heirs are going to *ruin* the racecourse. You can see it a mile off. The rows! Suspicion. Violent hatreds. They set on each other before the old man was even cold."

"It's civil war," Oliver Wells said miserably. "Anarchy. Roger is the manager and I'm the Clerk of the Course, and we are running things ourselves now, trying to keep the place going, but we can't do it much longer. We've no *authority,* do you see?"

I looked at the deep concern on their faces and thought about the difficulty of finding employment of that caliber at fifty-something in the unforgiving job climate.

Lord Stratton, my non-grandfather, had owned three-quarters of the shares in the racecourse and had for years run the place himself as a benevolent despot. Under his hand, at any rate, Stratton Park had earned a reputation as a popular well-run racecourse to which trainers sent their runners in dozens. No Classics, no Gold Cups took place there, but it was accessible and friendly and had a well-laid-out racing circuit. It needed new stands and various face-lifts but old die-hard Stratton had been against change. He appeared genially on television sometimes, an elder conservative statesman consulted by interviewers when the sport lurched into controversy. One knew him well by sight.

Occasionally out of curiosity I'd spent an afternoon on the racecourse, but racing itself had never compulsively beckoned me, nor had my non-grandfather's family.

Roger Gardner hadn't made the journey to give up easily.

"But your *sister* is part of the family," he said.

"Half-sister."

"Well, then."

"Mr. Gardner," I explained, "forty years ago my mother abandoned her infant daughter and walked out. The Stratton family closed ranks behind her. Her name was mud, spelt in capitals. That daughter, my half-sister, doesn't acknowledge my existence. I'm sorry, but nothing I could say or do would carry any weight with any of them."

"Your half-sister's father . . ."

"Particularly," I said, "not with him."

During the ensuing pause while the bad news got chewed and digested a tall fair-headed boy came out of one of the bedrooms on the gallery, skipped down the stairs, waved me a flapping hand and went into the kitchen, to reappear almost at once carrying the baby, now clothed. The boy took the baby upstairs, returned with him to his bedroom and shut the door. Silence fell.

Questions hovered on Roger's face but remained unasked, to my amusement. Roger—Lt. Colonel R. B. Gardner, according to the Stratton Park racecards—would have been a thorough flop as a journalist, but I found his inhibitions restful.

"You were our last hope," Oliver Wells complained, accusingly.

If he hoped to instill guilt, he failed. "What would you expect me to *do?*" I asked reasonably.

"We hoped . . ." Roger began. His voice faded away, then he rallied and manfully tried again. "We *hoped,* do you see, that you might knock some sense into them."

"How?"

"Well, for one thing, you're big."

"Big?" I stared at him. "Are you suggesting I *literally* knock some sense into them?"

It did seem that my appearance had given them instant ideas. It was true that I was tall and physically strong; very useful for building houses. I couldn't swear I'd never found those facts conclusive in swinging an argument. But there were times when to tread softly and shrink one's shoulder-span produced more harmonious results, and I leaned by nature more to the latter course. Lethargic, my wife called me. Too lazy to fight. Too placid. But the ruins got restored and left no trails of rancor in local officials minds, and I'd learned how to get around most planning officers with conciliation and reason.

"I'm not your man," I said.

Roger clutched at straws. "But you do own those shares. Can't you stop the war with those?"

"Is that," I asked, "what you mainly had in mind when you sought me out?"

Roger unhappily nodded. "We don't know where else to turn, do you see?"

"So you thought I might gallop into the arena waving my bits of paper and crying 'enough,' and they would all throw down their prejudices and make peace?"

"It might help," Roger said, straightfaced.

He made me smile. "For one thing," I said, "I own very few shares. They were given to my mother all those years ago as a divorce settlement, and I inherited them when she died. They pay a very small dividend now and then, that's all."

Roger's expression went from bewilderment to shock. "Do you mean," he demanded, "that you haven't heard what they are fighting *about?*"

"I told you, I have had no contact with them." All I knew was what I'd learned from a brief paragraph in *The Times*'s business pages ("Stratton heirs dispute over family racecourse") and some blunter remarks in a tabloid ("Long knives out at Stratton Park").

"I'm afraid you will soon hear from them," Roger said. "One faction of them want to sell off the racecourse to developers. As you know, the course lies just to the northeast of Swindon, in an area that's growing all the time. That town has exploded into a center of industry. All sorts of firms are moving there. It's heaving with new life. The racecourse land is increasing in value all the time. Your few shares might now be worth quite a lot, and they might be worth even more in the future. So some of the Strattons want to sell now, and some want to wait, and some don't want to sell at all, but to go on running the racecourse for racing, and the sell-now lot should have been onto you by now, I would have thought. Anyway, someday soon they'll remember your shares and they'll drag you into the fight whether you like it or not."

He stopped, feeling he'd made his point; and I supposed he had. My sincere desire *not* to be dragged into any fracas looked like being a casualty of "the real world," as one of my sons described all calamities.

"And naturally," I commented, "you are with the faction that wants racing to continue."

"Well, yes," Roger admitted. "Yes, we are. Frankly we hoped to persuade you to vote your shares *against* selling."

"I don't know that my shares even have a vote and there aren't enough of them to sway anything. And how did you know I had any?"

Roger briefly consulted his fingernails and decided on frankness.

"The racecourse is a private limited company, as I expect you know. It has directors and board meetings and the shareholders are informed each year when the annual general meeting is to take place."

I nodded resignedly. The notice came every year and every year I ignored it.

"So last year the secretary who sends out the notice was ill, and Lord Stratton told me just to do it, there's a good chap . . ."—his voice mimicked the old man's splendidly—"so I sent out the notice and it happened that I put the list of names and addresses in a file for the future . . ." He paused, hovering, ". . . in case I had to do it again, do you see?"

"And the future's upon us," I said. I pondered. "Who else owns shares? Did you by any chance bring the list with you?"

I saw from his face both that he had brought it and also that he was unsure of the ethics of passing it over. The threat to his job, though, conquered all, and after the briefest of hesitations he reached into an inner pocket in the tweed jacket and produced a clean once-folded sheet of paper. A fresh copy, by the looks of things.

I opened it and read the ultra-short list. Shorn of addresses it read:

> William Darlington Stratton (3rd Baron).
> Hon. Mrs. Marjorie Binsham.
> Mrs. Perdita Faulds.
> Lee Morris Esq.

"Is that all?" I inquired blankly.

Roger nodded.

Marjorie Binsham was, I knew, the old lord's sister. "Who is Mrs. Perdita Faulds?" I asked.

"I don't know," Roger said.

"So you haven't been to see her? You came here, though?"

Roger didn't answer, but he didn't need to. That sort of ex-soldier felt more at home with other men than with women.

"And" I said, "who inherits the old man's shares?"

"I don't *know,*" Roger answered exasperatedly. "The family aren't saying. They've shut up like clams about the will, and of course it's not open to public inspection before probate, which may be *years* away, at the rate they're going. If I had to guess, I'd say Lord Stratton left them all equal shares. He was fair, in his way. Equal shares would mean that no single one of them has control, and that's the nub of the problem, I'd think."

"Do you know them personally?" I asked, and they both nodded gloomily. "Like that, is it?" I asked. "Well, I'm sorry, but they'll have to sort it out themselves."

The young fair-haired woman strolled out of the kitchen with a glass in one hand and a feeding bottle of milk in the other. She nodded vaguely in our direction and went up the staircase and into the room where the boy had taken the baby. My visitors watched in silence.

A brown-haired boy rode a bicycle up the passage from the front door and made a controlled circuit of the room, slowing slightly as he passed behind me and saying "Yeah, yeah, you told me not to," before returning along the passage towards the outside world. The bicycle was scarlet, the clothes purple and pink and fluorescent green. The very air seemed to quiver with vibrant color, settling back to quiet slate when he'd gone.

Tactfully, no one said anything about obedience or keeping children in order.

I offered the visitors a drink but they had nothing to celebrate and murmured about the length of the drive home. I went with them into the softening sunlight and proffered polite apologies for their non-success. They nodded unhappily. I walked across with them to their car.

The three pirate-ambushers had dematerialized from the oak. The scarlet bicycle flashed in the distance. My visitors looked back at the long dark bulk of the barn, and Roger finally came out with a question.

"What an interesting house," he said civilly. "How did you find it?"

"I built it. The interior, that is. Not the barn itself, of course. That's old. A listed building. I had to negotiate to be allowed windows."

They looked at the neat dark oblongs of glass set unobtrusively into the timber cladding, the only outward indication of the dwelling within.

"You had a good architect," Roger commented.

"Thank you."

"That's another thing the Strattons are fighting over. Some of them want to tear down the stands and rebuild, and they've engaged an architect to draw up plans."

His voice was thick with disgust.

I said curiously, "Surely new stands would be a good thing? Crowd comfort, and all that?"

"Of course new stands would be good!" Irritation finally swamped him. "I implored the old man for years to rebuild. He always said, yes, one day, one day, but he never meant to, not in his lifetime, and now his son Conrad, the new Lord Stratton, he's invited this dreadful man to design new stands, and he's been striding about the place telling me we need this and we need that, and it's all rubbish. He's never designed stands of any sort before and he knows bugger-all about racing."

His genuine indignation interested me a lot more than a fight about shares.

"Building the wrong stands would bankrupt everybody," I said thoughtfully.

Roger nodded. "They'll have to borrow the money, and racing people are fickle. The punters stay away if you don't get the bars right, and if the owners and trainers aren't pampered and comfortable, the buggers will run their horses somewhere else. This lunatic of an architect looked totally blank when I asked him what he thought the crowds did between races. Look at the horses, he said. I ask you! And if it's raining? Shelter and booze, I told him, that's what brings in the customers. He told me I was old-fashioned. And Stratton Park will get a horrendously expensive white elephant that the public will shun. And, like you said, the place will go bust."

"Only if the sell-now or sell-later factions don't get their way."

"But we *need* new stands," Roger insisted. "We need *good* new stands." He paused. "Who designed your house? Perhaps we need someone like *him.*"

"He's never designed any stands. Only houses . . . and pubs."

"Pubs." Roger pounced on it. "At least he'd understand the importance of good bars."

I smiled. "I'm sure he would. But you need big-building specialists. Engineers. Your own input. A team."

"Tell that to Conrad." He shrugged dejectedly and slid behind his steering wheel, winding down the window and peering out for one more question. "Could I possibly ask you to let me know if or when the Stratton family contact you? I probably shouldn't trouble you, but I *care* about the racecourse, you see. I know the old man believed it would carry on as before, and he wanted it that way, and perhaps there's something I can do, but I don't know *what,* do you see."

He reached into his jacket again and produced a business card. I took it and nodded, making no promise one way or another, but he took the acknowledgment as assent.

"Thank you very much," he said.

Oliver Wells sat impassively beside him, showing his certainty that their mission had been, as he'd all along expected, unproductive. He still failed to raise guilt in me. Everything I knew of the Strattons urged me strongly to stay away from them in every way I could.

Roger Gardner gave me a sad farewell and drove off, and I went back into my house hoping I wouldn't see him again.

"WHO WERE THOSE people?" Amanda said. "What did they want?"

The fair-haired woman, my wife, lay at the far side of our seven-foot-square bed, emphasizing as usual the distance between us.

"They wanted a white knight act on Stratton Park racecourse."

She worked it out. "A rescue job? You? Those old

shares of yours? I hope you said no."

"I said no."

"Is that why you're lying there wide awake in the moonlight, staring at the canopy?"

The pleated silk canopy roofed our great four-poster like a medieval sleeping tent, the only way to achieve privacy in those days before separate bedrooms. The theatrical glamour of the tester, the tassels and the bed's cozy promise beguiled friends: only Amanda and I understood the significance of its size. It had taken me two days of carpentry and stitching to construct, and it was understood by both of us to be a manifestation of a hard-won compromise. We would live in the same house, and also in the same bed, but apart.

"The boys start their Easter holiday this week," Amanda said.

"Do they?"

"You said you'd take them somewhere for Easter."

"Did I?"

"You know you did."

I'd said it to defuse an argument. Never make rash promises, I told myself. An incurable failing.

"I'll think of something," I said.

"And about this house . . ."

"If you like it, we'll stay here," I said.

"Lee!" It briefly silenced her. I knew she had a thousand persuasions ready: the scattered hints and sighs had been unmistakable for weeks, ever since the gravel had been laid in the drive and the building inspector had called for the last time. The house was freehold, finished and ready for sale, and we needed the money. Half my working capital lay cemented into its walls.

"The boys need a more settled existence," Amanda said, not wanting to waste her reasons.

"Yes."

"It's not fair to keep dragging them from school to school."

"No."

"They worry about leaving here."

"Tell them not to."

"I can't believe it! Can we afford it? I thought you'd say you couldn't afford it. What about the mansion near Oxford, with the tree growing in the drawing room?"

"With luck I'll get planning permission this week."

"But we're not going there, are we?" Despite my assurance, her anxiety rose sharply.

"I'll go there," I said. "You and the boys will stay here for as long as you want. For years. I'll commute."

"You *promise.*"

"Yes."

"No more *mud?* No more *mess?* No more tarpaulins for roofs and brick dust in the cornflakes?"

"No."

"What made you decide?"

The mechanics of decision, I thought, were mysterious. I could have said it was indeed because it was time to settle down for the children's sake, that the eldest had reached the examination time zone and needed continuity in teaching. I could have said that this area, the smiling countryside on the Surrey-Sussex border, was as wholesome as anywhere nowadays. I could have made the decision sound eminently logical.

Instead, I knew in my private mind that the decider had been the old oak. It had appealed to me powerfully, to the inner boy who had been brought up in London traffic, surrounded by landscapes of stone.

I'd seen the oak first a year earlier, fuzzy then as now with the promise of leaf. Mature, perfect, its boughs invited climbers, and as I'd gone there alone I climbed it without embarrassment, sitting at home in its ancient embrace, looking at the rotting great eyesore of a barn that the hard-up landowner had been forbidden to demolish. A historic tithe barn! A local landmark! It would have to stay there until it actually fell down.

A lot of crap, I'd thought, descending from the tree and walking into the ruin through a creaking gap doing duty as a doorway. History-worship gone mad.

Parts of the roof far above were missing. Along the west side the timbers all leaned drunkenly at wild angles, their supports wholly weathered away. A rusted abandoned tractor and heaps of other assorted junk lay among saplings struggling up from the cracked concrete floor. A stiff breeze blew through the tangled desolation, unfriendly and cold.

I'd seen almost at once what could be built within there, almost as if the design had been hovering for a long time in my mind, awaiting life. It would be a house for children. Not necessarily for my own children, but for any. For the child I'd been. A house with many rooms, with surprises, with hiding places.

The boys had hated the place at first and Amanda, heavily pregnant, had burst into tears, but the local planners had been helpful and the landowner had sold me the barn with a surrounding acre of land as if he couldn't believe his luck. When each son found he would be having a separate bedroom as a domain all his own, the objections miraculously ceased.

I'd brought in a conservationist to check the oak. A superb old specimen, he'd said. Three hundred years in the growing. It would outlive us all, he said; and its timeless strength seemed to give me peace.

Amanda repeated, "What made you decide?"

I said, "The oak."

"What?"

"Common sense," I said, which satisfied her.

ON WEDNESDAY I received two direction-changing letters. The first, from an Oxford District Council, turned down my third application for planning permission for restoring the mansion with the beech tree growing in its drawing room. I telephoned to discover why, as I'd understood the third plan had met with their unofficial approval. They now were of the opinion, a repressive voice told me, that the mansion should be restored as one dwelling, not divided into four smaller houses, as I'd suggested. Perhaps I would care to submit revised plans. Sorry, I said. Forget it. I phoned the mansion's owner to say I was no longer a potential buyer, sending him into predictable orbital rage: but no planning permission, no sale, had been our firm agreement.

Sighing, I disconnected and dropped three months' work into the wastepaper basket. Back, literally, to the drawing board.

The second letter came from the lawyers acting for the Stratton family, inviting me to a Stratton Park shareholders' extraordinary meeting the following week.

I phoned the lawyers. "Do they expect me to go?" I asked.

"I don't know, Mr. Morris. But as you are a shareholder, they were required to alert you to the meeting."

"What do you think?"

"Entirely your decision, Mr. Morris."

The voice was cautious and noncommittal, no help at all.

I asked if I held voting shares.

"Yes, you do. Each share has one vote."

* * *

ON FRIDAY I did the end-of-term school run, collecting the boys for their Easter break: Christopher, Toby, Edward, Alan and Neil.

What, they wanted to know, had I planned for their holidays?

"Tomorrow," I said calmly, "we go to the races."

"Motor?" Christopher asked hopefully.

"Horses."

They made vomiting noises.

"And next week . . . a ruin hunt," I said.

Deafening disapproval lasted all the way home.

"If I don't find another nice ramshackle ruin, we'll have to sell this house after all," I said, pulling up outside. "Take your pick."

Sobered, they grumbled, "Why can't you get a *proper* job?" which I took as it was meant, resigned acceptance of the program ahead. I'd always told them where the money came from for food and clothes and bicycles and because they'd suffered no serious shortage they had inexhaustible faith in ruins, and were apt to point them out to me unprompted.

Since the thumbs-down letter on the mansion I'd checked through the files of replies I'd had to an advertisement I'd run in the *Spectator* three months earlier—"Wanted, an uninhabitable building. Anything from castle to cowshed considered"—and had inquired of several interesting propositions to see if any were still available. As, owing to a recent severe slump in property prices, it seemed they all were, I promised an inspection and made a list.

I hardly admitted to myself that the uninhabitable buildings niggling away on the fringes of my mind were the grandstands at Stratton Park.

Only I knew the debt I owed to the third baron.

2

I T RAINED on Stratton Park's steeplechase meeting, but
my five elder sons—Christopher, fourteen, to Neil,
seven—grumbled not so much about the weather as about
having to wear tidy, unobtrusive clothing on a Saturday.
Toby, twelve, the rider of the red bicycle, had tried to avoid
the trip altogether, but Amanda had packed him firmly
into the mini-van with the others, providing a picnic of
Coca-Cola and ham omlettes in burger buns, which we
dealt with in the parking lot on arrival.

"OK, ground rules," I said, collecting the wrappings into
a single bag. "First, no running about and banging into
people. Second, Christopher looks after Alan, Toby takes
Edward, Neil goes with me. Third, when we've chosen a
rallying point, everyone turns up there immediately after
each race."

They nodded. The family crowd control measures were
long established and well-understood. The regular head
counts reassured them rather than irked.

"Fourth," I went on, "you don't walk behind horses as

they're apt to kick, and fifth, notwithstanding the classless society, you'll get on very well on a racecourse if you call every man 'sir.' "

"Sir, sir," Alan said, grinning, "I want to pee, sir."

I trooped them in through the gates and acquired Club enclosure tickets all round. The white cardboard badges fluttered on cords from the sliders of the zips on five blue-hooded anoraks. The five young faces looked serious and well-intentioned, even Toby's, and I went through a rare moment of being both fond and proud of my children.

The rallying point was established under shelter not far from the winner's unsaddling enclosure and within sight of the men's room. We then went all together through the entrance gate into the Club itself and round to the front of the stands and, once I was sure they all had the hang of the whereabouts, I let the paired elder ones go off on their own. Neil, brainy but timid when not in a crowd of brothers, slid his hand quietly into mine and left it there as if absentmindedly, transferring his hold to my trousers occasionally but running no risk of getting lost.

For Neil, as for imaginative Edward, getting lost was the ultimate nightmare. For Alan, it was a laughing matter; for Toby, an objective. Christopher, self-contained, never lost his bearings and habitually found his parents, rather than vice versa.

Neil, easy child, made no objection to walking around in the stands instead of going to see the horses currently plodding wetly round the parade ring before the first race. ("What are the stands, Dad?" "All those buildings.") Neil's agile little brain soaked up vocabulary and impressions like a sponge, and I'd grown accustomed to hearing observations from him that I would hardly have expected from adults.

We popped our heads into a bar that in spite of the

rain was uncrowded, and Neil, wrinkling his nose, said he didn't like the smell in there.

"It's beer," I said.

"No, it smells like that pub we lived in before the barn, like it smelled when we first went there, before you changed it."

I looked down at him thoughtfully. I'd reconstructed an ancient unsuccessful and dying inn and turned its sporadic trade into a flood. There had been many factors— reorganized ground plan, colors, lighting, air management, parking. I'd deliberately *added* smells, chiefly of bread baking, but I didn't know what I'd taken away, beyond stale beer and old smoke.

"What smell?" I asked.

Neil bent his knees and put his face near the floor. "It's that horrid cleaning stuff in the water the pub man used to wash his lino tiles with, before you took them all up."

"Really?"

Neil straightened. "Can we go out of here?" he asked.

We left hand in hand. "Do you know what ammonia is?" I said.

"You put it down drains," he explained.

"Was it that smell?"

He thought it over. "Like ammonia but with scent in it."

"Disgusting," I said.

"Absolutely."

I smiled. Apart from the wondrous moment of Christopher's birth I'd never been a good man for babies, but once the growing and emerging minds had begun expressing thoughts and opinions all their own, I'd been continually entranced.

We watched the first race, with my lifting Neil up so that he could see the bright action over the hurdles.

One of the jockeys, I noticed in the racecard, was named Rebecca Stratton, and after the race, when the horses returned to be unsaddled (R. Stratton unplaced), we happened to pass by while she was looping girths round her saddle and speaking over her shoulder to downcast owners before setting off back to the changing rooms.

"He moved like a torpid stumblebum. Might try him in blinkers next time."

She was tall with a flat body and a thin scrubbed face with high hard cheekbones, no compromise with femininity in sight. She walked not in a heel-down scurry like the male jockeys but in a sort of feline loping strut on her toes, as if she were not only aware of her own power but aroused by it.

"What's a torpid stumblebum?" Neil asked, after she'd gone.

"It means slow and clumsy."

"Oh."

We met the others at the rallying point and I issued popcorn money all round.

"Horse racing is boring," Toby said.

"If you can pick a winner I'll pay you Tote odds," I said.

"What about me?" Alan said.

"Everyone."

Brightening, they went off to look at the next race's runners in the parade ring, with Christopher explaining to them how to read the form lines in the racecard. Neil, staying close to me, said without hesitation that he would choose number seven.

"Why seven, then?" I asked, looking it up. "It's never won a race in its life."

"My peg in the cloakroom at school is number seven."

"I see. Well, number seven is called Clever Clogs."

Neil beamed.

The other four returned with their choices. Christopher had picked the form horse, the favorite. Alan had singled out Jugaloo because he liked its name. Edward chose a no-hoper because it looked sad and needed encouragement. Toby's vote went to Tough Nut because it had been "kicking and bucking in the ring and winding people up."

They all wanted to know my own choice, and I ran a fast eye over the list and said randomly, "Grandfather," and then wondered at the mind's subliminal tricks and thought it perhaps not so random after all.

Slightly to my relief, Toby's Tough Nut not only won the race but had enough energy left for a couple of vicious kicks in the unsaddling enclosure. Toby's boredom turned to active interest and, as often happened, the rest responded to his mood. The rain stopped. The afternoon definitely improved.

I took them all down the course later to watch the fourth race, a three-mile steeplechase, from beside one of those difficult jumps, an open ditch. This one, the second to last fence on the circuit, was attended by a racecourse employee looking damp in an orange fluorescent jacket, and by a St. John's Ambulance volunteer whose job it was to give first aid to any jockeys who fell at his feet. A small crowd of about thirty racegoers had made the trek down there besides ourselves, spreading out behind the inside rails of the track, both on the take-off and the landing sides of the fence.

The ditch itself—in steeplechasing's past history a real drainage ditch with water in it—was in modern times, as at Stratton Park, no real ditch at all but a space about four feet wide on the take-off side of the fence. There was a large pole across the course on the approach side to give an eye-line to the horses, to tell them when to jump, and the fence itself, of dark birch twigs, was four feet six inches high and at least a couple of feet thick: all in all a regular jump presenting few surprises to experienced 'chasers.

Although the boys had seen a good deal of racing on television I'd never taken them to an actual meeting before, still less down to where the rough action filled the senses. When the ten-strong field poured over the fence on the first of the race's two circuits, the earth quivered under the thudding hooves, the black birch crackled as the half-ton 'chasers crashed through the twigs, the air parted before the straining bunch risking life and limb off the ground at thirty miles an hour: the noise stunned the ears, the jockeys' voices cursed, the colored shirts flashed by kaleidoscopically . . . and suddenly they were gone, their backs receding, silence returning, the brief violent movement over, the vigor and striving a memory.

"Wow!" Toby said, awestruck. "You didn't say it was like *that.*"

"It's only like that when you're close to it," I said.

"But it must be always like that for the jockeys," Edward said thoughtfully. "I mean, they take the noise with them all the way." Edward, ten, had led the pirate ambush up the oak. Misleadingly quiet, it was always he who wondered what it would be like to be a mushroom, who talked to invisible friends, who worried most about famine-struck children. Edward invented make-believe games for his brothers and read books and lived an intense inner life, as reserved as Alan, nine, was outgoing and ebullient.

The racecourse employee walked along the fence on the landing side, putting back into place with a short-handled paddle all the dislodged chunks of birch, making the obstacle look tidy again before the second onslaught.

The five boys waited impatiently while the runners continued round the circuit and came back towards the open ditch for the second and last time before racing away to the last fence and the sprint to the winning post. Each boy had picked his choice of winner and had registered it with me, and when people around us began yelling for their fancy the boys yelled also, Neil jumping up and down in excitement and screaming, "Come on seven, come on seven, come on *peg.*"

I had put my own trust on Rebecca Stratton who was this time partnering a gray mare called Carnival Joy, and as they neared the fence she seemed to be lying second, to my mild surprise, my own expertise at picking winners being zero.

At the last minute the horse in front of her wavered out of a straight line, and I glimpsed the strain on the jockey's face as he hauled on a rein to get himself out of trouble, but he was meeting the fence all wrong. His mount took off a stride too soon and landed right in the space between take-off pole and fence, where, frightened, it dumped its jockey and veered across into the path not only of Carnival Joy, but of all the runners behind.

Things happen fast at thirty miles an hour. Carnival Joy, unable to see a clear path ahead, attempted to jump both the fence *and* the horse on the take-off side, a near-impossible task. The gray's hooves caught the loose horse so that its whole weight crashed chest-first into the fence. Its jockey willy-nilly flew catapulting out forwards over the birch and in a flurry of arms and legs thudded onto the turf. Carnival Joy fell over the fence onto its head, somersaulted, came down on its side and lay there winded, lethally kicking in an attempt to get up.

The rest of the field, some trying to stop, some unaware of the melee, some trying to go round it, compounded the debacle like cars crashing in a fog. One of the horses, going too fast, too late, with no chance of safety, took what must have seemed to him a possible way out and tried to jump right off the course through the nearside wing.

Wings, on the take-off side of each fence, were located there precisely to stop horses running out at the last moment and, to be effective, needed to be too high to jump. Trying to escape trouble by jumping the wings was therefore always a disaster, though not so bad as in the old days when all wings had been made of wood, which splintered and ripped into flesh. Wings at Stratton Park, conforming to the current norm, were made of plastic, which bent and gave way without injuring, but this particular horse, having crashed through unscathed, then collided with the bunch of onlookers, who had tried to scatter too late.

One minute, a smooth race. In five seconds, carnage. I was peripherally aware that three more horses had come to grief on the landing side of the fence with their jockeys either unconscious or sitting up cursing, but I had eyes only for the knocked-down clutch of spectators and chiefly, and I confess frantically, I was counting young figures in blue anoraks, and feeling almost sick with relief to find them all upright and unscathed. The horror on their faces I could deal with later.

Alan, born seemingly without an understanding of danger, suddenly darted out onto the course, ducking under the rails, intent on helping the fallen jockeys.

I yelled at him urgently to come back, but there was too much noise all around us and, powerfully aware of all the loose horses charging about in scared bewilderment, I bent under the rails myself and hurried to retrieve him. Neil, little Neil, scrambled after me.

Terrified for him also, I hoisted him up and ran to fetch Alan who, seemingly oblivious to Carnival Joy's thrashing legs, was doing his best to help a dazed Rebecca Stratton to her feet. In something near despair I found that Christopher too was out on the course, coming to her aid.

Rebecca Stratton returned to full consciousness, brushed crossly at the small hands stretched to help her and in a sharp voice said to no one in particular, "Get these brats out of my way. I've enough to contend with without that."

She stood up furiously, stalked over to the jockey whose mount had caused the whole pile-up and who was now standing forlornly beside the fence, and uttered loud and uncomplimentary opinions about his lack of horsemanship. Her hands clenched and unclenched as if, given half a chance, she would hit him.

My brats predictably detested her immediately. I hustled them with their wounded feelings off the course and out of further trouble, but as we passed near to the lady jockey Neil said, suddenly and distinctly, "Torpid stumblebum."

"What?" Rebecca's head snapped round, but I'd whirled my small son hastily away from her and she seemed more disconcerted than actively directing fire at anyone except the other unfortunate rider.

Toby and Edward, impervious to her, were more concerned with the mown-down spectators, two of whom looked badly hurt. People were in tears, people were stunned, people were awakening to anger. Somewhere in the distance, people were cheering. One of the few horses that had side-stepped the calamity had gone on to win the race.

As on most racecourses, the runners had been followed all the way round by an ambulance driven along on a narrow private roadway on the inner side of the track, so that help was at hand. The racecourse official had unfurled and urgently waved two flags, one red and white, one orange, signaling to the doctor and the vet sitting in a car out in the middle of the course that they were both needed at once.

I collected the boys together and we stood in a group watching the ambulance men and the doctor, in an identifying arm band, kneeling beside the fallen, fetching stretchers, conferring, dealing as best they could with broken bones and blood and worse. It was too late to worry about what the boys were seeing: they resisted my suggestion that we should go back to the stands, so we remained with most of the spectators already there, and were joined by the steady stream of new spectators ghoulishly attracted down the course by chaos and disaster.

The ambulance drove off slowly with the two racegoers who'd been felled by the crash through the wing. "The horse jumped on one man's face," Toby told me matter-of-factly. "I think he's dead."

"Shut up," Edward protested.

"It's the real world," Toby said.

One of the horses couldn't be saved. Screens were erected round him, which they hadn't been for the kicked-in-the-face man.

Two cars and a second ambulance swept up fast from the direction of the stands and out leapt another doctor, another vet, and racecourse authority in the shape of the Clerk of the Course, Oliver Wells, one of my visitors from Sunday. Hurrying from clump to clump, Oliver checked with the doctors, checked with the vets behind the screens, checked with the first-aid men tending a flat-out jockey, listened to a horse-battered spectator sitting on the ground with his head between his knees and finally paid attention to Rebecca Stratton, whose brief spell of daze was still resulting in hyperactivity and a het-up stream of complaints.

"Pay *attention*, Oliver." Her voice rose imperiously. "This little shit caused the whole thing. I'm reporting him to the Stewards. Careless riding! A fine. Suspension, at least."

Oliver Wells merely nodded and went to have a word with one of the doctors, who looked across at Rebecca and, leaving his unconscious patient, attempted to feel the all-too-conscious lady's pulse.

She pulled her wrist away brusquely. "I'm perfectly all right," she insisted. "You stupid little man."

The doctor narrowed his eyes at her and took his skills elsewhere, and across Oliver Wells's bony features flitted an expression that could only be described as glee.

He caught me looking at him before he'd rearranged his expression, and changed the direction of his thoughts with a jolt.

"Lee Morris," he exclaimed, "isn't it?" He looked at the children. "What are they all doing here?"

"Day at the races," I said dryly.

"I mean . . ." He glanced at his watch and at the clearing up going on around us. "When you go back up the course, will you call in at my office before you go home. It's right beside the weighing room. Er . . . *please?*"

"OK," I agreed easily. "If you like."

"Great." He gave me a half-puzzled final glance and dived back into his duties and, with things improving on the turf and slowly losing their first intense drama, the five boys at length unglued their feet and their eyes and walked back with me towards the stands.

"That man came to our house last Sunday," Toby told me. "He's got a long nose and sticking-out ears."

"So he has."

"The sun was making shadows of them."

Children were observant in an uncomplicated way. I'd been too concerned with why the man was there to notice the shadows on his face.

"He's the man who mostly organizes the races here," I said. "He runs things on race days. He's called the Clerk of the Course."

"A sort of field marshal?"

"Quite like that."

"I'm hungry," Alan said, quickly bored.

Neil said "Torpid stumblebum" twice, as if the words themselves pleased his lips.

"What are you talking about?" Christopher demanded, and I explained.

"We were only trying to help her," he protested. "She's a cow."

"Cows are nice," Alan said.

By the time we reached the stands the fifth race, over hurdles, was already being run, but none of my five much cared about the result, not having had a chance to pick their fancy.

No one had won on the fourth race. Everyone's hopes had ended at the ditch. Edward's choice was the horse that died.

I gave them all tea in the tea-room: ruinously expensive but a necessary antidote to shock. Toby drowned his brush with the real world in four cups of hot sweet milky pick-you-up and every cake he could cajole from the waitress.

They ate through the sixth race. They all went to the men's room. The crowds were pouring homewards out of the gates when we made our way to the Clerk of the Course's office beside the weighing room.

The boys entered quietly behind me, unusually subdued and giving a misleading impression of habitual good behavior. Oliver Wells, sitting at a busy-looking desk, eyed the children vaguely and went on speaking into a walkie-talkie. Roger Gardner, racecourse manager, was also in attendance, sitting with one hip on the desk, one foot swinging. The Colonel's worry-level had if anything intensified during the week, lines having deepened across his forehead. Civilized habits of behavior would see him through, though, I thought, even if he rose to full height at our entrance looking as if he had expected Lee Morris but not five smaller clones.

"Come in," Oliver said, putting down his instrument. "Now, what shall we do with these boys?" The question seemed to be merely rhetorical as he had recourse again to his walkie-talkie, pressing buttons. "Jenkins? To my office, please." He switched off again. "Jenkins will see to them."

An official knocked briefly on an inner door and came in without waiting for a summons: a middle-aged messenger in a belted navy raincoat, with a slightly stodgy expression and slow-moving reassuring bulk.

"Jenkins," Oliver said, "take these boys into the jockeys' changing rooms and let them collect autographs."

"Won't they be a nuisance?" I asked, as parents do.

"Jockeys are quite good with children," Oliver said, making shooing motions to my sons. "Go with Jenkins, boys, I want to talk to your father."

"Take them, Christopher," I encouraged, and all five of them went cheerfully with the safe escort.

"Sit down," Oliver invited, and I pulled up a chair and sat round the desk with the two of them. "We're not going to get five minutes without interruptions," Oliver said, "so we'll come straight to the point." The walkie-talkie crackled. Oliver picked it up, pressed a switch and listened.

A voice said brusquely. "Oliver, get up here, pronto. The sponsors want a word."

Oliver said reasonably, "I'm writing my report of the fourth race."

"Now, Oliver." The domineering voice switched itself off, severing argument.

Oliver groaned. "Mr. Morris . . . Can you wait?" He rose and departed, whether I could wait or not.

"That," Roger explained neutrally, "was a summons from Conrad Darlington Stratton, the fourth baron."

I made no comment.

"Things have changed since we saw you on Sunday," Roger said. "For the worse, if possible. I wanted to go and see you again, but Oliver thought it was useless. And now . . . well, here you are! Why are you here?"

"Curiosity. But with what the boys saw at that fence today, I shouldn't have come."

"Terrible mix-up." He nodded. "A horse killed. It does racing no good."

"What about the spectators? My son Toby thought one of them, too, was dead."

Roger said disgustedly, "A hundred dead spectators wouldn't raise marches against cruel sports. The stands could collapse and kill a hundred, but racing would go on. Dead *people* are irrelevant, don't you know."

"So . . . the man *was* dead?"

"Did you see him?"

"Only with a dressing covering his face."

Roger said gloomily, "It'll be in the papers. The horse came through the wing into him and slashed him across the eyes with a foreleg—those racing plates on their hooves cut like swords—it was gruesome, Oliver said. But the man died of a snapped neck. Died instantly under half a ton of horse. Best that can be said."

"My son Toby saw the man's face," I said.

Roger looked at me. "Which is Toby?"

"The second one. He's twelve. The boy who rode his bike into the house."

"I remember. Poor little bugger. Nightmares ahead, I shouldn't wonder."

Toby was anyway the one I most worried about, and this wouldn't help. He'd been born rebellious, grown into a cantankerous toddler and had never since been easy to persuade. I had a sad feeling that in four years' time he would develop, despite my best efforts, into a sullen world-hating youth, alienated and miserable. I could sense that it would happen and I ached for it not to, but I'd seen too many other suffering families where a much-loved son or daughter had grown destructively angry in the mid-teens, despising attempts to help.

Rebecca Stratton, I surmised, might have been like that, ten years earlier. She came into Oliver's office now like a whirlwind, smashing the door open until it hit the wall, bringing in with her a swirl of cold outside air and a towering attack of fury.

"Where's that bloody Oliver?" she loudly demanded, looking round.

"With your father . . ."

She didn't listen. She still wore breeches and boots, but with a tan sweater in place of her racing colors. Her eyes glittered, her body looked rigid, she seemed half-way demented. "Do you know what that stupid bloody doctor's done? He's stood me down from racing for *four* days. Four days! I ask you. He says I'm concussed. Concussed, my arse. Where's Oliver? He's got to tell that bloody man I'm going to ride on Monday. Where is he?"

Rebecca spun on her heel and strode out with the same energy expenditure as on the way in.

I said, closing the door after her, "She's concussed to high heaven, I'd have said."

"Yes, but she's always a bit like that. If I were the doctor I'd stand her down for life."

"She's not your favorite Stratton, I gather."

Caution returned to Roger with a rush. "I never said . . ."

"Of course not." I paused. "So what has changed since last Sunday?"

He consulted the light cream walls, the framed print of Arkle, the big calendar with days crossed off, a large clock (accurate) and his own shoes, and finally said, "Mrs. Binsham came out of the woodwork."

"Is that so momentous?"

"You know who she *is?*" He was curious, a little surprised.

"The old lord's sister."

"I thought you didn't know anything about the family."

"I said I had no contact with them, and I don't. But my mother talked about them. Like I told you, she was once married to the old man's son."

"Do you mean Conrad? Or Keith? Or . . . Ivan?"

"Keith," I said. "Conrad's twin."

"Fraternal twins," Roger said. "The younger one."

I agreed. "Twenty-five minutes younger, and apparently never got over it."

"It does make a difference, I suppose."

It made the difference between inheriting a barony, and not. Inheriting the family mansion, and not. Inheriting a fortune, and not. Keith's jealousy of his twenty-five-minute-elder brother had been one—but only one, according to my mother—of the habitual rancors poisoning her ex-husband's psyche.

I had my mother's photographs of her Stratton wedding day, the bridegroom tall, light-haired, smiling, strikingly good-looking, all the promise of a splendid life ahead in the pride and tenderness of his manner towards her. She had that day been exploding with bliss, she'd told me; with an indescribable floating feeling of happiness.

Within six months he'd broken her arm in a fight and punched out two of her front teeth.

"Mrs. Binsham," Roger Gardner said, "has insisted on a shareholders' meeting next week. She's a dragon, they say. She's Conrad's aunt, of course, and apparently she's the only living creature who makes him quake."

Forty years back she had implacably forced her brother, the third baron, to behave harshly in public to my mother. Even then Mrs. Binsham had been the dynamo of the family, the manipulator, the one who laid down the program of action and forced the rest to follow.

"She never gave up," my mother said. "She would simply wear down any opposition until you would do what she wanted just to get some peace. In her own eyes, you see, she was always *right,* so she was always certain that what she wanted was *best.*"

I asked Roger, "Do you know Mrs. Binsham yourself?"

"Yes, but not well. She's an impressive old lady, very upright. She comes to the races here quite often with Lord Stratton—er, not Conrad, but the old lord—but I've never had any really private conversations with her. Oliver knows her better. Or at least," he faintly grinned, "Oliver has obeyed her instructions from time to time."

"Perhaps she'll sort out the present squabbles and quiet things down," I said.

Roger shook his head. "What she says might go with Conrad and Keith and Ivan, but the younger generation may rebel, especially since they're all coming into some shares of their own."

"You're sure?"

"Certain."

"So now you have an informant in the nest?"

His face grew still; wary almost. "I never said that."

"No."

Oliver returned. "The sponsors are unhappy about the dead horse, bless their little hearts. Bad publicity. Not what they pay for. They'll have to reconsider before next year, they say." He sounded dispirited. "I'd framed that race well, you know," he told me. "Ten runners in a three-mile 'chase. That's good, you know. Often you'll only attract five or six, or even less. If the sponsor pulls out, it'll be a poorer affair altogether, next year."

I made sympathetic noises.

"If there *is* a next year," he said. "There's a share-holders' meeting next week . . . did they tell you?"

"Yes."

"They're holding it here on the racecourse, in the Strattons' private dining room," he said. "Conrad hasn't moved into the big house yet, and anyway this is less personal, he says. Will you be coming?" It was less a question, I thought, than an entreaty.

"I haven't decided," I said.

"I do hope you will. I mean, they need an *outside* view, do you see? They're all too *involved.*"

"They wouldn't want me there."

"All the more reason for going."

I doubted that, but didn't bother to argue. I suggested collecting the boys, and found them "helping" the valets pack the jockeys' saddles and other gear into large laundry hampers while eating fruitcake.

They'd been no trouble, I was told, and hoped I could believe it. I thanked everyone. Thanked Roger. "Vote your shares," he said anxiously. Thanked Jenkins. "Well-behaved little sods," he said helpfully. "Bring them again."

"We called everyone 'sir,' " Neil confided to me as we left.

"We called Jenkins 'sir,' " Alan said. "He got us the cake."

We reached the mini-van and climbed in, and they showed me all the jockeys' autographs in their racecards. They'd had a good time in the changing room, it seemed.

"Was that man dead?" Toby asked, reverting to what was most on his mind.

"I'm afraid so."

"I thought he was. I've never seen anyone dead before."

"You've seen dogs," Alan said.

"That's not the same, plank-head."

Christopher asked, "What did the Colonel mean about voting your shares?"

"Huh?"

"He said 'Vote your shares.' He looked pretty upset, didn't he?"

"Well," I said, "do you know what shares are?"

"Pieces of cake," Neil guessed. "One each."

"Say you had a chessboard," I said, "there would be sixty-four squares, OK? Say you called each square a share. There would be sixty-four shares."

The young faces told me I wasn't getting the idea across.

"OK," I said, "say you have a floor made of tiles."

They nodded at once. As a builder's children they knew all about tiles.

"Say you lay ten tiles across and ten tiles down, and fill in the square."

"A hundred tiles," Christopher nodded.

"Yes. Now call each tile a share, a hundredth part of the whole square. A hundred squares. OK?"

They nodded.

"What about voting?" Christopher asked.

I hesitated. "Say you owned some of the tiles, you

could vote to have yours blue . . . or red . . . whatever you'd like."

"How many could *you* vote on?"

"Eight," I said.

"You could have eight blue tiles? What about the others?"

"All the others, ninety-two, belong to other people. They could all choose whatever color they liked for the tiles they owned."

"It would be a mess," Edward pointed out. "You wouldn't get everyone to agree on a pattern."

"You're absolutely right," I said, smiling.

"But you're not really meaning *tiles,* are you?" Christopher said.

"No." I paused. For once, they were all listening. "See, say this racecourse is like a hundred tiles. A hundred squares. A hundred shares. I have eight shares of the racecourse. Other people have ninety-two."

Christopher shrugged. "It's not much, then. Eight's not even one row."

Neil said, "If the racecourse was divided up into a hundred squares . . . Dad's eight squares might have the stands on!"

"Plank-head," Toby said.

3

WHY DID I go?

I don't know. I doubt if there is such a thing as a wholly free choice, because one's choices are rooted in one's personality. I choose what I choose because I am what I am, that sort of thing.

I chose to go for reprehensible reasons like the lure of unearned gain and from the vanity that I might against all odds tame the dragon and sort out the Stratton feuds peacefully, as Roger and Oliver wanted. Greed and pride . . . powerful spurs masquerading as prudent financial management and altruistic good works.

So I disregarded the despairing plea from my mother's remembered wisdom and took my children into desperate danger and by my presence altered forever the internal stresses and balances of the Strattons.

Except, of course, that it didn't seem like that on the day of the shareholders' meeting.

It took place on Wednesday afternoon, on the third day of the ruin hunt. On Monday morning the five boys and I had set off from home in the big converted single-decker bus that had in the past served as mobile home for us all during periods when the currently-being-rebuilt ruin had been truly and totally uninhabitable.

The bus had its points: it would sleep eight, it had a working shower room, a galley, sofas and televisions. I'd taken lessons from a yacht builder in creating storage spaces where none might seem to exist, and we could in fact store a sizable household very neatly aboard. It did not, all the same, offer privacy or much personal space, and as the boys grew they had found it increasingly embarrassing as an address.

They packed into it quite happily on Monday, though, as I had promised them a real holiday in the afternoons if I could visit a ruin each morning, and in fact with map and timetables I'd planned a series of the things they most liked to do. Monday afternoon we spent canoeing on the Thames, Tuesday they beat the hell out of a bowling alley, and on Wednesday they'd promised to help Roger Gardner's wife clean out her garage, a chore they bizarrely enjoyed.

I left the bus outside the Gardner house and with Roger walked to the stands.

"I'm not invited to the meeting," he said as if it were a relief, "but I'll show you to the door."

He took me up a staircase, round a couple of corners, and through a door marked "Private" into a carpeted world quite different from the functional concrete of the public areas. Silently pointing to paneled and polished double doors ahead, he gave me an encouraging pat on the shoulder and left me, rather in the manner of a colonel avuncularly sending a rookie into his first battle.

Regretting my presence already, I opened one of the double doors and went in.

I'd gone to the meeting in business clothes (gray trousers, white shirt, tie, navy blazer) to present a conventional boardroom appearance. I had a tidy normal haircut, the smoothest of shaves, clean fingernails. The big dusty laborer of the building sites couldn't be guessed at.

The older men at the meeting all wore suits. Those more my own age and younger hadn't bothered with such formality. I had, I thought in satisfaction, hit it just right.

Although I had arrived at the time stated in the lawyer's letter, it seemed that the Strattons had jumped the clock. The whole tribe was sitting round a truly imposing Edwardian dining table of old French-polished mahogany, their chairs newer, nineteen-thirtyish, like the grandstands themselves.

The only one I knew by sight was Rebecca, the jockey, dressed now in trousers, tailored jacket and heavy gold chains. The man sitting at the head of the table, gray-haired, bulky and authoritative, I took to be Conrad, the fourth and latest baron.

He turned his head to me as I went in. They all, of course, turned their heads. Five men, three women.

"I'm afraid you are in the wrong place," Conrad said with scant politeness. "This is a private meeting."

"Stratton shareholders?" I asked inoffensively.

"As it happens. And you are . . . ?"

"Lee Morris."

The shock that rippled through them was almost funny, as if they hadn't realized that I would even be notified of the meeting, let alone had considered that I might attend; and they had every reason to be surprised, as I had never before responded to any of their official annual bits of paper.

I closed the door quietly behind me. "I was sent a notification," I said.

"Yes, but—" Conrad said without welcome. "I mean, it wasn't necessary . . . You weren't expected to bother . . ." He stopped uncomfortably, unable to hide what looked like dismay.

"As I'm here," I said amiably, "I may as well stay. Shall I sit here?" I indicated an empty chair at the foot of the table, walking towards it purposefully. "We've never met," I went on, "but you must be Conrad, Lord Stratton."

He said, "Yes," tight-lipped.

One of the older men said violently, "This is a disgrace! You've no right here. Don't sit down. You're *leaving.*"

I stood by the empty chair and brought the lawyer's letter out of a pocket. "As you'll see," I answered him pleasantly, "I *am* a shareholder. I was properly given advance notice of this meeting, and I'm sorry if you don't like it, but I do have a legal right to be here. I'll just sit quietly and listen."

I sat down. All of the faces registered stark disapproval except for one, a younger man's, bearing a hint of a grin.

"Conrad! This is ridiculous." The man who most violently opposed my presence was up on his feet, quivering with fury. "Get rid of him at once."

Conrad Stratton realistically took stock of my size and comparative youth and said defeatedly, "Sit down, Keith. Who exactly is going to throw him out?"

Keith, my mother's first husband, might have been strong enough in his youth to batter a miserable young wife, but there was no way he could begin to do the same to her thirty-five-year-old son. He hated the fact of my existence. I hated what I'd learned of him. The antagonism between us was mutual, powerful and lasting.

The fair hair in the wedding photographs had turned a blondish gray. The good bone structure still gave him a more patrician air than that of his elder twin. His looking glass must still constantly be telling him that the order of his birth had been nature's horrible mistake, that *his* should have been the head that engaged first.

He couldn't sit down. He strode about the big room, snapping his head round in my direction now and then and glaring at me.

Important chaps who might have been the first and second barons looked down impassively from gold-framed portraits on the walls. The lighting hung from the ceiling in convoluted brass chandeliers with etched glass shades around candle bulbs. Upon a long polished mahogany sideboard stood a short case clock flanked by heavy old throttled-neck vases that, like the whole room, had an air of having remained unchanged for most of the old lord's life.

There was no daylight: no windows.

Next to Conrad sat a ramrod-backed old lady easy to identify as his aunt, Marjorie Binsham, the convener of this affair. Forty years earlier, on my mother's wedding day, she had stared grimly at the camera as if a smile would have cracked her facial muscles, and nothing in that way, either, seemed to have been affected by passing years. Now well into her eighties, she flourished a still-sharp brain under disciplined wavy white hair and wore a red and black hound's-tooth dress with a white, ecclesiastical-looking collar.

Rather to my surprise she was regarding me more with curiosity than rigid dislike.

"Mrs. Binsham?" I said from the other end of the table. "Mrs. Marjorie Binsham?"

"Yes." This monosyllable came out clipped and dry, merely acknowledging information.

"I," said the man whose grin was now in control, "am Darlington Stratton, known as Dart. My father sits at the head of the table. My sister Rebecca is on your right."

"This is unnecessary!" Keith snapped at him from somewhere behind Conrad. "He does not need introductions. He's leaving."

Mrs. Binsham said repressively and with exquisite diction, "Keith, do stop prowling, and sit down. Mr. Morris is correct, he has a right to be here. Face facts. As you cannot eject him, ignore him."

Mrs. Binsham's direct gaze was bent on me, not on Keith. My own lips twitched. Ignoring me seemed the last thing any of them could do.

Dart said, with a straight face covering infinite mischief, "Have you met Hannah, your sister?"

The woman on the other side of Conrad from Mrs. Binsham vibrated with disgust. "He's not my brother, he's *not.*"

"Half-brother," Marjorie Binsham said, with the same cool fact-facing precision. "Unpalatable as you may find it, Hannah, you cannot change it. Just ignore him."

For Hannah, as for Keith, the advice was impossible to follow. My half-sister, to my relief, didn't look like our joint mother. I'd been afraid she might: afraid to find familiar eyes hating me from an echo of a loved face. She looked more like Keith, tall, blonde, fine-boned and, at the moment, white with outrage.

"How dare you!" She shook. "Have you no decency?"

"I have shares," I pointed out.

"And you shouldn't have," Keith said harshly. "Why Father ever gave them to Madeline, I'll never know."

I refrained from saying that he must know perfectly well why. Lord Stratton had given shares to Madeline, his daughter-in-law, because he knew why she was leaving. In my mother's papers, after she'd died, I came across old letters from her father-in-law telling her of his regret, of his regard for her, of his concern that she shouldn't suffer financially, as she had physically. Though loyal in public to his son, he had privately not only given her the shares "for the future" but had endowed her also with a lump sum to keep her comfortable on the interest. In return she had promised never ever to speak of Keith's behavior, still less to drag the family name through a messy divorce. The old man wrote that he understood her rejection of Hannah, the result of his son's "sexual attacks." He would care for the child, he wrote. He wished my mother "the best that can be achieved, my dear."

It was Keith who later divorced my mother—for adultery with an elderly illustrator of children's books, Leyton Morris, my father. The resulting devoted marriage lasted fifteen years, and it wasn't until she was on her own one-way road with cancer that my mother talked of the Strattons and told me in long night-time outpourings about her sufferings and her fondness for Lord Stratton; and it wasn't until then that I learned that it was Lord Stratton's money that had educated me and sent me through architectural school, the foundations of my life.

I had written to thank him after she died, and I still had his reply.

> My dear boy,
>   I loved your mother. I hope you gave her the joy she deserved. I thank you for your letter, but do not write again.
>   Stratton.

I didn't write again. I sent flowers to his funeral. With him alive, I would never have intruded on his family.

With Conrad identified, and Keith, and Marjorie Binsham, and Conrad's offspring Dart and Rebecca, there remained two males at the meeting still to be named. One, in late middle age, sat between Mrs. Binsham and Keith's vacated chair, and I could make a guess at him.

"Excuse me," I said, leaning forward to catch his attention. "Are you . . . Ivan?"

The youngest of the old lord's three sons, more bullish like Conrad than greyhound like Keith, gave me a hard stare and no reply.

Dart said easily, "My uncle Ivan, as you say. And opposite him is his son Forsyth, my cousin."

"Dart!" Keith objected fiercely. "Be quiet."

Dart gave him an impassive look and seemed unintimidated. Forsyth, Ivan's son, was the one, I thought, that had reacted least to my attendance. That is to say he took it less personally than the others, and he slowly revealed, as time went on, that he had no interest in me as Hannah's regrettable half-brother, but only as an unknown factor in the matter of shares.

Young and slight, he had a narrow chin and dark intense eyes, and was treated by the others without the slightest deference. No one throughout the meeting asked his opinion about anything and, when he gave it regardless, his father, Ivan, regularly interrupted. Forsyth himself seemed to find this treatment normal, and perhaps for him it was.

Conrad, coming testily to terms with the inevitable, said heavily, "Let's get on with the meeting. I called it . . ."

"*I* called it," corrected his aunt sharply. "All this squabbling is ridiculous. Let's get to the point. There has been racing on this racecourse for almost ninety years, and it will go on as before, and that's an end to it. The arguing must stop."

"This racecourse is dying on its feet," Rebecca contradicted impatiently. "You have absolutely no idea what the modern world is all about. I'm sorry if it upsets you, Aunt Marjorie, but you and Grandfather have been left behind by the tide. This place needs new stands and a whole new outlook, and what it doesn't need is a fuddy-duddy old colonel for a manager and a stick-in-the-mud Clerk of the Course who can't say boo to a doctor."

"The doctor outranks him," Dart observed.

"You shut up," his sister ordered. "You've never had the bottle to ride in a race. I've raced on most courses in this country and I'm telling you, this place is terminally old-fashioned and it's got my name on it too, which makes me open to ridicule, and the whole thing *stinks*. If you won't or can't see that, then I'm in favor of cashing in now for what we can get."

"Rebecca!" Conrad's reproof seemed tired, as if he'd heard his daughter's views too often. "We need new stands. We can all agree on that. And I've commissioned plans . . ."

"You'd no right to do that," Marjorie informed him. "Waste of money. These old stands are solidly built and are thoroughly serviceable. We do *not* need new stands. I'm totally opposed to the idea."

Keith said with troublemaking relish, "Conrad has had this pet architect roaming round the place for weeks. *His* choice of architect. None of us has been consulted, and I'm against new stands on principle."

"Huh!" Rebecca exclaimed. "And where do you think the women jockeys have to change? In a partitioned-off space the size of a *cupboard* in the ladies' loo. It's pathetic."

"All for want of a horseshoe nail," Dart murmured.

"What do you mean?" Rebecca demanded.

"I mean," her brother explained lazily, "that we'll lose the racecourse to feminism."

She wasn't sure enough of his meaning to come up with a cutting answer so instead ignored him.

"We should sell at once," Keith exclaimed, still striding about. "The market is good. Swindon's growing. The industrial area is already on the racecourse boundary. Sell, I say. I've already sounded out a local developer. He's agreed to survey and consider."

"You've done *what?*" Conrad demanded. "And *you've* consulted no one, either. And that's never the way to sell *anything*. You know nothing about business dealings."

Keith said huffily, "I know if you want to sell something you have to advertise."

"No," Conrad said flatly, as if that settled it. "We're not selling."

Keith's anger rose. "It's all right for *you*. You inherit most of Father's residual estate. It's not fair. It was *never* fair, leaving nearly all to eldest sons. Father was hopelessly old-fashioned. *You* may not need money, but none of us is getting any younger and I say take out our capital *now*."

"Later," Hannah said intensely. "Sell when there's less land available. Wait."

Conrad remarked heavily, "Your daughter, Keith, fears that if you take the capital now you'll squander it and there'll be none left for her to inherit."

Hannah's face revealed it to be a bull's-eye diagnosis, and also showed disgust at having had her understandable motives so tellingly disclosed.

"What about you, Ivan?" his aunt inquired. "Still of the same indecisive mind?"

Ivan scarcely responded to the jibe, even if he recognized it as one. He nodded with a show of measured sagacity. "Wait and see," he said. "That's the best."

"Wait until you've lost the opportunity," Rebecca said scathingly. "That's what you mean, isn't it?"

He said defensively, "Why are you always so *sharp*, Rebecca? There's nothing wrong with patience."

"Inaction," she corrected. "Making no decision's as bad as making the wrong decision."

"Rubbish," Ivan said.

Forsyth began, "Have we thought about tax on capital gains . . ." but Ivan was saying, "It's clear we ought to shelve a decision until . . ."

"Until the bloody cows come home," Rebecca said.

"Rebecca!" Her great-aunt's disapproval arrived automatically. "Now stop it, all of you, because at the moment I and I alone can make decisions and I have the impression that none of you realize that."

From their expressions it was clear that they neither knew nor cared to be told.

"Aunt," Conrad said repressively, "you have ten shares only. You cannot make unilateral decisions."

"Oh, but I can," she said triumphantly. "You're so ignorant, all of you. You fancy yourselves as men— oh, and *women*, Rebecca—of affairs but none of you seems to realize that in any company it is the directors, not shareholders, who make the decisions, and *I* . . ." she looked round, collecting undivided attention, "I am at present the sole remaining director. *I* make the decisions."

She brought the meeting to its first taste of silence.

After a pause, Dart laughed. Everyone else scowled, chiefly at him, disapproval of a grandson being more prudent than defying the dragon.

The splendid old lady took folded sheets of paper from an expensive leather handbag and shook them open with an almost theatrical flourish.

"This is a letter," she said, putting on reading glasses, "from the Stratton Park racecourse lawyers. I won't bother you with the introductory paragraphs. The heart of the matter is this." She paused, glanced around at her attentive and apprehensive audience and then read from the letter. "As two directors are sufficient, it was quite proper for yourself and Lord Stratton to comprise the whole Board and for him, as by far the major shareholder, to make all the decisions. Now that he has died you may wish to form a new Board with more directors, and while these *may* be members of the Stratton family, there is no bar to your electing outside, non-shareholding directors if you should wish.

"We would accordingly suggest you call an extraordinary meeting of shareholders for the purpose of electing new directors to serve on the Board of Stratton Park Racecourse Ltd., and we will be happy to assist you in every possible way."

Marjorie Binsham looked up. "The lawyers were willing to conduct this meeting. I said I could do it and they weren't to bother. As the sole remaining director of the company I make a motion that we elect new directors, and as director I also second the motion, and although this may not be exactly regulation procedure, it will have the desired effect."

Conrad said, feebly for him, "Aunt . . ."

"As you, Conrad, are now titular head of the family, I propose that you become a director forthwith." She looked down at the letter. "It says here that any director may be elected if he obtains at least fifty percent of the votes cast at a shareholders' meeting. Each share, in this company, bears one vote. According to this letter, if I and the inheriting family shareholders all attend this meeting, there will be eighty-five votes available. That is to say, my ten shares, and the seventy-five now inherited by the rest of you." She paused and looked down the table to where I sat. "We did not expect Mr. Morris to attend, but as he is here, he has eight votes to cast."

"No!" Keith said furiously. "He has no *right.*"

Marjorie Binsham replied implacably. "He has eight votes. He can cast them. You cannot prevent it."

Her verdict had surprised me as much as it had astounded the others. I'd gone there out of curiosity as much as anything else, ready to upset them slightly, but not to this fundamental extent.

"It's *disgraceful,*" Hannah yelled, rising compulsively from her seat like her still-pacing father. "I won't have it!"

"According to our lawyers," her great-aunt went on, totally ignoring the tantrum, "once we have elected a Board of Directors it is *they* who decide the future of this racecourse."

"Make *me* a director," Rebecca demanded.

"You need forty-seven votes," murmured Dart, having done some arithmetic. "Any director needs forty-seven, minimum."

"I propose we elect Conrad at once," Marjorie reiterated. "He has my ten votes." She looked round, challenging them to disagree.

"All right," Ivan said. "Conrad, you have my twenty-one."

"I suppose I can vote for myself," Conrad said. "I vote my own twenty-one. That's, er, fifty-two."

"Elected," Marjorie said, nodding. "You can now conduct the rest of the meeting."

Conrad's manner regained confidence and he seemed literally to swell to fill his new role. He said kindly, "Then I think we should vote to keep Marjorie on the Board. Only right."

No one demurred. The Honorable Mrs. Binsham looked as if she would chew any dissenter for breakfast.

"I, too, must be a director," Keith asserted. "I also have twenty-one shares. I vote them for me."

Conrad cleared his throat. "I propose Keith for director . . ."

Forsyth said too quickly, "That's asking for trouble."

Conrad, not hearing, or at least choosing not to, hurried on. "Keith's twenty-one, then, and mine. Forty-two. Aunt?"

Marjorie shook her head. Keith took three fast paces towards her with his hands outstretched as if he would attack her. She didn't flinch or shrink away. She stared him down.

She said with starch, "That's exactly why I won't vote for you, Keith. You never had any self-control, and you've grown no wiser with age. Look elsewhere. Ask Mr. Morris."

A wicked old lady, I saw. Keith went scarlet. Dart grinned.

Keith walked round behind Ivan. "Brother," he said peremptorily, "I need your twenty-one votes."

"But I say," Ivan dithered, "Aunt Marjorie's right. You'd fight Conrad all the time. No sensible decisions would ever get made."

"Are you *refusing* me?" Keith could hardly believe it. "You'll be sorry, you know. You'll be sorry." The violence in his character had risen too near the surface even for his daughter, Hannah, who had subsided into her seat and now said uneasily, "Dad, don't bother with him. You can have my three votes. Do calm down."

"That's forty-five," Conrad said. "You need two more, Keith."

"Rebecca has three," Keith said.

Rebecca shook her head.

"Forsyth, then," Keith said furiously, at least not begging.

Forsyth looked at his fingers.

"Dart?" Keith shook with anger.

Dart glanced at his sweating uncle and took pity on him.

"OK, then," he said, making nothing of it. "My three."

Without much emotion, a relief after the storm, Conrad said flatly, "Keith's elected."

"And to be fair," Dart said, "I propose Ivan also."

"We don't need four directors," Keith said.

"As I voted for *you,*" Dart told him, "you can do the decent thing and vote for Ivan. After all, he has twenty-one shares, just like you, and he's got just as much right to make decisions. So, Father," he said to Conrad, "I propose Ivan."

Conrad considered his son's proposal and shrugged: not because he disapproved, I guessed, but because he didn't think much of his brother Ivan's brains.

"Very well. Ivan. Anyone against?"

Everyone shook their heads, including Marjorie.

"Mr. Morris?" Conrad asked formally.

"He has my votes."

"Unanimous, then," Conrad said, surprised. "Any more nominations?"

Rebecca said, "Four is a bad number. There should be five. Someone from the younger generation."

She was suggesting herself again. No one, not even Dart, responded. Rebecca's thin face was in its way as mean as Keith's.

Not one of the four grandchildren was going to give power to any other. The three older brothers showed no wish to pass batons. The Board, with undercurrents of gripe and spite, was established as the old lord's three sons and their enduring aunt.

Without difficulty they agreed that Conrad should be chairman (*"Chair,"* Rebecca said. "Don't be ridiculous," said Keith), but Marjorie had another squib in reserve.

"The lawyer's letter also says," she announced, "that if the shareholders are dissatisfied with any director, they can call a meeting and vote to remove him. They need a fifty-one percent vote to achieve it." She stared beadily at Keith. "If it should become advisable to save us all from an irresponsible director, I will make certain that Mr. Morris and his eight votes are encouraged to attend the meeting."

Hannah was as affronted as Keith, but Keith, besides being infuriated, seemed almost bewildered, as if the possibility of his aunt's vitriolic disapproval had never occurred to him. Similarly it had never occurred to me that she wouldn't demand my execution rather than my presence. Marjorie, I then reckoned, would use any tool that came to hand to achieve a desired end: a wholly pragmatic lady.

Dart said with deceptive amiability, "Isn't there some rule in the setup of this company that says all board meetings are open? I mean, all shareholders may attend."

"Rubbish," Keith said.

Forsyth said, "Attend but not interrupt. Not speak unless asked . . ."

Ivan's voice drowned his son's. "We'll have to read the articles, or whatever."

"I did," Forsyth said. No one paid any attention.

"It never mattered before," Conrad observed. "The only shareholders besides Father and Aunt Marjorie were Mr. Morris, and of course before him, Madeline, and . . . er . . . Mrs. Perdita Faulds."

"Who exactly *is* Mrs. Perdita Faulds?" Rebecca demanded.

No one replied. If they knew, they weren't telling.

"Do you," Dart asked me directly, "know who Mrs. Perdita Faulds is?"

I shook my head. "No."

"We'll find her if necessary," Marjorie declared, making it sound ominous. "Let's hope we won't have to." Her malevolent gaze swept over Keith, warning him. "If we have to remove a director, we will find her."

On the brief list of shareholders that Roger had shown me, Mrs. Faulds's address had been care of a firm of lawyers. Messages to the lady would no doubt routinely be relayed, but actually finding her in person might take ingenuity. Take a professional bloodhound, perhaps. Marjorie wouldn't blink at that, I guessed, if it suited her.

It also occurred to me that if she were so certain the mysterious Mrs. Faulds would vote as Marjorie wanted, then Marjorie, at least, knew who she was. Not really my business, I thought.

Conrad said, with a show of taking a grip on the meeting, "Well, now that we have directors, perhaps we can make some firm decisions. We must, in fact. We have another race meeting here next Monday, as you know, and we cannot ask Marjorie indefinitely to be responsible for authorizing everything. There was a lot Father used to do that none of us know about. We simply have to learn fast."

"The first thing to do is sack the Colonel and stupid Oliver," Rebecca said.

Conrad merely glanced at his daughter and spoke to the others. "The Colonel and Oliver are the only people at present who can keep this place running. We need, in fact we rely entirely on, their expertise, and I intend to go on consulting them over every detail."

Rebecca sulked angrily. Marjorie's disapproval grew vigorous runners in her direction, like a rampant strawberry plant.

"I put forward a motion," Ivan said surprisingly, "that we continue to run the races as before, with Roger and Oliver in their normal roles."

"Seconded," Marjorie said crisply.

Keith scowled. Conrad, ignoring him, made a note on a pad in front of him. "The Board's first decision is to continue without change, for now." He pursed his lips. "I suppose we ought to have a secretary to write the minutes."

"You could use Roger's secretary," I suggested.

"No!" Rebecca jumped on it. "Everything we said would go straight to bloody Roger. And no one asked you to speak. You're an outsider."

Dart launched into verse, "Oh wad some power the giftie gie us to see oursels as others see us! It wad frae monie a blunder free us, an' foolish notion."

"What?" Rebecca demanded.

"Robert Burns," Dart said. " 'To a Louse.' "

I smothered the least appearance of a laugh. No one else seemed to think it funny.

I said to Rebecca mildly, "You could reposition the women jockeys' changing room."

"Oh really?" She was sarcastic. "Exactly where?"

"I'll show you. And," I went on speaking to Conrad, "you could double the take in the bars."

"Ye *gods,*" Dart said comically, "what have we here?"

I asked Conrad, "Are there already detailed plans for new stands?"

"We're not having new stands!" Marjorie was adamant.

"We must," Conrad said.

"We sell the land," Keith insisted.

Ivan dithered.

"New stands," Rebecca said. "New management. New everything. Or sell."

"Sell, but later," Hannah repeated obstinately.

"I agree," Forsyth nodded.

"Not in my lifetime," Marjorie said.

4

WHEN THE meeting broke up it became apparent why it had been held impersonally on the racecourse, as none of the people attending lived with any of the others.

They walked out as individuals, each in a seeming barbed-wire enclosure of self-righteousness, none of them anxious to acknowledge my continued presence.

Only Dart, half-way out of the door, looked back to where I stood watching the exodus.

"Coming?" he said. "The fun's done."

With a smile I joined him by the door as he thoughtfully looked me over.

"Care for a jar?" he said and, when I hesitated, added, "There's a pub right outside the main gates that's open all day. And, frankly, I'm curious."

"Curiosity's a two-way street."

He nodded. "Agreed, then." He led the way downstairs by a different route than the one I'd come up, and we emerged into an area, within the paddocks and near the unsaddling enclosures, that had been crowded with people on the race day but now contained only a number of parked cars. Into each car a single Stratton was climbing, none of the brothers, offspring or cousins grouping for friendly family chat.

Dart took it for granted and asked where my car was.

"Down there." I pointed vaguely.

"Oh? Hop in, then. I'll drive you."

Dart's car, an old dusty economical runabout, was standing next to Marjorie's chauffeur-driven blackly-gleaming Daimler, and she lowered her rear window as she glided slowly away, staring in disbelief at my acceptance by Dart. Dart waved to her cheerfully, reminding me vividly of my son Alan's similar disregard of the power of dragons, a lack of perception as much as a matter of courage.

Car doors slammed, engines purred, brake lights went on and off; the Strattons dispersed. Dart put his own car into gear and steered us straight to the main entrance, where a few forlorn-looking individuals were slowly walking up and down bearing placards saying "BAN STEEPLE-CHASING" and "CRUELTY TO ANIMALS."

"They've been here trying to stop people coming in, ever since that horse died here last Saturday," Dart observed. "The woolly head brigade, I call them."

It was an apt enough description, as they wore a preponderance of knitted hats. Their placards were handwritten and amateurish, but their dedication couldn't be doubted.

"They don't understand horses," Dart said. "Horses run and jump because they want to. Horses try their damnedest to get to the front of the herd. Racing wouldn't exist if it weren't for horses naturally busting their guts to get out in front and win." The grin came and went. "I don't have the instincts of a horse."

But his sister had, I thought.

Dart bypassed the demonstrators and drove across the road into the parking lot of the Mayflower Inn opposite, which looked as if it had never seen Plymouth, let alone sailed the Atlantic.

Inside, it was resolutely decorated with 1620 imitation memorabilia, but not too bad for all that. Murals of Pilgrim fathers in top hats (an anachronism) and white beards (wrong, the Pilgrims were young) were reminiscent of Abraham Lincoln two hundred years later, but who cared? The place was warm and welcoming and had at least tried.

Dart bought us two unadventurous half pints and put them carefully on a small dark oak table, settling us into wooden-armed reasonably comfortable old oak chairs.

"So why," he said, "did you come?"

"Eight shares in a racecourse."

He had steel-gray eyes: unusual. Unlike his sister, he hadn't honed his bone structure to angular leanness. Not for him the agonies and bad-temper-inducing deprivations of an unremitting battle with weight. Thirty or thereabouts, Dart already showed the roundness which could develop into the all-over weightiness of his father. Unlike his father he was also showing early signs of baldness, and this did, I slowly discovered, upset him radically.

"I'd heard about you," Dart said, "but you were always cast as a villain. You don't look villainous in the least."

"Who cast me as a villain?"

"Hannah, mostly, I suppose. She's never got over being rejected by her mother. I mean, mothers aren't supposed to dump infants, are they? Fathers do, regularly, male prerogative. Rebecca would kill me for saying that. Anyway, your mother dumped Hannah but not *you*. I'd look out for knives between the shoulder blades, if I were you."

His voice sounded light and frivolous and I had the impression I'd received a serious warning.

"What do you do?" I asked neutrally. "What do you all do?"

"Do? I farm. That is to say, I look after the family estates." Perhaps he read polite surprise on my face because he grimaced self-deprecatingly and said, "As it happens, we have a farm manager who runs the land and also an agent who sees to the tenants, but I make the decisions. That is to say, I listen to what the manager wants to do and to what the agent wants to do, and then I decide that that's what *I* want them to do, so they do it. Unless Father has different ideas. Unless Grandfather had different ideas, in the old days. And of course unless they've all been listening to my great-aunt Marjorie whose ideas are ultimate." He paused quite cheerfully. "The whole thing's bloody boring, and not what I'd like to do at all."

"Which is?" I asked, entertained.

"Fantasy land," he said. "Private property. Keep out." He meant no offense. The same words in Keith's mouth would have been a curse. "What do *you* do, yourself?" he asked.

"I'm a builder," I said.

"Really? What of?"

"Houses, mostly."

It didn't interest him greatly. He trotted briefly through the occupations of the other Strattons, or at least the ones I'd met.

"Rebecca's a jockey, I suppose you guessed? She's been besotted with horses all her life. She's two years younger than me. Our papa owns a racehorse or two and goes hunting. He used to do my own job until he decided I was too idle, so now he does even less. But to be fair, he does no harm, which in these days invests him with sainthood. My uncle Keith . . . heaven knows. He's supposed to be in finance, whatever that means. My uncle Ivan has a garden center, all ghastly gnomes and things. He potters about there some days and trusts his manager."

He paused to drink and gave me a glimmering inspection over the glass's rim.

"Go on," I said.

"Hannah," he nodded. "She's never done a hard day's work. My grandfather poured money over her to make up for her mother—*your* mother—rejecting her, but he never seemed to love her . . . I suppose I shouldn't say that. Anyway, Hannah's not married but she has a son called Jack who's a pain in the arse. Who else is there? Great-aunt Marjorie. Apart from Stratton money, she married a plutocrat who did the decent thing by dying fairly early. No children." He considered. "That's the lot."

"What about Forsyth?" I asked.

A shutter came down fast on his easy loquacity.

"Grandfather divided his seventy-five shares of Stratton Park among all of us," he stated. "Twenty-one shares each to his three sons, and three shares each to his four grandchildren. Forsyth gets his three like the rest of us." He stopped, his expression carefully noncommittal. "Whatever Forsyth does isn't my business." He left the clear implication that it wasn't mine, either.

"What will you all do," I asked, "about the racecourse?"

"Besides quarrel? In the short term, nothing, as that's what the great-aunt is set on. Then we'll get some hopeless new stands at enormous cost, then we'll have to sell the land to pay for the stands. You may as well tear up your shares right away."

"You don't seem unduly worried."

His quick grin shone and vanished. "To be honest, I don't give a toss. Even if I get myself disinherited by doing something diabolical, like voting to abolish hunting, I can't help but get richer as time goes by. Grandfather gave me millions nine years ago, for a start. And my father has his good points. He's already given me a chunk of his own fortune, and if he lives another three years it'll be clear of tax." He stared at me, frowning. "Why do I tell you that?"

"Do you want to impress me?"

"No, I don't. I don't care a bugger what you think." He blinked a bit. "I suppose that's not true." He paused. "I have irritating holes in my life."

"Like what?"

"Too much money. No motivation. And I'm going bald."

"Marry," I said.

"That wouldn't grow hair."

"It might stop you minding."

"*Nothing* stops you minding. And it's damned unfair. I go to doctors who say I can't do a bugger about it, it's in the genes, and how did it get *there,* I'd like to know? Father's OK and Grandfather had the full thatch, even though he was eighty-eight his last birthday, and look at Keith with enough to brush back with his hands all the time like a ruddy girl. I hate that mannerism. And even Ivan has no bare patches, he's going thin all over but that's not as *bad.*" He looked balefully at my head. "You're about my age, and yours is *thick.*"

"Try snake oil," I suggested.

"That's typical. People like you have *no idea* what it's like to find hair all over the place. Washbasin. Pillow. Hairs which ought to stay growing in my scalp, dammit. How did you know I wasn't married, anyway? And don't give me the stock answer that I don't look worried. I *am* worried, dammit, about my hair."

"You could try implants."

"Yes. Don't laugh, I'm going to."

"I'm not laughing."

"I bet you are, inside. Everybody thinks it's hilarious, someone else going bald. But when it's you, it's tragic."

There were irretrievable disasters, I saw, that could only get worse. Dart drank deep as if beer would irrigate the failing follicles and asked if I were married, myself.

"Do I look it?"

"You look stable."

Surprised, I said yes, I was married.

"Children?"

"Six sons."

"*Six!*" He seemed horrified. "You're not old enough."

"We married at nineteen, and my wife likes having babies."

"Good Lord." Other words failed him, and I thought back, as I did pretty often, to the heady student days when Amanda and I had taken to each other with excitement. Friends around us were pairing and living together: it was accepted behavior.

"Let's get married," I said impulsively. "No one gets *married,*" Amanda said. "Then let's be *different,*" I said.

So we married, giggling happily, and I paid no attention to my mother, who tried to tell me I was marrying Amanda with my eyes, marrying a half-grown woman I didn't really know. "I married Keith Stratton for his beauty," she told me, "and it was a dreadful mistake. It's always a mistake."

"But Amanda's lovely."

"She's lovely to look at and she's kind and she clearly loves *you,* but you're both so young, you'll change as you grow older and so will she."

"Mum, are you coming to the wedding?"

"Of course."

I married Amanda for her long legs and her blonde hair and her name, Amanda, which I loved. It took ten years for me to face a long-repressed recognition that my mother had been right about changes.

Neither Amanda nor I had known at nineteen that she would almost at once develop a hunger for babies. Neither of us could possibly have envisaged that she would ecstatically enjoy the actual birth process, or that she would plan the next pregnancy as soon as the last was accomplished.

Both Christopher and Toby had been born by the time I'd struggled through my qualifying exams, and feeding and housing the four of us had seemed an impossible task. It was then, in my first week out of college, that I'd gone to drown my sorrows in a depressing old pub and found the landlord weeping bankrupt tears into warm beer amid the crash of his own personal dream. The place had been condemned as unfit to live in, he owed money everywhere, his wife had left him and his license to sell liquor would run out the next day.

We negotiated a rock-bottom price. I went to the council to get a stay of demolition. I begged and borrowed and mortgaged my soul, and Amanda, the two boys and I moved into our first ruin.

I began to make it habitable while I looked around for a job, and I found a lowly position in a large firm of architects, an existence I disliked but stuck to grimly for the pay packets.

Unlike Dart, I knew well what it was like to sweat at night over which bill to pay next, over how to pay *any* bill next, over which did I need most, electricity or a telephone (electricity), and do I pay the plumber (yes, but I learn his job) or do I pay first for roof tiles (yes) or new bricks (no).

I'd carted away free rubble and improvised and sanded old mortar off by the bucketful and given glamour to old stones and built a chimney that never smoked. The ruin came to life again, and I left the firm of architects and irrevocably grew and changed.

I hadn't known at nineteen that I would be unsuited to work as part of a team, or that my true *métier* was hands-on construction, not simply the drawing board. Amanda hadn't imagined that life with an architect could mean dirt, upheaval and months without income; but to the extent that we'd settled for what we hadn't expected, she had coped with the ruins and I had agreed to the babies, and each of us had had what we needed for our own private fulfillment, even if we'd grown apart until even our sexual interest in each other had become perfunctory and sporadic, an effort, not a joy.

After Neil's birth, during a patch when nothing had seemed to go right, we had nearly split finally asunder, but the economics of feeding the nestlings had prevailed. I took to sleeping alone under the tarpaulins while the rest slept in the bus. I worked eighteen hours a day as a form of escape. After four increasingly prosperous but unhappy years, when neither of us had met anyone to supplant the other, we'd made a great effort to "start again." Jamie had been the result. He still kept Amanda happy and, even though the new start had slowly fizzled, we had, because of it, achieved a sort of tolerant to-our-mutual-advantage stand-off which I reckoned enough for the foreseeable future, at least until the boys were grown.

So where was free choice in all of that? I chose to marry to be different and to stick to what it brought me because of an inability to admit failure. I'd chosen to work alone because I hadn't the qualities needed for a team. Every choice a result of given factors. No free choice at all.

"I choose to be what I am," I said.

Dart, startled, said, "What?"

"Nothing. Only a theory. Was it inevitable that Conrad, Keith, Ivan and the rest of you should make the choices you all have about the future of the racecourse?"

He looked at his beer for answers and glanced up at me briefly. "Too deep for me," he said.

"Would you ever have expected your father to want to sell? Or Keith to potter along as things are?"

"Or Rebecca to love men?" He grinned. "No, in all three cases, I wouldn't."

"What do you yourself want for the racecourse?" I asked.

"You tell me," he said amiably, "you're the expert."

I felt in him an encompassing lassitude. Not the sort of thing to say to a virtual stranger.

"Another half?" I suggested, indicating our almost empty glasses.

"No, don't bother. What about totally random choice? Pick a card, that sort of thing. What about rational choices? Like do I take an umbrella because it's raining."

"Many people don't."

"Because it isn't in their natures? Because they think it wimpish?"

"More or less."

"How did we get into this?" He seemed to tire of the subject. "Go back to the meeting. When you asked Father if he already had detailed plans of the new stands he's set on, was it because you're a builder?"

"Yes," I nodded.

"Well . . . if you could see the proposals, would you have an opinion?"

"I might."

He thought it over. "I do know where you could see the plans, but no one will want you to, except me. If I get you a look at them, will you tell just *me* what you think of them? Then at least I'd have some idea of whether new stands are a good idea or not. I mean, I don't know *how* to vote about the future of the racecourse, because I don't really know the significance of the options. So yes, you're right, if I had to choose now it would be a gut reaction. I'd choose because of the way I am. Right?"

"Right."

"How about taking a look-see at Conrad's pet architect's plans, then?"

"Yes," I said.

He grinned. "This choice game's a knock-out. Come on then, we'll do a bit of breaking and entering." He stood up decisively and turned towards the door. "Can you pick locks?"

"It depends on the lock. But given due warning and high need, possibly."

"Good."

"How long," I asked, "will it take?"

He paused, eyebrows rising. "Half an hour, maybe."

"OK."

I followed him out of the Mayflower and into his run-about, and we set off with a jolt to a destination undisclosed.

"How about I choose not to go bald?" It amused him in a bitter sort of way.

"Not a choice."

We were heading east, Swindon behind us, Wantage, according to the signposts, ahead. Long before we reached there, however, Dart put his foot on the brake and swerved in through some open gates set in a stone wall. Up a short driveway he came to a halt in front of a large house built of smooth gray bricks with bands of smooth pink bricks and inset patterns of smooth yellowish bricks, all in all (to me) an eyesore.

"I was brought up here," Dart said encouragingly. "What do you think of it?"

"Edwardian," I said.

"Near enough. Last year of Victoria."

"Solid, anyway."

A turret. Big sash windows. A conservatory. Affluent middle-class display.

"My parents rattle around in it now," Dart said frankly. "They're out, by the way. Father was going to meet Mother from the racecourse. They won't be back for hours." He pulled a bunch of keys out of the ignition and stood up out of the car. "We can get in round the back," he said, sorting out one key. "Come on."

"No breaking and entering?"

"Later."

At close quarters the walls were still repulsive and also slippery to the touch. The path around to the rear was edged with gloomy evergreen shrubs. At the back of the house, a red brick extension had been added to provide bathrooms: brown-painted drains zig-zagged over the exterior, an invitation to ice. Dart unlocked a brown-painted door and let us into the bowels (well, literally) of the house.

"This way," he said, marching past a cloakroom and other plumbing, briefly glimpsed through half-open doors. "Through here." He pushed aside a swing door which led from utility to opulence; to the black-and-white tiled floor of a large entrance hall.

We made our way across this to a polished door and into a cluttered oak-paneled room whose chief eyecatchers were endless pictures of horses; some, in oil paintings, hanging thickly on the walls with individual lights on the frames, some in black-and-white photographs in silver frames standing on every surface, some on book jacket covers. Horse-head bookends supported leather-bound classics like the *Irish R.M.* and *Handley Cross.* A silver fox held down papers on a busy desk. Silver and gold coins were displayed in collections. A hunting crop lay casually coiled on a broken-springed chair. Copies of *Horse and Hound* and *Country Life* filled a magazine rack to overflowing.

"Father's sanctum," Dart said unnecessarily. He strolled unconcernedly across the room, skirted the desk and the large chair behind it, and stopped beside a section of paneling which he said was a cupboard door always kept carefully locked by his parent.

"The racecourse plans are inside," Dart said. "How about opening it?"

"Your father wouldn't approve."

"I dare say not. Don't tell me you're going all moral and starchy. You pretty well said you could do it."

"This is too personal."

I went round beside him, however, and bent to take a closer look at the lock. All that was to be seen from the outside was an inconspicuous keyhole: without Dart's knowledge of its existence the door itself would have remained more or less invisible, particularly as a painting of a meet with huntsman and foxhounds adhered on it, to make it indistinguishable from the walls around.

"Well?" Dart asked.

"What does its key look like?"

"How do you mean?"

"I mean, is it a small short key, or one with a longish narrow shaft with a clump of wards on the end?"

"A long shaft."

I straightened up and gave him the bad news.

"I'll not touch it," I said. "Won't the key be somewhere in this room?"

"I tried to find it for years in my teens. No good at all. How about a bit of force?"

"Absolutely not."

Dart fiddled around with things on the desk. "What about this paper-knife? Or this?" He held up a long button-hook. "It isn't as if we're going to *steal* anything. Just to take a look."

"Why does your father have the plans locked up?"

Dart shrugged. "He's secretive by nature. It takes such a lot of *energy* to be secretive. I can never be bothered."

The lock was an old and undoubtedly simple warded-bit key job, probably surface-mounted on the inside of the door. The keyhole itself was about an inch from top to bottom, a healthy size that made picking it a cinch. Failing a filed-down key, two wires would have been enough. I was not, however, going to undo it, on the grounds that Conrad would be legitimately furious if he found out, and also because my interest in seeing the plans was not uncontrollable.

"Wasted journey, then?" Dart asked.

"Sorry."

"Oh, well." It seemed his appetite for the enterprise had easily subsided, as if common sense had somewhere raised its wiser head. He looked at me assessingly. "I've a distinct feeling you *could,* but you won't."

The trip had been an anticlimax. I looked at my watch and asked if he would mind taking me back to the racecourse. He agreed, seeming to feel the same deflation. I had not, it was clear, come up to his expectations.

We set off again in his car and I asked where he lived now, himself.

"Actually," he said, "in Stratton Hays."

"Is that a village?"

"Lord, no." He was amused. "A house. Though, come to think of it, it's as big as a village. Grandfather's house. The old fellow was lonely when Gran died, so he asked me to stay for a while. That was about ten years ago. Keith didn't like it, of course. He tried to get me out and himself in. He'd lived there a lot of his life, after all. He said it wasn't natural for a twenty-year-old boy to move in there, but Grandfather wouldn't have Keith back. I remember all the shouting. I used to get out of the way whenever Keith was around. That wasn't anything new, mind you. Anyway, I *liked* Grandfather, and we got on fine. We used to dine together every evening and I drove him most days round the estate and the racecourse. He ran the racecourse himself, really. That's to say, the colonel that Rebecca was complaining about, Colonel Gardner, he's the racecourse manager, he would do whatever Grandfather wanted. He's an excellent manager, whatever Rebecca says. Grandfather had a real knack of picking people to run things, like Colonel Gardner, and those two that I depend on, the farm manager and the land agent. Just as well, because to be frank we only ever had one genius in the family and that was the first baron, who was a merchant banker with a super-plus Midas touch." His voice was light and self-deprecating, but there was a depth of feeling in his next statement. "I miss the old man rotten, you know."

We droned along until the woolly-head marchers were again in sight.

"Stratton Hays," Dart said, "is straight on past the gates. Not far. On the edge of the racecourse land. Do you want to see it? It's where your mother lived with Keith. Where she dumped Hannah."

I looked at my watch, but curiosity prevailed over parental responsibility. I said I would be very interested, and on we went.

Stratton Hays was everything Conrad's house was not, an ancient homogenous pile in the manner of a smaller Hardwicke Hall. Early seventeenth-century stone and glass in lighthearted proportional harmony, built by the golden fortunes of the Elizabethan age, it looked exactly as it had done for almost four hundred years and certainly as it had forty years earlier when my mother had gone there as a bride.

She had spoken of "the Stratton house" as a heartless heap, projecting her own unhappiness into its walls, so that I was unprepared for its easygoing grandeur. It looked friendly to me, and welcoming.

"My great-great-grandfather bought it," Dart said off-handedly, "as being a suitable seat for a newly ennobled baron. The first baroness is on record as thinking it not aristocratic enough. She wanted Palladian pillars, pediments and porticos."

As before, we went into the house via an unobtrusive side door, and as before found ourselves in a black-and-white hall, this time floored with marble. There was more space than furniture and no curtains at the high windows and, as my mother had said, it echoed with vanished generations.

"Keith used to have the west corridor," Dart said, heading up a wide staircase. "After he divorced your mother he got married again, and Grandfather made him and his new wife take Hannah and find somewhere else to live. Before I was born, of course. It seems Keith didn't want to go but Grandfather insisted."

Dart headed across a large unfurnished area and turned a corner into a long wide corridor with a dark wood floor, a runner of crimson carpet and a tall window at the far end.

"West corridor," Dart said. "The doors are all unlocked. The rooms get dusted once a month. Browse around, if you like."

I browsed, feeling uncomfortable. This was where my mother had suffered beatings and what was now called marital rape. Time had stood still in their bedroom. I shivered there.

A dressing room, a boudoir, a study and a sitting room, all with tall uncurtained windows, also opened onto the corridor. A Victorian bathroom and a twentieth-century kitchen had been fitted into what had probably once been another bedroom. No sign of a nursery.

I went back along the corridor and thanked Dart.

"Did these rooms never have curtains?" I asked.

"They rotted away," Dart said. "Grandfather got rid of them and wouldn't let Gran replace them." He walked towards the stairs. "Grandfather and Gran lived in the east corridor. It's the same architecturally but it's a proper home. Carpets, curtains, pretty. Gran chose everything there. It feels so empty, now, without either of them. I used to spend most evenings with Grandfather in their sitting room, but I don't go along there much any more."

We went down the stairs.

"Where do you live, then?" I asked.

"This house is E-shaped," he said. "I have the ground floor of the south wing." He pointed to a wide passage leading away from the main hall. "Father has inherited this house but he and Mother don't want to live here. They say it's too big. I'm negotiating with Father to be allowed to stay here as a tenant. Keith wants me out and himself in, sod him."

"It must cost a fortune to run," I commented.

"There's no roof on the north wing," he said. "Ridiculous, but if part of the house is uninhabitable, they reduce the tax on it. The north wing needed a new roof, but it was more economical to take the roof right off and let the weather do its worst. The north wing's a ruin. The outside walls still look all right, but it's a shell."

I would come back one day soon, I thought, and ask to see the ruin, but at the moment was concerned only to relieve the Gardners of their extended baby-sitting.

Dart obligingly drove me the mile back to the main gate, where our way in through them was barred by a large bearded man in a woolly hat who stepped into the path of our car. Dart, swearing, jolted to a stop, his only option.

"They were doing this earlier," he said. "They stopped Aunt Marjorie on her way to the shareholders' meeting. And Father, and Keith. They were furious."

Owing to Roger Gardner having directed me to his house through a down-the-course entrance, I hadn't had to run the gauntlet myself. The boys, I knew, would have enjoyed it from the safe, high ground of the bus.

The large beard carried a red message on a placard— "HORSES RIGHTS COME FIRST." He stood without budging in front of the car while a sharp-faced woman rapped on Dart's window, signaling that he should lower it. Dart stolidly refused, which made her screech her own message, which was that all persons to do with racing were murderers. Her thin intensity reminded me vividly of Rebecca, and I wondered which came to them both first, a leaning towards obsession or an activity worthy of it.

She carried a black-edged placard saying ominously "DOOM TO RACEGOERS," and she was joined at the window by a jollier woman whose notice-on-a-stick read "SET HORSES FREE."

Someone rapped peremptorily on the window my side, and I turned my head and looked straight into the glaring eyes of a fanatical young man showing the blazing fervor of an evangelist.

He yelled "Murderer" at me and shook for my attention a blown-up photograph of a horse lying dead beside white racecourse rails. "Murderer," he repeated.

"They're potty," Dart said, unconcerned.

"They're doing their thing."

"Poor buggers."

The proselytizing group had now all gathered round the car, but were staring balefully rather than making overtly threatening movements. Their dedication to the cause stopped short of physically harming us. Their kicks would be a nice warm glow that evening at having expressed their caring natures. They would be unlikely, by themselves, to close down an industry that employed the sixth-largest workforce in the country, but that probably made them feel all the safer in attacking it.

So far, I thought, looking at their angry committed faces, they hadn't been adopted by professional bully-boy saboteurs. A matter of time, perhaps.

Dart, having had enough, began edging his car forward. The bearded way-barrer leaned against the bonnet. Dart waved to the obstruction to remove itself. The obstruction shook its fist and continued leaning. Dart pushed his hand down irritably on the horn and the obstruction jumped to one side, galvanized. Dart rolled slowly ahead. The placard bearer stalked beside us for several paces but stopped abruptly as we crossed through the gates themselves. Someone, it seemed, must have instructed them about trespass.

"Such a bore," Dart said, accelerating. "How long do you think they'll keep it up?"

"For your race meeting here next Monday," I suggested, "I would get a police cordon."

5

"WHERE'S YOUR car?" Dart asked. "I'm going out the back way. I'm tired of those hate merchants. Where's your car?"

"I came in the back way," I said. "Drop me somewhere down there."

His eyebrows rose, but all he said was, "Fine," and he headed on the inner way past the grandstands and down the narrow private inconspicuous road to the racecourse manager's house.

"What's that monstrous bus doing there?" he demanded rhetorically when he saw it.

I said, "It's mine," but the words were lost in a sharp horrified exclamation from my driver who had seen, past the bus, the black parked shape of his great-aunt's chauffeured Daimler.

"Aunt Marjorie! What the hell is *she* doing here?"

He braked his rusty runabout beside the gleaming ostentation and without much enthusiasm decided to investigate. The view that presented itself as we rounded a corner of the manager's neat modern house had me helplessly laughing, even if I laughed alone.

Double garage doors stood open. Within the garage, empty space, swept clean. Out on the drive, the former contents lay untidily in clumps of gardening tools, cardboard boxes, spare roof tiles and rolls of netting for covering strawberry beds. To one side a discard section included a gutted refrigerator, a rotted baby buggy, a battered metal trunk, a mouse-eaten sofa and a heap of rusty wire.

Standing more or less to attention in a ragged row stood five young helpers deep in trouble, with Mrs. Roger Gardner, sweet but threatened by authority, trying ineffectually to defend them.

Marjorie's penetrating voice was saying, "It's all very well you boys carrying all that stuff out, but you're not to leave it there. Put everything back at once."

Poor Mrs. Gardner, wringing her hands, was saying, "But Mrs. Binsham, all I wanted was for them to empty the garage . . ."

"This mess is insupportable. Do as I tell you, boys. Put it all back."

Christopher, looking desperately around, latched onto my arrival with Dart as if saved at the eleventh hour from the worst horror movie.

"Dad!" he said explosively. "We cleared out the garage."

"Yes, well done."

Marjorie swiveled on one heel and directed her disapproval towards Dart and me, at which point my identification as the father of the workforce left her temporarily speechless.

"Mr. Morris," Roger Gardner's wife said hurriedly, "your children have been great. Please believe me."

It was courageous of her, I thought, considering her husband's vulnerability to the Stratton family's whims. I thanked her warmly for keeping the children employed while I'd attended the shareholders' meeting.

Marjorie Binsham stared at me piercingly but spoke to Dart, her displeasure a vibration in the air.

"What are you doing here with Mr. Morris?"

Dart said with cowardice, "He wanted to see Stratton Hays."

"Did he, indeed? Stratton Hays is no business of his. This racecourse, however, is *yours,* or so I should have thought. Yours and your father's. Yet what have either of you done to look after it? It is I who have had to drive round to see that everything is in order. Colonel Gardner and I, not you and your father, have made a thorough inspection of the course."

I could see, as easily as she could, that it had never occurred to Dart that he had any responsibility for the state of the racecourse. It had never been his domain. He opened and closed his mouth a couple of times but came up with no protest or defense.

A frazzled-looking Colonel drove up in a jeep and, springing out, assured Marjorie Binsham that he had already put in hand her requirement that spectators should be kept further away from the fences, to save them from injury henceforth.

"It isn't my job," she complained to Dart. "A few posts, and some rope, some instructions to stand back, that's all it takes. *You* should have thought of it. The racecourse has had too much bad publicity. We cannot afford another debacle like last Saturday."

No one mentioned that it had been the horses, not the spectators, which had caused the grief.

"Also," Marjorie continued, "you and your father must

get rid of those people at the main gates. If you don't, they will attract extremists from all over the place, and the race crowds will stay away because of the aggravation. The racecourse will be killed off as quickly as by any of the crackpot schemes of Keith and your father. And as for Rebecca! If you notice, there's a woman just like her in that group at the gate. It's only a group now. Make sure it doesn't grow into a mob."

"Yes, Aunt Marjorie," Dart said. The task was beyond him, perhaps beyond anybody.

"Demonstrators don't want to succeed," Marjorie pointed out. "They want to *demonstrate*. Go and tell them to demonstrate for better conditions for stable lads. The horses are pampered enough. The lads are not."

No one remarked that injured stable lads usually lived.

"You, Mr. Morris." She fixed me with a sharp gaze. "I want to talk to *you.*" She pointed to her car. "In there."

"All right."

"And you children, clear this mess up at once. Colonel, I don't know what you're thinking of. This place is a *dump.*"

She headed off vigorously towards her car and didn't look around to make sure I followed, which I did.

"Mark," she told her chauffeur, who was sitting behind the steering wheel, "please take a walk."

He touched his chauffeur's cap to her and obeyed her as if accustomed to the request, and his employer waited beside one of the rear doors until I opened it for her.

"Good," she said, climbing into the spacious rear seat. "Get in beside me and sit down."

I sat where she pointed and closed the door.

"Stratton Hays," she said, coming at once to the point, "was where your mother lived with Keith."

"Yes," I acknowledged, surprised.

"Did you ask to see it?"

"Dart offered, very kindly. I accepted."

She paused, inspecting me.

"I never saw Madeline again, after she left," she said at length. "I disapproved of her leaving. Did she tell you?"

"Yes, she told me, but after so many years she bore you no animosity. She said you had urged your brother to close family ranks against her, but she was fond of your brother."

"It was a long time," she said, "before I found out what sort of a man Keith is. His second wife killed herself, did you know? When I said to my brother that Keith was an unlucky picker he told me it wasn't bad luck, it was Keith's own nature. He told me your mother couldn't love or nurse the baby Hannah because of the way the child had been conceived. Your mother told my brother that touching the baby made her feel sick."

"She didn't tell me that."

"I am now," Marjorie said, "offering you a formal apology for the way I behaved to your mother."

I paused only briefly to check what my parent would have wanted. "It's accepted," I said.

"Thank you."

I thought that that must conclude the conversation, but it seemed not.

"Keith's third wife left him and divorced him for irretrievable breakdown of marriage. He now has a fourth wife, Imogen, who spends half of the time drunk."

"Why doesn't she leave him too?" I asked.

"She won't or can't admit she made a mistake."

It was close enough to my own feelings to strike me dumb.

"Keith," his aunt said, "is the only Stratton short of money. Imogen told me. She can't keep her mouth shut after six glasses of vodka. Keith is in debt. That's why he's pushing to sell the racecourse. He needs the money."

I looked at the appearance Marjorie presented to the world: the little old lady well into her eighties with wavy white hair, soft pink and white skin and hawk-like dark eyes. The pithy, forceful mind and the sinewy vocabulary were, I imagined, the nearest in quality in the Stratton family to the financial genius who had founded them.

"I was furious with my brother for giving Madeline those shares," she said. "He could be obstinate sometimes. Now, all these years later, I'm glad that he did. I am glad," she finished slowly, "that someone outside the family can bring some sense of proportion into the Stratton hothouse."

"I don't know that I can."

"The point," she said, "is whether you want to. Or rather, how much you want to. If you hadn't been in the least bit interested, you wouldn't have turned up here today."

"True."

"You could oblige me," she said, "by finding out how much money Keith owes, and to whom. And by finding out what relationship Conrad has with the architect he's committed to, who Colonel Gardner tells me knows nothing about racing and is designing a monstrosity. The Colonel tells me we need an architect more like the one who built your own house, but that your architect only designs on a small scale."

"The Colonel told you he'd visited me?"

"Most sensible thing he's done this year."

"You amaze me."

"I want you as an ally," she said. "Help me make the racecourse prosper."

I tried to sort out my own jumbled responses, and it was

out of the jumble and not from thought-through reasons that I gave her my answer.

"All right, I'll try."

She held out a small hand to formalize the agreement, and I shook on it, a binding commitment.

MARJORIE WAS DRIVEN away without returning to the gutted garage, which was just as well as I found the mess unchanged and the boys, the Gardners and Dart all in the Gardners' kitchen with their attention on cake. Warm fragrant pale-colored fruitcake, that minute baked. Christopher asked for the recipe "so that Dad can make it in the bus."

"Dad can cook?" Dart asked ironically.

"Dad can do anything," Neil said, munching.

Dad, I thought to myself, had probably just impulsively set himself on a high road to failure.

"Colonel . . ." I started.

He interrupted. "Call me Roger."

"Roger," I said, "can I . . . I mean, may the architect of my house come here tomorrow and make a thorough survey of the grandstands as they are at present? I'm sure you have professional advisers about the state of the fabric and so on, but could we take a fresh detached survey with a view to seeing whether new stands are or are not essential for a profitable future?"

Dart's cake came to a standstill in mid-chew and Roger Gardner's face lost some of its habitual gloom.

"Delighted," he said, "but not tomorrow. I've got the course-builders coming, and the full complement of groundsmen will be here getting everything in shape for next Monday's meeting."

"Friday, then?"

He said doubtfully, "That'll be Good Friday. Easter, of

course. Perhaps your man won't want to work on Good Friday."

"He'll do what I tell him," I said. "It's me."

Both Dart and Roger were surprised.

"I am," I said gently, "a qualified architect. I did five arduous years at the Architectural Association, one of the most thorough schools in the world. I do choose houses in preference to high rises, but that's because horizontal lines that fit in with nature please me better. I'm a Frank Lloyd Wright disciple, not a Le Corbusier, if that means anything to you."

"I've heard of them," Dart said. "Who hasn't?"

"Frank Lloyd Wright," I said, "developed the cantilever roof you see on all new grandstands everywhere."

"We don't have a cantilever," Roger said thoughtfully.

"No, but let's see what you *do* have, and what you can get away with not having."

Dart's view of me had changed a little. "You said you were a builder," he accused.

"Yes, I am."

Dart looked at the children. "What does your father do?" he asked.

"Builds houses."

"With his own hands, do you mean?"

"Well," Edward amplified, "with spades and trowels and a saw and everything."

"Ruins," Christopher explained. "We're on a ruin hunt for our Easter holidays."

Together they described the pattern of their lives to an ever more astonished audience. Their matter-of-fact acceptance of not every child's experience seemed especially to amaze.

"But we're going to keep the last one he did. Aren't we, Dad?"

"Yes."

"Promise."

I promised for roughly the twentieth time, which was an indication of the depth of their anxiety, as I'd always kept the promises I'd made them.

"You must all be so tired of moving on," Mrs. Gardner said sympathetically.

"It's not that," Christopher told her, "it's the house. It's brilliant." Brilliant in his teenage vocabulary meant only the opposite of awful (pronounced *ah*-fal, ironically).

Roger nodded and agreed, however. "Brilliant. Hell to heat, I should think, though, with all that space."

"It has a hypocaust," Neil said, licking his fingers.

The Gardners and Dart gazed at him.

"What," Dart asked, giving in, "is a hypocaust?"

"Central heating invented by the Romans," said my seven-year-old composedly. "You make hollow spaces and runways under a stone floor and drive hot air through, and the floor stays warm all the time. Dad thought it would work and it does. We ran about without shoes all winter."

Roger turned his head my way.

"Come on Friday, then," he said.

WHEN I DROVE the bus back to the same spot on a sunny morning two days later the ground outside the garage was cluttered not with the debris of decades but with horses.

My sons gazed out of their safe windows at a moving clutch of about six large quadrupeds and decided not to climb down among the hooves, even though every animal was controlled by a rider.

The horses, to my eyes, weren't fine-boned enough to be racehorses, nor were the riders as light as the average stable lad, and when I swung down from the cab Roger came hurrying across from his house, side-stepping round massive hindquarters, to tell me these were Conrad's working hunters out for their morning exercise. They were supposed to be out on the road, Roger said, but they'd been practically attacked by the six or seven woolen hats still stubbornly picketing the main gates.

"Where do they come from?" I asked, looking around.

"The horses? Conrad keeps them here on the race-course in a yard down near the back entrance, where you came in."

I nodded. I'd seen the back of what could well have been the stables.

"They're trotting up and down the inner road instead," Roger said. "It's not ideal, but I won't let them out on the course, where they sometimes go, because everything is ready for Monday's meeting. Wouldn't your boys like to get out and see them?"

"I don't think so," I said. "Since the slaughter at the open ditch last Saturday they are a bit afraid of them. They were very shocked, you know, by that dead spectator's injuries."

"I'd forgotten they'd seen him, poor man. Will they just stay in the bus, then, while you and I go over the stands? I've spread out some of the original drawings in my office. We'll look at those first, if you like."

I suggested driving bus and boys as near to the office as possible, which resulted in our parking where the Stratton family's cars had been gathered two days earlier. The boys, relieved by the arrangement, asked if they could play a hide-and-seek game in the stands, if they promised not to do any damage.

Roger gave assent doubtfully. "You'll find many of the doors are locked," he told them. "And the whole place was cleaned yesterday, ready for Monday, so don't make any mess."

They promised not to. Roger and I left them beginning to draw up rules for their game and made our way to a low white-painted wooden building on the far side of the parade ring.

"Is it pirates again?" Roger asked, amused.

"I think it's storming the Bastille this time. That's to say, rescuing a prisoner without being captured yourself. Then the rescued prisoner has to hide and not be recaptured."

I looked back as Roger unlocked his office door. The boys waved. I waved back and went in, and began to sort my way through ancient building plans that had been rolled up so long that straightening them out was like six bouts with an octopus.

I took off my jacket and hung it on the back of a chair, so as to come to grips with things more easily, and Roger made a comment about the warmth of the spring day and hoped the sunshine would last until Monday.

Most of the plans were in fact working drawings, which gave detailed specifications for every nut and bolt. They were thorough, complete and impressive, and I commented on it.

"The only problem is," Roger said, with a twisting smile, "that the builder didn't stick to the specs. Concrete that should be six inches thick with reinforcing bars well covered has recently proved to be barely four and a half inches and we're having endless trouble with the private balcony boxes with water getting in through cracks and rusting the bars, which then of course expand because of the rust and crack the concrete more. *Crumble* the concrete, in some places."

"Spalling," I nodded. "Can be dangerous."

"And," Roger went on, "if you look at the overall design of the water inlets and outlets and sewer lines, the drawings make very good sense, but the water and drain pipes don't actually go where they should. We had one set of ladies' lavatories backing up for no reason we could think of and flooding the floor, but the drain seemed clear, and then we found we were checking the wrong drain, and the one from the lavatories went in an entirely different direction and was blocked solid."

It was familiar territory. Builders had minds of their own and often ignored the architect's best instructions, either because they truly thought they knew better or because they could make a fatter profit by shaving the quality.

We uncurled a dozen more sheets and tried to hold them flat with pots of pens for paperweights, a losing battle. I acquired, all the same, an understanding of what should have been built, with some picture of stress points and weaknesses to look for. I'd studied ancient plans a great deal less trustworthy than these, and these grandstands weren't ruins after all: they'd withstood gales and rot for well over half a century.

Basically, the front of the stands, the viewing steps themselves, were of reinforced concrete supported by steel girders, which also held up the roof. Backing the concrete and steel, solid brick pillars formed the weight-bearers for the bars, dining rooms and private rooms for the owners and stewards. Centrally there was a stairway stretching upward through five stories giving access outwards and inwards throughout. A simple effective design, even if now out of date.

The door of the office was suddenly flung open, and Neil catapulted himself inside.

"Dad," he said insistently, "Dad . . ."

"I'm busy, Neil."

"But it's urgent. Really really urgent."

I let a set of drawings recurl by accident. "How urgent?" I asked, trying to open them again.

"I found some white wires, Dad, going in and out of some walls."

"What wires?"

"You know when they blew up the chimney?"

I left the plans to their own devices and paid full attention to my observant son. My heart jumped a beat. I did indeed remember the blowing up of the chimney.

"Where are the wires?" I asked, trying for calmness.

Neil said, "Near that bar with the smelly floor."

"What on earth is he talking about?" Roger demanded.

"Where are your brothers?" I said briefly.

"In the stands. Hiding. I don't know where," Neil's eyes were wide. "Don't let them be blown up, Dad."

"No." I turned to Roger. "Can you switch on a public address system that can be heard everywhere in the stands?"

"What on earth . . ."

"*Can you?*" I felt my own panic rising: fought it down.

"But . . ."

"For God's sake," I half yelled at him, quite unfairly. "Neil's saying he's seen det cord and demolition charges in the stands."

Roger's own face went taut. "Are you *serious?*"

"Same as the factory chimney?" I asked Neil, checking.

"Yes, Dad. *Exactly* the same. Do come on."

"Public address system," I said with dreadful urgency to Roger. "I have to get those children out of there at once."

He gave me a dazed look but at last went into action, hurrying out of his office and half running across the parade ring towards the weighing room, sorting through his bunch of keys as he went. We came to a halt beside the door into Oliver Wells's office, the lair of the Clerk of the Course.

"We tested the system yesterday," Roger said, fumbling slightly. "Are you *sure?* This child's so young. I'm sure he's mistaken."

"Don't risk it," I said, practically ready to shake him.

He got the door open finally and went across to unlatch a metal panel which revealed banks of switches.

"This one," he said, pressing down with a click. "You can speak direct from here. Let me plug in the microphone."

He brought an old-fashioned microphone from a drawer, fitted plug to socket, and handed me the instrument.

"Just speak," he said.

I took a breath and tried to sound urgent but not utterly frightening, though utterly frightened was what I myself felt.

"This is Dad," I said as slowly as I could, so they could hear clearly, "Christopher, Toby, Edward, Alan, the grandstands are not safe. Wherever you're hiding, leave the stands and go to the gate in the rails where we went through and down the course last Saturday. Go out in front of the stands, and gather by that gate. The gate is the rallying point. Go *at once.* The Bastille game is over for now. It's *urgent* that you go at once to the gate where we went out onto the course. It's quite near the winning post. Go there now. The grandstands aren't safe. They might blow up at any moment."

I switched off temporarily and said to Neil, "Do you remember how to get to that gate?"

He nodded and told me how, correctly.

"Then you go there too, will you, so that the others can

see you? And tell them what you saw."

"Yes, Dad."

I said to Roger, "Have you the key to the gate?"

"Yes, but . . ."

"I'd be happier if they could go out through that gate and across to the winning post itself. Even that might not be far enough."

"Surely you're exaggerating," he protested.

"I hope to God I am."

Neil hadn't waited. I watched his little figure run.

"We went to see an old factory chimney being blown up," I said to Roger. "The boys were fascinated. They saw some charges being set. It was only three months ago." I spoke again into the microphone, "Boys, go down to the gate. It's very very urgent. The stands are unsafe. They might blow up. Just run." I turned to Roger. "Could you unlock the gate for them?"

He said, "Why don't you?"

"I'd better check those wires, don't you think?"

"But . . ."

"Look, I've got to make sure Neil is right, haven't I? And we don't know *when* the charges are set for, do we? Maybe five minutes, maybe five hours, maybe after dark. Can't risk it for the boys, though. Have to get them out at once."

Roger swallowed and made no more objections. Together we ran from his office round to the front of the stands, he taking the key with him, I wanting to check that all five were safe.

The little knot by the gate grew to four as Neil reached them. Four, not five.

Four. *Not Toby.*

I sprinted back to Oliver's office and picked up the microphone.

"Toby, this is not a game. Toby, get off the stands. The stands are not safe. Toby, for Christ's sake do what I say. *This is not a game.*"

I could hear my voice reverberating round and through the building and out in the paddocks. I repeated the urgent words once more and then ran round the stands again to check that Toby had heard and obeyed.

Four boys. Four boys and Roger, walking across the track to the winning post. Not running. If Toby were watching, he'd see no reason for haste.

"Come on, you little *bugger*," I said under my breath. "For once in your life, *be told.*"

I went back to the microphone and said it loud and baldly. "There are demolition charges in the stands, Toby, are you listening? Remember the chimney? The stands can blow up too. Toby, get out of there quickly and join the others."

I went back yet again to the front of the stands, and yet again Toby failed to appear.

I was not a demolitions expert. If I wanted to take a building down to its roots I usually did it brick by brick, salvaging everything useful. I'd have felt happier at that moment if I'd known more. The first priority, though, was obviously to look at what Neil had seen, and to do that I needed to enter and climb the central stairway, off which led the bar with the smelly floor; the members' bar which should have been much busier than it was.

It was the same staircase, I'd noticed, that on one landing led off through double doors to the Strattons' carpeted and cosseted private rooms. According to the plans and also from what I myself remembered of it, that staircase was the central vertical artery feeding all floors of the grandstand; the central core of the whole major building.

At the top was a large windowed room like a control tower from where the Stewards with massive binoculars watched the races. A modern offshoot from there ran up yet again to an eyrie inhabited by race-callers, television equipment and the scribbling classes.

At other levels on its upward progress the staircase branched off inwards to a members' lunch room and outwards to ranks of standing-only steps open to the elements. A corridor on the first floor led to a row of private balcony boxes where prim little light white wooden chairs gave respite to rich and elderly feet.

I went into the staircase from the open front of the stands and sprinted up to the level of the smelly members' bar. The door of the bar was locked, but along the white-painted landing wall outside, at about eighteen inches from the ground, ran a harmless-looking thick white filament that looked like the sort of washing line used for drying laundry in back gardens.

At intervals along the wall the line ran into the wall itself and out again, and finally a hole had been drilled from the landing through into the bar, so that the white line ran into it, disappearing from view.

Neil had made no mistake. The white washing line look-alike was in fact itself an explosive known as "det cord," short for detonating cord, along which detonation could travel at something like eighteen thousand meters a second, blowing apart everything it touched. At every spot where the cord went into the wall and out again there would be a compressed cache of plastic explosive. All explosives did more damage when compressed.

Det cord was not like old fuses spluttering slowly towards a bomb marked "BOMB," as in comics and ancient westerns. Det cord *was* the explosive; and it seemed to be winding up and down through the walls of the stairwell for at least one floor above me and another below.

I yelled "Toby" with full lungs and whatever power I could muster. I yelled "Toby" up the staircase and I yelled "Toby" down the staircase, and got no response at all.

"Toby, if you're here, this place is full of explosives." I yelled it up the stairs, and down.

Nothing.

He had to be somewhere else, I thought. But where? *Where?* There could be det cord festooned throughout the length of all the buildings; throughout the Club, through the big secondary enclosure known as "Tattersalls" where on race days the bookies had their pitches, through the cheapest of three enclosures where there were almost more bars than viewing steps.

"Toby," I yelled: and got silence.

There was no possibility that I could miraculously dismantle what looked like a thoroughly planned attack. I didn't know enough, nor where to start. My first priority, anyway, was the safety of my son, so with silence continuing, I turned to go back out into the open air, to run further down the sprawling complex and try again.

I'd already pivoted to run when I heard the tiniest noise, and it seemed to me it came from above, from somewhere up the stairs, over my head.

I sprinted up two levels, to the landing outside the Stewards' vantage point, and yelled again. I tried the Stewards' room door, but like so much else, it was locked. He couldn't be in there, but I yelled anyway.

"Toby, if you're here, *please* come out. This place can blow up at any moment. Please, Toby. *Please.*"

Nothing. False alarm. I turned to go down again, to start searching somewhere else.

A wavery little voice said, "Dad?"

I whirled. He was climbing with difficulty out of his perfect tiny hiding place, a small sideboard with spindly legs beside an empty row of pegs meant for the Stewards' hats and coats.

"Thank God," I said briefly. "Now come on."

"I was the escaped prisoner," he said, slithering out and standing up. "If they'd found me they would have put me back in the Bastille."

I hardly listened. I felt only urgency along with relief.

"Will it really blow up, Dad?"

"Let's just get out of here."

I reached for his hand and tugged him with me towards the stairs, and there was a sort of *crrrump* from below us, and then a brilliant flash of light and a horrendous bang and a swaying all about us, and it was like what I imagined it must be like to be caught in an earthquake.

6

IN THE fraction of time when thought was possible, both knowledge and instinct screamed that the stairs themselves, wreathed and tied with explosive like a parcel, were the embrace of death.

Enclosing Toby in my arms I spun on the heaving floor and hurled us with slipping feet and every labor-trained muscle back towards Toby's hiding-place cupboard beside the Stewards' box door.

The core of Stratton Park racecourse imploded, folding inwards. The staircase ripped and cracked and crashed as its walls collapsed into the well, splitting open into jagged caverns all the rooms alongside.

The Stewards' door blew open, its glass viewing walls splintering and flying in slicing spears. The terrifying noise deafened. The stands shrieked as they tore apart, wood against wood against brick against concrete against stone against steel.

With Toby beneath me, I fell forwards, scrabbling and

seeking for footing so as not to slide back towards the gutted stairs; and the high precarious tower atop all else, the press and television vantage point, came smashing down through the ceiling beams and plaster above us, plunging in sharp-edged pieces at crazy angles across my back and legs. I seemed to stop breathing. Sharp stabs of passing agony stapled me to the floor. Movement became impossible.

Billowing black smoke poured up from the stairs, lung-filling, choking, setting off convulsive coughing when there was no room to cough.

The thunderous noise gradually stopped. Far below, small creaks and intermittent crashes. Everywhere black smoke, gray dust. In me, pain.

"Dad," Toby's voice said, "you're squashing me." He was coughing also. "I can't breathe, Dad."

I glanced vaguely down. The top of his head, brown-haired, came up as far as my chin. Inappropriately, but how can one help the things one thinks, I thought of his mother's once frequent complaint—"Lee, you're squashing me"— and I would raise my weight off her by leaning on my elbows and I'd look into her gleaming laughing eyes and kiss her, and she'd say that I was too big and that one day I would collapse her lungs and break her ribs and suffocate her from love.

Collapse her lungs, snap her ribs, suffocate . . . dear God.

With a good deal of effort I levered my elbows up into the familiar supporting position and spoke to Amanda's twelve-year-old son.

"Wriggle out," I said, coughing. "Wriggle up this way, head first."

"Dad . . . you're too heavy."

"Come on," I said, "you can't lie there all day." I meant,

I didn't know for how long I could lift myself off him, so as not to kill him.

I felt like Atlas, only the world lay not on my shoulders, but beneath them.

Incongruously, sunlight fell all around us. Blue sky above, glimpsed through the hole in the roof. The black smoke funneled up through there, slowly dispersing.

Toby made convulsive little heaves until his face came up level with mine. His brown eyes looked terrified and, uncharacteristically, he was crying.

I kissed his cheek, which normally he didn't like. This time he seemed not to notice and didn't wipe it away.

"It's all right," I said. "It's over. We're both all right. All we have to do is get out. Keep on wriggling, you're doing fine."

He inched out with difficulty, pushing bits of masonry out of his way. There were some sobs but no complaints. He made it onto his knees by my right shoulder, panting quietly, coughing now and then.

"Well done," I said. I let my chest relax onto the floor. Not an enormous relief, except for my elbows.

"Dad . . . you're bleeding."

"Never mind."

A few more sobs.

"Don't cry," I said.

"That man," he said. "The horse kicked his eyes out."

I moved my shirt-sleeved right forearm in his direction. "Hold my hand," I said. His own fingers slid slowly across my palm. "Look," I said, gripping lightly, "dreadful things do happen. There's never going to be a time in your whole life when you won't remember that man's face. But you'll remember it less and less often, not all the time, like now. And you'll remember us being here, with all the stands blown inwards. A lot of people's memories are full of truly awful things. Any time you want to talk about that man, I'll listen."

He squeezed my hand fiercely, and let it go.

"We can't just sit here forever," he said.

Despite our fairly disadvantaged state, I was smiling.

"It's quite likely," I remarked, "that your brothers and Colonel Gardner will have noticed the stands have been rearranged. People will come."

"I could go and wave out of those broken windows, to tell them where we are . . ."

"Stay right here," I said sharply. "Any floor might collapse."

"Not this one, Dad." He looked around wildly. "Not this one, that we're on, will it, Dad?"

"It'll be all right," I said, hoping I spoke the truth. The whole landing, however, now sloped towards where the stairs had been, and I wouldn't have cared to jump up and down on it with abandon.

The pressures of the chunks of ceiling roof and press tower were unremitting across my back and legs, pinning me comprehensively. I could, though, move my toes inside my shoes, and I could certainly feel. Unless the building subsided more from accumulated internal stress, it looked possible I might escape with a clear head, an intact spinal cord, both hands and feet and an undamaged son. Not bad, considering. I hoped, all the same, that rescuers would expedite.

"Dad."

"Mm?"

"Don't shut your eyes."

I opened them, and kept them open.

"When will people come?" he asked.

"Soon."

"It wasn't my fault the stands exploded."

"Of course not."

After a pause, he said, "I thought you were kidding."

"Yep."

"It's not my fault you're hurt, is it?"

"No." He wasn't, I saw, reassured. I said, "If you hadn't been hiding right up here I could have been lower down the stairs when the explosion happened, and would now very likely be dead."

"Are you sure?"

"Yes."

It seemed very quiet. Almost as if nothing had happened. If I tried to move, different story . . .

"How did you know the stands would explode?" Toby said.

I told him about Neil seeing the det cord. "It's thanks to him," I said, "that all five of you weren't killed."

"I didn't notice any cord."

"No, but you know what Neil's like."

"He *sees* things."

"Yes."

In the distance, at what seemed long last, we could hear sirens. One, at first, then several, then a whole wailing orchestra.

Toby wanted to move but again I told him to stay still, and before very long there were voices on the racecourse side, outside and below, calling my name.

"Tell them we're here," I told Toby, and he shouted with his high voice, "We're here. We're up here."

After a brief silence a man's voice yelled, "Where?"

"Tell them beside the Stewards' box," I said.

Toby shouted the information and got another question in return.

"Is your father with you?"

"Yes."

"Is he talking?"

"Yes." Toby looked at me and spontaneously gave them more news. "He can't move. Some roof fell in."

"Stay there."

"OK?" I said to Toby. "I told you they would come."

We listened to clanging and banging and businesslike shouting, all far away and outside. Toby was shivering, not with cold, as the midday sun still warmed us, but with accumulated shock.

"They won't be long," I said.

"What are they *doing?*"

"Putting up some sort of scaffolding, I should think."

They came up from the racecourse side, where the reinforced concrete viewing steps on the steel girders had, it transpired, survived the onslaught pretty well unscathed. A fireman in a big hard hat and a bright yellow jacket suddenly appeared outside the broken windows of the Stewards' box and peered inwards.

"Anyone home?" he cheerfully called.

"Yes." Toby stood up joyfully and I told him abruptly to stay still.

"But Dad . . ."

"Stay still."

"You stay there, young 'un. We'll have you out in no time," the fireman told him, and vanished as quickly as he'd come. Returning, he brought with him a colleague and a secure metal walkway for Toby to cross onto the window, and almost in no time, as he'd promised, he'd picked the boy out of the window and out of danger. As Toby disappeared from my view, I felt weak. I trembled from relief. A lot of strength seemed to drain away.

The colleague, a moment later, stepped through the window and crossed the walkway in reverse, stopping at the end of it, some several feet from where I lay.

"Lee Morris?" he asked. Dr. Livingstone, I presume.

"Yes," I said.

"It won't be long."

They came in personal harnesses with jacks and canti-levers and slings and cutting equipment and a mini-crane, and they knew what they were doing, but the whole area where I was lying proved wickedly unstable, and at one point another big section of the press box came crashing through the roof and, missing my feet by millimeters, bounced and plummeted down the five-story hole where the stairs were meant to be. One could hear it colliding with wrecked walls all the way down until it reached the bottom with a reverberating disintegrating thud.

The firemen sweated and put jacks from floor to ceiling wherever they could.

There were three men working, moving circumspectly, taking no sudden unpremeditated steps. One of them, I slowly realized, seemed to be operating a video camera, of all things. The whirring came and went. I twisted my head round to check and found the busy lens pointing straight at my face, which I found deeply embarrassing but could do nothing about. A fourth man arrived, again in yellow, again with a rope to his waist, and he too brought a camera. Too much, I thought. He asked the first three for a progress report and I read his identification—"Police"—in black on his yellow chest.

The building *creaked*.

The men all stopped moving, waiting. The sounds ceased and the firemen with extreme caution moved again, cursing, dedicated, brave, prosaically taking risks.

I lay gratefully inert on my stomach and thought I hadn't had a bad life, if this should prove to be the end of it. The firemen had no intention of letting me come to the end of it. They brought up and slid a harness under my chest and fastened it round my arms and across my shoulders so that if I slid I wouldn't go down the gaping hole and, bit by bit, they levered the extensive chunks of brick and plaster slightly off me and freed me from splintered beams until, by pulling on the harness, they could move me a couple of feet up the sloping floor towards the threshold of the Stewards' box. The footing was more solid there, they said.

I wasn't of much help to them. I'd lain squashed for so long that my muscles wouldn't move properly on demand. Many of them developed pins and needles and then throbbed as if released from tourniquets, which I didn't much mind. The cuts caused by spears of wood felt worse.

A man in a fluorescent green jacket came through the window, crossed the safe walkway and, pointing to the information lettered in black across his chest, told me he was a doctor.

Dr. Livingstone? No, Dr. Jones. Oh, well.

He bent down by my head, which I'd tired of holding up.

"Can you squeeze my hand?" he asked.

I squeezed his hand obligingly and told him I wasn't much hurt.

"Good."

He went away.

It wasn't until much later, when I watched one of the videotapes, that I learned he hadn't totally believed me because, except for the collar and sleeves, my white shirt showed scarlet and had been ripped here and there like bits of skin underneath. In any case, when he returned it wasn't to expect me to stand up and walk out: instead he brought what looked to me like a sled, not a flat stretcher that one could easily fall off, but with raised rails down the sides, better for carrying.

One way or another, with one of the fireman levering the last chunk of timber off my legs and the other two pulling me forwards by the harness, with me tugging myself forward handhold by handhold, I slithered along face down onto the offered transport. When my center of gravity was more or less onto the safe walkway, and I was supported from the thighs up, the ominous creaking started again in the building, this time worse, this time with tremors.

The fireman behind my feet said "Christ" and leapt onto the walkway, edging past me with infectious urgency. As if rehearsed he and the others abandoned slow care, caught hold of the side rails of my sled-stretcher and yanked it with me hanging on like a limpet across the narrow path to the windows.

The building shuddered and shook. The rest of the press room—by far the largest part—toppled up high, broke loose, smashed down lethally through what was left of the ceiling right onto the place where I'd been lying, and with its weight tore the whole landing away from its walls and, roaring and thundering, plunged horribly downwards. Grit, dust, bricks, chunks of splintered plaster and slivers of glass fog-filled the air. Mesmerized, I glanced back over my shoulder and saw Toby's hiding place, the small sideboard, topple over forwards and slide to oblivion. The floor of the Stewards' box subsided and left the cantilevered safe walkway protruding inward from the sill of the window, life-saving still but now with nothing beneath. My legs, from above the knees, stuck out over space.

Incredibly, the policeman, now just outside the window, went on filming.

I gripped the rails of the stretcher, my hands fierce with the elemental fear of falling. The firemen clutched the harness round my shoulders, lifted the stretcher, hurled themselves and me toward safety, and the whole lot of us popped out into sunshine, an untidy group, disorganized, coughing from dust, but alive.

Nothing even then proved simple. The concrete viewing steps of the stands reached only as far as a story below the Stewards' box, and to bring the rescue equipment up the last nine or ten feet had demanded many struts ingeniously bolted together. Below near the racecourse rails, where crowds on race days cheered the finishes, the asphalt and grass viewing areas were packed with vehicles—fire engines, police cars, ambulances—and, worst, a television station's van.

I said that it would be much easier and less embarrassing if I simply stood up and walked down, and no one paid any attention. The doctor reappeared talking about internal injuries and not giving me any chance to make things worse, so rather against my will I got covered with a dressing or two and a blanket and was secured to the stretcher with straps and slowly carried step by careful step to the ground and across to where the emergency vehicles waited. I thanked the firemen. They grinned.

At the end of the journey five boys stood in a row, frightened and terribly strained.

I said, "I'm fine, chaps," but they seemed unconvinced.

I said to the doctor, "They're my children. Tell them I'm OK."

He glanced at me and at their young distressed faces.

"Your father," he said with common sense, "is a big strong fellow and he's quite all right. He has some bruises and cuts which we'll stick a few bandages on. You don't need to worry."

They read the word "Doctor" on the front of his bright green jacket and they decided, provisionally, to believe him.

"We're taking him to the hospital," the man in green

said, indicating a waiting ambulance, "but he'll be back
with you soon."

Roger appeared beside the boys and said he and his wife
would look after them. "Don't worry," he said.

Ambulance men began feeding me feet first into their
vehicle.

I said to Christopher, "Do you want your mother to
come and take you home?"

He shook his head. "We want to stay in the bus."

The others nodded silently.

"I'll phone her," I said.

Toby said urgently, "No, Dad. We want to stay in the
bus." His anxiety level, I saw, was still far too high. Anything that would reduce it had to be right.

"Play marooned, then," I said.

They all nodded, Toby, looking relieved, included.

The doctor, writing notes to give the ambulance men to
take with me asked, "What's play marooned?"

"Making do on their own for a bit."

He smiled over his notes. *Lord of the Flies?*

"I never let it get that far."

He gave the notes to one of the ambulance men and
glanced back at the boys. "Good kids."

"I'll look after them," Roger said again. "Be glad to."

"I'll phone you," I said. "And thanks."

The busy ambulance men shut the door on me, and Mrs.
Gardner, I found later, made fruitcake for the boys until
they couldn't face another slice.

Judged solely as a medical casualty I was fairly low
in priority in the hospital's emergency department but all
too high on the local media's attention list. The airwaves
were buzzing, it seemed, with "terrorist bombing of a racecourse." I begged the use of a telephone from some half-
cross, half-riveted nurses and got through to my wife.

"What the *hell's* going on?" she demanded, her voice high. "Some ruddy newspaper just phoned me to ask if I knew my husband and sons had been blown up. Can you *believe* it?"

"Amanda . . ."

"You obviously *haven't* been blown up."

"Which paper?"

"What does it matter? I can't remember."

"I'll complain. Anyway, just listen. Someone with a grudge put some explosive in Stratton Park racecourse, and yes, the stands did slightly blow up."

She interrupted, "The *boys*. Are they all right?"

"Unharmed. Totally all right. Only Toby was anywhere near, and some fireman carried him out. I promise you, none of them has a scratch."

"Where are you now?"

"The boys are with the racecourse manager and his wife."

"Aren't they with *you?* Why aren't they with you?"

"I've just . . . um. I'll be back with them in no time. I've got a couple of grazes that the local hospital's putting stuff on, then I'm going back to them. Christopher will phone you."

Every evening, from the mobile phone in the bus, the boys talked to their mother; family routine on expeditions.

Amanda took a bit of placating as well as reassuring. It was obviously my fault, she said, that the children had been put in danger. I didn't deny it. I asked her if she wanted them home.

"What? No, I didn't say that. You know I've a lot of things planned this weekend. They'd better stay with you. Just take more care of them, that's all."

"Yes."

"So what do I say if any other newspapers ring up?"

"Say you talked to me and everything's fine. You might see something about it on television, there were news cameras on the racecourse."

"Do take more *care,* Lee."

"Yes."

"And don't phone this evening. I'm taking Jamie over to Shelly's for the night. It's her birthday dinner, remember?"

Shelly was her sister. "Right," I said.

We said goodbye; always polite. Acid, by effort, diluted.

The variety of gashes and grazes that I had minimized as much as possible eventually got uncovered and tut-tutted over. Dust and rubble got washed out, impressive splinters were removed with tweezers and rows of staples got inserted with local anesthetic.

"You'll be sore when this wears off," the stitcher cheerfully told me. "Some of these wounds are deceptively deep. Are you *sure* you won't stay here overnight? I'm certain we can find a bed for you."

"Thanks," I said, "but no thanks."

"Lie on your stomach for a few days then. Come back in a week and we'll take the staples out. You should be healed by then."

"Thanks a lot," I said.

"Keep on taking the antibiotics."

The hospital dredged up an ambulance to take me back to Roger Gardner's house (by the back road, at my insistence) and with a bit of help from a borrowed walker and dressed in a blue dressing gown/robe from the hospital shop, I made the end of the journey upright.

The bus, I gratefully noted, had been driven down and parked outside the tidied garage. Its five younger inhabitants were in the Gardners' sitting room watching television.

"Dad!" they exclaimed, springing up, then, at the sight of the walking aid to the elderly, falling uncertainly silent.

"Yes," I said, "we will have no giggles about this, OK? A lot of bricks and ceiling fell on my back and legs and made a few cuts, which have now been stitched up. Some cuts were on my back and quite a lot on my legs and one cut is straight across my bottom so that I can't very easily sit down, and we will *not laugh* about that."

They did, of course, chiefly from relief, which was fine.

Mrs. Gardner offered sympathy.

"What can I get you?" she asked. "Hot cup of tea?"

"Treble scotch?"

Her sweet face creased. She poured the hard stuff generously and told me Roger had been busy all day along at the stands and was worn out by the police and by the news people and by most of the Stratton family, who had flocked to the place in fury.

The boys and Mrs. Gardner were, it appeared, waiting for the television news to start, which presently happened, with the bombing of Stratton Park racecourse prominently featured. Various shots showed the rear of the stands, from where the central column of damage couldn't be missed. A five-second interview with Conrad revealed his innermost thoughts ("shocked and angry"). "Fortunately only one minor casualty," said a voice over a shot of myself (luckily unrecognizable) being carried down the steps.

"That's you, Dad," Neil told me excitedly.

A brief shot of Toby walking down hand in hand with a fireman had the boys cheering. Next, ten seconds of Roger—"Colonel Gardner, racecourse manager"—saying the Stratton family promised the Monday race meeting would be held as scheduled. "Important not to give in to terror tactics." Finally a shot of the woolly hats with their placards at the gates, leaving viewers with an unspoken but sinister implication. Unfair, I thought.

When the news slid away into a plethora of politicians, I told Mrs. Gardner and the boys that I would go and put some clothes on, and I limped slowly with the walker over to the bus and winced without it up the steps, and although I'd meant to get dressed I lay down instead on the long sofa that was also my bed, and felt shivery and ill, and finally admitted to myself that I was a good deal more injured than I wanted to be.

After a while the outer door opened and I expected a child, but it was in fact Roger who had come.

He sat on the other long sofa opposite and looked weary.

"Are you all right?" he asked.

"Yes," I said, not moving.

"My wife says you look gray."

"You don't look too rosy yourself."

He smiled briefly and massaged his nose with a finger and thumb; a lean, neat, disciplined soldier allowing himself a gesture of tiredness after a long day's maneuvers.

"The police and all the safety-first people came out like bloodhounds. Oliver dealt with them—I phoned him at once—and he's bloody marvelous with those sort of people always. He had them agreeing immediately that, taking precautions, we could hold the races on Monday. Silver-tongued magician, he is." He paused. "The police have driven off to the hospital to interview you," he said. "Surely there was a bed for you there, in your state?"

"I didn't want to stay."

"But I told you we would look after your boys."

"I know. One or two might have been all right, but not five."

"They're easy children," he protested.

"They're subdued, today. It was best I came back."

He made no more demur but, as if unready yet to talk of the things uppermost in his thoughts, asked which was which. "To get them straight in my mind," he said.

I answered him in much the same way, postponing for a breathing space the questions that would have to be asked and answered.

"Christopher, the tall fair one, he's fourteen. Like most oldest children, he looks after the others. Toby, the one with me today in the stands, he's twelve. Edward's ten. He's the quiet one. Any time you can't find him, he's sitting in a corner somewhere reading a book. Then there's Alan."

"Freckles and a grin," Roger said, nodding.

"Freckles and a grin," I agreed, "and a deficient sense of danger. He's nine. Leaps first. Oops after."

"And Neil," Roger said. "Little bright-eyed Neil."

"He's seven. And Jamie, the baby, ten months."

"We have two daughters," Roger said. "Both grown and gone and too busy to marry."

He fell silent, and I also. The respite from gritty life slowly evaporated. I shifted with sharp discomfort on the sofa and Roger noted it but made no comment.

I said, "The stands were cleaned yesterday."

Roger sighed. "They were cleaned. They were clean. No explosives. Certainly no det cord running round that staircase. I walked everywhere myself, checking. I make rounds continually."

"But not on Good Friday morning."

"Late yesterday afternoon. Five o'clock. Went round with my foreman."

"It wasn't a matter of killing people." I said.

"No," he agreed. "It was to kill one main grandstand, on one of the very few weekdays in the year when there are no race meetings anywhere in Britain. Precisely *not* to kill people, in fact."

"I expect you have a night watchman," I said.

"Yes, we do." He shook his head frustratedly. "He makes his rounds with a dog. He says he heard nothing. He didn't hear people drilling holes in the walls. He saw no lights moving in the stands. He clocked out at seven this morning and went home."

"The police asked him?"

"The police asked him. I asked him. Conrad asked him. The poor man was brought back here soggy with sleep and bombarded with accusing questions. He's not ultra-bright at the best of times. He just blinked and looked stupid. Conrad blames me for employing a thicko."

"Blame will be scattered like confetti," I said.

He nodded. "The air's dense with it already. Mostly, everything's my fault."

"Which Strattons came?" I asked.

"Which didn't?" He sighed. "All of them except Rebecca that were here for the shareholders' meeting, plus Conrad's wife, Victoria, plus Keith's wife Imogen who was squinting drunk, plus Hannah's layabout son Jack, plus Ivan's mousy wife, Dolly. Marjorie Binsham used her tongue like a whip. Conrad can't stand up to her. She had the police pulverized. She wanted to know why you, particularly, hadn't stopped the stands blowing up once your infant child had done the trouble-spotting for you."

"Dear Marjorie!"

"Someone told her you'd damn nearly been killed and she said it served you right." He shook his head. "Sometimes I think the whole family's unhinged."

"There's some scotch and glasses in that cupboard above your head," I said.

He loosened into a smile and poured into two tumblers.

"It won't make you feel better," he observed, placing one on the built-in table with drawers under it that marked the end of my bed. "And where did you get this splendid bus? I've never seen anything like it. When I drove it down here with the boys on board they showed me all round it. They seemed to think you built the interior with your own hands. I reckon you had a yacht designer."

"Both right."

He tossed off his drink neat in two gulps, army fashion, and put down the glass.

"We can't give your boys beds, not enough room, but we could do food."

"Thanks, Roger. I'm grateful. But there's enough food in this bus for a battalion, and the battalion's had a good deal of practice in do-it-yourself."

Despite his assurances I could see his relief. He was indeed, if anything, more exhausted than myself.

I said, "Do me a favor, though?"

"If I can."

"Be vague about my whereabouts tonight? If, say, the police or the Strattons should ask."

"Somewhere to the left of Mars do you?"

"One day," I said, "I'll repay you."

THE REAL WORLD, as Toby would have said, had a go in the morning.

Traveling uncomfortably, I went along with Roger in his jeep to his office beside the parade ring, having left the five boys washing the outside of the bus with buckets of detergent, long-handled brushes and mops and the borrowed use of the Gardners' outdoor tap and garden hose.

Such mammoth splashy activity terminated always in five contentedly soaked children (they loved water-clown acts in circuses) and an at least half-clean bus. I'd advised

Mrs. Gardner to go indoors and close her eyes and windows, and after the first bucketful of suds had missed the windscreen and landed on Alan, she'd given me a wild look and taken my advice.

"Don't you mind their getting wet?" Roger asked as we left the scene of potential devastation.

"They've a lot of compressed steam to get rid of," I said.

"You're an extraordinary father."

"I don't feel it."

"How are the cuts?"

"Ghastly."

He chuckled, stopped beside the office door and handed me the walker once I was on my feet. I would have preferred not to have needed it, but the only strength left anywhere, it seemed, was in my arms.

Although it was barely eight-thirty the first carload of trouble drew up on the tarmac before Roger had finished unlocking his office door. He looked over his shoulder to see who had come, and said a heartfelt *"Bugger,"* as he recognized the transport. "Bloody Keith."

Bloody Keith had not come alone. Bloody Keith had brought with him his Hannah, and Hannah, it transpired, had brought with her her son Jack. The three of them climbed out of Keith's car and began striding purposefully round to Roger's office.

He finished unlocking, opened the door, and said to me abruptly, "Come inside."

At walker pace I willingly followed him around towards the far side of his desk, where, as it happened, my jacket still hung over the back of his chair, abandoned since the previous morning. A lifetime, almost a deathtime, ago.

Keith, Hannah and Jack crowded in through the door, all three faces angry. Keith had reacted to the sight of me as if to an allergy, and Hannah wouldn't have admired her own shrewish expression. Jack, a loose-lipped teenager, mirrored his grandfather too thoroughly; handsome and mean.

Keith said, "Gardner, get that damned man out of here! And you're sacked. You're incompetent. I'm taking over your job, and you can clear out. As for you . . ." He turned his glare fully my way. "Your bloody children had no right to be anywhere near the grandstands, and if you're thinking of suing us because you were stupid enough to get yourself blown up you've another think coming."

I hadn't thought of it at all, actually. "You've given me ideas," I said rashly.

Roger, too late, made a warning movement with his hand, telling me to cool it, not stir. I had myself seen the speed with which Keith's violence had risen in him at the shareholders' meeting, and I remembered the complacency with which I'd reflected that he'd have no physical chance against Madeline's thirty-five-year-old son.

Things had changed slightly since then. I now needed a walker if I were to stay upright. And besides, there were three of them.

7

ROGER SAID *"Hell"* under his breath.

I muttered to him similarly, "Get out of here."

"No."

"Yes. Keep your job."

Roger stayed.

Keith kicked the office door shut and though he, for a second or two, seemed to hesitate, Hannah had no doubts or restraints. I was, to her, the hated symbol of every resentment she'd fed and festered on for forty years. Keith, who could and should have soothed from childhood her hurt feelings, had no doubt encouraged them. Hannah's loathing was beyond her control. A dagger between the shoulder blades . . . it was there in her eyes.

She came towards me fast in the same leonine stride I'd seen in Rebecca and used her full weight to thrust me back against the wall while at the same time aiming with sharp clawed fingernails to rip my face.

Roger tried civilized protest. "Miss Stratton . . ."

The stalking cat pounced, oblivious.

I'd have liked to have punched her hard at the base of the sternum and to have slapped her into concussion, but hindering taboos bristled in my subconscious, and maybe I couldn't floor that particular woman because of Keith's hitting my mother. My mother, Hannah's mother. A jumble. In any case, I tried merely to grasp my wretched half-sister's wrists, which involved taking both my hands off the walker, and this gave Keith an opportunity he had no qualms in seizing.

He tweaked up the frame, barged Hannah out of the way and delivered a damaging clout in my direction in the shape of sturdy chromium tubing with black rubber-tipped feet. Not good. On the stapled-shut cuts, rotten.

Roger held on to Keith's arm to prevent a second strike and I held Hannah's wrists and tried to avoid her spitting in my face. All in all it had developed into a poorish Saturday morning.

It got worse.

Keith lashed out at Roger with the frame. Roger ducked. Keith swung the tubes round my way and again connected and, what with Hannah tugging furiously to get free and Keith crowding in with the four black-tipped legs aimed roughly now at my stomach, my legs inefficiently decided against continued support and to all intents buckled, so that I wavered and wobbled and in the end folded up ignominiously onto the floor.

Hannah yanked her wrists out of my grasp and put her boot in. Her son, who didn't even know me, stepped into the fracas and kicked me twice with equal venom, but also without considering any consequences to himself. I grabbed the foot coming forward for a third time and jerked hard, and with a yell of surprise he overbalanced, falling down within my reach.

His bad luck. I grabbed him and hit him crunchingly

in the face and banged his head on the floor, which set Hannah screeching over us like a banshee. Her shoes, I learned, had sharp toes and spikes for heels.

I was aware that Roger, somewhere above, was trying to stop the fray, but what the Colonel really needed was a gun.

Keith took his heavy feet to me, stamping and kicking. There were deep shudders in my body under his weight and his savagery. Roger to his credit did his best to pull him off, and roughly at that time, and not a moment too soon, the outer door opened again, bringing a welcome interruption.

"I say," a man's voice bleated, "what's going on here?"

Keith, shaking off Roger's clutch and undeterred, said, "Go away, Ivan. It's none of your business."

Ivan, I supposed, might have done as he was told, but on his heels came a much tougher proposition.

Marjorie's imperious voice rose above the general noise of battle.

"Keith! Hannah! What on earth do you think you're doing? Colonel, call the police. Call the police this minute."

The threat worked instantaneously. Hannah stopped kicking and screeching. Keith, panting, stepped back. Jack slithered away from me on all fours. Roger put the walker next to me and stretched out a hand to haul me to my feet. It took him more effort than he'd expected, but by martial perseverance he succeeded. I propped myself upright on the walker by force of arms and leaned wearily against the wall, and found that not only Ivan and Marjorie had arrived, but also Conrad and Dart.

For a moment of speechlessness Marjorie took stock of things, noting the still-scorching fury in Hannah's manner, the brutish force unspent in Keith and the sullen nose-bleeding vindictiveness of Jack. She glanced at Roger and lastly flicked her gaze over me, head to foot, coming to rest on my face.

"Disgraceful," she said accusingly. "Fighting like animals. You ought to know better."

"He shouldn't be here," Keith said thickly, and added, lying easily, "He punched me. He started it."

"He's broken my nose," Jack complained.

"Don't tell me he attacked all three of you," Dart mocked. "Serves you right."

"You shut up," Hannah told him with bile.

Conrad gave his opinion. "He must have done *something* to start all this. I mean, it's obvious." He became the examining magistrate, the heavyweight of the proceedings, the accuser; pompous.

"Well, Mr. Morris, why precisely did you punch my brother and attack his family? What have you to say?"

Time, I thought, for the prisoner at the bar to defend himself. I swallowed. I felt weak. Also angry enough not to give in to the weakness, or to let them all see it and enjoy it.

When I could trust my voice not to come out as a croak, I said neutrally, "I didn't punch your brother. I did nothing. They had a go at me for being who I am."

"That doesn't make sense," Conrad said. "People don't get attacked just for being who they are."

"Tell that to the Jews," Dart said.

It shocked them all, but not much.

Marjorie Binsham said, "Go outside, the lot of you. *I* will deal with Mr. Morris, in here." She turned her head to Roger. "You too, Colonel. Out."

Conrad said, "It's not safe."

"Rubbish!" Marjorie interrupted. "Off you go."

They obeyed her, shuffling out without looking at each other, losing face.

"Close the door," she commanded, and Roger, last out, closed it.

She sat down composedly, wearing that day a narrow tailored navy blue overcoat with a white band of collar again showing beneath. The waved white hair, the fragile-looking complexion and the piercing hawk eyes, all those were as before.

She inspected me critically. She said, "You got yourself blown up yesterday and trampled today. Not very clever, are you?"

"No."

"And get off the wall. You're bleeding on it."

"I'll paint it, later."

"From where, exactly, are you bleeding?"

I explained about the multitude of bruises, cuts and staples. "Some of those," I said, "feel as if they've popped open."

"I see."

She seemed for a few moments undecided, not her usual force. Then she said, "I will free you, if you like, from our agreement."

"Oh?" I was surprised. "No, the agreement stands."

"I did not expect you to be hurt."

I briefly considered things. Hurt, even if grievous, was in some ways immaterial. I ignored it as best I could. Concentrated on anything else.

"Do you know," I asked, "who set the explosive?"

"No, I don't."

"Which Strattons could have the knowledge?"

"None of them."

"What about Forsyth?"

Shutters came down in her, too.

"Whatever Forsyth is or isn't," she said, "he is not expert in blowing things up."

"Does he have a motive for getting someone else to do it?"

After a pause, she said, "I don't think so."

My forehead was sweating. I put a hand up automatically to wipe it and started swaying, and regripped the walker urgently, fighting to regain balance and not to fall down. Too many crushed muscles, too many cut fibers, too much damned battering overall. I stood quietly, breathing deeply, crisis over, my weight on my arms.

"Sit down," Marjorie commanded.

"That might be worse."

She stared. I smiled. "My children think it funny."

"But not."

"Not very."

She said slowly, "Are you going to charge Keith with assault? Hannah also?"

I shook my head.

"Why not? They were kicking you. I saw them."

"And would you say so in court?"

She hesitated. She had used the police as a threat to end the fight, but that was all it had been, a threat.

I thought of the pact my mother had made with Lord Stratton, to keep quiet about Keith's violent behavior. I had hugely benefited from that silence. My unthought-out instinct was to do the same as my mother.

I said, "I will even things one day, with Keith. But not by embroiling you against your family in public. It will be a private matter, between him and me."

With evident relief and formality, she said, "I wish you well."

There was a brief single wail of a police siren outside the window, more an announcement of arrival than of hurry.

The police had arrived anyway. Marjorie Binsham looked not enchanted and I felt very tired, and presently the office door opened to let in far more people than the space had been designed for.

Keith was making abortive attempts to persuade the law that I had caused actual bodily harm to his grandson, Jack.

"Jack," observed Roger calmly, "shouldn't try to kick people when they're down."

"And you," Keith said to him viciously, "you can clear out. I told you. You're sacked."

"Don't be ridiculous," Marjorie snapped. "Colonel, you are *not* sacked. We need you. Please stay here. Only by a majority vote of the Board can you be asked to leave, and there will be no such majority."

"One of these days, Marjorie," Keith said, his voice heavy and shaking with humiliation, "I will get rid of you."

"Look here, Keith . . ." Conrad began.

"And you shut up," Keith said with hatred. "It was you or your blackmailing architect that put paid to the stands."

Into the shocked silence, which left all Stratton mouths dropping open, the police with bathos consulted a notebook full of pre-arranged agenda and asked which of the family normally drove a dark green six-year-old Granada with rusted near fenders.

"What's that got to do with anything?" Dart demanded.

Without answering that question the police presence repeated their own.

"I do, then," Dart said. "So what?"

"And did you drive that car through the main gates of the racecourse at eight-twenty yesterday morning, and did you oblige Mr. Harold Quest to leap out of your path to avoid serious injury, and did you make an obscene gesture to him when he protested?"

Dart nearly laughed, and prudently thought better of it at the last moment.

"No, I didn't," he said.

"Didn't do what, sir? Didn't drive through the gates? Didn't make Mr. Quest leap out of the way? Didn't make an obscene gesture?"

Dart said unworriedly, "I didn't drive through the main gates at twenty past eight yesterday morning."

"But you identified the car, sir . . ."

"I wasn't driving it at eight-twenty yesterday morning. Not through the main gates, here. Not anywhere."

The police asked the inevitable question, politely.

"I was in my bathroom, since you ask," Dart said, and left his actual activity there to the collective imagination.

I asked, "Is Mr. Quest a large man with a beard, a knitted hat and a placard reading 'HORSES RIGHTS COME FIRST'?"

The police admitted, "He does answer to that description, yes, sir."

"That man!" exclaimed Marjorie.

"Should be shot," Conrad said.

"He walks straight out in front of one's car," Marjorie told the policemen severely. "He will, no doubt, achieve his aim in the end."

"Which is, madam?"

"To be knocked down, of course. To fall down artistically at the slightest contact. To suffer for the cause. One has to be frightfully careful with that sort of man."

I asked, "Are you sure that Mr. Quest was actually outside the gates himself at twenty past eight yesterday morning?"

"He insisted that he was," said the policeman.

"On Good Friday? It's a day when no one goes to racecourses."

"He said he was there."

I left it. Lack of energy. Dart and the car had gone in and out of the gates often enough for every picketer to be able to describe it down to its tattered rear bumper-sticker, which read, "If you can read this, drop back." Dart had annoyed big-beard the day I'd been with him. Big-beard, Harold Quest, felt compelled to make trouble. Where lay the truth?

"And you, Mr. Morris . . ." The notebook's pages were flipped over and were consulted, "We were told you were to be detained in hospital but when we went to interview you they said you had discharged yourself. They hadn't officially released you."

"Such punitive words!" I said.

"What?"

"Detained and released. As in prison."

"We couldn't find you," he complained. "No one seemed to know where you'd gone."

"Well, I'm here now."

"And . . . er . . . Mr. Jack Stratton alleges that at approximately eight-fifty this morning you attacked him and broke his nose."

"Jack Stratton alleges nothing of the sort," Marjorie said with certainty. "Jack, speak up."

The sullen young man, dabbing his face with a handkerchief, took note of Marjorie's piercing displeasure and mumbled he might have walked into a door, like. Despite Keith's and Hannah's protestations, the policeman resignedly drew a line across the entry in his notebook and said his superiors wanted information from me on the whereabouts of the explosive charges "prior to detonation." Where, they asked, could I be found?

"When?" I asked.

"This morning, sir."

"Then . . . here, I suppose."

Conrad, looking at his watch, announced that he had summoned a demolitions expert and an inspector from the local council to come to advise how best to remove the old stands and clear the area ready for rebuilding.

Keith, in a rage, said, "You've no right to do that. It's my racecourse just as much as yours, and I want to sell it, and if we sell to a developer *he* will clear away the stands at no expense to us. We are *not* rebuilding."

Marjorie, fierce-eyed, said they needed an expert opinion on whether or not the stands could be restored as they had been, and whether the racecourse insurance would cover any other course of action.

"Add the insurance to the profit from selling, and we will all benefit," Keith obstinately said.

The policemen, uninterested, retired to their car outside and could be seen talking on their private phone line, consulting their superiors, one supposed.

I said doubtfully to Roger, "*Can* the stands be restored?"

He answered with caution. "Too soon to say."

"Of course they can." Marjorie was positive. "Anything can be restored, if one insists on it."

Replaced as before, or copied, she meant. A mistake, I thought it would be, for Stratton Park's racing future.

The family went on quarreling. They had all turned up early, it appeared, precisely to prevent any unilateral decision making. They left the office in an arguing mass, bound together by fears of what any one could do on his own. Roger watched them go, his expression exasperated.

"What a way to run a business! And neither Oliver nor I have been paid since before Lord Stratton died. He used to sign our checks personally. The only person empowered to pay us since then is Mrs. Binsham. I explained it to her when we were walking round the course last Wednesday, and she said she understood, but when I asked her again yesterday after the stands blew up, when she came here with all the others, she told me not to bother her at such a time." He sighed heavily. "It's all very well, but it's over two months now since we had any salary."

"Who pays the racecourse staff?" I asked.

"I do. Lord Stratton arranged it. Keith disapproves. He says it's an invitation to fraud. Judges me by himself, of course. Anyway, the only paychecks I can't sign are Oliver's and my own."

"Have you made them out already?"

"My secretary did."

"Give them to me, then."

"To you?"

"I'll get the old bird to sign them."

He didn't ask how. He merely opened a desk drawer, took out an envelope and held it towards me.

"Put it in my jacket," I said.

He looked at the walker, shook his head at his thoughts, and tucked the checks into my jacket pocket.

"Are the stands," I asked, "a total loss?"

"You'd better see for yourself. Mind you, no one can get close. The police have cordoned everything off."

From the office window, little damage was visible. One could see the end wall, the roof and an oblique side view of the open steps.

"I'd rather see the holes unaccompanied by Strattons," I said.

Roger almost grinned. "They're all afraid to let the others out of their sight."

"I thought so too."

"I suppose you do know you're bleeding."

"Staining the wall, Marjorie said." I nodded. "It's stopped by now, I should think."

"But . . ." He fell silent.

"I'll go back for running repairs," I promised. "Though God knows when. They keep one waiting so long."

He said diffidently, "One of the racecourse doctors would be quicker. I could ask him for you, if you like. He's very obliging."

"Yes," I said tersely.

Roger reached for his telephone and reassured the doctor that racing was still going ahead as planned on Monday. Meanwhile, as a favor, could a casualty be stitched? When? At once, preferably. Thanks very much.

"Come on, then," he said to me, replacing the receiver. "Can you still walk?"

I could and did, pretty slowly. The police protested at my vanishing again. Back in an hour or so, Roger said soothingly. The Strattons were nowhere in sight, though their cars were still parked. Roger aimed his jeep towards the main gates, and Mr. Harold Quest refrained from planting his obsessions in our path.

The doctor was the one who had attended the fallers at the open ditch, businesslike and calm. When he saw what he was being asked to do, he didn't want to.

"GPs don't do this sort of thing any more," he told Roger. "They refer people to hospitals. He should be in a hospital. This level of pain is ridiculous."

"It comes and goes," I said. "And suppose we were out in the Sahara Desert?"

"Swindon is not the Sahara."

"All life's a desert."

He muttered under his breath and stuck me together again with what looked like adhesive tape.

"Haven't I seen you before?" he asked, puzzled, finishing.

I explained about the fence.

"The man with the children!" He shook his head regretfully. "They saw a horror, I'm afraid."

Roger thanked him for his services to me, and I also. The doctor told Roger that the racing authorities had received a complaint from Rebecca Stratton about his professional competency, or lack of it. They wanted a full report on his decision to recommend that she should be stood down for concussion.

"She's a bitch," Roger said, with feeling.

The doctor glanced my way uneasily.

"He's safe," Roger assured him. "Say what you like."

"How long have you known him?"

"Long enough. And it was Strattons that kicked his wounds open again."

It had to be hellish, I thought, being in even the smallest way reliant on the Strattons for employment. Roger truly lived on the edge of an abyss: and out of his job would mean out of his home.

He drove us carefully back to the racecourse, forbearing from lecturing me about the hand I clamped over my face, or my drooping head. As far as he was concerned, what I chose to do about my troubles was my own affair. I developed strong feelings of friendship and gratitude.

Big-beard stepped in front of the jeep. I wondered if his name were really Quest, or if he'd made it up. Not a tactful question to ask at that time. He barred our way through the main gates peremptorily, and Roger, to my surprise, smartly backed away from him, swung the jeep round and drove off down the road, continuing our journey.

"It just occurred to me," he said judiciously, "that if we

go in by the back road we not only avoid words with that maniac, but you could call at your bus for clean clothes."

"I'm running out of them."

He glanced across doubtfully. "Mine aren't really big enough."

"No. It's OK."

I was down to a choice between well-worn working jeans and racegoing tidiness. I opted for the jeans and a lumberjack-type wool checked shirt and dumped the morning's bloodied garments in a washing locker already filled with sopping smaller clothes.

The boys had finished sluicing both the bus and themselves. The bus looked definitely cleaner. The boys must be dry, even though nowhere in sight. I descended slowly to the ground again and found Roger walking round the home-from-home, interested but reticent, as ever.

"It used to be a long-distance touring coach," I said. "I bought it when the bus company replaced its cozy old fleet with modern glass-walled crowd-pleasers."

"How . . . I mean, how do you manage the latrines?"

I smiled at the army parlance. "There were huge spaces for suitcases, underneath. I replaced some of them with water and sewage tanks. Every rural authority runs pump-out tankers for emptying far-flung cesspits. And there are boatyards. It's easy to get a pump-out, if you know who to ask."

"Amazing." He patted the clean coffee-colored paint-work, giving himself another interval, I saw again, before having to go back to the distasteful present.

He sighed. "I suppose . . ."

I nodded.

We climbed back into the jeep and returned to the grand-stands, where, leaning again on the walker, I took my first objective look at the previous day's destructive mayhem.

We stood prudently outside the police tapes, but movement had ceased in the pile.

First thought: *incredible* that Toby and I had come out of that mess alive.

The building had been centrally disemboweled, its guts spilling out in a monstrous cascade. The weighing room, changing rooms and Oliver Wells's office, which jutted forward from the main structure, had been crushed flat under the spreading weight of the collapsing floors above. The long unyielding steel and concrete mass of the course-facing viewing steps had meant that all the explosive force had been directed one way, into the softer resistance of the brick, wood and plaster of dining rooms, bars and staircase.

Above the solidly impacted rubble a hollow column of space rose through the upper floors like an exclamation mark, topped with a few stark remaining fingers of the Stewards' viewing box pointing skyward.

I said slowly, under my breath, "Jesus Christ."

After a while, Roger asked, "What do you think?"

"Chiefly," I said, "how the hell are you going to hold a race meeting here the day after tomorrow?"

He rolled his eyes in frustration. "It's Easter weekend. More weddings today than on any other day of the year. Monday, horse shows, dog shows, you name it, all over the place. I spent all yesterday afternoon trying to get hire firms to bring marquees. *Any* sort of tent. But every scrap of canvas is already out in service. We're shutting off the whole of this end of the stands, of course, and are having to move everyone and everything along into Tattersalls, but so far I've only managed a promise of a couple of Portakabins for the changing rooms and it looks as if we're going to have to have the scales out in the open air, as they used to do at point-to-points. And as for food and extra bars . . ." He shrugged helplessly. "We've told the caterers to make their own arrangements and they say they're stretched already. God help us if it rains, we'll be working under umbrellas."

"Where were you planning to put tents?" I asked.

"In the members' parking lot." He sounded disconsolate. "The Easter Monday holiday meeting is our biggest money-maker of the year. We can't afford to cancel it. And both Marjorie Binsham and Conrad are adamant that we go ahead. We've told all the trainers to send their runners for the races. The stables are all right. We'll still comply with all the regulations such as six security boxes, and so on. The saddling stalls are fine. The parade ring's OK. Oliver can use my office."

He turned away from his gloomy contemplation of the ruined grandstand and we began a slow traverse towards his telephone. He had to confirm some electrical plans, he said.

His office was full of Strattons. Conrad sat in Roger's chair behind the desk. Conrad was talking on Roger's telephone, taking charge.

Conrad was saying, "Yes, I know you told my manager that all your tents were out, but this is Lord Stratton himself speaking, and I'm telling you to dismantle and bring in a suitable marquee from anywhere at all, and put it up here tomorrow. I don't care where you get it from, just get it."

I touched Roger's arm before he could make any protest, and waved to him to retreat. Outside the office, ignored by all the Strattons, I suggested he drive us both back to the bus.

"I've a telephone in it," I explained. "No interruptions."

"Did you hear what Conrad was saying?"

"Yes, I did. Will he be successful?"

"If he is, my job's gone."

"Drive down to the bus."

Roger drove and, to save having to get in and out of the bus again, I told him where to find the mobile phone and asked him to bring it out, along with a book of private phone numbers he would find beneath it. When he climbed down the steps with the necessary, I looked up a number and made a call.

"Henry? Lee Morris. How goes it?"

"Emergency? Crisis? The roof's fallen in?"

"How did you guess?"

"Yes, but Lee, my usual big top is out as an indoor pony school. Little girls in hard hats. They've got it for the year."

"What about the huge one that takes so much moving?"

A resigned sigh came down the wire. Henry, long-time pal, general large-scale junk dealer, had acquired two big tops from a bankrupt traveling circus and would rent them out to me from time to time to enclose any thoroughly gutted ruin I wanted to shield from the weather.

I explained to him what was needed and why, and I explained to Roger who he was going to be talking to, and I leaned peacefully on the walker while they discussed floor space, budget and transport. When they seemed to be reaching agreement I said to Roger, "Tell him to bring all the flags."

Roger, mystified, relayed the message and got a reply that made him laugh. "Fine," he said, "I'll phone back to confirm."

We took the telephone and the numbers book with us in the jeep and returned to the office. Conrad was still shouting down the phone there but, judging from the impatience now manifest in the Stratton herd, was achieving nil results.

"You're on," I murmured to Roger. "Say *you* found the tent."

It didn't come naturally to him to take another man's credit, but he could see the point in it. The Strattons could perversely turn down any suggestion of mine, even if it were to their own advantage to adopt it.

Roger walked over to his desk as Conrad slammed down the receiver in fury.

"I . . . er . . . I've located a tent," he said firmly.

"About time!" Conrad said.

"Where?" Keith demanded, annoyed.

"A man in Hertfordshire has one. He can ship it here by tomorrow morning, and he'll send a crew to erect it."

Conrad was grudgingly pleased but wouldn't admit it.

"The only thing is," Roger continued, "that he doesn't supply this tent on short leases. We would need to keep it for a minimum of three months. However," he hurried on, sensing interruptions, "that condition could be to our advantage, as the grandstands will be out of operation for much longer than that. We could keep the tent for as long as we need. And this tent has a firm floor and versatile dividing partitions and sounds stronger than a normal marquee."

"Too expensive," Keith objected.

"Less expensive, actually," Roger said, "than erecting tents separately for each meeting."

Marjorie Binsham's gaze bypassed both Roger and her family and fastened on me.

"Any ideas?" she asked.

"Ignore him," Keith insisted.

I said neutrally, "All four directors are here. Hold a board meeting and decide."

A smile, quickly hidden, tugged at Marjorie's lips. Dart, though, grinned openly.

"Give us the details," Marjorie commanded Roger, and he, consulting his notes, told them the space and price involved, and said the insurance from non-availability of the stands would easily cover it.

"Who arranged that insurance?" Marjorie asked.

"Lord Stratton and I and the insurance brokers."

"Very well," Marjorie said crisply. "I put forward a motion that the Colonel arranges a contract for the tent on the terms proposed. And Ivan will second it."

Ivan, galvanized, said vaguely, "Oh? Yes, rather."

"Conrad?" Marjorie challenged him.

"Well . . . I suppose so."

"Carried," Marjorie said.

"I object," Keith seethed.

"Your objection is noted," Marjorie said. "Colonel, summon the tent."

Roger turned the leaves of my phone book and spoke to Henry.

"Very well done, Colonel!" Marjorie congratulated him warmly when all was arranged. "This place could not function without you."

Conrad looked defeated; Ivan, bewildered; and Keith, murderous.

Jack, Hannah and Dart, minor players, put no thoughts into words.

The brief ensuing pause in the proceedings came to an end with the arrival of two more cars, one containing, it transpired, two senior policemen with an explosives expert, and the other, Conrad's demolition man and a heavily mustached manifestation of local authority.

The Strattons, as a flock, migrated into the open air.

Roger wiped a hand over his face and said service in Northern Ireland had been less of a strain.

"Do you think we had an Irish bomb here?" I said.

He looked startled but shook his head. "The Irish boast of it. No one so far has done any crowing. And this one wasn't aimed at people, don't forget. The Irish bombers aim to maim."

"So who?"

"Crucial question. I don't know. And you don't need to say it . . . this may not be the end."

"What about guards?"

"I've press-ganged my groundsmen. There are relays of them in pairs patrolling the place." He patted the walkie-talkie clipped to his belt. "They're reporting all the time to my foreman. If anything looks wrong, he'll report it to me."

The newly arrived policemen came into the office and introduced themselves as a detective chief inspector and a detective sergeant. An accompanying intense-looking young man was vaguely and anonymously introduced as an explosives expert, a defuser of bombs. It was he who asked most of the questions.

I answered him simply, describing where the det cord had been and how it had looked.

"You and your young son both knew at once what it was?"

"We'd both seen it before."

"And how close to each other were the charges in the walls?"

"About three feet apart. In some places, less."

"And how extensive or widespread?"

"All round the stairwell and the landing walls on at least two floors. Perhaps more."

"We understand you're a builder. How long, do you think, would it have taken you personally to drill the holes for the charges?"

"Each hole? Some of the walls were brick, some were

composition, like cinder block, all of them plastered and
painted. Thick and load-bearing, but soft, really. You'd
hardly need a hammer drill, even. The holes would
probably have to be five inches deep, about an inch in
diameter—given a wide drill bit and electricity, I could
do perhaps two a minute if I was in a hurry." I paused.
"Threading the holes with det cord and packing them with
explosives obviously takes longer. I've been told you need
to compress and tamp it all in very carefully with something
wooden, no sparks, like a broom handle."

"Who told you?"

"Demolitions people."

The chief inspector asked, "How are you so sure the
walls were made of brick and cinder block? How could
you possibly tell, if they were plastered and painted?"

I thought back. "On the floor beneath each charge there
was a small pile of dust caused by drilling the hole. Some
piles were pink brick dust, others were gray."

"You had time to see that?"

"I remember it. At the time, it just made it certain that
there was a good deal of explosive rammed into those
walls."

The expert said, "Did you look to see where the circuit
began or ended?"

I shook my head. "I was trying to find my son."

"And did you see anyone else at all in the vicinity of
the stands near that time?"

"No. No one."

They asked me and Roger to walk with them as far as the
safety cordon, so that we could explain to the expert where
the staircase and walls had been before the explosion. The
expert, it seemed, would then put on a protective suit and
a hard hat and go in wherever he could to take a look
from the inside.

"Rather you than me," I commented.

They watched the best I could do at walking with them. When we reached the point of maximum visual bad news, the bomb-defusing expert looked upwards to the fingers of the Stewards' box and down to my walker. He put on his large head-sheltering hat and gave me a twisting self-mocking smile.

"I'm old in my profession," he said.

"How old?"

"Twenty-eight."

I said, "All of a sudden, I can't feel a thing."

His smile broadened. "People sometimes get lucky."

"Good luck, then," I said.

8

"YOU KNOW what?" Roger said to me.

"What?"

We were standing on the tarmac a little apart from the policemen but looking still at the rubble.

"I'd think our demolitionist got more bang for his bucks than he intended."

"How do you mean?"

He said, "High explosives are funny things. Unpredictable, often. They weren't my speciality in the army, but of course most soldiers learn about them. There's always a tendency to use too much explosive for the job in hand, just to make sure of effective results." He smiled briefly. "A colleague of mine had to blow up a bridge, once. Just to blow a hole in it, to put it out of action. He overestimated how much explosive it would take, and the whole thing totally disintegrated into invisible dust which was carried away in the river below. Not a thing left. Everyone thought he'd done a brilliant job, but he was laughing about it in private. *I* wouldn't have known how much to use to cause this much damage here in the grandstands. And I've been thinking that whoever did it probably meant only to put the stairway out of action. I mean . . . setting all those careful charges rounds its walls . . . if he'd meant to destroy the whole stand, why not use one single large bomb? Much easier. Less chance of being spotted setting it up. See what I mean?"

"Yes, I do."

He glanced directly at my face. "Look," he said awkwardly, "I know it's not my business, but wouldn't you be better lying down in your bus?"

"I'll go if I have to."

He nodded.

"Otherwise," I said, "it's better to have other things to think about."

He was happy with that. "Just say, then."

"Yes. Thanks."

The Strattons were suddenly all around us. Dart said in my ear, "Conrad's architect has come. Now for some fireworks!" I looked at his impish enjoyment. "Did Keith really *kick* you?" he asked. "Ivan says I missed a real pretty sight by a few seconds."

"Too bad. Where's the architect?"

"That man beside Conrad."

"And is he a blackmailer?"

"God knows. Ask Keith."

He knew as well as I did that I wouldn't ask Keith anything.

"I reckon Keith made that up," Dart said. "He's a terrible liar. He can't tell the truth."

"And Conrad? Does he lie?"

"My father?" Dart showed no anger at the possible slur. "My father tells the truth on principle. Or else from lack of imagination. Take your pick."

"The twins at the fork in the road," I said.

"What the heck are you talking about?"

"Tell you later."

Marjorie was saying formidably, "We do *not* need an architect."

"Face facts," Conrad pleaded. "Look at this radical destruction. It's a heaven-sent opportunity to build something meaningful."

Build something meaningful. The words vibrated in memory. "Build something meaningful" had been one of the precepts repeated ad nauseam by a lecturer at college.

I looked carefully at Conrad's architect, turning the inward eye back more than sixteen years. Conrad's architect, I slowly realized, had been a student like myself at the Architectural Association School of Architecture: senior to me, one of the elite, a disciple of the future. I remembered his face and his glittering prospects, and I'd forgotten his name.

Roger left my side and went across to put in a presence at the Marjorie-Conrad conflict, a hopeless position for a manager. Conrad's architect nodded to him coolly, seeing Roger as critic, not ally.

Dart, waving a hand towards the rubble, asked me, "What do you think they should do?"

"I, personally?"

"Yes."

"They don't care what I think."

"But I'm curious."

"I think they should spend their time finding out who did it, and why."

"But the police will do that."

"Are you saying that the family doesn't want to find out?"

Dart said, alarmed, "Can you see through brick?"

"Why don't they want to know? I wouldn't think it safe not to."

"Marjorie will do anything to keep family affairs private," Dart said. "She's worse than Grandfather, and he would pay the earth to keep the Stratton name clean."

Keith must have cost them a packet, I thought, from my own mother onwards; and I wondered fleetingly again what Forsyth could have done to cause them such angst.

Dart looked at his watch. "Twenty to twelve," he said. "I'm fed up with all this. What do you say to the Mayflower?"

On reflection I said yes to the Mayflower, and without fanfare retreated with him to the green six-year-old Granada with rusted near fenders. Harold Quest, it seemed, never interfered with exits. We made an unhindered passage to imitation 1620 A.D., where Dart accepted a half pint and I ordered also fifteen fat rounds of cheese, tomato, ham and lettuce homemade sandwiches and a quart tub of ice cream.

"You can't be *that* hungry!" Dart exclaimed.

"I've five beaks to fill."

"Good God. I'd forgotten."

We drank the beer while waiting for the sandwiches, and then he good-naturedly drove us down through the back entrance to park outside Roger's house, near the bus.

Beside the main door into the bus, in a small outside compartment, I'd long ago installed a chuck-wagon-type bell. Dart watched in amusement when I extended it on its arm outward, and set it clanging with vigor.

The cowboys came in from the prairie, hungry, dry and virtuous, and sat around on boxes and logs for their open-air lunch. I stood with the walker. Getting used to it, the boys took it for granted.

They had built a stockade from sticks, they said. Inside the fort were the United States cavalry (Christopher and Toby) and outside were the Indians (the rest). The Indians were (of course) the Good Guys, who hoped to over-run the stockade and take a few scalps. Sneaky tactics were needed, Chief Edward said. Alan Redfeather was his trusty spy.

Dart, eating a sandwich, said he thought Neil's lurid warpaint (Mrs. Gardner's lipstick) a triumph for political correctness.

None of them knew what he meant. I saw Neil storing the words away, mouthing them silently, ready to ask later.

Locust-like, they mopped up the Mayflower's food and, as it seemed a good time for it, I said to them, "Ask Dart the riddle of the pilgrim. He'll find it interesting."

Christopher obligingly began, "A pilgrim came to a fork in the road. One road led to safety, and the other to death. In each fork stood a guardian."

"They were twins," Edward said.

Christopher, nodding, went on, "One twin always spoke the truth and the other always lied."

Dart turned his head and stared at me.

"It's a very *old* riddle," Edward said apologetically.

"The pilgrim was allowed only one question," Toby said. "Only one. And to save his life he had to find out which road led to safety. So what did he ask?"

"He asked which way was safe," Dart said reasonably.

Christopher said, "Which twin did he ask?"

"The one who spoke the truth."

"But how did he know which one spoke the truth? They both looked the same. They were twins."

"Conrad and Keith aren't identical," Dart said.

The children, not understanding, pressed on. Toby asked

again, "What question did the pilgrim ask?"

"Haven't the foggiest."

"Think," Edward commanded.

Dart turned my way. "Save me!" he said.

"That's not what the pilgrim said," Neil informed him with relish.

"Do you all know?"

Five heads nodded. "Dad told us."

"Then Dad had better tell *me.*"

It was Christopher, however, who explained. "The pilgrim could only ask one question, so he went to one of the twins and he asked, 'If I ask your brother which way leads to safety, which way will he tell me to go?' "

Christopher stopped. Dart looked flummoxed. "Is that all?" he asked.

"That's all. So what did the pilgrim do?"

"Well . . . he . . . I give in. What did he do?"

They wouldn't tell him the answer.

"You're *devils,*" Dart said.

"One of the twins was a devil," Edward said, "and the other was an angel."

"You just made that up," Toby accused him.

"So what? It makes it more interesting."

They all tired abruptly of the riddle and trooped off, as was their habit, back to their make-believe game.

"For Christ's sake!" Dart exclaimed. "That's not bloody fair."

I laughed in my throat.

"So what did the pilgrim do?"

"Work it out."

"You're as bad as your children."

Dart and I got back into his car. He put the walker onto the back seat and observed, "Keith really hurt you, didn't he?"

"No, it was the explosion. Bits of roof fell in."

"Fell in on you. Yes, I heard."

"From the shoulder blades down," I agreed. "Could have been worse."

"Oh, sure." He started the engine and drove up the private inner road. "What did the pilgrim do, then?"

I smiled. "Whichever road either twin told him was safe, he went down the other one. Both twins would have pointed to the road leading to death."

He thought very briefly. "How come?"

"If the pilgrim asked the truthful twin which way his brother would send him to safety, the truthful twin, knowing his brother would lie, would point to the road to death."

"You've lost me."

I explained over again. "And," I said, "if the pilgrim happened to ask the lying twin which way his brother would send someone to safety, the lying twin, though knowing his brother would speak the truth, lied about what he would say. So the lying twin also would point to the road to death."

Dart relapsed into silence. When he spoke he said, "Do your boys understand it?"

"Yes. They acted it out."

"Don't they ever quarrel?"

"Of course they do. But they've been moved around so much that they've made few outside friendships. They rely on each other." I sighed. "They'll grow out of it, shortly. Christopher's already too old for half their games."

"A pity."

"Life goes on."

Dart braked his rusty car gently to a halt in the impromptu parking lot outside Roger's office.

I said diffidently, "Did you, in fact, drive here yesterday morning in this car, as Harold Quest said?"

"No, I didn't." Dart took no offense. "And what's more I *was* in my bathroom from eight to eight-thirty, and don't bloody laugh, I'm not telling anyone else, but I've got a new scalp vibrator thing that's supposed to stop hair falling out."

"Snake oil," I said.

"Bugger you, I said don't laugh."

"I'm not laughing."

"Your face muscles are *twitching.*"

"I do believe, anyway," I said, "that because of your hair you didn't arrive at the racecourse at eight-twenty yesterday morning with your old jalopy bulging with detonating cord and plastic explosive."

"Thanks a bunch."

"The thing is, could anyone have borrowed your car without you knowing? And would you mind very much if the bomb expert or the police tested this car for the presence of nitrates?"

He looked aghast. "You can't mean it!"

"Someone," I pointed out, "brought explosives to the stairs in the grandstands yesterday. It's probably fair to say it was plugged into the walls after the night watchman went home at seven. It was fully light by then. There was no one else about because of its being Good Friday. There was only Harold Quest and his pals at the gate, and I don't know how much one can trust him."

"The lying twin," Dart said.

"Maybe."

I tried to imagine easygoing Dart, with his thickening frame and his thinning hair, his ironic cast of mind and his core of idleness, ever caring enough about anything to blow up a grandstand. Impossible. But to lend his car? To lend his car casually for an unspecified purpose, yes, certainly. To lend it knowing it would be used for a crime?

I hoped not. Yet he would have let me open the locked cupboard in his father's study. Had taken me there and given me every illegal chance. Hadn't cared a jot when I'd backed off.

A sloppy sense of right and wrong, or a deep alienation that he habitually hid?

I liked Dart; he lifted one's spirits. Among the Strattons, he was the nearest to normal. The nearest, one should perhaps say, to a rose among nettles.

I said neutrally, "Where's your sister Rebecca today? I'd have thought she'd have been here, practically purring."

"She's racing at Towcester," he said briefly. "I looked in the newspaper. No doubt she's thrilled the stands have had it, but I haven't spoken to her since Wednesday. She's talked to Father, I think. She's riding one of his horses here on Monday. It's got a good chance of winning, so no way would she have put the meeting in jeopardy, with dynamite shenanigans, if that's what you're thinking."

"Where does she live?" I asked.

"Lambourn. Ten miles away, roughly."

"Horse country."

"She lives and breathes horses. Quite mad."

I lived and breathed building. I got fulfillment from putting brick on brick, stone on stone: from bringing a dead thing to life. I understood a single-minded encompassing drive. Not much in the world, for good or for evil, gets done without it.

The rest of the Strattons came round from the racecourse side of the grandstands, bringing Conrad's architect with them. The police and the bomb expert seemed to be sifting carefully through the edges of the rubble. The mustached local authority was scratching his head.

Roger came over to Dart's car and asked where we'd been.

"Feeding the children," I said.

"Oh! Well, the Honorable Marjorie wants to demolish you. Er . . ." He went on more prudently in the presence of Dart, "Mrs. Binsham wants to see you in my office."

I clambered stiffly onto the tarmac and plodded that way. Roger came along beside me.

"Don't let her eat you," he said.

"No. Don't worry. Do you happen to know that architect's name?"

"What?"

"Conrad's architect."

"It's Wilson Yarrow. Conrad calls him Yarrow."

"Thanks."

I stopped walking abruptly.

Roger said, "What's the matter? Is it worse?"

"No." I looked at him vaguely, to his visible alarm. I asked, "Did you tell any of the Strattons that I'm an architect?"

He was perplexed. "Only Dart. You told him yourself, remember? Why? Why does it matter?"

"Don't tell them," I said. I did a one-eighty back towards Dart, who got out of his car and came to meet us.

"What's the matter?" he said.

"Nothing much. Look . . . did you happen to mention to any of your family that I'm a qualified architect?"

He thought back, frowning. Roger, reaching us, looked thoroughly mystified. "What does it matter?" he asked.

"Yes," Dart echoed, "what does it matter?"

"I don't want Conrad to know."

Roger protested. "But Lee, why ever not?"

"That man he's brought here, Wilson Yarrow, he and I were trained at the same school. There's something about him . . ." I dried up, thinking hard.

"What's odd about him?" Roger demanded.

"That's the trouble, I can't quite remember. But I can easily find out. I'd just rather find out without his knowing about it."

"Do you mean," Dart asked, "that he blew up the stands to get the commission to build the new ones?"

"God," Roger said. "You do jump to conclusions."

"Keith thinks so. He said so."

"I think they just know you're a builder," Roger said to me thoughtfully, "and to be honest, at the moment that's just what you look like."

I glanced down at my loose checked shirt and my baggy faded working jeans and acknowledged the convenient truth of it.

"Won't he know *you,*" Roger asked, "if you trained at the same place?"

"No. I was at least three years behind him and not very noticeable. He was one of the flashing stars. Different firmament to me. I don't think we ever spoke. People like that are too wrapped up in their own affairs to learn the faces and names of junior intakes. And it wasn't last week. It's seventeen years now since I enrolled there."

When two architects met, the most normal opening gambit between them was, "Where were you taught?" And one took preconceived ideas from the answer.

To have learned architecture at Cambridge, for instance, indicated a likelihood of cautious conservation; at Bath, of anatomy before beauty; and at the Mackintosh in Glasgow, of partisan Scottishness. People who'd been to any of them knew how their fellows had been influenced. One understood a stranger because of the experiences shared.

The Architectural Association, alma mater of both Yarrow and myself, tended to turn out innovative ultra-modernists who saw into the future and built people-coercive edifices cleverly of glass. The spirit of Le

Corbusier reigned, even though the school itself stood physically in Bedford Square in London, in a Georgian, beautifully proportioned terraced mansion often at odds with the lectures within.

The library windows shone out, brightly lit always, into the night shadows of the square, celebrating distinction of knowledge, and if a certain arrogance crept into self-satisfied star students, perhaps the supreme excellence and thoroughness of the tuition excused it.

The Association was mostly outside the state education system, which meant few student grants, which in turn meant that chiefly paying students went there, the intake having consequently changed slowly over the years from a preponderance of indigenous bohemian English to the off-spring of wealthy Greeks, Nigerians, Americans, Iranians and Hong Kong Chinese, and I reckoned I'd learned a good deal and made unexpected friends from the mixture.

I myself had emerged from the exhaustively practical, and sometimes metaphysical, teaching with Le Corbusier technology and humanist tendencies, and would never be revered in the halls that had nurtured me: restoring old ruins carved no fame for posterity.

Dart asked curiously, "Do you have letters after your name?"

I hesitated. "What? Yes, I do. They're AA Dipl, which stands for Architectural Association Diploma. It may not mean much to the outside world generally, but to other architects, and to Yarrow, it's pretty revealing."

"Sounds like Alcoholics Anonymous Dipsomaniac," Dart said.

Roger laughed.

"Keep that joke under wraps," I begged, and Dart said maybe he would.

Mark, Marjorie's chauffeur, joined us and told us disapprovingly that I was keeping Mrs. Binsham waiting. She was sitting in the office tapping her foot.

"Tell her I'll come instantly," I said, and Mark went off with the message.

"That brave man deserves the Victoria Cross," Dart grinned, "for conspicuous valor." I set off in Mark's wake. "So do you," Dart shouted.

Marjorie, stiff-backed, was indeed displeased but, it transpired, not with Mark or myself. The chauffeur had been told to go for a walk. As for myself, I was invited to sit.

"I'd rather stand, really."

"Oh, yes, I forgot." She gave me a short shirt-by-jeans inspection, as if uncertain how to categorize me because of my changing appearance.

"I believe you're a builder by trade," she began.

"Yes."

"Well, as a builder, now that you've had a good look at the extent of the damage to the grandstand, what do you think?"

"About restoring things as they were?"

"Certainly."

I said, "As much as I understand that that's what you'd like, I frankly think it would be a mistake."

She was obstinate. "But could it be done?"

I said, "The whole structure may prove to be unsafe. The building's old, though well built, I grant you. But there may be fractures that can't be seen yet, and undoubtedly there are new stresses. Once the rubble is removed, more of the building could fall in. It would all need shoring up. I'm really sorry, but my advice would be to take it down and rebuild it from scratch."

"I don't want to hear that."

"I know."

"But could it be done so it was the same as before?"

"Certainly. All the original plans and drawings are here, in this office." I paused. "But it would be a lost opportunity."

"Don't tell me you side with Conrad!"

"I don't side with anyone. I'm just telling you honestly that you could improve the old stands enormously for modern comfort if you redesigned them."

"I don't like the architect that Conrad's thrusting down our throats. I don't understand half of what he says, and the man's *condescending,* can you believe?"

I could certainly believe it. "He'll find out his mistake," I said, smiling. "And, incidentally, if in the end you decide to modify the stands, it would be sensible to announce a competition in magazines architects read, asking for suggestions and drawings to be submitted to a jury, which you could appoint. Then you'd have a choice. You wouldn't be in a take-it-or-leave-it situation with Wilson Yarrow who, the Colonel assures me, doesn't know a jot about racing. One wouldn't choose even a chair without sitting in it. The stands need to be comfortable as well as good-looking."

She nodded thoughtfully. "You were going to look into this Yarrow's background. Have you done it?"

"It's in hand."

"And about Keith's debts?"

"Working on it."

She made a "Hmph" noise of disbelief, justifiably. "I suppose," she added, trying to be fair, "you're finding it difficult to get about."

I shrugged. "It's a holiday weekend, that's another of the problems." I thought briefly. "Where does Keith live?"

"Above his expectations."

I laughed. Marjorie primly smiled at her own wit.

She said, "He lives in the Dower House on the estate. It was built for the widow of the first baron and, as she had a taste for ostentation, it is large. Keith pretends he owns it, but he doesn't, he rents it. Since my brother has died, ownership passes to Conrad, of course."

I asked tentatively, "And . . . Keith's source of income?"

Marjorie disapproved of the question but on reflection answered: it was she, after all, who'd set me in motion.

"His mother left him provided for. He was a beautiful-looking little boy and young man, and she doted on him. Forgave him anything. Conrad and Ivan were always clumsy and plain and never made her laugh. She died ten years ago, I suppose. Keith inherited his money then, and I'd say he's lost it."

I thought a bit, and asked, "Who is Jack's father?"

"That's none of your business."

"Not relevant?"

"Certainly not."

"Does Keith gamble on horses? Or anything? Cards? Backgammon?"

"Perhaps you'll find out," she said. "He will never, of course, tell me anything."

I could think of only one way of getting a window into Keith's affairs, and even that was problematical. I would have to borrow a car and drive it, for a start, when it was hard enough to walk. Give it two or three days, I thought. Say Tuesday.

"What does Keith do with his time?" I asked.

"He says he has a job in the City. He may have had once, but I'm sure he's lying about it now. He does lie, of course. He's sixty-five, anyway. Retiring age, I'm told." She more or less sniffed. "If one has obligations, my brother used to say, one *never* retires."

Retiring wasn't always one's own choice, but why argue? Not everyone was a hereditary baron with dependent

Honorables and a paternal nature. Not everyone had wealth enough to oil wheels and calm storms. My non-grandfather, I thought, must have been a nice man, whatever his faults; and my mother had liked him, and Dart also.

"How about Ivan?" I asked.

"Ivan?" Her eyebrows rose. "What do you mean?"

"He has a garden center?"

She nodded. "My brother made over to him fifty acres of the estate. Years ago, that was, when Ivan was young. He's good at growing things." She paused, and went on, "One doesn't need to be intellectual to lead a contented and harmless life."

"One needs to be lucky."

She considered me, and nodded.

I asked her, as it seemed she had run out of inquisition, if she would sign Roger's and Oliver's paychecks.

"What? Yes, I said I would. Tell the Colonel to remind me sometime again."

"They're here," I said, picking the envelope out of my still-chair-draping jacket. "Do you have a pen with you?"

She resignedly rummaged in a large handbag for a pen, took the checks out of the envelope and wrote her name with precision, no flourish, on the lines provided.

I said diffidently, "To save you the trouble in future, you directors could enable Conrad or Ivan or Dart to sign checks. It only needs to have their signatures registered with the bank. There are bound to be many things, and not only salary checks, needing signatures in the future. The Colonel has to have authorizations, in order to run things."

"You seem to know a lot about it!"

"I know about business. I have a limited company."

She frowned. "Very well. All three of them. Will that do?"

"Make it any two of the four of you. Then you will have safeguards, and the Colonel's honesty will be beyond being queried by Keith or Rebecca."

She didn't know whether to be annoyed or amused. "It's taken you no time at all, has it, to lay bare our Stratton souls?"

Without warning, and before I could answer, the office door opened fast and Keith and Hannah came in. Ignoring my presence they complained loudly to Marjorie that Conrad was talking to his architect as if the new plans would definitely be agreed.

"He's saying *when,*" Keith griped, "not *if.* I'm wholly against this ridiculous project and you've got to stop it."

"Stop it yourself," his aunt told him tartly. "You make a lot of noise, Keith, but you don't get things done. You want to get rid of me one minute, and you ask me to fight battles for you the next. And as you and Hannah are both here, you can apologize to Mr. Morris for attacking him."

Keith and Hannah gave me matching looks of malevolence from between narrowed eyelids. From their point of view, I understood, their ultimate purpose had been frustrated by Marjorie and Ivan's fortuitous arrival. I was still present, still standing, still and forever the symbol of their having been detested and rejected unbearably. That their hatred was irrational made no difference. Irrational hatred, the world over, set the furrows flooding with an impure blood—though it was only France that actively encouraged massacre in its patriotic war cry, the "Marseillaise" still glorifying the sentiments of 1792.

The impure blood at that time had been Austrian. Two hundred or so years later, blood-hatred flourished around the globe. Blood-hatred could almost be smelled in the manager's office of Stratton Park. I had by my presence there already activated responses beyond Keith and Hannah's control, and felt no confidence whatever that we'd come to the end of it.

Only Marjorie, at that moment, stood between me and a continuation of what they'd intended to do earlier that morning. I thought wryly that every big and usually powerful weakling should have a staunch octogenarian bodyguard.

Marjorie waited only briefly for the apology that would never come: and I could happily dispense forever with apologies, I thought, if they would clearly see that no amount of Stratton money could cancel charges of manslaughter.

Or half-brother slaughter. Or ex-wife's son slaughter. Whatever.

Amoeba-like, Strattons followed Strattons as if components of one organic mass, and Conrad with Jack and Ivan joined the company, also swelled by the foreign substance of Wilson Yarrow and completed by Dart, looking mischievously entertained, and Roger, trying to be inconspicuous. The crowd again was too big for the space.

Wilson Yarrow didn't know me. I gave him a flicking glance only, but he'd accorded me barely that. His attention was chiefly engaged by Conrad, whose suspicions had been aroused by Keith's talking to Marjorie behind a closed door.

Physically, Wilson Yarrow was remarkable not so much for his actual features as for his posture. His reddish brown hair, tall narrow-shouldered body, and square heavy jaw made no indelible statement. The way he held his head back, so that he could look down his nose, was unforgettable.

Condescending, Marjorie had said of him. Convinced of his own superiority, I thought, and without modesty to cloak it.

Conrad said, "Wilson Yarrow is of the opinion we should clear the site and start rebuilding immediately, and I've agreed to that proposal."

"My dear Conrad," Marjorie said in her stop-the-world voice, "you may *not* make such a decision. Your father had the right to make such decisions because he owned the racecourse. It now belongs to us all, and before anything is done, a majority of our Board must agree to it."

Conrad looked affronted and Wilson Yarrow impatient, obviously thinking the old lady a no-account interruption.

"It is clear," Marjorie went on in her crystal diction, "that we have to have a new grandstand."

"No," Keith interrupted. "We sell!"

Marjorie paid him no attention. "I am sure Mr. Yarrow is a highly competent architect, but for something as important as new stands I propose we put an advertisement in a magazine read by architects, inviting any who are interested to send us plans and proposals in a competition so that we could study various possibilities and then make a choice."

Conrad's consternation was matched by Yarrow's.

"But Marjorie . . ." Conrad began.

"It would be the normal course of activity, wouldn't it?" she asked with open-eyed simplicity. "I mean, one wouldn't buy even a chair without considering several for comfort and appearance and usefulness, would one?"

She gave me a short, expressionless, passing glance. Double bravo, I thought.

"As a director," Marjorie said, "I put forward a motion that we seek a variety of suggestions for a grandstand, and of course we will welcome Mr. Yarrow's among them."

Dead silence.

"Second the motion, Ivan?" Marjorie suggested.

"Oh! Yes. Sensible. Very sensible."

"Conrad?"

"Now look here, Marjorie . . ."

"Use common sense, Conrad," she urged.

Conrad squirmed. Yarrow looked furious.

Keith unexpectedly said, "I agree with you, Marjorie. You have my vote."

She looked surprised, but although she may have reckoned, as I did, that Keith's motive was solely to impede the rebuilding, she pragmatically accepted his help.

"Carried," she said without triumph. "Colonel, could you possibly find a suitable publication for an advertisement?"

Roger said he was certain he could, and would see to it.

"Splendid." Marjorie leveled a limpid gaze on the discomfited personage who'd made the error of condescension. "When you have your plans ready, Mr. Yarrow, we'd be delighted to see them."

He said with clenched teeth, "Lord Stratton has a set."

"Really?" Conrad squirmed further under a similar gaze. "Then, Conrad, we'd all like to see them, wouldn't we?"

Stratton heads nodded with various gradations of urgency.

"They're in my house," Conrad informed her grudgingly. "I suppose I could bring them to you sometime."

Marjorie nodded. "This afternoon, shall we say? Four o'clock." She looked at her watch. "My goodness! We're all terribly late for lunch. Such a busy morning." She rose to her small feet. "Colonel, as our private dining room in the stands is, as I suppose, out of action, perhaps you could arrange somewhere suitable for us on Monday? Most of us, I imagine, will be attending."

Roger said again, faintly, that he would see to it.

Marjorie, nodding benignly, made a grande dame exit

and, surrendering herself to Mark's solicitous care, was driven away.

More or less speechlessly, the others followed, Conrad taking an angry Yarrow, leaving Roger and myself in quiet occupancy of the combat zone.

"The old battleaxe!" Roger said with admiration.

I handed him his paychecks. He looked at the signature.

"How did you do that?" he said.

9

ROGER SPENT the afternoon with the racecourse's consultant electrician, whose men bypassed the main grandstand while restoring power to everywhere else. Circuits that hadn't fused by themselves had been disconnected prudently by Roger, it seemed. "Fire," he explained, "is the last thing we need."

A heavy-duty cable in an insulating tube was run underground by a trenching machine to the members' parking lot, for lights, power and refrigerators in the big top. "Never forget champagne on a racecourse," Roger said, not joking.

The investigators in the ruins had multiplied and had brought in scaffolding and cutters. At one point they erected and bolted together a long six-foot-high fence, replacing the cordoning tape. "We could lose priceless clues to souvenir hunters," one told me. "Monday's crowd, left alone, could put piranhas to shame."

I said to one of the bombfinders, "If you'd been drilling

upwards of thirty holes into the walls of a stairway, would you have posted a lookout?"

"Christ, yes." He thought for a bit. "Course, you know, when you have someone drilling, you mostly can't tell where the noise is coming from. Drilling's deceptive, like. You can think it's next door and it's a hundred yards away; and the other way round. If anyone heard the drilling, is what I'm trying to say, one, they wouldn't know where it was happening, and two, they wouldn't think nothing of it, not in a place this big."

Only Roger, I thought, would have known drilling was wrong: and Roger had been in his house half a mile out of earshot.

I used my mobile phone, still in Roger's jeep, to try to locate friends and staff from my student days to ask about Yarrow, but almost no one answered. I raised one wife, who said she would give Carteret my number but, sorry, he was busy in St. Petersburg, and I spoke also to a very young daughter who told me Daddy didn't live with them any more. This sort of thing, I thought ruefully, didn't happen to the best private eyes.

In the office, Roger and I drew up plans for the positioning of the big top and of the two Portakabins he'd been promised. Jockeys were to change in one, with the scales and attendant officials given housing in the other. We placed both structures near the parade ring within a few steps of Roger's office, and agreed that if his men took down the fence between the pad-dock and the members' parking lot, the access to the big top would be unhampered for the public. It meant rerouting the horses round the big top to get them out onto the course, but all, Roger promised, could be accomplished.

"Rebecca!" he exclaimed at one point, clapping palm

to aghast forehead. "Women jockeys! Where do we put them?"

"How many of them?"

"Two or three. Six, max."

I phoned Henry, got an answering machine, and left a message begging for side tents of any description. "Also send anything pretty," I added. "Send Sleeping Beauty's castle. We need to cheer people up."

"This is a racecourse, not a fairground," Roger said, a touch disapprovingly, as I finished the call.

"This is Easter Bank Holiday," I reminded him. "This is restore-confidence day. This is ignore-bombs day, feel-more-secure day, have-a-good-time day. On Monday people coming here are going to forget there's a frightening disaster lying behind that new fence." I paused. "And we're going to have lights over the whole area tonight and tomorrow night, and as many people patrolling the stables and Tattersalls and the cheap rings as you can possibly press-gang."

"But the expense!" he said.

"Make a success of Monday, and Marjorie will pay for the guards."

"You're infectious, you know that?" He gave me an almost lighthearted smile and was about to hurry back to his electricians when the telephone rang.

Roger said, "Hallo," and "Yes, Mrs. Binsham," and "At once, of course," and put down the receiver.

He relayed the news. "She says Conrad and Yarrow are with her, and they've shown her his plans, and she wants a copy made here on the office copier."

"And did Conrad agree?" I asked with surprise.

"It seems so, as long as we lock the copy in the office safe."

"She's amazing," I said.

"She's got Conrad in some sort of hammerlock. I've noticed before. When she applies pressure, he folds."

"They all blackmail each other!"

He nodded. "Too many secrets, paid for and hushed up."

"That's what Dart says, more or less."

Roger pointed to the door of his secretary's office. "Both the copier and the safe are in there. Conrad and Yarrow are coming straight over."

"In that case, I'll vanish," I said. "I'll wait in your jeep."

"And when they've gone—back to your bus?"

"If you don't mind."

"Long after time," he said briefly, and opened the door for my clip-clomping progress outwards.

I sprawled sideways in the jeep and watched Conrad and Wilson Yarrow arrive with a large-sized folder and later leave, both of them striding stiff-legged in annoyance.

When they'd gone, Roger brought the new copies over to the jeep and we looked at them together.

He said the plans had been on three large sheets, with blue lines on pale gray paper, but owing to the size of the office machine, the copies came on smaller sheets with black lines. One set of copies laid out a ground-floor plan. One set showed elevations of all four sides. The third looked a maze of thin threadlike lines forming a three-dimensional viewpoint, but hollow, without substance.

"What's *that*?" Roger asked, as I frowned over it. "I've never seen anything like that."

"It's an axonometric drawing."

"A what?"

"An axonometric projection is a method of representing a building in three dimensions that is easier than fiddling about with true perspectives. You rotate the plan of the building to whatever angle you like and project verticals upwards . . . Well," I apologized, "you did ask."

Roger was more at home with the elevations. "It's just one big slab of glass," he protested.

"It's not all that bad. Incomplete, but not bad."

"Lee!"

"Sorry," I said. "Anyway, I wouldn't build it in Stratton Park, and probably not anywhere in England. It's crying out for tropical weather, vast air-conditioning and millionaire members. And even those aren't going to be ultra-comfortable."

"That's better," he said, relieved.

I looked at the top left-hand corner of each set of copies. All three were inscribed simply "Club Grandstands, Wilson Yarrow, AA Dipl." A lone job. No partners, no firm.

"The best racing grandstands ever built," I said, "are at Arlington Park, near Chicago."

"I thought you didn't go racing much," Roger said.

"I haven't been there. I've seen pictures and prints of the plans."

He laughed. "Can we afford stands like that?"

"You could adapt their ideas."

"Dream on," he said, shuffling the copies into order. "Wait while I tuck these into the safe." He went off on the short errand and returned to drive the scant half-mile to his house, which was quiet and empty: no children, no wife.

We found them all in the bus. The boys had invited Mrs. Gardner to tea (tuna sandwiches with crusts on, potato chips and chocolate wafer biscuits) and they were all watching the soccer results unwaveringly on television.

When the guest of honor and her husband had gone, Christopher gave her the highest of accolades. "She understands even the off-side rule!"

Soccer coverage went on. I claimed my own bed, dis-

lodging a viewer or two, and lay on my stomach to watch
the proceedings. After the last possible report had been
made (ad infinitum reruns of every goal that afternoon),
Christopher made supper for everyone of tinned spaghetti
on toast. The boys then chose a video from the half dozen
or so I'd rented for the ruin-hunt journey and settled down
to watch that. I lay feeling that it had been a pretty long
day and, somewhere during the film, went to sleep.

I awoke at about three in the morning, still face down,
fully dressed.

The bus was dark and quiet, the boys asleep in their
bunks. I found that they had put a blanket over me instead
of waking me up.

On the table by my head stood a full glass of water.

I looked at it with grateful amazement, with a lump in
the throat.

The evening before, when I'd stood a glass there, Toby,
to whom, since the explosion, anything out of routine was
a cause of quivering anxiety, had asked what it was for.

"The hospital," I explained, "gave me some pills to take
if I woke up in the night and the cuts started hurting."

"Oh. Where are the pills?"

"Under my pillow."

They'd nodded over the information. I hadn't slept much
and I had taken the pills, which they'd commented on in
the morning.

So now, tonight, the glass of water was back, standing
ready, put there by my sons. I took the pills, drinking, and
I lay in the dark feeling grindingly sore and remarkably
happy.

IN THE MORNING, a fine one, the boys opened all the windows to air out the bus, and I gave them the Easter presents
Amanda had packed into the locker under my bed. Each

boy received a chocolate Easter egg, a paperback book and a small hand-held computer game, and all spoke to their mother to thank her.

"She wants to talk to you, Dad," Alan said, handing me the telephone, and I said, "Hi," and "Happy Easter," and "How's Jamie?"

"He's fine. Are you feeding the boys properly, Lee? Sandwiches and tinned spaghetti aren't enough. I asked Christopher . . . he says you didn't buy fruit yesterday."

"They've had bananas and cornflakes for breakfast today."

"Fruit and fresh vegetables," she said.

"OK."

"And can you stay out a bit longer? Say Wednesday or Thursday?"

"If you like."

"Yes. And take their clothes to a launderette, won't you?"

"Sure."

"Have you found a good ruin yet?"

"I'll keep looking."

"We're living on savings," she said.

"Yes, I know. The boys need new sneakers."

"You could get them."

"All right."

Conversation, as usual, confined itself mostly to childcare. I said, trying my best, "How did your sister's party go?"

"Why?" She sounded almost, for a moment, wary: then she said, "Great, fine. She sends you her love."

"Thanks."

"Take care of the boys, Lee."

"Yes," I said, and "Happy Easter," and "Goodbye, Amanda."

"She asked us to phone her tomorrow night," Christopher said.

"She cares about you. She wants us to go on hunting ruins for another day or two."

None of them objected, surprisingly. They were eyes-down, of course, to their bleep-bleeping flickering games.

There was a bang on the door, which was opened without pause by Roger, who stuck his head in while still standing outside.

"Your pal Henry," he told me, "has himself arrived with a crane on a low-loader and brought the big top on about six vast lorries and he won't unload a thing without talking to you first."

"Henry's big top!" Christopher exclaimed. "The one we had over the pub, before you built our house?"

"That's right."

The boys shut the windows instantly and presented themselves fast in the driveway, looking hopeful. Roger resignedly gestured towards the jeep and they all packed into the back, jostling and fighting for their favorite seats.

"Sit down or get out," Roger commanded in his best parade-ground bark and, subdued, they sat down.

"I'll swap you the boys for Marjorie," I suggested.

"Done." He careered in battle fashion up the private road, did a flourish of a four-wheel drift stop outside his office, and informed my progeny that any sign of disobedience would incur immediate banishment to the bus for the rest of the day. The troops, very impressed, took the warning respectfully, but ran off to greet Henry with out-of-school whoops.

Henry, huge, bearded, always made me feel short. He lifted Neil effortlessly to sit on his shoulders and beamed in my direction, walker and all.

"Nearly got yourself squelched, then?" he said.

"Yeah. Careless."

He gestured with a huge hand to his heavily laden monster trucks, currently cluttering the tarmac.

"I brought the whole razzmatazz," he said, pleased with it.

"Yes, but, look here . . ." Roger began.

Henry looked down on him kindly. "You trust Lee, here," he said. "He knows what people like. He's a bloody wizard, is Lee. You let him and me set you up here for tomorrow, and six weeks from now, when you've got another Bank Holiday meeting—I looked it up, so I know—you won't have enough room in the parking lot. Word of mouth, see? Now, do you want crowds here, or don't you?"

"Er . . . yes."

"Say no more."

Roger said to me despairingly, "Marjorie . . ."

"She'll love it. She wants the racecourse to prosper, above all."

"Are you sure?"

"Hundred per cent. Mind you, she'll take five seconds to get over the shock."

"Let's hope it takes longer for her to drop down dead from a heart attack."

"Did you get those electrical cables laid?" Henry asked him. "Heavy-duty?"

"As you specified," Roger said.

"Good. Then . . . site plans?"

"In the office."

For most of the day Roger directed his groundsmen to help where they could and himself stood in long spells of wonderment as Henry and his crew built before his eyes a revolutionary vision of grandstand comfort.

First they erected four pylon-like towers in crane-lifted

sections, towers strong enough, Henry told Roger, for trapeze artists to swing from: then with thick wire cables and heavy electric winches they raised tons of strong white canvas and spread them wide. The final height and the acreage matched those of the old stands, and easily outdid them for splendor.

Henry and I discussed crowd movement, racegoers' behavior, provision for rain. We set out the essentials, rubbed out the bottlenecks, made pleasure a priority, gave owners their due, allocated prime space for Strattons, for Stewards, for trainers' bars. Throughout the big top we planned solid-seeming flooring, with a wide center aisle, firm partition walls, and tented ceilings in each "room" of pale peach-colored thin pleated silk-like material. "I buy it by the mile," Henry assured a disbelieving Roger. "Lee told me sunlight shining through canvas and peach was more flattering to old faces than yellow, and it's seniors who pay the bills, mostly. I used to use yellow. Never again. Lee says the right light is more important than the food."

"And what Lee says is gospel?"

"Have you ever seen anyone transform a derelict no-customer pub into a human beehive? He's done it twice before my eyes, and more times before that, so I'm told. He knows what *attracts* people, see? They don't know exactly *what* attracts them. They just feel attracted. But Lee knows, you bet your sweet life he knows."

"Just what attracts people?" Roger asked me curiously.

"A long story," I said.

"But *how* do you know?"

"For years I asked hundreds, literally hundreds of people, why they'd bought the old houses they lived in. What was the decider, however irrational, that made them choose that house and no other? Sometimes they said bits of trellis, sometimes hidden winding secondary staircases, sometimes Cotswold stone fireplaces, or mill wheels, or sometimes split levels and galleries. I asked them also what they disliked, and would change. I simply grew to know how to rebuild near-ruins so that people hunger to live in them."

Roger said slowly, "Like your own house."

"Well, yes."

"And pubs?"

"I'll show you one day. But with pubs it's not just rebuilding. It's good food, good prices, fast service and a warm welcome. It's essential to learn the customers' faces and greet them as friends."

"But you always move on?"

"Once they're up and running," I nodded. "I'm a builder, not a restaurateur."

To Henry's men, many of them circus people themselves and accustomed to raising magic from an empty field overnight, twenty-four hours to gate-opening time was a luxury. They heaved on ropes, they swung mallets, they sweated. Henry bought a barrel of beer from the Mayflower for his "good lads."

Henry had brought not only the big top but a large amount of the iron piping and planking that, bolted together, had formed the basis of the tiered seating round the circus ring.

"Thought you might need it," he said.

"Grandstands!" I breathed. "You broth of a boy."

Henry beamed.

Roger couldn't believe it. His own workmen, under Henry's circus men's direction, erected all the steps not round a ring but in the open air along beside the rails of the track, their backs to the big top and their slanting face towards the action, with a wide strip of grass for access between the bottom step and the racecourse rails.

"We could do better given more time," Henry said, "but at least some of the customers will be able to see the races from here, without all squeezing onto the Tattersalls' steps."

"We probably need planning permission," Roger said faintly. "Safety officers. Heaven knows what."

Henry waved a couple of licenses under his nose. "I'm a licensed contractor. This is a temporary structure. Get who you like. Get them on Tuesday. Everything I do is safe and legal. I'll show you."

Grinning, he waved a huge hand and hey-prestoed an army of fire extinguishers from one of the trucks.

"Happier?" he asked Roger.

"Speechless."

Henry at one point drew me aside. "Who are those arse-holes blocking the gates? We as near as buggery knocked one of them over when we came across with the beer. He walked straight out. Raving lunatic."

I explained about Mr. Harold Quest, his followers and their quest to get steeplechasing banned. "Weren't they here when you first arrived?" I asked.

"No, they weren't. Do you want them shifted?"

"You mean physically shifted?"

"What other way is there?"

"Persuasion?" I suggested.

"Come off it."

"If you stamp on one wasp, fifty come to the funeral."

He nodded. "See what you mean." He rubbed his beard. "What do we do, then?"

"Put up with them."

"That's pathetic."

"You could tell them that banning steeplechasing would mean hundreds of horses being killed, once there was no use for them. Not just one horse would die occasionally, but all of them within a year. Tell Harold Quest he's advocating equine massacre and turning horses into an endangered species."

"Right." He looked as if he would do it immediately.

"But," I said, "quite likely he's not really fussed about the horses. Quite likely he's looking for a way to stop people enjoying themselves. *He's* enjoying himself, that's his main aim. He's been trying for days to get knocked down gently. Tomorrow he may manage to get himself arrested. If he does, he'll be ecstatic."

"All fanatics are nutters," he said.

"What about suffragettes and the twelve apostles?"

"Want a beer?" he said. "I'm not arguing with *you*."

"What we really want is a counterdemonstration," I suggested. "People marching alongside Harold Quest with placards saying, 'ADD TO UNEMPLOYMENT.' 'PUT STABLELADS OUT OF WORK.' 'SEND ALL STEEPLECHASE HORSES TO THE GLUE FACTORY.' 'PUT BLACKSMITHS ON THE DOLE.'"

"Farriers," Henry said.

"What?"

"Farriers shoe horses. Blacksmiths make wrought-iron gates."

"Let's have that beer," I said.

Beer got postponed however by the arrival of two cars, both driven by boiling tempers as a result of near-contact with Harold Quest.

Stuck behind the leading bumper came the torn remains of a placard saying "BAN CRUELTY," but as so often in such confrontations, a bossy platitudinous admonition had evoked an opposite response.

In the driver, Oliver Wells, the veneer of gentlemanly affability had rawly peeled to disclose a darker, heavier authority; and I was seeing, I thought, the equivalent of the ramming force of the pistons usually hidden within a smooth-running engine. More power, more relentlessness than on display to the world. Cruelty, in this unveiling of the man, could be considered a possibility.

His long nose and sticking-out ears quivering with the strength of his anger, he gave me a brief dismissive glance and demanded, "Where's Roger?"

"In his office," I said.

Oliver strode towards the office door, seemingly oblivious to the hammering activity all around him. The second car, a scarlet Ferrari, arrived to park beside his with a burning of tires and from it, self-ejecting, came the scowling fury of Rebecca.

She was, it briefly occurred to me, the first Stratton of the day, infinitely less welcome to me than her hair-fixated brother.

Rebecca too, in well-cut fawn trousers and brilliant scarlet sweater, resonated hotly with maximum outrage.

"I'll kill that verminous cretin," she told the world. "He's begging to be run down, and I'll do it, I swear it, if he dares to call me 'ducky' again."

I had difficulty swallowing the inappropriate laugh. Henry, having no inhibitions and sizing up the bristling feminism instantly, simply guffawed.

She half lowered her expressive eyelids and delivered a look of whole-hearted venom which left Henry unmoved.

"Where's Oliver?" Her voice, like her manner, conveyed uncontrolled arrogance. "The man who drove in ahead of me?"

"In that office," Henry said, pointing; and I swear the word "ducky" got as far as his teeth.

He watched her pantherish gait as she set off away
from us and for comment raised comical eyebrows, a real
dagger-between-the-shoulders invitation if she'd chanced
to turn round.

"She's good-looking and brave," I said. "Pity about
the rest."

"Who is she?"

"The Honorable Rebecca Stratton, steeplechase jockey."

Henry lowered his eyebrows and shrugged her out of
his immediate attention.

"Beer," he announced.

Another car again frustrated him; a small black Porsche
this time, coasting up like a shadow from the private inner
road and coming to an inconspicuous halt half hidden by
one of Henry's trucks. No driver emerged. The tinted side
windows obstructed identification.

Henry frowned in the newcomer's direction. "Who's
that skulking behind my trucks?"

"Don't know," I said. "Go and see."

He padded over, inspected briefly, padded back.

"He's thin, young, looks like Ducky. He's sitting in
there with the doors locked. He wouldn't speak to me."
Henry leered. "He made an Italian truck driver's gesture!
Are you any the wiser?"

"He just might be Forsyth Stratton. Ducky's cousin. He
looks very like her."

Henry shrugged, his interest waning. "What do you want
done with the empties in the bars?"

"The caterers will deal with them."

"Beer, then."

"Beer."

We finally lifted the elbows, discussing things as yet
undone. His crew would work to midnight or later, he

promised. They would sleep in the cabs of the trucks, as they often did, and would finish setting up early in the morning. His trucks would be gone by nine-thirty, all except the smallest, his own personal traveling workshop, which contained everything for maintenance and urgent repairs.

"I'll stay for the races," he said. "Can't miss them, after all this."

Roger joined us, a lot of strain showing.

"Oliver's in one of his vilest tempers," he reported. "And as for Rebecca . . ."

Rebecca herself came fast on his heels but bypassed our group and tried to find a way through the bolted-together fence that hid the gutted grandstand. Failing, she powered back to Roger and said forcefully, "Let me through that fence. I want to see how much damage has been done."

"I'm not in charge of the fence," Roger said with restraint. "Perhaps you should ask the police."

"Where are the police?"

"On the other side of the fence."

She narrowed her eyelids. "Fetch me a ladder, then."

When Roger failed to move fast to obey her, she turned instead to a passing workman. "Fetch me a stepladder," she told him. She gave him no "please," nor "thank you" when he brought one. She merely told him where to place it and gave him the slightest nod of ungracious approval when he stepped back to let her climb.

She went up the steps with assured liquid movement and looked for a long time at what the fence hid.

Henry and Roger sloped off fast like wily old soldiers and left me alone to benefit from Rebecca's scalpel-sharp opinions. She descended the steps with the same athletic grace, cast a disparaging look at my still-useful walker and told me to leave the racecourse at once, as I had no right to be there. I had also had no right to be in the stands two days earlier, on Friday morning, and if I were thinking of suing the Strattons for damages because of my injuries, the Strattons would sue me for trespass.

"OK," I said.

She blinked. "OK what?"

"Have you been talking to Keith?"

"That's none of your business, and I'm telling you to leave."

"The prosperity of this racecourse is my business," I said, unmoving. "I own eight hundredths of it. You, after probate, will own three hundredths. So who has the better right to be here?"

She narrowed the brilliant eyes, impatiently ducking the majority-of-interest issue but targeting the truly significant. "What do you mean, after probate? Those shares are mine, in the will."

"Under English law," I said, having discovered it in settling my mother's affairs, "no one actually owns what has been bequeathed to them until the will has been proved genuine, until taxes have been paid and a certificate of probate issued."

"I don't believe you."

"Doesn't alter the facts."

"Do you mean," she demanded, "that my father and Keith and Ivan have no right to be directors? That all their stupid decisions are null and void?"

I dashed her awakening hopes. "No, it doesn't. Directors don't have to be shareholders. Marjorie could have appointed anyone she liked, whether or not she was aware of it."

"You know too damned much," Rebecca said with resentment.

"Are you pleased," I asked, "that the main stands are now rubble?"

She said defiantly, "Yes, I am."

"And what would you want done?"

"New stands, of course. Modern. Glass-walled. New everything. Get rid of bloody Oliver and fuddy-duddy Roger."

"And run things yourself?" I said it without seriousness, but she seized on it fervently.

"I don't see why not! Grandfather did. We need change, now. New ideas. But this place should be run by a Stratton." Her zeal shone out like a vision. "There's no one else in the family who knows a rabbet from a raceway. Father has to leave Stratton Hays to his heir, but the racecourse land is not entailed. He can leave his racecourse shares to *me*."

"He's only sixty-five," I murmured, wondering what galvanizing effect this conversation would have had on Marjorie and Dart, not to mention Roger and Oliver, and Keith.

"I can wait. I want to ride for at least two more seasons. It's time a woman reached the top five on the jockeys' list, and I'm going to do that this year, bar falls and bloody stand-downs by stupid doctors. After that, I'll manage the place."

I listened to her confidence, not sure whether she were self-deluded or, in fact, capable.

"The directors would have to appoint you," I said prosaically.

She sharpened her gaze on me assessingly. "So they would," she said slowly. "And I've two whole years to make sure that they do." She paused. "Whoever they are, by then."

Deciding abruptly that she'd given me enough of her

time she prowled back to her scarlet car, casting hungry looks left and right at the domain she aimed to rule. Marjorie, of course, would frustrate her: but couldn't forever, consequence of the difference in decades. Rebecca had had that in mind.

Henry and Roger cravenly returned as Rebecca's exhaust pipe roared towards the exit.

"What was she saying to you?" Roger asked curiously. "She looked almost human."

"I think she wants to take charge here, like her grandfather."

"Rubbish!" He began a laugh which turned uneasily into a frown. "The family won't let her."

"No, they won't." Not this year, I thought, nor next year: but thereafter?

Roger shrugged away the untenable thought. "Don't tell Oliver," he said. "He'd strangle her first."

A policeman and the twenty-eight-year-old bomb expert came through a section of the fence, swinging it partly open, revealing the slow sifting activity of others within.

Roger and I walked to meet them and looked curiously at what they were carrying.

"Remains of an alarm clock," the expert said cheerfully, holding up a cog wheel. "One nearly always comes across pieces of timing devices. Nothing actually vaporizes with this type of explosive."

"What type?" I asked.

"P.E.4. Not Semtex. Not fertilizer and diesel oil. Not do-it-yourself terrorism. I'd say we're handling regular army here, not Irish Republican."

Roger, the colonel, said stiffly, "The army keeps strict control of detonators. P.E.4 is pussy-cat stuff without detonators."

The expert nodded. "You can pat it and mold it like marzipan. I wouldn't hit it with a hammer, though. But detonators under lock and key? Don't make me laugh. My life would be easier if it were true. But the army's been known to mislay tanks. What's a little fulminate of mercury between friends?"

"Everyone is very careful about detonators," Roger insisted. .

"Oh, sure." The expert grinned wolfishly. "Old soldiers could liberate a field-gun from under your nose. And—you know what they say—there's nothing as good as a fire."

From the look on Roger's face, the saying was all too familiar.

"When a certain large depot the size of five soccer fields went up in flames a few years ago," the expert enlarged to me with unholy relish, "enough stuff was reported lost to fill double the space. The army produced tons of constructive paperwork to prove that all sorts of things had been sent to the depot during the week before the fire. Things that had earlier gone missing, and might have had to be accounted for, were all reported as having been 'sent to the depot.' Things were reported to have been 'sent to the depot' that had, after the fire, marched out of their home bases by the suitcaseful to much nearer destinations. A good fire is a godsend, right, Colonel?"

Roger said formally, "You don't expect me to agree."

"Of course not, Colonel. But don't tell me it's impossible for a caseful of detonators to fail to be counted." He shook his head. "I'll grant you no one but a fool or an expert would handle them, but a word here, a word there, and there's a market for anything under the sun."

10

THE WORK went on.

Electric cables snaked everywhere and were gradually assimilated invisibly into the canvas. Lighting grew, looking as if it belonged there inevitably. White silently whirling fans hung beneath roof vents, to get rid of smells and used air. Henry himself understood tent management and crowd comfort in a way that sweltering guests in sunbaked marquees had never imagined, and as I too put climate control near the top of all living priorities, the Stratton Park racegoers were going to breathe easily without knowing why.

The nineteenth-century chimney-born updraughts in houses had created a boom then in footstools, winged chairs and screens; twentieth-century wind tunnels meant gale-ridden city street corners.

Air pressure, air movement, air temperature; dust removal, mite reduction, dehumidification: all were not just a matter of soft self-indulgence indoors, but of positive no-allergy health and the deterrence of rot, rust, fungus and mildew. The Lazarus act on old buildings began, in my no doubt obsessional mind, with the provision of clean dry air, unobtrusively circulating.

We fed everyone from the Mayflower's kitchen. My sons fetched and carried, acted as waiters, willingly collected rubbish and generally behaved as they never did normally unless bullied.

Roger and I consulted the racecourse's water-main maps, and his men laid a branch pipe to the side-tents' catering areas, with a twiglet off to the female jockeys' changing room especially for Rebecca. Cold water, of course, but perhaps better than none. Persistent telephoning finally wrung out a promise of one Portalet van and, from Ivan, Roger bravely cajoled a truckload of garden center potted plants.

"He says it's one of the top-selling days in his year," Roger commented, putting down the receiver. "He says the racecourse must pay for what he sends."

"Charming."

We discussed a few more arrangements before Roger bustled away, leaving me in the office. I'd begun in the past hour to find walking easier but on the other hand I felt weary across the shoulders and glad of a chance to perch a rump on the desk, avoiding the worst winces but resting arms and legs. I thought of the admonition card back home in my workshop, given me in happier times by Amanda, which read "If everything is going well you have obviously overlooked something," and idly wondered what hadn't occurred to Roger and Henry and me that could become a hopeless disaster on the morrow.

The door opened abruptly to reveal Forsyth Stratton striding over the threshold. None of the Strattons seemed capable of entering a room slowly.

"What are you doing in here?" he demanded.

"Thinking," I said. Thinking in fact that I was not pleased to see him, particularly if he had similar ideas to Hannah and Keith. It appeared, however, and somewhat to my relief, that his attack would be verbal, not physical.

He said with rage, "You've no right to take charge here."

"The Colonel's in charge," I replied mildly.

"The Colonel consults you before he does anything." His dark eyes glittered in the same way as Rebecca's, and I wondered fleetingly whether either or both of them wore contact lenses. "And that huge man whose staff are putting up tents, he asks the Colonel for decisions, then they come and ask *you,* or he bypasses the Colonel and comes to you first. You're much younger than them, but whatever *you* say, that's what they do. I've been sitting for hours watching and getting angrier and angrier, so don't tell me I don't know what I'm talking about. None of us want you here . . . just who the hell do you think you are?"

I said dryly, "A builder."

"A sodding builder shouldn't be running our race-course."

"A shareholder then. A part owner."

"Sod that! I'm a *Stratton.*"

"Bad luck," I said briefly.

He was furiously affronted. His voice rose a couple of octaves and, with a vindictive twist to his mouth, he practically shouted, "Your sodding mother had no right to those shares. Keith should have given her a good hiding instead. And Jack says that's just what you got from Keith yourself yesterday only not enough and you've a sodding nerve to stick your snout into our affairs and if you're thinking of screwing money out of us you can piss in the wind."

The incoherence of his speech only added to the bile pouring out of him. As far as I was concerned I'd taken one insult too many from the Strattons and it annoyed me into a brutality I seldom felt. I said, with intention to wound, "*You* don't have an ounce of authority in your own family. They ignore you. They won't even look at you. What have you done?"

His hands rose fast, closing into fists. He took a fierce step forward. I stood up straight, not looking (I hoped) the pushover I actually was and, regardless of the threat, and with hot blood, I taunted him, "I'd guess it's cost them a fortune to keep you free, walking about and out of prison."

He yelled, "Shut up, shut up. I'll complain to Aunt Marjorie." One of his fists made a pass near my chin.

"Complain," I said. I strove unsuccessfully to regain the tatters of my temper, but even to my own ears, my words came out hurtful and rough. "You're a fool, Forsyth, and no doubt also a knave, and Marjorie despises you enough already, without you sniveling to her to have your pitiful nose wiped. And if you could see the ugly mess hate's making of your face, you'd run a mile and hide."

That last childish jibe pierced him keenly. He clearly liked his own good looks. The spiteful facial contortions slackened, the lips lost their rigidity and covered the teeth and his sallow skin reddened.

"You *shit.*" He shook with humiliations past and present. The fists unclenched and fell away. He unraveled fast into a pathetic failure, all sound and posture, no substance.

I abruptly felt ashamed of myself. Oh great, I thought, unleashing the artillery on the least of the Strattons. Where were my brave words yesterday when I'd been faced with Keith?

"I make a better ally than enemy," I said, cooling down. "Why don't you try me?"

He looked confused besides defeated: softened enough maybe to answer a few questions.

I said, "Was it Keith who told you I'd come here to screw money out of your family?"

"Of course." He nodded weakly. "Why else would you come?"

I did not say, "Because your grandfather's money paid for my schooling." I did not say, "Perhaps to avenge my mother." I said, "Did he say it before or after the stands blew up?"

"What?"

I didn't repeat the question. He stared sullenly for a bit and finally answered, "After, I suppose."

"When exactly?"

"Friday. The day before yesterday. In the afternoon. A lot of us came here when we heard about the explosion. They'd taken you off to hospital. Keith said you'd be exaggerating a few grazes far more than their worth. Bound to, he said."

"Which you naturally believed?"

"Of course."

"All of you?"

He shrugged. "Conrad said we'd have to be prepared to buy you off and Keith said they couldn't afford it, not after . . ." His voice stopped suddenly, his confusion worsening.

"Not after what?" I asked.

He shook his head miserably.

"Not after," I guessed, "what it had cost them to get *you* out of trouble?"

"I'm not listening," he said, and like a child put his hands over his ears. "Shut up."

He was twenty-something, I thought. Unintelligent, unemployed and apparently unloved. Also, primarily, a

Stratton. Buying people off had become standard Stratton behavior, but from the way the others had behaved to Forsyth at the Wednesday board meeting, he had cost them too much. If they had had any affection for him earlier, by that meeting it had turned to resentment.

Within the family there were levers and coercions: I could see they existed, couldn't know what they were. Forsyth's actual sin was probably not as important to them as the expense of it on one hand, and the power gained over him on the other. If the threat of disclosure could still be applied to him, he would now do, I reckoned, whatever the family told him.

Roger had said that Marjorie held Conrad in some sort of hammerlock; that he would always give in to her when she demanded it.

I myself had agreed, without realizing the possible significance of it, to try to find out for her how much Keith owed and to whom, and also to discover what pressure was being put on Conrad by the would-be architect of the new stands, who had proved to be Wilson Yarrow, of whom I knew something but had forgotten more.

Was I, I wondered, being used by Marjorie to seek out facts for her chiefly to give her more leverage for ruling her family? Had she shrewdly guessed I would help her if she engaged my interest in the prosperity of the racecourse? Was she that clever, and was I that dumb? Probably, yes.

I still did believe, though, that she genuinely did want the racecourse to prosper, even if she'd intended to use me as a tool in the achievement of her no-change policy.

Marjorie herself would not, and could not, have blown the grandstand apart. If, through me or in any other way, she found out who had, or who had arranged it, and if it should turn out to be one of themselves, she would not necessarily, I now thought, seek any public or law-driven retribution. There would be no trial or conviction or official penal sentence for the culprit. The Stratton family, and Marjorie above all, would assimilate one more secret into the family pool, and use it for internal family blackmail.

I said to Forsyth, "When you were at school, did you join a cadet corps?"

He stared. "No, of course not."

"Why 'of course'?"

He said impatiently, "Only a fool wants to march around in uniform being shouted at."

"Field marshals begin that way."

He sneered, "Power-hungry cretins."

I tired of him. It was unlikely he'd ever handled det cord or explosives himself: boys in the cadet forces might have done. Forsyth didn't seem even to understand the drift of my question.

Christopher, Toby and Edward all came into the office, close together as if for strength, looking anxious.

"What's the matter?" I asked

"Nothing, Dad." Christopher relaxed slightly, his gaze on Forsyth. "The Colonel asked us to bring you over to position the taps for the water."

"You *see?*" Forsyth said bitterly.

Still using the walker, I went past Forsyth and out of the door with my boys and, though I could hear Forsyth coming behind me, I neither expected nor received any more trouble from that quarter. Trouble enough manifested itself irritatingly in a bunch of the Strattons issuing from the big top's main entrance like a posse intent on intercepting me mid-way on the tarmac. My three sons stopped walking, too young, too inexperienced for this sort of thing.

I took one step past them and stopped also. The Strattons formed a semi-circle in front of me; Conrad on my left, then a woman I didn't know, then Dart, Ivan, Jack with a bruised swollen face, then Hannah and Keith. Keith, on my right, stood just out of my peripheral vision, to me an unsatisfying state of affairs. I took a half-pace backwards so that I could see if he made any unwelcome movement; a step that the Strattons seemed to interpret as a general retreat. They all, in fact, took an equal step forward, crowding a shade closer, with Keith again behind my vision unless I turned my head his way.

Christopher, Toby and Edward hesitated, wavered and separated from each other behind me. I could sense their fright and dismay. They sidled off and round into my view, backing away behind the Strattons, then frankly turning and running off, disappearing into the big top. I didn't blame them: felt like running myself.

"No Marjorie?" I asked flippantly of Dart. And where, I might have added, was my bodyguard when I might need her?

"We went to church," Dart said unexpectedly. "Marjorie, Father, Mother and I. Easter Sunday, and all that." He grinned insouciantly. "Marjorie gave us lunch afterwards. She didn't want to come here with us. She didn't say why."

No one bothered with introductions, but I gathered that the woman between Conrad and Dart was Dart's mother, Lady Stratton, Victoria. She was thin, cool, well-groomed and looked as if she would rather be anywhere else. She regarded me with full-blown Stratton disdain, and I wondered fleetingly if Ivan's wife Dolly and Keith's fourth victim, Imogen, fitted as seamlessly into the family ethos.

Forsyth came to a halt on my left, beside Conrad, who paid him not the slightest attention.

Across the tarmac Roger appeared briefly in the big top entrance, took note of the Stratton formation, and went back inside.

I surveyed the half-circle of disapproving faces and hard eyes and decided on attack. Better one shot than none, I supposed.

"Which of you," I said flatly, "blew up the stands?"

Conrad said, "Don't be ridiculous."

Talking to Conrad meant turning too much of my back towards Keith, but though the skin on my neck might creep with alarm, it was Conrad, I reckoned, who might deter Keith from action.

I said to him, "One of you did it, or otherwise arranged it. Blowing up the stands was Stratton work. Not outside terrorism. Homegrown."

"Rubbish."

"The real reason you want to be rid of me is fear that I'll find out who did it. You're afraid because I saw how the explosive charges looked before they were set off."

"No!" The strength of Conrad's denial was in itself an admission.

"And fear that if I find out who did it, I'll offer silence for money."

None of them uttered.

"Which you can't easily afford," I went on, "after Forsyth's adventure."

They looked furiously at Forsyth.

"I didn't tell him," he begged desperately. "I didn't say *anything*. He guessed." He summoned a flash of healthier rage. "He guessed because you've all been so *beastly* to me, so serve you all right."

"Shut up, Forsyth," Hannah said viciously.

I said to Conrad, "How do you like your tent grand-stand?"

For half a second Conrad looked instinctively, genuinely pleased, but Keith said violently behind my right ear, "It won't stop us selling the land."

Conrad gave him a glance of disgusted dislike and told him that without the tents now, disgruntled race-goers would stay away in droves in the future, the course would go bust and be left with huge debts that would cut deep into anything the land could be sold for.

Keith fumed. Dart smiled secretly. Ivan said judiciously, "The tents are *essential*. We're lucky to have them."

All except Keith nodded agreement. Keith growled in his throat, much too close to my shoulder. I could feel his intent.

I said with fierceness to Conrad, "Keep your brother off me."

"What?"

"If he," I said, "or any of you lays another finger on me, the big top comes down."

Conrad stared.

I leaned on the walker. I said, "Your brother knows he can still knock me over. I'm telling you that if he or Hannah or Jack has any idea of continuing what they were stopped from doing yesterday, tomorrow morning you'll find an empty field over there." I nodded towards the canvas.

Hannah sneered, "Don't be stupid."

Conrad said to me, "You can't do that. It isn't in your power."

"Want to bet?"

Henry came out of the big top, all my boys with him. They stood near the entrance, watching, awaiting events. Conrad followed the direction of my gaze and looked back at me thoughtfully.

"Henry," I told him, "that giant of a man, he brought the big top here to help you out because I asked him to. He's a friend of mine."

Conrad protested, "The Colonel found the tent."

"I told him where to look. If I get one more threat, one more bruise from you lot, Henry takes everything home."

Conrad knew the truth when it battered his eardrums. He was, moreover, a realist when it came to being persuaded by a threat he knew could be carried out. He turned away, breaking the alarming half-circle, taking his wife and Dart with him. Dart, looking back, gave me a gleam from his teeth. The crown of his head showed pink under the thinning fuzz, which he would not like to know.

I turned towards Keith, who still stood with hunched shoulders, head sticking forward, jaw prominent, eyes angry; a picture overall of unstable aggression.

I had nothing to say. I simply stood there, not daring him, just trying to convey that I expected nothing at all: not any onslaught, not a backing down, no loss of face on his part or on mine.

Forsyth, from behind me, said meanly, "Go on, Keith, give it to him. What are you waiting for? Kick him again, while you can."

The spiteful urging had the opposite effect. Keith said as if automatically, "Keep your stupid mouth shut, Forsyth," and shook with frustration as much as rage, the dangerous moment defusing into a more general state of continuing hatred.

I found my son Alan appearing at my side, holding on to the walker and watching Keith apprehensively, and a moment later Neil joined us, on my other side, giving Keith a wide perplexed stare. Keith, for all his bullying years, looked slightly unnerved at being opposed by children.

"Come on, Dad," Alan said, tugging at the frame, "Henry wants you."

I said, "Right," with decisiveness and began moving forward, with Hannah and Jack straight ahead in my way. Uncertainly, they parted to let me go by: no lack of ill will in their faces, but not the unstoppable boiling fury of the previous morning.

The other three boys trickled across and crowded round also, so that I reached Henry finally as if guarded by a young human hedge.

"You saw them off, then," he said.

"Your size was the ultimate deterrent."

He laughed.

"Also I told them that you would pack up the big top and go home if there were any more messing about, and they can't afford that."

"Right little raver, aren't you?" he said.

"I'm not keen on their sort of football."

He nodded. "The Colonel told me about that. Why the heck do you bother to help them?"

"Cussedness."

Christopher said unhappily, "We left you, Dad."

"We went to get help," Edward assured me, believing it.

Toby, whispering as much to himself as to me, said, "We were frightened. We just . . . ran away."

"You came into the office to fetch me," I pointed out, "and that was brave."

"But afterwards . . ." Toby said.

"In the real world," I said mildly, "no one's a total hero day in and day out. No one expects it. You can't do it."

"But Dad . . ."

"I was glad you went to find the Colonel, so forget it."

Christopher and Edward sensibly believed me, but Toby looked doubtful. There were too many things, that Easter school holidays, that he would never forget.

Roger and Oliver Wells came out of the big top chatting amicably. The fireball of Oliver's temper had been extinguished that morning by a conducted tour of the emerging arrangements inside the tents. Who cared about Harold Quest, he finally said. Henry's work was miraculous: all would be well. He and Roger had planned in detail how best to distribute racecards to all, and entry badges to the Club customers. At Oliver's insistence a separate viewing stand for the Stewards was being bolted together directly behind the winning post on the inside of the course. It was imperative, he said, that since that high-up box was no more, the Stewards should have an unimpeded all-round view of every race. Roger had found a sign-painter who'd agreed to forfeit his afternoon's television viewing in favor of "Stewards Only," "Club Enclosure," "Private Dining Room," "Women Jockeys' Changing Room" and "Members' Bar."

Roger and Oliver crossed to Roger's jeep, started the engine and set off on an unspecified errand. They'd gone barely twenty yards in the direction of the private road, however, when they smartly reversed, did a U-turn and pulled up beside me and the boys.

Roger stuck his head out and also a hand, which grasped my mobile phone.

"This rang," he said. "I answered it. Someone called Carteret wants to speak to you. Are you at home?"

"Carteret! Fantastic!"

Roger handed me the instrument, and went on his way.

"Carteret?" I inquired of the phone. "Is it you? Are you in Russia?"

"No, dammit," a long-familiar voice spoke in my ear. "I'm here in London. My wife says you told her it was urgent. After years of nothing, not even Christmas cards, everything's urgent! So what gives?"

"Er . . . what gives is that I need a bit of help from your long-term memory."

"What the hell are you talking about?" He sounded pressed and not over-pleased.

"Remember Bedford Square?"

"Who could forget?"

"I've come across an odd situation, and I wondered . . . do you by any chance remember a student called Wilson Yarrow?"

"Who?"

"Wilson Yarrow."

After a pause Carteret's voice said indecisively, "Was he the one three years or so ahead of us?"

"That's right."

"Something not right about him."

"Yes. Do you remember what, exactly?"

"Hell, it was too long ago."

I sighed. I'd hoped Carteret, with his oft-proven retentive memory, would come out snapping with answers.

"Is that all?" Carteret asked. "Look, sorry, mate, but I'm up to my eyes in things here."

Without much hope, I said, "Do you still have all those diaries you wrote at college?"

"I suppose so, well, yes, somewhere."

"Could you just look at them and see if you wrote anything about Wilson Yarrow?"

"Lee, have you *any* idea what you're asking?"

"I've seen him again," I said. "Yesterday. I *know* there's something I ought to remember about him. Honestly, it might be important. I want to know if I should . . . perhaps . . . *warn* some people I know."

A few moments of silence ended with, "I got back from St. Petersburg this morning. I've tried the number you gave my wife several times without success. Nearly gave up. Tomorrow I'm taking my family to Euro Disney for six days. After that, I'll look in the diaries. Failing that, come to think of it, if you're in more of a hurry, you could come over here, tonight, and take a quick look yourself. Would that do? You *are* in London, I suppose?"

"No. Near Swindon, actually."

"Sorry, then."

I thought briefly and said, "What if I came up to Paddington by train? Will you be at home?"

"Sure. All evening. Unpacking and packing. Will you come? It'll be good to see you, after all this time." He sounded warmer, as if he suddenly meant it.

"Yes. Great. I'd like to see you, too."

"All right then." He gave me directions for coming by bus from Paddington Station and clicked himself off. Henry and the children gave me blank stares of disbelief.

"Did I hear right?" Henry said. "You hang on to a walker with one hand and plan to catch a train to London with the other?"

"Maybe," I said reasonably, "Roger could lend me a stick."

"What about us, Dad?" Toby said.

I glanced at Henry who nodded resignedly. "I'll see they come to no harm."

"I'll be back by their bedtime, with a bit of luck."

I phoned Swindon railway station and asked about time-tables. If I ran, it seemed, I could catch a train in five minutes. Otherwise, yes, possibly I could get to London even on the reduced Sunday service and be back in Swindon by bedtime. Just. With luck.

Roger, returning from his errand, offered not one but two walking sticks, plus, at my cajoling, a copy of Yarrow's grandstand plans ("You'll get me *shot*"), plus a ride to the station, though as we set off he said he doubted my sanity.

"Do you want to know if Wilson Yarrow can be trusted?" I asked.

"I'd be happy to know he can't be."

"Well, then."

"Yes, but . . ."

"I'm healing," I said briefly.

"I'll say no more."

I paid for my ticket by credit card, tottered onto the train, took a taxi from Paddington and arrived without incident on Carteret's doorstep near Shepherd's Bush. (Bay-windowed terrace built for genteel but impoverished Edwardians.)

He opened the door himself and we took stock of each other, the years of no contact sliding away. He was still small, rounded, bespectacled and black-haired, an odd genetic mixture of Celt and Thai, though born and educated in England. We had paired as strangers to share digs together temporarily during our first year in architectural school and had gone through the whole course helping each other where necessary.

"You look just the same," I said.

"So do you." He eyed my height, curly hair and brown eyes; raised his eyebrows not at the working clothes but at the sticks I leaned on.

"Nothing serious," I said. "I'll tell you about it."

"How's Amanda?" he asked, leading me in. "Are you still married?"

"Yes, we are."

"I never thought it would last," he said frankly. "And how are the boys? Three, was it?"

"We have six, now."

"Six! You never did anything by halves."

I met his wife, busy, and his two children, excited about going to meet Mickey Mouse. I told him, in his untidy, much-lived-in sitting room, about the present and possible future of Stratton Park racecourse. I explained a good deal.

We drank beer. He said he hadn't remembered anything else about Wilson Yarrow except that he had been one of the precious elite tipped for immortality.

"And then . . . what happened?" he asked. "Rumors. A cover-up of some sort. It didn't affect us, personally, and we were always working so hard ourselves. I remember his name. If he'd been called Tom Johnson or something, I'd have forgotten that too."

I nodded. I felt the same. I asked if I could look at his diaries.

"I did find them for you," he said. "They were in a box in the attic. Do you seriously think I'd have written anything about Wilson Yarrow?"

"I hope you did. You wrote about most things."

He smiled. "Waste of time, really. I used to think my life would go by and I'd forget it, if I didn't write it down."

"You were probably right."

He shook his head. "One remembers the great things anyway, and all the dreadful things. The rest doesn't matter."

"My diaries are balance sheets," I said. "I look at the old ones and remember what I was doing, when."

"Did you go on with rebuilding old wrecks?"

"Yeah."

"I couldn't do that."

"I couldn't work in an office. I tried it."

We smiled ruefully at each other, old improbable friends, unalike in everything except knowledge.

"I brought an envelope," I said, having clutched its large brown shape awkwardly along with one of the walking sticks during the journey. "While I read the diaries, you look at the way Wilson Yarrow thinks a grandstand should be built. Tell me your thoughts."

"All right."

A sensible plan, but no good in the performance. I looked with dismay as he brought out his diaries and piled them on his coffee table. There were perhaps twenty large spiral-bound notebooks, eight inches by ten and a half, literally thousands of pages filled with his neat cramped handwriting; a task of days, not half an hour.

"I didn't realize," I said weakly. "I didn't remember . . ."

"I told you you didn't know what you were asking."

"Could you . . . I mean, *would* you, lend them to me?"

"To take away, do you mean?"

"You'd get them back."

"You swear?" he said doubtfully.

"On my diploma."

His face lightened. "All right." He opened the brown envelope and took a look at the contents, pausing with raised eyebrows at the axonometric drawing. "That's showing off!" he said.

"Yeah. Not necessary."

Carteret looked at the elevations and floor plans. He made no comment about the amount of glass: building in difficult ways with glass was typical Architectural Association doctrine. We'd been taught to regard glass as avant-garde, as the pushing back of design frontiers. When I'd murmured that surely building with glass had been old hat since Joseph Paxton stuck together the old Crystal Palace in Hyde Park in 1851, I'd been reviled as an iconoclast, if not ruthlessly expelled for heresy. In any case, glass was acceptable to Carteret in futuristic ways that I found clever for the sake of cleverness, not for grace or utility. Glass for its own sake was pointless to me: except as a source of daylight, it was normally what one could see through it that mattered.

"Where are the rest of the plans?" Carteret asked.

"This is all Yarrow showed the Strattons."

"How does he get crowds up five stories?"

I smiled. "Presumably they walk, like they did in the old grandstand that exploded . . ."

"No lifts. No escalators in the floor plan." He looked up. "No client would buy this, not in this day and age."

"I'd guess," I said, "that Conrad Stratton has committed himself and the racecourse to whatever Yarrow produced."

"Signed a contract, do you mean?"

"I don't know. If he did, it's not binding, as he hadn't the power to."

He frowned. "Bit of a mess, though."

"Not if Wilson Yarrow's disqualified himself in some way."

"Literally? Do you mean disbarred? Struck off?"

"More like dishonest."

"Well, good luck with the diaries. I don't remember anything like that."

"But . . . something?"

"Yes."

I looked at my watch. "Do you have a number I could ring for a taxi?"

"Sure. It's in the kitchen. I'll do it for you." He went away on the errand and presently returned, carrying a tote bag and followed by his wife, who hovered in the doorway.

"Take the diaries in this," he said, beginning to transfer them to the tote, "and my wife says I must drive you to Paddington myself. She says you're in pain."

Disconcerted, I glanced at his wife and rubbed a hand over my face while I sought for a response.

"She's a nurse," Carteret said. "She thought you had arthritis until I explained about the roof falling in. She says you're forcing yourself to move and you need to rest a bit."

"Haven't time."

He cheerfully nodded. "Like, I may have a roaring temperature today but I can't fit in flu until, let's say, next Tuesday?"

"Quite right."

"So I will drive you to Paddington."

"I'm truly grateful."

He nodded, satisfied that I meant it.

"Anyway," I said, "I thought the current medical theory was 'get up and go.'"

Carteret's wife gave me a sweetly indulgent smile and went away, and Carteret himself put the toteful of diaries in his car and on arrival at Paddington Station drove around the back taxi road to park close between platforms, among the trains.

On the way there I said, "Stratton Park racecourse will be advertising a competition for its new stands. Why don't you ask your firm to put in for it?"

"I don't know anything about grandstands."

"I do," I said. "I could tell you what's needed."

"Why don't you do it yourself?"

I shook my head. "Not my sort of thing."

"I'll see what my firm says," he remarked doubtfully.

"Tell them to write and express interest and ask for how large a crowd the stands are envisaged to cater. You can't even begin to design stands until you've an idea of the size needed. Someone must have told Yarrow, because he got that about right."

"My firm can but try, I suppose," Carteret said. "There are fifteen thousand architects in Britain currently out of work. People don't think they *need* architects. They don't want to pay the fees, then they complain if they knock down a wall and the bedrooms fall into the basement."

"Life's rotten," I said dryly.

"Still the same cynic, I see."

He carried the diaries to the train and stored them and me into a seat. "I'll phone you when I get back from Disney. Where will you be?"

I gave him my home number. "Amanda may answer. She'll take a message."

"Don't let's leave it another ten years," he said. "OK?"

SWAYING TOWARDS SWINDON I dipped into the diaries and finally drowned in nostalgia. How young we'd been! How unformed and trusting! How serious and certain.

I came to a deep thrust of the knife.

Carteret had written:

Lee and Amanda got married today in church, the whole bit, like she wanted. They're both nineteen. I think he's a fool but have to admit they looked very pleased with themselves. She's dreamy. Trust Lee. Her father, ultra pukkah, he paid for it all. Her young sister Shelly was bridesmaid, a bit spotty. Lee's mother came. Madeline. A knockout. Fancied her rotten. She says I'm too young. Went to Amanda's folks' house after, for champagne and cake etc. About forty people. Amanda's cousins, girl friends, old uncles, that sort of thing. I had to toast the bridesmaid. Who'd be a best man? Lee says they'll live on air. Must say they were walking on it. They went off to practice being Mr. and Mrs. in Paris for three days.

Amanda's parents gave it to them for a wedding present.

God, I thought, I remembered that wedding day in every
tiny detail. I'd been positive we'd be blissful for ever and
ever. Sad, sad illusion.

On the next page, Carteret had written:

Lee and Amanda's party last night. Most of our year came.
A rave up. Bit different from last week's wedding!! They
still look ecstatic. Beer and pizza this time. Lee was paying. I went to bed at six and slept through old Hammond's
lecture this morning. I miss Lee in our lodgings. Didn't
realize what I'd got. Better start looking for a replacement,
can't afford this place on my own, bleak though it is.

Watching lights flash by in the dark countryside outside
the train's windows, I wondered what Amanda was doing
at that moment. Was she quietly alone at home with Jamie?
Or was she, as I couldn't help speculating, embarking on
an adventure of her own; had she met a new man at her sister's party? Had she *been* to her sister's party? Why did she
want me and the boys to stay away for two more days?

I wondered how I would deal with it if she had finally,
after all these years, fallen seriously in love with someone else.

For all the fragile state of our marriage, I desperately
wanted it to continue. Perhaps because I myself hadn't
been engulfed by an irresistible new passion, I still saw
only advantages in staying, even unsatisfactorily, together;
and top of that list came stability for six young lives. My
whole mind skittered away from the thought of breaking
everything up, from division of property, loss of sons,
uncertainty, unhappiness, loneliness, acrimony. That sort
of pain would disintegrate me into uselessness as nothing
physical could.

Let Amanda have a lover, I thought: let her light up with excitement, go off on trips, even bear a child not mine; but dear God, let her stay.

I would find out, I thought, when we went home on Thursday. I would see, then. I would know. I didn't want Thursday to come.

With an effort I turned back to dipping into Carteret's diaries for the rest of the journey, but Wilson Yarrow might never have existed for all I found of him.

It was after ten o'clock when I directed the Swindon taxi to drive into the racecourse by the back road and stop at the bus.

The boys were all there, drowsily watching a video, Neil fast asleep. Christopher, relieved, went off, as he'd promised, to tell the Gardners I'd come safely back. I lay down gratefully myself with an intense feeling that *this* was home, this bus, these children. Never regret that unwise wedding day, this had grown out of it. Now, keeping it together was all that mattered.

Sleep enfolded us all, peacefully; but there was a fire in the night.

11

THE BOYS and I surveyed the smoking ruins of the fence at the open ditch. Black, scorched to stumps and ash, it stretched across the course, smelling healthily of garden bonfire, thirty feet long by three feet wide.

Roger was there, unworried, with three groundsmen who had apparently doused the flames earlier and were now waiting with spades and a truck for the embers to cool to dismantling point.

"Harold Quest?" I asked Roger.

He shrugged resignedly. "His sort of thing, I suppose, but he left no signature. I'd have expected a 'BAN CRU-ELTY' poster, at the least."

"Will you doll off the fence?" I asked.

"Lord, no. Once we get this mess cleared away, we'll rebuild it. No problem. It's just a nuisance, not a calamity."

"No one saw who set it alight?"

" 'Fraid not. The night watchman spotted the flames from the stands at about dawn. He phoned me, woke me

up, and of course I drove up here, but there was no one
about. It would have been handy to catch someone with
a can of gasoline, but no dice. It was a pretty thorough
job, as you see. Not a cigarette. The whole width of the
fence burned at once. There isn't much wind. It had to be
gasoline."

"Or firelighters," Christopher said.

Roger looked interested. "Yes. I didn't think of that."

"Dad won't let us light fires with gasoline," my son
explained. "He says we could easily light ourselves."

"Firelighters," Roger said thoughtfully.

All the boys nodded.

"Lots of twigs," Neil said.

"Birch," Edward corrected.

Toby said, shuddering, "I don't like this place."

Roger and I both abruptly remembered that it was here
that Toby had seen the racegoer with his eyes kicked out.
Roger said briskly, "Jump in the jeep, boys," and as they
tumbled to obey him, added to me, "You *walked* up here
from the bus!"

"It's not far," I pointed out, "and it's getting easier all
the time." I'd taken only one stick: felt stiff and creaky
but definitely stronger.

Roger said, "Good. Well, get in the jeep yourself. Henry's a genius!"

He drove up to the by now familiar roadway and parked
outside his office and positively beamed at the sight before
us.

The fine weather, though cooling, had lasted. The sky
was a washed pale blue with a few streaky clouds slowly
thinning and vanishing. The morning sun shone unhampered on strings of bright flags, which fluttered gently
from the ridge lines of the big top's spreading roof right
down to the ground in a blizzard of strings, arcading the

whole huge tent like an arch of honor. Merrie Englande come again to gorgeous lighthearted life, uplifting the spirits, making one laugh.

I breathed, "Oh, my boy," and Roger said, "There are your flags. Henry said he brought every last one. When his men unfurled them all less than an hour ago, and that big white spread of canvas blossomed like that . . . well, you'd have to have been a sneering misanthrope not to have been moved."

"Colonel, you're a sentimentalist!"

"Who's talking!"

"I'm a hard-headed businessman," I said, only half truthfully. "The flags make people ready to spend more. Don't ask for the psychology, it just happens."

He said contentedly, "That's the perfect squelch for possible cynics. Mind if I use it?"

"Be my guest."

Henry's vast trucks had gone. Henry's own personal van, Roger said, was now parked out of sight at the far end of the big top. Henry was somewhere about.

Two Portakabins now stood, neatly aligned end to end, where Henry's trucks had been. Into one of them jockeys' valets were carrying saddles and hampers from their nearby vans, setting up the changing room for the male riders. Through the open door of the other could be seen an official weighing machine, borrowed from an obliging Midlands course.

A row of caterers' vans were drawn up outside the small feeder tents on the side of the big top furthest from the track, with busy hands carrying tables and trestles and folding chairs through the specially made passages into what would soon be fully fledged dining rooms and bars.

"It's all working," Roger said in wonderment. "It's bloody amazing."

"It's great."

"And the stables, of course, are OK. Horses have been arriving as usual. The canteen for drivers and lads is open, serving hot food. The press are here. The stable security staff say that for once everyone seems to be in a holiday mood. Like the Blitz, there's nothing like a bloody disaster to make the English good-humored."

We climbed out of the jeep and went into the big top itself. Each "room" now had a high-rising Moorish-looking tented ceiling of pleated peach "silk" above white solid-seeming walls, some of which were in fact taut whitened canvas laced onto poles. The floor throughout was of brown matting glued onto wooden sections slotted levelly together, firm and easy to the feet. Lights shone everywhere, discreetly. The fans up by the high roof silently circled, changing the air. Each room had an identifying board at its entrance. It all looked spacious, organized and calm. A rebirth; marvelous.

"What have we forgotten?" I said.

"You're such a comfort."

"Can I ask you something?"

"Of course."

"You remember, a week or so ago, that you learned about the precise distribution of shares among the Strattons, that they wouldn't tell you before?"

He flicked a glance at me, mentally a fraction off balance.

"Yes," he said slowly. "You noticed."

"Was it Forsyth who told you?"

"What does it matter?"

"Was it?" I asked.

"As a matter of fact, yes. Why did you think it was him?"

"He resents the way the others treat him, which makes

him untrustworthy from their point of view. He knows he thoroughly earned the way they treat him. They think they control him, but they could compress him too far."

"Like plastic explosive."

"Yeah. Too close to home."

Roger nodded. "He told me in a moment of spite against them, and then said he was only guessing. He's not very bright."

"Very unhappy, though."

"I don't like him, don't trust him and, no, I really don't know what he did. When the Strattons hide something, they do a good job."

We walked out of the big top and found a van and a car parked near the entrance. The van, green with white lettering, announced "Stratton Garden Center." The car, door opening, disgorged Ivan.

He stood with his hands on his hips, head back, staring up in utter amazement at the sunlit splendor of flags. I waited for his disapproval, forgetting the little boy in him.

He looked at Roger, his eyes shiny with smiling.

"Colonel," he said, "what *fun.*" He transferred his gaze first to my walking stick and then up to my face. "Would you mind," he said awkwardly, "if I reconsidered a bit?"

"In what way?"

"Actually," he said, "I think Keith's wrong about you, don't you know." He turned away, embarrassed, and instructed his driver to get out of the cab and open the rear doors of the van. "I talked it over with Dolly—that's my wife—last night," he went on, "and we thought it didn't make sense. If you were meaning to blackmail the family, why would you help us by getting this tent? And then, don't you know, you don't seem a bad fellow at all, and Hannah has had bees in her bonnet about her mother—

your mother—all her life. So we decided I might just, don't you know, *apologize,* if the occasion arose."

"Thank you," I said.

His face lightened, his errand achieved. His man opened the van's rear doors and disclosed a packed blaze of color inside. A whole army of flourishing pots.

"Superb!" Roger said, genuinely delighted.

"You see," Ivan explained, pleased, "when I saw the big top yesterday I understood why you'd asked me for plants, and this morning I went along to the center myself and told my manager to load not just green stuff, but *flowers.* Lots of flowers. The least I could do, don't you know."

"They're wonderful," I assured him.

He beamed, a heavy-set man in his fifties, not clever, not charismatic, polished in a way, but at heart uncomplicated. He hadn't been much of an enemy and wouldn't be much of a friend, but any neutralized Stratton could, in my terms, be counted a blessing.

Under Ivan's happy direction, my children enthusiastically carried and positioned all the flowers. I guessed they would be missing when it became time to collect them up again, except that Ivan in good humor gave them a pound each for their labors, making anything possible.

"You don't *have* to," Christopher told him earnestly, pocketing his coin, "but thanks very much."

"Forsyth," Ivan told me wistfully, "was a nice little boy."

I watched Toby stagger by with a huge pot of hyacinths. I would give almost anything, I thought, to have my own problem son grow into a well-balanced man, but it had to come from within him. He would make his own choices, as Forsyth had, as everyone did.

The plants positioned, Ivan and his van drove away and Roger asked if I would like to see the burned fence rebuilt. I glanced down at Neil who happened to be holding my hand and Roger resignedly yelled "Boys!" in his parade-ground voice and waited while they came running and piled into the jeep.

Toby refused to get out when he found where we'd got to, but I and the others watched the ultimate in prefabrication.

"It used to take days to put a new fence together," Roger said. "That was when we positioned poles as framework and filled the frame with bundle after bundle of birch, finally cutting the rough top edges into shape. Now we build fences in sections away in a separate area, take them to wherever's needed, and stake them into the ground. We can replace a whole fence or part of one at very short notice. Today's fire was at dawn and we don't race over this fence until two-thirty this afternoon. Piece of cake!"

His men, already having cleared the embers, were busy manhandling the first of the new sections into place.

"All our fences are built like this, now," Roger said. "They're good to jump but not as hard and unforgiving as the old sort."

I asked, "Did your men find any . . . well, *clues* . . . in the ashes to say who started the fire?"

Roger shook his head. "We always have trouble with vandalism. It's hopeless bothering to find out who did it. It's nearly always teenagers, and the courts hardly give them a slap on the wrist. We simply write vandalism into the budget and find ways to minimize the nuisance."

"How many people would know you could replace a fence this fast?" I asked.

"Trainers might," he said judiciously. "Jockeys, perhaps. Not many others, unless they worked here."

Roger went to speak to his foreman who looked at his watch, nodded, and got on with the job.

"Right," Roger said, returning and shepherding us back to his jeep. "Now, boys, muster at the jeep up by my office at eleven-thirty, right? I'll drive you and your father down to the bus then, and go on to my house. We all change for racing. At noon precisely I drive you back to the paddock. Understand?"

The boys were near to saluting. Roger, the peak of his tweed cap well pulled down over his eyes like a guards officer, was, with his clipped, very civilized voice and his spare decisive manner, the sort of senior soldier it was natural to obey. I could see I was never going to achieve such effortless mastery of my children's behavior.

We returned to Roger's office to find a flourishing row in full progress out on the tarmac. All the protesters from outside the gate were now inside, all of them clustered around Henry who held Harold Quest's elbow in an unyielding grip. The fierce woman was using a placard saying "ANIMAL RIGHTS" to belabor Henry as with a paddle. Four or five others howled verbal abuse with stretched ugly mouths and Henry shook Harold Quest without respect or mercy.

When he saw us Henry yelled, his voice rising as effortlessly above the screeching din as his height above everyone else, "This fellow's an imposter! A bloody imposter. They all are. They're rubbish."

He stretched out the hand not busy with shaking Quest and tweaked the placard away from the harpy attacking him.

"Madam," he roared, "go back to your kitchen."

Henry stood eighteen inches above her. He towered

over Quest. Henry's beard was bigger than Quest's, Henry's voice mightier, Henry's strength double, Henry's character—no contest.

Henry was laughing. Harold Quest, the scourge of entering vehicles, had more than met his match.

"This man," Henry yelled, shaking Quest's elbow, "do you know what he was doing? I went over to the Mayflower and when I came back I found him *eating a hamburger.*"

My sons stared at him in perplexity. Eating hamburgers came well within normal behavior.

"Animal rights!" Henry shouted joyously. "What about hamburgers' rights? This man was *eating an animal.*"

Harold Quest squirmed.

"Three of these dimwits," Henry yelled, glancing at the screeching chorus, "were *dripping* with hamburgers. Animal rights, my *arse.*"

My boys were fascinated. Roger was laughing. Oliver Wells came out of Roger's office primed to disapprove of the noise only to crease into a smile once he understood Quest's dilemma.

"This jacket he's wearing," Henry yelled, "feels like *leather.*"

"No." Quest shook his head violently, tipping his woolly hat over one ear.

"And," Henry yelled, "when I accused him of eating an animal he put the hamburger in his *pocket.*"

Alan jumped up and down, loving it, his freckled face grinning.

Henry flung the "ANIMAL RIGHTS" placard far and wide and plunged his hand into the pocket of Harold Quest's leather-like jacket. Out came a wrapper, a half-eaten bun, tomato ketchup and yellow oozing mustard and a half-moon of meat with the Quest bite marks all over it.

Out of the pocket, too, unexpectedly, fell a second ball of plastic wrapper which had never seen a short-order cook.

In the general melee, no one saw the significance of the second wrapper until Christopher, from some obscure urge to tidiness, picked it up. Even then it would have meant nothing to most people, but Christopher was different.

"Come on," Henry yelled at his hapless captive, "you're not a real protester. What are you doing here?"

Harold Quest didn't answer.

"Dad," Christopher said, pulling my sleeve, "look at this. Smell it."

I looked at the ball of wrapping material he'd picked up, and I smelled it. "Give it," I said, "to the Colonel."

Roger, hearing my tone of voice, glanced at my face and took the crumpled ball from Christopher.

There were two brown transparent wrappers scrunched together, with scarlet and yellow printing on them. Roger smoothed one of them out and looked up at Henry who, no slouch on the uptake, saw that more had been revealed than a hamburger.

"Bring him into the office," Roger told Henry.

Henry, receiving the message, roared at Quest's followers, "You lot, clear off before you get prosecuted for being a nuisance on the highway. You with the leather shoes, you with the hamburgers, next time get your act right. Shove off, the lot of you."

He turned his back on them, marching Quest effortlessly towards the office door, the rest of us interestedly watching while Quest's noisy flock collapsed and deserted him, straggling off silently towards the way out.

The office filled up again: Oliver, Roger, myself, five boys trying to look unobtrusive, Harold Quest and, above all, Henry who needed the space of three.

"Could you," Roger said to Henry, "search his other pockets?"

"Sure."

He must have loosened his grip a little in order to oblige because Quest suddenly wrenched himself free and made a dash for the door. Henry plucked him back casually by the collar and swung his arm before letting go. With anyone else's strength it wouldn't have much mattered, but under Henry's easy force Quest staggered across the room and crashed backwards against the wall. A certain amount of self-pity formed moisture round his eyes.

"Take the jacket *off*," Henry commanded, and Quest, fumbling, obeyed.

Roger took the jacket, searched the pockets and laid the booty out on the desk beside the blotter where Henry had parked the half-eaten hamburger. Apart from a meager wallet with a return bus ticket to London, there were a cigarette lighter, a box of matches and three further dark brown transparent wrappers with scarlet and yellow overprinting.

Roger smoothed out one of these flat on the desk and read the writing aloud.

" 'Sure Fire,' " he announced. " 'Clean. Non-toxic. Long-burning. Infallible. A fire every time. Twenty sticks.' " He did brief sums. "Five empty wrappers; that means one hundred firelighters. Now what would anyone want with one hundred firelighters on a racecourse?"

Harold Quest glowered.

Henry stood over him, a threat simply by size.

"As you're *unreal*," he boomed, "what were you up to?"

"Nothing," Quest weakly said, mopping his face with his hand.

Henry's loud voice beleaguered him, "People who burn

fences can blow up grandstands. We're turning you over to the force."

"I never blew up the grandstand," said Quest, freshly agitated.

"Oh really? You were here, Friday morning. You admitted it."

"I never . . . I wasn't here then."

"You definitely *were,*" I said. "You told the police you saw Dart Stratton's car drive in through the gates between eight and eight-thirty in the morning."

Harold Quest looked baffled.

"And it was *pointless,*" Roger added, "to be picketing the gates of a racecourse at that hour on a day none of the public would come."

"A day the TV cameras came, though," I said, "after the explosion."

"We saw you," Christopher said vehemently. "They said on the telly you'd done it. You nearly got my brother killed and you hurt my dad badly."

"I *didn't!*"

"Who did, then?" Henry roared. "You did it! You've been a bloody nuisance, you're not a real protester, you've destroyed racecourse property and you're heading for jail. Colonel, fetch the police, they're here already poking around behind that fence. Tell them we've caught their terrorist."

"No!" Quest squealed.

"Then *give,*" Henry commanded. "We're listening."

"All right then. All right. I did burn the fence." Quest was not confessing, but pleading. "But I never touched the grandstand. I didn't, as God's my witness."

"As to God, that's one thing. You've got to convince *us.*"

"*Why* did you burn the fence?" Roger demanded.

"Why?" Quest looked around desperately as if the answer might be written on the walls.

"Why?" Henry bellowed. "Why? Why? Why? And don't give us any shit about animal rights. We know that's all crap as far as you're concerned." He waved a hand at the hamburger relics. "So why did you do it? You're in dead trouble unless you come up with the goods."

Quest saw hope. "If I tell you, then, will that be the end of it?"

"It depends," Henry said. "Tell us first."

Quest looked up at the big man and at all of us staring at him with sharp hostile eyes and at the wrappers and the hamburger on the desk and, from one second to the next, lost his nerve.

He sweated. "I got paid for it," he said.

We met this announcement with silence.

Quest cast an intimidated look round the accusing faces and sweated some more.

"I'm an actor," he pleaded.

More silence.

Quest's desperation level rose with the pitch of his voice. "You don't know what it's like, waiting and waiting for jobs and sitting by the telephone forever and living on crumbs . . . you take anything, anything . . ."

Silence.

He went on miserably. "I'm a good actor . . ."

I thought that none of us, probably, would refute that.

". . . but you have to be lucky. You have to know people . . ."

He pulled off his askew woolly hat and began to look more credibly like Harold Quest, out-of-work actor, and less like Harold Quest, psyched-up fanatic.

He said, "I got this phone call from someone who'd seen me play a hunt saboteur in a TV film . . . only a bit part, no dialogue, just screaming abuse, but my name was there in the credits, hunt saboteur leader, Harold Quest."

Extraordinarily, he was proud of it: his name in the credits.

"So this phone caller said would I demonstrate for real, for money? And I wouldn't have to pay any agents' fees as he'd looked me up in the phone directory and just tried my number on the off-chance . . ."

He stopped, searching our faces, begging for understanding but not getting much.

"Well," he said weakly, "I was being evicted from my flat for non-payment of rent and I'd nowhere to go and I lived rough on the streets once before and anything's better than that."

Something in this recital, some tinge in the self-pity, reminded me sharply that this was an actor, a good one, and that the sob-stuff couldn't be trusted. Still, I thought, let him run on. There might be truth in him somewhere.

He realized himself that the piteousness wasn't achieving an over-sympathetic response and reacted with a more businesslike explanation.

"I asked what was wanted, and they said to come here and make a bloody intolerable nuisance of myself . . ."

"They?" Roger asked.

"He, then. *He* said to try to get some real demonstrators together and persuade them to come here and rant and rave a bit, so I went to a foxhunt and got that loud-mouthed bitch Paula to bring some of her friends . . . and I tell you, I've spent nearly a week with them and they get on my wick something chronic . . ."

"But you've been paid?" I suggested. "You've taken the money?"

"Well . . ." grudgingly, "some up front. Some every day. Yes."

"Every day?" I repeated, incredulously.

He nodded.

"And for burning the fence?"

He began to squirm again and to look mulishly sullen. "He didn't say anything about burning the fence, not to begin with."

"Who," Roger asked without threat, "is *he?"*

"He didn't tell me his name."

"Do you mean," Roger said in the same reasonable voice, "that you mounted a threatening demonstration here for someone unknown?"

"For *money.* Like I said."

"And you just trusted you'd get paid?"

"Well, I *was."* His air of defiance was of no help to him; much the reverse. "If I *hadn't* been paid, all I'd have laid out was the bus fare from London, but he promised me, and he kept his promise. And every day that I caused trouble, I got more."

"Describe him," I said.

Quest shook his head, rear-guarding.

"Not good enough," Roger said crisply. "The race-course will lay charges against you for willful destruction of property, namely burning down the fence at the open ditch."

"But you *said . . ."* began Quest, impotently protesting.

"We promised nothing. If you withhold the identity of your, er, *procurer,* we fetch the police across here immediately."

Quest, looking hunted, caved in.

"He told me," he said, seeking to persuade us, "to stop every car and be as much nuisance as I could, and one of the cars would be *his,* and he would wind down the window and tell me my telephone number, and I would know it was *him,* and I would put my hand into the car and he would put money into my hand, and I was not to ask questions or speak to him—as God's my judge."

"Your judge will be a damn sight nearer than God," Henry bellowed, "if you're not telling us straight."

"As God's my . . ." Quest began, and collapsed into speechlessness, unable to deal with so many accusers, with such complete disbelief.

"All right," Roger told him prosaically, "you may not have wanted to look at him in the face, to be able to identify him, but there's one thing you do now know, which you can tell us."

Quest simply looked nervous.

"Which car?" Roger said. "Describe it. Tell us its number."

"Well . . . I . . ."

"After the first payment," Roger said, "you'd have been looking out for that car."

I suppose that rabbits might look at snakes as Quest looked at Roger.

"Which car?" Henry yelled in Quest's ear.

"A Jaguar XJ6. Sort of silver." He mumbled the number.

Roger, slightly aghast but not disbelieving, said to me succinctly, *"Keith's."*

He and I digested the news. Henry raised his eyebrows our way. Roger flapped a hand, nodding. Henry, perceiving that the really essential piece of information had surfaced, looked more benignly upon his demoralized captive.

"Well, now," he said, at only medium fortissimo, "when did you get hold of the firelighters?"

After a moment, meekly, Quest said, "I bought them."

"When?" Roger asked.

"Saturday."

"On *his* instructions?"

Quest said feebly, "There was a piece of paper in with the money. He said to burn the open ditch fence, where a horse had been killed on the Saturday. He said douse it with gasoline, to make sure."

"But you didn't."

"I'm not *daft.*"

"Not far off it," Henry told him.

"Where do I get gasoline?" Quest asked rhetorically. "Buy a can from a garage, buy five gallons of gasoline, then burn a fence down? I ask you! He took me for daft."

"Eating a hamburger was daft," Henry said.

"Do you still have the paper with the instructions?" I asked.

"The paper said to burn the instructions."

"And you did?"

He nodded. "Of course."

"Silly," I said. "You're not much of a villain. Who's going to believe you, without those instructions?"

"But," he spluttered, "I mean, but . . ."

"How did you actually do it?" I asked. "I mean, how did you position the firelighters?"

He said matter-of-factly, "I pushed them into the fence in bunches. Then I lit a roll of newspaper and went along lighting the bunches all at once." He almost smiled. "It was easy."

He should have burned the wrappers as well, I thought, but then people were fools, especially actors who weren't practiced criminals.

"I think," I said to Roger and Henry and Oliver, "that we might do a spot of Strattoning here."

"How do you mean, exactly?"

"Could I borrow your typewriter?"

"Of course," Roger said, pointing to the inner office. "In there."

I went through to the machine, switched on the electricity and typed a short statement:

> I, Harold Quest, actor, agreed that in return for money I would mount nuisance demonstrations at the main gates of Stratton Park racecourse, ostensibly but not actually in support of a movement to discredit the sport of steeplechasing. For this service I received payments on several occasions from a man driving a silver Jaguar XJ6, registration number as follows: To comply with instructions received from this driver I also bought one hundred "Sure Fire" firelighters and, using them, burned to the ground the birch fence at the open ditch in the straight, at approximately six A.M. Monday, Easter Bank Holiday.

Roger, Oliver and Henry read it and presented it to Quest for signing. He was predictably reluctant. We told him to add the date and his address.

"You might as well," I said, when he shrank from it, "as you're in the phone book and we can find you any time, I should think, if your photo's in *Spotlight* with the name of your agent."

"But this is an admission of guilt," he protested, not disputing our ability to track him down, as one could with any actor, through their professional publication.

"Of course," I said, "but if you sign it, you can buzz off now, at once, and use your return bus ticket, and with luck we won't give your confession to the police."

Quest searched our faces, not finding much to reassure or comfort him; but he did sign the paper. He did, in his own handwriting, fill in the car registration (verified by Roger), and also his address and the date.

The others scrutinized the pages.

"Is that everything?" Roger asked me.

"I'd think so."

Roger said to Henry, "Let him go," and Henry opened the office door to freedom and jerked his thumb in that direction, giving Quest a last order, "Out!"

Quest, an amalgam of relief and anxiety, didn't wait for a change of heart on our part but took himself off at the double.

Henry looked at the abandoned bits of hamburger and said disgustedly, "We should have rubbed the little shit's nose in that mustard."

I said with mock seriousness, "Quest's not all bad. Remember, he did call Rebecca 'ducky.' "

Henry guffawed. "So he did."

Roger picked up the signed confession. "What do we do with this, then? Do we, in fact, give it to the police?"

"No," I said. "We give it to Marjorie Binsham."

12

NOTWITHSTANDING OUR threats to Quest, the police presence behind the partitioning wall had by that morning fallen to two constables, both there more to prevent the public from entering and hurting themselves in the unstable building than to investigate further for evidence.

As far as Roger and Oliver had been able to discover the previous afternoon, after I'd left, the higher ranks and the bomb expert had completed their work with the discovery and reassembling of a blown-apart clock face, and had said their further inquiries would be conducted "elsewhere," unspecified.

"They don't know who did it," Roger baldly interpreted.

In front of the boring and forbidding partition fence there now rose an inflated Sleeping Beauty's Bouncing Castle, complete with fairytale towers and a child-minder in the shape of Henry's one remaining maintenance man.

Ivan, in a flush of generosity, had returned with a second vanload of (free) plants, this time young bushy trees in pots, which he spread out on each side of the castle, making the fence in consequence a tamer, even decorative, part of the scenery.

By the time Roger drove us toward his house at eleven-thirty, neither he nor I nor Henry could think of any improvements that could be managed in time for that afternoon, though many that could be achieved afterwards, before the next meeting.

The boys changed into tidy clothes with only medium grumbles. I changed from navvy to gentleman and with my walking stick clumsily managed to knock to the floor the pile of Carteret's diaries that had been on the table by my bed. Edward obligingly picked them up for me, but held one awkwardly open, its pages tearing halfway along from the spiral wire binding.

"Hey, careful!" I said, taking it from him. "You'll get me shot."

I concentrated on closing the book to minimize the damage, and there, leaping out at me from the page, was the name I'd sought for unsuccessfully on the train.

Wilson Yarrow.

"Wilson Yarrow," Carteret had written, "that paragon we've had stuffed down our throats, they say he's a fraud!"

The next paragraph didn't explain anything but merely consisted of remarks about a lecture on miniaturization of space.

I groaned. "They say he's a fraud" got me no further. I flicked forward a few pages and came to:

There's a rumor going round that Wilson Yarrow won the Epsilon Prize last year with a design he pinched from someone else! Red faces on the staff! They're refusing to discuss it, but perhaps we'll hear less about the *brilliant* Wilson Yarrow from now on.

The Epsilon Prize, I remotely remembered, had been given each year for the most innovative design of a building by a senior student. I hadn't won it. Nor had Carteret. I couldn't remember ever having submitted an entry.

Roger banged on the bus door, stuck his head in and said, "Ready?" and the Morris family, dressed to impress, trooped out for his inspection.

"Very good," he approved. He gave us all racecards, entry badges and lunch tickets out of an attaché case.

"I don't want to go to the races," Toby said, suddenly frowning. "I want to stay here and watch soccer."

Roger left the decision to me.

"OK," I said to my son peaceably. "Get yourself some lunch, and if you change your mind, walk up later to the office."

Toby's worried frown turned to a more carefree expression. "Thanks, Dad," he said.

"Will he be all right by himself?" Roger asked, driving away with the rest of us, and Edward assured him, "Toby *likes* being by himself. He hides from us often."

"He goes off on bike rides," Christopher said.

Roger's mind switched to the day ahead. "We've done all we could," he said dubiously.

"Don't worry so much," I told him. "Do you know a rabbet from a raceway?"

"What on earth are you talking about?"

"Testing a theory."

"Is it a riddle, Dad?" Neil asked.

"Sort of. But don't ask, it hasn't an answer."

Roger parked the jeep at the end of the office building, where it would be ready if he needed to drive around the course. The boys paired off, Neil with Christopher, Edward and Alan together, with a rallying point near the office door for after the first, third and fifth races.

People were coming: a busload of Tote operators, the St. John's Ambulance people, the squad of policemen for traffic control and the general prevention of fights in the betting rings, the bookies with their soapboxes and chalkboards, the gate-men, the racecard sellers; and then the jockeys, the sponsors of the races, the Stewards, the trainers, the Strattons and, finally, the racegoers with all bets still to lose.

I stood near the main entrance, watching the faces, seeing on almost all of them the holiday pleasure we'd aimed for. Even the TV crew, invited by Oliver, seemed visibly impressed, cameras whirring outside the big top and within.

Mark drove the Daimler right up to the gate into the paddock so that Marjorie wouldn't have to walk from the parking lot. She saw me standing not far away, and beckoned as one seldom refused.

Without comment she watched me limp, with the stick, to her side.

"Flags," she said dubiously.

"Watch the faces."

She was sold, as I'd thought she would be, by the smiles, the chatter, the hum of excitement. A fairground it might be, but something to talk about, something to give Stratton Park races a more positive face than a bomb-blasted grandstand.

She said, "The Colonel promised us *lunch . . .*"

I showed her the way to the Strattons' own dining room, where she was greeted by the same butler and waitresses who always served her at the races, and obviously she felt instantly at home. She looked around carefully at every-thing, at the table the caterers had brought and laid with linen and silver, and up at the shimmering tent-ceiling with its soft oblique lighting and hidden air-vents.

"Conrad told me," she said slowly. "He said . . . a miracle. A miracle is saving us. He didn't say it was *beautiful*." She stopped suddenly, swallowing, unable to go on.

"There's champagne for you, I think," I said, and her butler was already bringing her a glass on a salver and pulling out a chair for her to sit down—a collapsible plastic-seated chair at base, covered now, as were ten round the table, with flowery material tied with neat bows.

Since pleasing Marjorie herself would mean the success of the whole enterprise, nothing we could think of that would make her comfortable had been left undone.

She sat primly, sipping. After a while she said, "Sit down, Lee. That is, if you can."

I sat beside her, able by now to do it without openly wincing.

Lee. No longer Mr. Morris. Progress.

"Mrs. Binsham . . ."

"You can call me Marjorie . . . if you like."

My great old girl, I thought, feeling enormous relief. "I'm honored," I said.

She nodded, agreeing with my assessment.

"Two days ago," she said, "my family treated you shamefully. I can hardly speak of it. Then you do this for us." She gestured to the room. "*Why* did you do it?"

After a pause I said, "Probably you know why. You're probably the only person who does know."

She thought. "My brother," she said, "once showed me a letter you wrote to him, after Madeline died. You said his money had paid for your education. You thanked him. You did all this for *him*, didn't you? To repay him?"

"I suppose so."

"Yes. Well. He would be pleased."

She put down her glass, opened her handbag, took out a small white handkerchief and gently blew her nose. "I

miss him," she said. She sniffed a little, put the handkerchief away and made an effort towards gaiety.

"Well now," she said. "Flags. Happy faces. A lovely
sunny spring day. Even those horrid people at the gate
seem to have gone home."

"Ah," I said, "I've something to show you."

I took Harold Quest's confession from my pocket and,
handing it over, explained about Henry and the out-of-
character hamburger.

She searched for spectacles and read the page, soon
putting a hand over her heart as if to still it.

"*Keith,*" she said, looking up. "That's Keith's car."

"Yes."

"Did you give a copy of this to the police?"

"No," I said. "That's a copy too, incidentally. The original is in the safe in the Colonel's office." I paused and
went on. "I don't think I can find out how much money
Keith owes, or to whom, but I did think this might do for
you as a lever instead."

She gave me a long inspection.

"You understand me." She sounded not pleased, nor
displeased, but surprised, and accepting.

"It took me a while."

A small smile. "You met me last Wednesday."

A long five days, I thought.

A woman appeared in the entrance to the dining room,
with a younger woman hidden behind her.

"Excuse me," she said, "I was told I could find Lee
Morris in here."

I stood up in my unsprightly fashion.

"I'm Lee Morris," I said.

She was plump, large-bosomed, friendly-looking, about
sixty, with large blue eyes and short grayish blonde curly

hair. She wore layers of blue and beige clothes with brown low-heeled shoes, and had an untidy multicolored silk square scarf tied in a bunched knot round her neck. Under her arm she carried a large brown handbag with its gold shoulder-chain dangling down, and there was altogether about her an air of being at home with herself: no mental insecurity or awkwardness.

Her gaze casually slid past me and fell on Marjorie, and there was a moment of extraordinary stillness, of suspension, in both women. Their eyes held the same wideness, their mouths the same open-lipped wonder. I thought in a flash of enlightenment that each knew the identity of the other, even though they showed no overt recognition nor made any attempt at polite speech.

"I want to talk to you," the newcomer said to me, removing her gaze from Marjorie but continuing to be tinglingly aware of her presence. "Not here, if you don't mind."

I said to Marjorie, "Will you excuse me?"

She could have said no. If she'd wanted to, she would have done. She cast an enigmatic glance at the newcomer, thought things over, and gave me a positive "Yes. Go and talk."

The newcomer backed out into the central aisle of the big top, with me following.

"I'm Perdita Faulds," the newcomer said, once outside. "And this," she added, stepping to her right and fully revealing her companion, "is my daughter, Penelope."

It was like being hit twice very fast with a hammer; no time to take in the first bit of news before being stunned by the second.

Penelope Faulds was tall, slender, fair-haired, long-necked and almost the double of Amanda: the young

Amanda I'd fallen in love with, the nineteen-year-old marvelous girl with gray smiling eyes going laughingly to her immature marriage.

I was no longer nineteen. I felt as breathless, however, as if I still were. I said, "How do you do," and it sounded ridiculous.

"Is there a bar in here?" Mrs. Faulds asked, looking around. "Someone outside told me there was."

"Er . . . yes," I said. "Over here."

I took her into one of the largest "rooms" in the big top, the members' bar, where a few early customers were sitting at small tables with sandwiches and drinks.

Perdita Faulds took easy charge. "Was it champagne that Mrs. Binsham was drinking? I think we should have some."

Faintly bemused, I turned towards the bar to do her bidding.

"My treat," she said, opening her handbag and providing the funds. "Three glasses."

Penelope followed me to the bar. "I'll carry the glasses," she said. "Can you manage the bottle?"

My pulse quickened. Stupid. I had six sons. I was too old.

The bar staff popped the cork and took the money. Mrs. Faulds watched in good-natured enjoyment while I poured her bubbles.

"Do you know who I am?" she demanded.

"You own seven shares in this racecourse."

She nodded. "And you own eight. Your mother's. I knew your mother quite well at one time."

I paused with the drinks. "Did you really?"

"Yes. Do get on. I'm thirsty."

I filled her glass, which she emptied fast. "And how

well," I asked, refilling it, "do you know Marjorie Binsham?"

"I don't exactly know her. I met her once, years ago. I know who she is. She knows who I am. You noticed, didn't you?"

"Yes."

I watched Penelope. Her skin looked smooth and enticing in the softly diffused peach light. I wanted to touch her cheek, stroke it, to kiss it, as I had with Amanda. For God's sake, I told myself astringently, take a grip on things. Grow up, you fool.

"I've never been here before," Mrs. Faulds said. "We saw on the television about the grandstand being bombed, didn't we, Pen? I got all curious. Then it was in Saturday's papers of course, with your name and everything, and they said the races would go on as planned. They said you'd been in the stands when they blew up, and that you were a shareholder, and in hospital." She looked at the walking stick. "They got that wrong, obviously. Anyway, I phoned the office here to ask where you were and they said you'd be here today, and I thought I'd like to meet you, Madeline's son, after all these years. So I told Pen I had some old shares in this place and asked if she would like to come with me, and here we are."

I thought vaguely that there was much she'd left out, but Penelope held most of my attention.

"Pen, darling," her mother said kindly. "This must be pretty boring for you, Mr. Morris and I talking about old times, so why don't you buzz off for a look at the horses?"

I said, "It's too early for there to be any horses in the parade ring yet."

"Hop off, Pen," her mother said, "there's a love."

Penelope gave a resigned conspiratorial smile, sucked her glass dry and amicably departed.

"She's a darling," her mother said. "My one and only. I was forty-two when I had her."

"Er . . . lucky," I murmured.

Perdita Faulds laughed. "Do I embarrass you? Pen says I'm embarrassing. She says I tell total strangers things I should never tell anyone. I do like to shock people a bit, to be honest. There are so many tight-lipped fuddy-duddies about. But secrets, they're different."

"What secrets?"

"What secret do you want to know?" she bantered.

"How you came by seven shares," I said.

She put down her glass and regarded me with eyes that were suddenly shrewd, besides being benign.

"Now, there's a question!" She didn't answer it at once. She said, "A couple of weeks ago the papers were saying the Strattons were rowing over the future of this racecourse."

"Yes, I read that too."

"Is that why you're here?"

"Basically, I guess so, yes."

She said, "I was brought up here, you know. Not here on the racecourse, but on the estate."

I said, puzzled, "But the Strattons—except Marjorie— say they don't know you."

"No, silly, they don't. Years ago, my father was Lord Stratton's barber."

She smiled at the surprise I hadn't hidden.

"You don't think I look like a barber's daughter?"

"Well, no, but then I don't know any barbers' daughters."

"My father rented a cottage on the estate," she explained, "and he had shops in Swindon, and Oxford and Newbury,

but he used to go to Stratton Hays himself to cut Lord
Stratton's hair. We moved before I was fifteen and lived
near the Oxford shop, but my father still went to Stratton
Hays once a month."

"Do go on," I said. "Did Lord Stratton give your father
the shares?"

She finished the pale liquid in her glass. I poured some
more.

"No, it wasn't like that." She considered a little, but
continued. "My father died and left me the barber business. You see, by that time I'd learned the whole beauty
trade, got diplomas, everything. Lord Stratton just strolled
into the Oxford shop one day when he was passing, to see
how I was getting on without my father, and he stayed to
have a manicure."

She smiled. She drank. I asked no more.

"Your mother used to come into the Swindon shop to
have her hair done," she said. "I could have told her
not to marry that vicious swine, Keith, but she'd done
it by then. She used to come into the shop with bruises
on her face and ask me personally to style her hair to
hide them. I used to take her into a private cubicle, and
she'd cling to me sometimes, and just cry. We were
about the same age, you see, and we liked each other."

"I'm glad she had someone," I said.

"Funny, isn't it, what happens? I never thought I'd be
sitting here talking to *you.*"

"You know about me?"

"Lord Stratton told me. During manicures."

"How long did you . . . look after his hands?"

"Until he died," she said simply. "But things changed,
of course. I met my husband and had Penelope, and
William—I mean, Lord Stratton, of course—he got *older*

and couldn't . . . well . . . but he still liked to have his nails done, and we would *talk.* Like old, old friends, you see?"

I saw.

"He gave me the shares at the same time he gave them to your mother. He gave them to his lawyers to look after for me. He said they might be worth something one day. It wasn't a great big deal. Just a present. A loving present. Better than money. I didn't ever want money from him. He knew that."

"He was a lucky man," I said.

"Oh, you *dear.* You're as nice as Madeline was."

I rubbed a hand over my face, finding no answer.

"Does Penelope know," I asked, "about you and Lord Stratton?"

"Pen's a *child!*" she replied. "She's eighteen. Of course she doesn't know. Nor does her father. I never told anyone. Nor did William . . . Lord Stratton. He wouldn't hurt his wife, and I didn't want him to."

"But Marjorie guesses."

She nodded. "She's known all these years. She came to see me in the Oxford shop. She made a special appointment. I think it was just to see what I was like. We just talked a bit, not about anything much. She never said anything afterwards. She loved William, as I did. She wouldn't have given him away. She didn't, anyway. She still hasn't, has she?"

"No, she hasn't."

After a pause, Perdita changed gears with her voice, shedding nostalgia, taking on business, saying crisply, "So what are we going to do now, about William's racecourse?"

"If the course is sold for development," I said, "you'll make a nice little capital gain."

"How much?"

"You can do sums as well as anyone. Seventy thousand pounds for every million the land raises, give or take a little capital gain."

"And you?" she asked frankly. "Would you sell?"

"You can't say it's not tempting. Keith's pushing for it. He's actually trying to put people off coming here, so that there's no profit in the course staying open."

"That puts me off selling, for a start."

I smiled. "Me, too."

"So?"

"So if we get a brilliant new stand built—and by brilliant, I don't mean huge, but clever, so that the crowds like to come here—our shares should pay us more regular dividends than they have in the past."

"You think, then, that horseracing as such will go on?"

"It's lasted in England so far for more than three hundred years. It's survived scandals and frauds and all sorts of accidental disasters. Horses are beautiful and betting's an addiction. I'd build a new stand."

"You're romantic!" she teased.

"I'm not deeply in debt," I said, "and Keith may be."

"William told me Keith was the biggest disappointment of his life."

I looked at her in sudden speculation, fifty questions rising like sharp rays of light; but before I could do anything constructive a racecourse official came to my side and said Colonel Gardner would like me to go urgently to the office.

"Don't go away without telling me how to find you," I begged Perdita Faulds.

"I'll be here all afternoon," she reassured me. "If I miss you, this is the phone number of my Swindon shop. That'll reach me." She gave me a business card. "And how do I find *you?*"

I wrote my mobile phone number and the Sussex house number on the back of another of her cards, and left her contentedly continuing with her champagne while I went to find out what crisis had overcome us.

The trouble, essentially, was the state of Rebecca's nerves. She was pacing up and down outside the office and gave me an angry stare as I went past her and through the door, and I'd never seen her look more unstable.

Roger and Oliver were inside, steaming and grinding their teeth.

"You are not going to believe this," Roger said tautly, when he saw me. "We have all the normal sort of troubles—we've caught a would-be nobbler in the stables, the lights on the Tote board have fused and there's a man down in Tattersalls having a heart attack—and we also have Rebecca creating the father and mother of a stink because there are no hangers in the women jockeys' changing tent."

"Hangers?" I said blankly.

"Hangers. She says they can't be expected to hang their clothes and colors up on the floor. We gave her a table, a bench, a mirror, a basin, running water and a drain. And she's creating a stink about *hangers."*

"Er . . ." I said helplessly. "How about a rope, for their clothes?"

Roger handed me a bunch of keys. "I wondered if you'd take the jeep down to my house—it's locked, my wife's somewhere here but I can't find her—and bring back some hangers. Take the clothes off them. It's madness, but do you mind? Can you do it? Will your legs be up to it?"

"Sure," I said, relieved. "I thought it was serious, when you sent for me."

"She's riding Conrad's horse in the first race. It would be serious enough for him—and for all of us—if she went completely off her rocker."

"OK."

Outside, I found Dart trying without success to pacify his sister. He gave it up when he saw me and walked with me to the jeep, asking where I was going. When I said to fetch some hangers he was at first incredulous and then offered to help, so I drove both of us on the errand.

"She gets into states," Dart said, excusing her.

"Yes."

"I suppose it's a strain, risking your life every day."

"Perhaps she should stop."

"She's just blowing off steam."

We disunited Roger's clothes from a whole lot of hangers and on the way back called at the bus, where I opened the door and stuck my head into a soccer roar, maximum decibels.

"Toby," I yelled, "are you all right?"

"Yes, Dad." He turned the volume down slightly. "Dad, they had Stratton Park on the telly! They showed all the flags and the bouncing castle and everything. They said people should come here, the racing was going ahead and it was a real Bank Holiday day out."

"Great!" I said. "Do you want to come up to the paddock?"

"No thanks."

"OK, see you later."

I told Dart about the television coverage. "That was Oliver's doing," he said. "I heard him screwing the arms off those camera guys to get them rolling. I must say, he and Roger and you, you've done a fantastic job here."

"And Henry."

"Father says the family got you wrong. He says they

shouldn't have listened to Keith."

"Good."

"He's worried about Rebecca, though."

So would I be, I thought, if she were my daughter.

Dart gave the hangers to his sister who stalked off with them, tight-mouthed. He also, to save my legs, he said, took the jeep's keys back into the office and told Roger and Oliver the big top had been news. Finally he suggested a beer and a sandwich in the bar so that he could skip the Stratton lunch. "Keith, Hannah, Jack and Imogen," he said. "Yuk." Then, "Did you know the police took my old wheels away for testing?"

"No," I said, looking for signs of worry on Dart's face, and finding none. "I didn't know."

"It's a bloody nuisance," he said. "I've had to rent a car. I told the police I would send them the bill and they just sneered. I'm fed up with this bomb thing." He grinned at my walking stick. "You must be, too."

Perdita Faulds had left the bar and was nowhere in sight when we reached it. Dart and I drank and munched and I told him I'd read a recipe once for curing falling hair.

He looked at me suspiciously. "You're kidding me."

"Well," I said judiciously, "it might be on a par with tearing off tree barks to cure malaria, or using mold growing on jelly to cure blood poisoning."

"Quinine," he said, nodding, "and penicillin."

"Right. So this cure for baldness came from a Mexican medicine-man's handbook written in 1552."

"I'll try *anything,*" he said.

"You grind up some soap plant," I said, "and you boil it in dog's urine, and you throw in a tree frog or two and some caterpillars . . ."

"You're a *shit,*" he said bitterly.

"That's what the book says."

"You're a bloody liar."

"The Aztecs swore by it."

"I'll throw you to Keith," he said. "I'll stamp on you myself."

"The book's called *The Barberini Codex*. It was all serious medicine five hundred years ago."

"What is soap plant, then?"

"I don't know."

"I wonder," he said thoughtfully, "if it works."

WE LEANED ON the parade ring rails before the first race, Dart and I, watching his father and mother, Conrad and Victoria, talking to their daughter-jockey, Rebecca, in a concerned little group that also included the horse's trainer. Other concerned little groups similarly eyed their four-legged performers stalking patiently around them, and hid their wild hopes under judicious appraisals.

"He won last time out," Dart said, appraising judiciously from his own sidelines. "She can ride well, you know, Rebecca."

"She must do, to get so high on the list."

"She's two years younger than me, and I can't remember when she wasn't besotted by ponies. I got kicked by one once, and that was enough for me, thanks very much, but Rebecca . . ." his voice held the familiar mix of exasperation and respect, "she's broken her bones as if they were fingernails . . . I can't imagine *ever* wanting *anything* as much as she wants to win."

"I think," I said, "that all top achievers are like that, at least for a while."

He turned his head, assessing me. "Are you?"

"Afraid not."

"Nor am I."

"So we stand here," I said, "watching your sister."

Dart said, "You have such a *damned* clear way of looking at things."

The signal was given for the jockeys to mount. Rebecca, wearing the distinctive Stratton colors of green and blue checks on the body with mismatched orange and scarlet sleeves and cap, swung her thin lithe shape into the saddle as softly as thistledown landing. The excessive strain brought on by the trivial annoyance of a lack of hangers had vanished: she looked cool, concentrated, a star on her stage, in command of her performance.

Dart watched her with all his ambivalent feelings showing; the female sibling whose prowess outshone him, whom he admired and resented, understood but couldn't love.

Conrad's runner, Tempestexi, a chestnut gelding, looked, by comparison with some of the others in the ring, to have a long back and short legs. The two-mile hurdle race, according to the card, was for horses that hadn't won a hurdle race before January first. Tempestexi, who had won one since, carried a seven-pound penalty for doing so, but had, all the same, been made favorite.

I asked Dart how many racehorses his father had in training and he said five, he thought, though they came and went a bit, he said, according to their legs.

"Tendons," he said succinctly. "Horses' tendons are as temperamental as violin strings. Tempestexi is Father's current white-hot hope. No leg problems, so far."

"Does Conrad bet?"

"No. Mother does. And Keith. He'd have put the Dower House on this one, if he'd owned it—the Dower House, that is. He'll have bet anything he can lay his hands on. If Rebecca doesn't win, Keith will kill her."

"That wouldn't help."

Dart laughed. "You of all people must know that logic never interferes with instinct, in Keith."

The horses streamed out of the parade ring on their way to the course, and Dart and I went to watch the race from the makeshift stands Henry had bolted together from the circus tiers.

The steps were packed to the point that I hoped Henry's boast of infallible safety would hold up. Crowds, in fact, had poured through the gates like a river during the past hour and had spread over the tarmac and into the big top and down to the betting rings in chattering thousands. The dining rooms were full, with customers waiting. There were crushes in all the bars and long lines at the Tote, and the booths by the entrance had sold out of regular racecards. The big office copier was churning out paper substitutes and running red-hot. Oliver, glimpsed briefly, sweated ecstatically.

"The television did it," he said, gasping.

"Yes, your work, well done."

Waiting for the race to start I said to Dart, "Perdita Faulds is here at the races."

"Oh? Who is she?"

"The other non-Stratton shareholder."

He showed minimal interest. "Didn't someone mention her at the family Board meeting the other day? Why did she come?"

"Like me, to see what was happening about her investment."

Dart cast it out of his mind. "They're off!" he said. "Now, come on, Rebecca."

It looked an uneventful race from the stands, though no doubt not from the saddle. The runners stayed bunched throughout the first circuit, clattered safely over the flights of hurdles, swept in an overlapping ribbon past the winning post for the first time and set off again into the country.

Down the far side the less fit, the less speedy, fell back, leaving Rebecca in third place round the last bend. Dart's genuine wish for his sister to win couldn't be doubted. He made scrubbing, encouraging movements with his whole body, and when she reached second place coming towards the last flight he raised his voice like the rest and yelled to her to win.

She did. She won by less than a length, accelerating, a thin streak of neat rhythmic muscle against an opponent who flapped his elbows and his whip but couldn't hang on to his lead.

The crowd cheered her. Dart oozed reflected glory. Everyone streamed down towards the winner's unsaddling enclosure where Dart joined his parents and Marjorie in a kissing and back-slapping orgy. Rebecca, pulling off the saddle, ducked the sentiment and dived purposefully into the Portakabin weighing room to sit on the scales. Very professional, fairly withdrawn; rapt in her own private world of risk, effort, metaphysics and, this time, success.

I took myself over to the office door and found four boys faithfully reporting there.

"Did you have lunch OK?" I asked.

They nodded. "Good job we went early. There were no tables left, pretty soon."

"Did you see Rebecca Stratton win that race?"

Christopher said reproachfully, "Even though she called us brats, we wanted to back her with you, but we couldn't find you."

I reflected. "I'll pay you whatever the Tote pays on a minimum bet."

Four grins rewarded me. "Don't lose it," I said.

Perdita Faulds and Penelope, passing, stopped by my side, and I introduced the children.

"All yours?" Perdita asked. "You don't look old enough."

"Started young."

The boys were staring at Penelope, wide-eyed.

"What's the matter?" she asked. "Have I got mud on my nose?"

"No," Alan said frankly, "you look like Mummy."

"Like your mother?"

They all nodded, and they moved off with her, as if it were natural, to go and look at the horses walking round for the next race.

"Like your wife, is she, my Pen?" Perdita said.

I dragged my gaze back. Heart thudded. Idiotic.

"Like she was then," I said.

"And now?"

I swallowed. "Yes, like now, too."

Perdita gave me a look born of long, knowing experience. "You can never go back," she said.

I would do it again, I thought helplessly. I'd marry with my eyes and find an unsuspected stranger inside the package. Did one never grow up?

I wrenched my mind away from it and said to Perdita, "Did Lord Stratton happen to know—and tell you—what it was that Forsyth Stratton did that has tied the whole family into knots?"

Her generous red mouth formed an O of amused surprise.

"You don't mess about, do you? Why should I tell you?"

"Because if we're going to save his racecourse, we have to unravel the strings that work the family. They all know things about each other that they use as threats. They blackmail each other to make them do—or not do—what they want."

Perdita nodded.

"And as a part of that," I said, "they pay people off, to keep the Stratton name clean."

"Yes, they do."

"Starting with my own mother," I said.

"No, before that."

"So you *do* know!"

"William liked to talk," she said. "I told you."

"And . . . Forsyth?"

Penelope and the boys were on their way back. Perdita said, "If you come to see me in my Swindon shop tomorrow morning, I'll tell you about Forsyth . . . and about the others, if you think up the questions."

13

KEITH'S RAGE, when he discovered that the runners in the second race would be jumping the open ditch as scheduled, verged on the spectacular.

Henry and I happened to be walking along behind the caterers' tents when the eruption occurred (Henry having had to deal with a leak in the new water main) and we hurried down a caterers' passage towards the source of vocal bellowing and crockery-smashing noises; into the Stratton's private dining room.

The whole family had clearly returned, after their victory, to finish their lunch and toast the winner, and typically, but perhaps luckily, had invited no outsiders to join them.

Keith, legs astride, shoulders back, mane of hair flying, had flung the entire dining table over and swept an arm along the line of bottles and glasses on the serving sideboard. Tablecloths, knives, plates, cheese, champagne, coffee, whipped-cream puddings, lay in a mess on the floor. Wine poured out of opened bottles. The waitresses pressed their hands to their mouths and various Strattons grabbed napkins and tried to clean debris from laps, trousers and legs.

"Keith!" screeched Conrad, equally furious, quivering on his feet, thunderous as a bull before charging. "You *lout.*"

Victoria's cream silk suit ran with coffee and Bordeaux. "I'm presenting the Cup," she yelled, wailing, "and *look* at me."

Marjorie sat calm, unspattered, icily furious. Ivan, beside her, said, "I say, Keith, I *say . . .*"

Hannah, trifle dripping down her legs, used unfilial language to her father and also to her son, who turned ineffectively to help her. The thin woman who sat beyond Ivan, unconcernedly continuing a relationship with a large snifter of brandy, I provisionally guessed to be Imogen. Dart wasn't there. Forsyth, sullenly seeming to be relieved that someone other than he was the focus of family obloquy, made his way to the doorway into the main passage, where we'd arranged a flap of canvas that could be fastened across to give privacy.

People were pulling the flap aside, trying to see in, to find out the cause of the commotion. Forsyth shouldered his way out, telling people rudely to mind their own business which, of course, they didn't.

The whole scene was laughable but, not far below the farcical surface, as each family member uneasily knew, lay the real cause of destructive violence, the melt-down in Keith that had so far gained most expression in hitting his wives and taking a belt at Lee Morris, but would one day go too far for containment.

Marjorie was holding in plain sight the copy of Harold Quest's confession; the cause of the debacle.

Keith suddenly seized it out of her hand, snatched the

brandy glass rudely from his wife, poured the alcohol over the letter, threw down the glass and with economic speed produced a lighter from his pocket and put a flame to the paper. Harold Quest's confession flared brightly and curled to ash and was dropped and stamped on, Keith triumphant.

"It was only a copy," Marjorie said primly, intentionally goading.

"I'll kill you," Keith said to her, his lower jaw rigid. His gaze rose over her and fastened on me. The animosity intensified, found a more possible, a more preferred target. "I *will* kill *you,*" he said.

In the small following silence I turned and went out the back way with Henry, leaving the poor waitresses to clear up the garbage.

"That was only half funny," Henry said thoughtfully.

"Yes."

"You want to be careful. He might just kill you next time. And *why? You* didn't bring Harold Quest here. *You* didn't smell out the hamburger."

"No," I sighed. "My pal Dart Stratton says logic never interferes with instinct, in Keith. But then, half the world's like that."

"Including murderers," Henry said.

"How inflammable," I asked, "is the big top?"

Henry stopped walking. "You don't think he'd try . . . ? He's pretty handy with that lighter. And burning the fence . . ." Henry looked angry but after a moment shook his head.

"This big top won't go on fire," he said positively. "Everything I brought here is flame retardant, flame resistant or can't burn, like all the metal poles and the pylons. There were disasters in circuses in the past. The regs now are stringent. This big top won't burn by accident.

Arson . . . well, I don't know. But we've got extinguishers all over the place, as you know, and I ran a bit of water main up to the roof in a sort of elementary sprinkler system." He took me along to see. "That bit of rising main," he pointed, "the pressure's very good in it. I fed a pipe up and connected it to a garden hose running along inside, below the ridge. The hose has small holes in it. The water squirts out OK."

"Henry! You're a genius."

"I had a bit of time yesterday, when you went off to London, and I reckoned the racecourse couldn't afford another calamity like the stands. A good precaution's never wasted, I thought, so I rigged up this very basic sprinkler. Don't know how long it would work. If ever flames got that high, they could melt the hose." He laughed. "Also, I, or someone who knows, has to be around to turn the tap on. I had to stick tape and those labels all over it saying, *'Do not touch this,'* in case someone turned it on while all the crowds were inside tucking into their smoked salmon sandwiches."

"My God!"

"Roger knows about it and Oliver, and now you."

"Not the Strattons?"

"Not the Strattons, I don't trust them."

Keith, definitely, would have soaked the paying customers to ruin their day.

Henry went on, trying to reassure me. "But Keith won't actually try to kill you, not after he said in public that he was going to."

"That wasn't public. That was the Stratton family."

"But *I* heard him, and the waitresses did."

"They would pay off the waitresses and swear you misheard."

"Do you mean it?"

"I'm certain they've done that sort of thing often. Maybe not for murder, but other crimes, certainly."

"But . . . what about newspapers?"

"The Strattons are rich," I said briefly. "Money will and does buy more than you'd think. Money's for using to get what you want."

"Well, obviously."

"The Strattons don't want scandal."

"But they can't bribe the press!"

"How about the sources that speak to the press? How about suddenly blind waitresses with healthy bank balances?"

"Not these days," he protested. "Not with our insatiable tabloids."

"I never thought I'd feel older than you, Henry. The Strattons can outbid the tabloids."

Henry's mind I knew to be agile, practical, inventive and straight, but of his home life and background I knew nothing. Henry the giant and I had worked together in harmony over a stretch of years, never intimate, always appreciative; on my part, at least. Henry's junk dealings had found me a whole untouched Adam room once, and dozens of antique fireplaces and door frames. Henry and I did business by telephone—"Can you find me . . ." or "I've come across this . . ." These Stratton Park days were the first I'd spent so much in his company and they would, I thought contentedly, lead to a positive friendship.

We rounded the far end of the big top and watched the runners for the second race walk by on their way out onto the track. I found I was liking more and more to watch them, having given them little thought for most of my life. Imagine the world without them, I thought: history itself would have been totally different. Land transport wouldn't have existed. Medieval battles wouldn't have been fought. No six hundred to ride into a valley of death. No Napoleon. The seafarers, Vikings and Greeks, might still rule the world.

Horses, fleet, strong, tamable, had been just the right size. I watched the way their muscles moved under the groomed coats; no architect anywhere could have designed anything as functional, economical, supremely proportioned.

Rebecca rode by, adjusting her stirrup leathers, her attentions inward on the contest ahead. I had never wanted to ride, but at that moment I envied her: envied her skill, her obsession, her absolute commitment to a physical— animal—partnership with a phenomenal creature.

People could bet; they could own, train, breed, paint, admire, write about thoroughbreds: the primeval urge to be first, in both runner and rider, was where the whole industry started. Rebecca on horseback became for me the quintessence of racing.

Henry and I stood on the ex–circus stands and watched the race together. The whole field jumped the restored open ditch without faltering. Rebecca finished well back, not taking part in the finish.

Henry said racing didn't grab him like rugger and went away to patrol his defenses.

The afternoon passed. "There were the usual disasters," Roger said, dashing about.

I came across the racecourse doctor taking a breather between casualties. "Come to see me on Thursday," he suggested. "I'll take all those staples out. Save you waiting around in the hospital."

"Great."

Oliver, in the office, dealt with inquiries and wrathful trainers and arranged for a Stewards' inquiry into an objection to the winner to take place in the inner office among the computers, copier and coffee machine.

On the whole, the pros whose business was everyone else's pleasure made allowances for the stopgap provisions, though it was interesting, as the day wore on, that they took the truly remarkable conjured-up arrangements more and more for granted and began to complain about the cramped weighing room and the inadequate view from the improvised stands.

"You give them a man-made miracle," Roger complained, "and they want the divine."

"Human nature."

"Sod them."

I spent some of the time with Perdita and Penelope, feeling disjointedly crazy, and some with my sons, thrust back into adulthood and paternity; but no more, thankfully, being told I was for the fairly immediate chop.

I did speak to Marjorie, who stood in for Victoria in the cup-presenting ceremony, her neat upright little figure being protected through the throng by the solicitous bulks of Conrad and Ivan. Photographs flashed, a hand-held microphone produced fuzzy noises; the winning owners floated, the trainer looked relieved, the jockey prosaic (his tenth pair of cufflinks) and the horse excited. A regular prizewinning; irregular day.

"Lee," Marjorie said, beginning to make her way back to the big top but pausing when she saw me nearby. "A cup of tea?"

I went with her obediently, though the tea idea was quickly abandoned in favor of vintage Pol Roger from Stratton Hays's cellars. Dismissing Conrad and Ivan, she took me alone into the tidied-up dining room, where the trusting staff had righted the table and laid it freshly with crustless cucumber sandwiches and small coffee éclairs.

Marjorie sat on one of the chairs and came straight to the point.

"How much is this all costing?" she peremptorily inquired.

"What is it worth?"

"Sit down, sit down." She waited while I sat. "It is worth, as you well know, almost anything your huge friend asks. We have been *flooded* with compliments all afternoon. People love this tent. The future of the racecourse, no less, has been saved. We may not make a cash profit on the day, but we have banked priceless goodwill."

I smiled at her business metaphor.

"I have told Conrad," she said collectedly, "not to quibble about the bills. Oliver Wells is so busy, I'm giving you this message for him instead. I've called for a family meeting on Wednesday, the day after tomorrow. Can you and Oliver and the Colonel draw up a list of costs and expenses for me before then?"

"Probably."

"Do it," she said, but more with persuasion than bossiness. "I've told Conrad to instruct our accountants to present an up-to-date realistic audit of the racecourse as soon as possible and not to wait for the end of its financial year. We need a survey of our present position, and it's imperative we sort out what we intend to do next." The clear voice paused briefly. "You have shown us today that we should not rebuild the old stand as it was before. You have shown us that people respond to a fresh and unusual environment. We must build some *lighthearted* stands."

I listened in awe. Eighty-four, was she? Eighty-five? A delicate-looking tough-minded old lady with a touch of tycoon.

"Will you come to the meeting?" she asked, far from sure.

"I expect so."

"Will Mrs. Faulds?"

I looked at her dryly. "She said you recognized her."

"Yes. What did she say to you?"

"Not a great deal. She said chiefly that if the racecourse can be run prosperously, she won't press for the land to be sold."

"Good." Marjorie's interior relief surfaced in a subtle loosening of several facial muscles that I hadn't realized were tight.

"I don't think she'll want to come to the meeting," I added. "She had read about the family disputes in the newspapers. She just wanted to know how things stood."

"The newspapers!" Marjorie shook her head in disgust. "I don't know how they heard of our arguments. Those reports were disgraceful. We cannot *afford* any more discord. What's more, we cannot afford *Keith.*"

"Perhaps," I said tentatively, "you should just let him . . . sink."

"Oh, no," she said at once. "The family name . . ."

The dilemma remained, age-old; unresolvable, from their point of view.

AT THE END of the day the crowds straggled off, leaving litter in tons. The big top emptied. The caterers packed their tables and chairs and departed. The afternoon sun waned in deep yellow on the horizon, and Henry, Oliver, Roger and I sat on upturned plastic crates in the deserted expanse of the members' bar, drinking beer from cans and holding anticlimactic post-mortems.

The five boys roamed around scavenging, Toby having joined them belatedly. The Strattons had left. Outside, horseboxes were loading the last winner and losers. The urgency was over, and the striving, and the glories. The incredible weekend was folding its wings.

"And for our next act . . ." I declaimed like a ring-master, waving an arm.

"We go home to bed," Roger said.

He drove me and the boys good-naturedly down to the bus, but in fact he himself returned to the buildings and the tents to oversee the clearing up, the locking, and the security arrangements for the night.

The boys ate supper and squabbled over a video. I read Carteret's diaries, yawning. We all phoned Amanda.

Carteret wrote:

Lee persuaded me to go to an evening lecture on the effects of bombing on buildings. (The I.R.A. work, more than air-strikes.) Boring, really. Lee said sorry for wasting my time. He's got a thing about tumbledown buildings. I tell him it won't get him bonus points here. He says there's life after college . . .

"Dad," Neil said, interrupting.

"Yes?"

"I asked Henry the riddle."

"What riddle?"

"Do you know a rabbit from a raceway?"

I gazed in awe at my super-retentive small son. "What did he say?"

"He said who wanted to know. I said you did, and he just laughed. He said if anyone knew the answer, you did."

I said, smiling, "It's like the Mad Hatter's riddle in *Alice in Wonderland:* 'What's the difference between a raven and a writing desk?' There's no answer at all."

"That's a silly riddle."

"I agree. I always thought so."

Neil, whose taste for Pinocchio had won the video fight (for perhaps the tenth time) returned his attention to the nose that grew longer with lying. Keith's nose, I reckoned, would in that line of fantasy make Cyrano de Bergerac a non-starter.

Carteret's diary:

The "great" Wilson Yarrow was there, asking questions to show off his own brilliance. Why the staff think he's so marvelous is a mystery. He sucks up to them all the time. Lee will get himself chucked out for heresy if the staff hear his comments on Gropius. Better stop writing this and get on with my essay on political space.

Pages and pages followed in a mixture of social events and progress on our courses: no more about Yarrow. I fast-forwarded in time to the partially ripped notebook and read onwards from the exclamation marks about the Epsilon Prize. There seemed, for all my searching, to be only one further comment, though it was damning enough in its way.

Carteret wrote:

More rumors about Wilson Yarrow. He's being allowed to complete his diploma! They're saying someone else's design was entered in his name for the Epsilon Prize *by mistake!!* Then old Hammond says a brilliant talent like that shouldn't be extinguished for one little lapse! How's that for giving the game away? Discussed it with Lee. He says choice comes from inside. If someone chooses to cheat once, they'll do it again. What about consequences, I asked? He said Wilson Yarrow hadn't considered consequences because he'd acted on a belief that he would get away with it. No one seems to know—or they're not telling—how the "mistake" was spotted. The Epsilon has been declared void for this year. Why didn't they give it to whoever's design it was that won it?

   * Just heard a red hot rumor. The design was by Mies!!! Designed in 1925, but never built. *Some* mistake!!!

I read on until my eyes ached over his handwriting but nowhere had Carteret confirmed or squashed the red-hot rumor.

One long-ago and disputed bit of cheating might be interesting, but even Marjorie wouldn't consider Carteret's old diaries a sufficient lever, all these years later, especially as no action had been taken at the time. To call Wilson Yarrow a cheat now would sail too close to slander.

I couldn't see any way that a dead ancient scandal, even if it were true, could have been used by Yarrow to persuade or coerce Conrad into giving him, alone, the commission for new stands.

Sighing, I returned the diaries to their tote bag, watched the last five minutes of *Pinocchio* and settled my brood for the night.

ON TUESDAY MORNING, with pressing errands of their own to see to, the Gardners took me and the boys with them to Swindon, dumping us outside the launderette and arranging a rendezvous later at a hairdressing salon called Smiths.

While almost our entire stock of clothes circled around washing and drying, we made forays to buy five pairs of sneakers (difficult—and expensive—as, for the boys, the colors and shapes of the decorative flashing had to be *right,* though to my eyes the "Yuk, Dad" shoes looked much the same), and after that (making a brief stop to buy a large bag of apples), I marched them relentlessly towards haircuts.

Their total opposition to this plan vanished like fruitcake the second they stepped over the threshold of Smiths, as the person who greeted us first there was Penelope Faulds. Blonde, tall, young Penelope, slapping hands with my children and deconstructing my every vestige of maturity.

Smiths, which I had expected somehow to be quiet and old-fashioned because of its age, proved to have skipped a couple of generations and now presented a unisex front of street smarts, blow-dries and rap music. Hairstyles in photographs on the walls looked like topiary. Chrome and multiple mirrors abounded. Young men in pigtails talked like Eastenders. I felt old there, and my children loved it.

Penelope herself cut their hair, consulting with me first about Christopher's instructions to have his head almost shaved, leaving only a bunch of his natural curls falling over his forehead. "Compromise," I begged her, "or his mother will slay me. It's she who normally gets their hair cut."

She smiled deliciously. I desired her so radically that the pain made a nonsense of falling-in roofs. She cut Christopher's hair short enough to please him, too short to my eyes. It was *his hair,* he said. Tell that to your mother, I told him.

Toby, interestingly, asked for his cut to be "ordinary": no statement of rebellion. Vaguely pleased, I watched Penelope fasten a gown round his throat and asked if her mother were anywhere about.

"Upstairs," she said, pointing. "Go up. She said she was expecting you." She smiled. Hop, skip and jump, heart. "I won't make your kids look like freaks," she promised. "They've got lovely-shaped heads."

I went upstairs reluctantly to find Perdita, and it was there, out of sight, that the old order persisted: the ladies with their hair in rollers, sitting under driers reading *Good Housekeeping.*

Perdita, vibrant in black trousers, a bright pink shirt and a long rope of pearls, led me past the grandmotherly customers who watched a large man with a walking stick go by as if he'd come from a different species.

"Never mind my old loves," Perdita teased me, beckoning me into a sheltered be-chintzed sanctum on the far side of the beautification. "Tanqueray do you?"

I agreed a little faintly that it would, and she pressed into my hand a large glass holding lavish gin and little tonic with tinkling ice and a thick slice of lemon. Eleven-fifteen on a Tuesday morning. Ah, well.

She closed the door between us and the old loves. "They have ears like bats for gossip," she said blithely. "What do you want to know?"

I said tentatively, "Forsyth . . . ?"

"Sit down, dear," she commanded, sinking into a rose-printed armchair and waving me into its pair.

She said, "I've thought all night about whether I should tell you these things. Well, half the night. Several hours. William always trusted me not to repeat what he told me, and I never have. But now . . . I don't really know if he would say I should be silent forever, but things are different now. Someone blew up his beloved race-course, and you saved the race meeting yesterday and I think . . . I really do think that, like you said, you can't finish the job for him unless you know what you're up against, so, well, I don't think he'd mind." She drank some gin. "I'll tell you about Forsyth first, and then we'll see."

"All right," I said.

She sighed deeply and began, gathering ease and momentum gradually as she went along.

"Forsyth," she said, "set out to defraud an insurance company, and the family had to come up with the whole pay-off or visit him behind bars for God knows how many years."

"I thought," I said slowly, "it might be something like that."

"William said . . ." She paused, still a little inhibited; uncertain, despite her decision. "It seems odd to be telling you these things."

I nodded.

"I wouldn't say a word if he were alive, but I don't care so much for his family. I often told him he ought to let them suffer properly for their criminal actions, but he wouldn't hear of it. Keeping the Stratton name clean . . . a sort of obsession."

"Yes."

"Well," she took a deep breath, "about a year ago, Forsyth borrowed a fortune from the bank, guaranteed by Ivan—his father—on the security of the garden center, and he started buying and selling radio-controlled lawn mowers. Ivan's no great businessman, but at least he listens to his manager and goes to Conrad or William . . . used to go, poor lamb . . . for advice, and has proper audits . . . but that know-it-all Forsyth, he went his own way and wouldn't listen to anybody and he bought a huge warehouse on a mortgage and thousands of lawn mowers that were supposed to cut the grass while you sat and watched, but they were already going out-of-date when he signed a contract for them, and also they kept breaking down. The people who sold them to him must have been laughing themselves sick, William said. William said Forsyth talked about 'cornering the market,' which no one can ever do, William said, in anything. It's a short cut to bankruptcy. So there is Forsyth with this vast stock he has contracted to buy but can't sell, paying a huge mortgage he can't afford, with the bank bouncing his checks and Ivan facing having to cover this enormous bank loan . . . and you can guess what happened." She paid attention to her drink.

"A little fire?" I suggested, swirling the ice around in my own glass.

"*Little!* Half an acre of it. Warehouse, mowers, radio controls, all cinders. William said everyone took it for granted it was arson. The insurance company sent investigators. The police were all over the place. Forsyth went to pieces and confessed to William in private."

She paused, sighing.

"So, what happened?" I asked.

"Nothing."

"*Nothing?*"

"No. It's not a crime to set fire to your own property. William paid it all off. He didn't claim the insurance. He paid off the warehouse mortgage with penalties and sold the land it had stood on. Paid off all the contracts for the rotten mowers, to avoid lawsuits. Repaid the money the bank had lent, plus all the interest, to save Ivan losing the garden center to the guarantee. It all cost an *enormous* amount. William told all the family that they would each inherit a good deal less from him because of Forsyth's business venture and criminal folly. None of them would speak to Forsyth after that. He whined to William about it and William told him it was Coventry or jail, and to be grateful. Forsyth said Keith had told him to burn the warehouse. Keith said Forsyth was lying. But William told me it was probably true. He said Keith always said you could get rid of things by burning them."

Like fences at open ditches, I thought. And grandstands, by blowing them up?

"There!" she said, as if surprised at herself for the ease of the telling, "I've told you! I can't feel William standing at my shoulder telling me to shut up. In fact . . . it's the other way round. I think he *approves,* dear, wherever he is."

I wasn't going to question that feeling. I said, "At least Forsyth's was a straightforward fraud. No rapes or drugs involved."

"Yes, dear, *much* harder to cover those up."

Some nuance in her voice, a quiet amusement, made me ask, "But not impossible?"

"You're encouraging me to be wicked!"

Once started, however, she'd been enjoying the saga.

"I won't tell them," I said. "I'll be like you, with William's secrets."

I don't know if she believed me. I don't know that I meant what I said. It encouraged her, all the same, to go on.

"Well . . . there was Hannah . . ."

"What about her?" I prompted, when she paused.

"She grew up so bitter."

"Yes, I know."

"No self-esteem, you see, dear."

"No."

"Keith never let her forget she'd been abandoned by her mother. By Madeline, poor dear. Madeline used to cry and tell me she'd give anything for a miscarriage, but we were both young then and we didn't know how to get her an abortion . . . you had to *know* someone in those days as you'd never get a family doctor to help you. No one would ever help a young married woman get rid of her first child. Keith got to hear she'd been *asking* about it and he flew into a terrible rage and knocked two of her teeth out." She drank deeply of gin at the memory. "William told me that Keith told Hannah her mother had wanted to abort her. Can you believe it? Keith had always been cruel, but saying that to your own daughter! He wanted Hannah to hate Madeline, and she did. William said he tried for Madeline's sake to love Hannah and bring her up properly, but Keith was there, poisoning her mind, and she was never a sweet little girl, William said, but always sullen and spiteful."

"Poor Hannah."

"Anyway, she grew up very pretty in a sharp sort of way, but William said young men were put off when they got to know her and she felt more and more rejected and hated everybody, and then she fell for this gypsy and let him have sex with her." Perdita shrugged, sighing. "William said he wasn't even a proper Romany, just a rough wanderer with a police record for thieving. William said he couldn't understand Hannah, but it was low self-esteem, dear. Low self-esteem."

"Yes."

"Well, she got pregnant of course. And this gypsy, he knew a good thing when it was shoved under his nose. He turned up on Keith's doorstep demanding money, else he'd go round the village telling everyone how he'd got Keith's posh daughter in the family way, and Keith knocked him down and kicked him and burst one of his kidneys."

Hell, I thought, I'd been lucky.

"Keith told William. Those three boys always loaded their troubles onto their father. William paid off the gypsy, and it cost ten times as much as the gypsy had been asking from Keith in the first place."

"Dire," I said.

"So Jack was born, and he didn't have much chance either of growing up decent. Hannah dotes on him. William, of course, paid and paid for his upbringing."

"William told you all this?"

"Oh yes, dear. Not all at once, like I told you. In little bits. Sort of squeezed out of him, over the years. He would come to me very tired of them all, and unburden some of his thoughts, and we'd have a little gin and—if he felt like it, well, *you know,* dear—and he'd say he felt better, and go off home . . ."

She sighed deeply for times past.

"Conrad," she said surprisingly, "years ago, he got addicted to heroin."

"Can't believe it!"

Perdita nodded. "When he was young. Kids nowadays, they know they face terrible dangers all the time from drugs. When Conrad was twenty, he thought it a great adventure, William said. He was at university. He was with another young man, both of them injecting themselves, and his friend had too much, and died. William said there was a terrible stink, but he got Conrad out and hushed it all up and sent him to a very private and expensive clinic for treatment. He got Conrad to write him a letter describing his drug experiences, what he felt and saw when he was high. William didn't show me what Conrad wrote, but he still had the letter. He said Conrad had been cured, and he was proud of him. Conrad didn't go back to university, though. William kept him at home on the estate."

Ah, I thought, *that* was Marjorie's hammerlock. Even after so many years, Conrad wouldn't want his youthful indiscretion made public.

Perdita finished her gin and poured some more. "Freshen your glass?" she asked me.

"No, I'm fine. Do go on, I'm riveted."

She laughed, talking easily now. "When Keith was about that age, when he was young and handsome and before all these really bad things, he spanked the daughter of one of the farm workers. Pulled down her knickers and spanked her. She hadn't done anything wrong. He said he wanted to know what it felt like. William paid her father a fortune—for those days—to keep him from going to the police. It wasn't a case of rape, though."

"Bad enough."

"Keith learned his lesson, William said. After that he only beat and raped his wives. You couldn't get done for it, then."

The fun went out of her face abruptly, and no doubt out of mine.

"Sorry, dear," she said. "I loved Madeline, but it was all forty years ago. And she did get out, and marry again and have you. William said Keith never forgave her for despising him."

Perhaps because I couldn't help having it on my mind, I said, "Keith said yesterday that he's going to kill me. Forty years on, he's trying to get even."

She stared. "Did he mean it?"

"He meant it when he said it."

"But dear, you have to take him seriously. He's a violent man. What are you going to do about it?"

I saw that she was basically more interested than anxious, but then it wasn't her life-or-death problem.

"It's the sight of me that enrages him," I said. "I could simply go away. Go home. Trust to luck he wouldn't follow me."

"I must say, dear, you take it very calmly."

I'd spent my own semi-wakeful night thinking about it, but I answered her casually. "It's probably because it seems so unreal. I mean, it's not exactly routine to be discussing the possibility of one's own murder."

"I do see that," she agreed. "So . . . are you going?"

I couldn't answer her, because I still didn't know. I had the five children to consider, and for their sakes I thought I should avoid any further confrontations as much as possible. The manic quality of Keith's hatred for me had been all too evident in the ferocity of his kicks and he

had now also the justification for an attack—in his eyes—
because of my involvement in the uncovering of Harold
Quest and the delivery of Quest's confession to Marjorie.
I had thrown him at her feet: he would kill me for it. I
did deep down believe he would try, and, although I didn't
want to, I feared him.

I could probably ensure the boys a live father by leaving
the arena.

I could . . . run away.

It was unrealistic, as I'd told Toby, to expect to be
steadfast every day of the week. It would be *prudent* to
go.

The trouble was that though I might long to, the part
of me that ultimately decided things *couldn't* go.

"I wish," I said fervently, "that I were able to do as
the Strattons do, and *blackmail* Keith into leaving me
alone."

"What a thought, dear!"

"No chance, though."

She put her head on one side, looking at my face and
thinking on my behalf.

"I don't know if it's of much help, dear," she said
slowly, "but Conrad might have something like that."

"What sort of thing? What do you mean?"

"I never knew exactly what it was," she said, "but
William did have a way of keeping Keith in order during the past few years. Only, for once he didn't tell me
everything. I'd have said he was too *ashamed* of Keith,
that time. He sort of winced away from his name, even.
Then one day he said there were things he didn't want
people to know, not even after he died, and he thought he
would have to give the knowledge to Conrad, his *heir,* you
see, dear, so that Conrad could use it if he had to. I'd never
seen him so troubled as he was that day. I asked him about

it the next time he came to see me, but he still didn't want to talk about it much. He just said he would give a sealed packet to Conrad with very strict instructions about when or if ever it should be opened, and he said he had always done the best he could for his family. The very best."

She stopped, overcome. "He was such a *dear,* you know."

"Yes."

The secrets were out. Perdita wept a few tears of fondness and felt clearly at peace. I stood up, kissed her cheek, and went downstairs to collect my newly shorn children.

They looked great. Penelope's pleased professionalism liquified my senses. The boys laughed with her, loving her easily, and I, who ached for her body, paid for their haircuts (despite her protestations) and thanked her, and took my sons painfully away.

"Can we go back there, Dad?" they asked.

I promised, "Yes, one day," and wondered "Why not?" and "Perhaps she would love me" and thought that the children liked her anyway, and fell into a hopeless jumble of self-justification, and was ready to dump my unsatisfactory marriage, that so recently, on the train, I had prayed to preserve.

The Gardners picked us up and took the clean clothes, the apples, the new sneakers and the haircuts back to the racecourse and ordinary life.

In the evening we telephoned Amanda. At eight o'clock, she sounded languorously sleepy.

I spent a long night unhappily, thinking both of my own obligations and desires, but also of Keith and whatever he might be plotting. I searched for ways to defeat him. I thought of fear and the need for courage, and felt unready and inadequate.

14

B Y WEDNESDAY morning Henry had gone home in his last truck, leaving everything so far accomplished ready for next time, and promising future improvements.

On Tuesday the flags over the big top had been furled into storage bags by ropes and pulleys and winches. The lights and the fans were switched off. The caterers' side-tents were laced tight, giving no casual access. The fire extinguishers remained in place, scarlet sentinels, unused. Henry's man and some of the groundsmen had scrubbed the tramp of a few thousand feet off the flooring with brooms and hoses.

On Wednesday morning Roger and I walked down the center aisle, desultorily checking the big empty rooms to each side. No chairs, no tables; a few plastic crates. The only light was daylight from outside, filtering through canvas and the peach roofing, and changing from dull to bright and to dull again as slow clouds crossed the sun.

"Quiet, isn't it?" Roger said.

A flap of canvas somewhere rattled in the wind but all else was silent.

"Hard to believe," I agreed, "how it all looked on Monday."

"We had the final gate figures yesterday afternoon," Roger said. "The attendance was eleven percent up on last year. Eleven percent! And in spite of the stands being wrecked."

"Because of them," I said. "Because of the television coverage."

"Yes, I suppose so." He was cheerful. "Did you see the papers yesterday? 'Plucky Stratton Park.' Goo like that. Couldn't be better!"

"The Strattons," I said, "said they were holding a meeting this morning. Do you know where?"

"Not here, as far as I've heard. There's only the office," he said doubtfully, "and it's really too small. Surely they'll tell you where, if they're meeting."

"I wouldn't bet on it."

We walked slowly back towards the office, unusually idle; and Dart in his beaten-up car drove onto the tarmac.

"Hello," he said easily, climbing out, "am I the first?"

Roger explained about his lack of instructions.

Dart's eyebrows rose. "When Marjorie said meeting, I took it for granted she meant here."

The three of us continued towards the office, amicably.

Dart said, "The police gave me my wheels back, as you see, but it's a wonder I'm not in the slammer. A matter of time, I dare say. They've decided I blew up the stands."

Roger paused briefly in mid-stride, astounded. *"You?"*

"Like, my car came up positive for HIV, hashish, mad cow disease, dirty finger-nails, you name it. Their dogs and their test-tubes went mad. Alarm bells all over the place."

"Nitrates," I interpreted.

"You've got it. The stuff that blew up the stands came to the racecourse in my car. Eight to eight-thirty, Good Friday morning. That's what they say."

"They can't mean it," Roger protested.

"Yesterday afternoon they gave me a bloody rough time." For all his bright manner, it was clear he'd been shaken. "They hammered away at where did I get the stuff, this P.E.4 or whatever. My accomplices, they kept saying. Who were they? I just goggled at them. Made a weak joke or two. They said it was no laughing matter." He made a comic-rueful face. "They accused me of having been in the army cadet corps at school. Half a lifetime ago! I ask you! I said so what, it was no secret. I marched up and down for a year or two to please my grandfather, but a soldier by inclination I am definitely *not*. Sorry, Colonel."

Roger waved away the apology. We all went into the office, standing around, discussing things.

Dart went on. "They said I would have handled explosives in the cadets. Not me, I said. Let others play at silly buggers. All I really remembered vividly of the cadets is crawling all over a tank once and having nightmares afterwards about falling in front of it. The *speed* it could go! Anyway, I said, talk to Jack, he's in the cadets for the same reason as I was, and he's still at school and hates it, and why didn't they ask *him* where you could get boom boom bang bangs, and they practically clicked on the handcuffs."

I said, when he paused, "Do you usually lock your car? I mean, who else could drive it at eight-thirty on a Good Friday morning?"

"Don't you believe me?" he demanded, affronted.

"Yes, I do believe you. I positively do. But if you weren't driving it, who was?"

"There *can't* have been explosives in my car."

"You'll have to face that there were."

He said obstinately, "I don't know anything about it."

"Well . . . er . . . *do* you lock your car?"

"Not often, no. Not when I'm outside my own door. I told the police that. I said it was just sitting there and yes, probably I'd left the key in it. I said *anyone* could have taken it."

Roger and I both looked away from Dart, not wanting to be accusatory. "Outside his own door" wasn't exactly in plain view of the general car-stealing public. Outside his own door was beside the back entrance of the family pile, Stratton Hays.

"What if it were Keith that took your car?" I asked. "Would your family loyalty stretch to *him?*"

Dart was startled. "I don't know what you're talking about. I don't know who took my car."

"And you don't want to find out."

He grinned a shade uneasily. "What sort of pal are you, anyway?"

Roger said neutrally, "Keith swore to Lee only the day before yesterday that he would kill him. There's no doubt he meant it. You can't blame Lee for wanting to know if Keith blew up the stands."

Dart gave me a long look. I smiled with my eyes.

"I don't think it was Keith," Dart said finally.

"I search under my bus," I said to him. "I won't let my children get into it before I'm as sure as I can be that it's safe."

"Lee!" It was a word full of shock. "No, he *wouldn't.* Not even Keith. I swear to you . . ." He stopped dead. He had, anyway, told me what I wanted to know. A fragment

of truth, even if not whole knowledge.

"From family feeling," I said, aiming at lightness, "would you consider helping me find a way of preventing Keith from carrying out his unpleasant threat? To save him and all of you, one might say, from the consequences?"

"Well, of course."

"Great."

"But I don't see what I can do."

"I'll tell you a bit later. At the moment, where is your meeting?"

"Holy hell, yes."

He picked up the office telephone and got through, it was evident, to his parents' home, where he talked to a cleaner who didn't know where either Lord or Lady Stratton could be found.

"Damn," Dart said, trying another number. "Ivan? Where's this bloody meeting? In *your* house? Who's there? Well—tell them I'm late." He put the receiver down and gave Roger and me the old carefree grin. "My parents are there, so are Rebecca and Hannah, Imogen and Jack, and they're waiting for Aunt Marjorie. I could hear Keith shouting already. Tell you the truth, I'm not keen to go."

"Don't then," I said.

"It's a three-line whip, Ivan says. The whole family. That means I have to."

Carpe diem, they say. Seize the day. Seize the moment. I'd been handed an opportunity I had been wondering how to achieve.

"How about," I said, "if you drive me to your parents' house, tell the cleaner I'm a friend of the family, and leave me there while you go to the meeting?"

He said, puzzled, "What ever for?"

"For luck," I said.

"Lee . . ."

"OK. For that look at the grandstand plans that I backed away from last time."

Roger made the beginnings of a gesture to remind me I'd already seen the plans, and then, to my relief, subsided.

Dart said with furrowed brow, "I don't honestly understand . . ."

As I didn't *want* him to understand I said confusingly, "It's for the sake of your family. Like I said, if you're not keen for Keith to bump me off, just trust me."

He trusted me more than anyone else in his family did, and his easygoing nature won the day.

"If that's what you want," he agreed, still not understanding—as how could he? "Do you mean *now?*"

"Absolutely. Except, do you mind going down the back road, as I'd better tell my boys I'll be off the racecourse for a while."

"You're extraordinary," Dart said.

"They feel safer if they know."

Dart looked at Roger, who nodded resignedly. "Christopher, the eldest, told me that when they're away from home, in that bus, they don't mind their father leaving them, as long as they know he's gone, and roughly when he'll be back. They look after themselves then without worrying. It does seem to work."

Dart rolled his eyes comically at the vagaries of my domestic arrangements but accompanied me out to his car. Lying on the front seat, when I went round there, was a large glossy magazine entitled *American Hair Club,* with a young well-thatched model-type man smiling broadly on the cover.

Dart, removing it to the door pocket beside him, said defensively, "It's all about bonding hair on with polymers. It does seem to be a good idea."

"Follow it up," I suggested.

"Don't laugh at me."

"I'm not."

He gave me a suspicious look, but drove me down amiably enough to report to my sons, who proved not to be in the bus, where I called to pick up a small tool or two, but to be elbow-deep in flour in Mrs. Gardner's kitchen, making her perfect pale fruitcake and eating most of it raw. She gave me a flashing smile and a kiss and said, "I'm having such *fun* here. Don't hurry back."

"Where do you find a wife who'll give you five sons?" Dart asked moodily, driving away. "Who the hell wants a pudgy going-bald thirty-year-old with no talents?"

"Who wants a good-natured easygoing nice guy not ridden by demons?"

"Me, do you mean?" He was surprised.

"Yes."

"No girls really want me."

"Have you asked any?"

"I've *slept* with some, but they all seem to have their sights on huge old Stratton Hays, and they tell me how great it would be for parties there, and one even talked about our daughter's coming-out *ball . . .*"

"And it frightens you?"

"They want to marry a *house.*"

"When I go home," I said, "you can come and stay, and I'll see you meet people who've never heard of Stratton Hays, and don't know about your father's title or your own millions, and you can be Bill Darlington, or whatever name you like, and see how you go."

"Are you *serious?*"

"Yes, I am." I thought for a moment and said, "What will happen in your family when Marjorie dies?"

"I don't think about it."

"You should be married by then. You'll be the head of the family one day, and the others should take that for granted, and respect you and your wife, and look ahead to a good well-rooted future."

"God," he protested, "you don't ask much!"

"You're the best of the Strattons," I said.

He swallowed; reddened; fell silent. He drove between the gateposts of his parents' ugly striped house and parked, and we walked round to the rear as before.

The back door was unlocked. We went past the plumbing and through into the black-and-white-floored hall, and Dart shouted out loudly, "Mrs. Chinchee? Mrs. Chinchee!"

A small middle-aged woman in a pink overall appeared at the top of a long flight of stairs saying, "Mr. Dart, I'm up here."

"Mrs. Chinchee," Dart called up to her, "this friend and I will be in the house for a while, but just carry on with the cleaning."

"Yes, sir. Thank you, sir."

Dart turned away and Mrs. Chinchee retreated towards her upstairs tasks, any awkward curiosity well neutralized.

"Right," Dart said. "Now what? I'm not going off to that meeting. You might need me here."

"OK," I said, vaguely relieved. "Now you go out to your car, and if either of your parents should come back sooner than we expect from the meeting, you put your palm on the horn and you give five or six urgent blasts to warn me."

"You mean . . . I'm just a lookout?"

"If your parents come back, blow the horn, then tell them you've lent me the phone, or the bathroom, or something."

"I don't like it," he frowned. "Suppose they find you looking at the plans?"

"You didn't mind before. You encouraged me, in fact."

He sighed. "Yes, I did. I didn't know you so well, then, or care . . . Look, don't be too long."

"No."

Still hesitantly he turned away and went back towards the rear door, and I went on into Conrad's private room where horse pictures crowded the walls and endless shiny bric-a-brac suggested a magpie disposition. Miniature silver horses, antique gold coins on a tray, a tiny gold hunting scene; every surface held treasures.

Without wasting time, I skirted the large cluttered desk and attended to the illegal act of picking someone else's lock, the keyhole fortunately living up to the promise of easy access. The small flat tool I'd brought with me slid obligingly past the ward that guarded the simple works and moved the tongue back from the socket. For picking simple locks, any flat filed-down narrow version of an ordinary key will do the job; the simpler, the better.

The paneled door, so like the walls, pushed easily open, revealing a cupboard large enough to walk into. Leaving the walking stick lying on the desk, I limped into the cupboard and pressed a light switch I found there, activating an overhead bulb in a simple shade.

Inside, the walls were lined throughout by shelves, on which stood endless boxes, all of different sizes, colors and shapes, and all unhelpfully unlabeled.

The drawings for the proposed new stands were in clear view, the large folder that Conrad and Wilson Yarrow had taken to Roger's office standing on the floor, leaning against one of the shelf-walls. Untying the pink tape bow that held the folder shut, I took out the drawings, laying them flat, outside, on Conrad's desk.

They were, I had to confess, a sort of window-dressing in case Dart came to find me, as the drawings were those I had already seen, without any additions.

The chief object of my risky enterprise had been to try to find the packet that Perdita had said William, Lord Stratton, third baron, had intended to entrust to Conrad, fourth baron; the packet containing enough dirt on Keith to keep him controlled. If I could but find it, I thought, I could use it perhaps to preserve my own life, promising for instance that if I should die violently, the packet's contents would become public knowledge inexorably.

Faced with the actual array of random containers, I had to rethink. Finding any particular packet in those could take hours, not minutes, particularly as I'd been given no clear description of what sort of packet I was looking for.

I took the lid off a box straight ahead. The box was the size of a large shoe box, made of stiff decorative cardboard in a mottled maroon color; the sort of box my mother had stored photographs in.

This box held no photographs and no mysterious packets, but only mementos of social events to do with the hunt of which Conrad was joint master; stiff gilt-edged invitations, menus, order of speeches. A longer box next to it held dozens of loose clippings from newspapers and magazines, all showing either future hunting programs or accounts of past sport.

Box after box contained the same sort of thing: Conrad was not so much secretive, as Dart had described him, as a compulsive collector of the minutiae of his life, far outdoing Carteret's diaries or my balance-sheet memories as a proof of existence.

I tried to think my way into Conrad's mind, to imagine just where he would have stowed the most sensitive knowledge: and balked at wondering if I should simply be searching his desk or the bookshelves. If the packet's existence had been enough to worry William Stratton into passing it on, Conrad wouldn't leave it anywhere where an unsuspecting person could open it accidentally. Given the hidden cupboard, for all that its lock was child's play, Conrad would use it.

I hurried along the rows, tipping open the lids, turning over reams of irrelevant papers, finding nothing worth the risk. It was in an ordinary shoe box that I finally came across a gem that I'd been hoping for, though not the ultimate jackpot.

I found myself looking at a black-and-white glossy photograph of Rebecca: not by any means a portrait, but a picture of her in ordinary clothes, not jockey's colors, holding out her hand and receiving a wad of what looked like banknotes from a man whose back was to the camera, but who wore a trilby hat with hair curling from beneath the brim and a jacket cut from a distinctive check cloth. The background, a shade out of focus, was nevertheless identifiable as a racecourse.

I turned the photograph over: no notes, no provenance, nothing.

In the same box, where the photograph had been lying, lay a recording tape. Apart from those two objects, the box was empty.

The tape, ordinary-looking, bore no information as to what it carried.

Even without believing in extra-sensory perception, I felt an unusual frisson over the juxtaposition of photograph and tape, and their sole occupancy of a box. I took them out and put them on Conrad's desk, meaning to look around for a tape recorder; but meanwhile I returned to the cupboard, still obstinately seeking a packet that was quite likely not there to be found.

Old out-of-date lists of hounds. Years-old estate accounts. Boxes packed with Dart's school reports. On the maxim thieves work by, that everyone hides valuable things at the *bottom* of drawers, and that the quickest way of finding profit is to empty the drawer out onto the floor, I began, not emptying exactly, but tipping up all the contents to look at the bottom-most in each box, and it was by doing that that I finally came across an ordinary brown envelope with the single word "Conrad" written on it.

I drew it out from under a pile of similar envelopes holding ancient insurance policies, long out of date. The "Conrad" envelope had been slit open. I looked inside without excitement, having by then concluded I'd been clutching at straws, that anything of critical importance would be somewhere else after all. Sighing, I drew out a single sheet of paper with a short note handwritten on it. It said:

> Conrad,
> This is the envelope I told you of.
> Take care with it.
> Knowledge is dangerous.
>
> S.

I looked into the brown envelope further. Inside it lay another brown envelope, this one smaller and unopened, but fatter, with more sheets than one or two inside.

Either it was what I was looking for, or it wasn't. In either case, I was taking it with me, and so as to conceal my pilfering even from Dart, I hid the outer envelope, with letter and unopened envelope inside it, in my clothes: in, to be exact, my close-fitting underpants, against the skin of my abdomen.

Looking round to make sure that all the boxes were

closed and appeared undisturbed, I went out to Conrad's desk to put the grandstand plans back in their folder, to prop them where they had been, to relock the cupboard door and beat an undiscovered retreat.

The photograph of Rebecca and the tape lay on top of the plans. Frowning, I unzipped my trousers again and put the photograph face down against my stomach, where the glossy surface stuck to me, the brown envelope outside it, both of them held snugly, too large and flat to slide out down my legs.

It was at that point that I heard voices out in the hall, near, coming nearer.

"But, Father," Dart's voice reached me loudly, desperately, "I want you to come and look at the fence along the five-acre covert—"

"Not now, Dart," Conrad's voice said. "And why were you not at the meeting?"

Bloody hell, I thought. I snatched up the tape and stuck it into my trousers pocket, and leaned over the set of grandstand plans as if they were the only interest in my life.

Conrad pushed open the door of the room, his until-then friendly expression becoming rapidly surprised and then thunderous, as anyone's would on seeing their most private heartland invaded.

Worse; behind him came Keith.

Conrad looked at his open cupboard with the light shining within, and at me by his desk. His bullish features darkened, his heavy eyebrows lowered, his mouth hardened implacably.

"Explain yourself!" he demanded, his voice harsh and scathing.

"I'm very sorry," I said awkwardly. I put the plans into the folder and closed it. "I can't excuse myself. I can only apologize. I do, very sincerely, apologize."

"It's not good enough!" His anger was deep and all the worse for being alien to his everyday nature, which was not quick to violence, like Keith's. "That cupboard was locked. I *always* lock it. How did you open it?"

I didn't answer him. The shaved key I'd used was still in the keyhole. I felt appallingly embarrassed, which no doubt he could see.

In an access of real rage he snatched up my walking stick, which lay on his desk, and raised it as if he would strike me.

"Oh no, Conrad," I said. "Don't."

He hesitated, his arm high. "Why not? Why bloody not? You deserve it."

"It's not your sort of thing."

"It's mine," Keith said loudly. He tugged the walking stick unceremoniously from his unprotesting twin and took a quick slash at my head.

I put an arm up in a reflex parrying action, caught the stick in my hand and, with more force then he'd envisaged, pulled it vigorously towards me. He held on long enough to overbalance, his weight coming forward, and he let go only in order to put both hands on the desk to steady himself.

All three of them, Conrad, Keith and Dart, looked stunned, but in truth that morning I'd felt some of my old strength returning like an incoming, welcome and familiar tide. They'd grown used to my weakness: had been unprepared for anything else.

I leaned on the stick, nevertheless; and Keith straightened himself, and in his eyes promised me death.

I said to Conrad, "I wanted to look at the plans."

"But why?"

"He's an architect," Dart said, defending me, though I wished he hadn't.

"A builder," contradicted his father.

"Both," I said briefly. "I'm very sorry. Very. I should have asked you to give me a sight of them, and not broken in here. I'm humbled . . . mortified . . ." And so I was, but not repentant nor truly ashamed.

Conrad interrupted my groveling, saying, "How did you know where the plans were?" He turned to Dart. "How did he know? He couldn't have found that cupboard by himself. It's practically invisible."

Dart, looking as uncomfortable as I felt, came round the desk and stopped a pace behind my left shoulder, almost as if sheltering from the parental ire brewing in Conrad.

"You told him where to look," Conrad accused his son indignantly. "You *showed* him."

Dart said weakly, "I didn't think it would matter. What's the big deal?"

Conrad gaped at him. "How can I explain if you can't see? But *you,*" he turned to me, "I'd just begun to think we might trust you." He shrugged defeatedly. "Get out, both of you. You disgust me."

"No," Keith protested, "how do you know he's not stolen anything?" He looked round the room. "You have all these silver and gold pieces in here. He's a *thief.*"

Damn bloody Keith, I thought, smothering panic. I'd stolen better than gold, and intended to keep what I'd taken. Stronger I might be, but couldn't yet swear to the outcome of a straightforward brawl, one against two. *Guile,* I told myself: all I had in the locker.

I raised my chin, until then tucked down in abashment. I looked as unworried as I could manage. I propped the walking stick against the desk, unzipped the front of the easy jacket which had spent several days earlier draped over the chair in Roger's office, slid my arms out of it and threw it to Conrad.

"Search it," I said.

He caught the bunched cloth. Keith seized the jacket and went through the pockets. No silver or gold. Nothing stolen.

I was wearing my loose wool checked shirt. I unbuttoned the cuffs and undid the front buttons, tugged off the shirt and threw it too to Conrad.

I stood bare to the waist. I smiled. I unzipped my fly and began to unbuckle my belt.

"Trousers next?" I asked Conrad lightly. "Shoes? Socks? Anything else?"

"No. No." He was confused. He made an upzipping gesture. "Put your shirt on again." He threw the shirt back to me. "You may be untrustworthy—I'm disappointed, I admit—but not a petty thief." He turned to Keith. "Let him go, Keith. Pick your fight somewhere else. Not in this room."

I put my shirt on and did up the buttons, but left the tails hanging down, like a coat.

Dart said abjectly, "Father, I'm sorry."

Conrad made a dismissive gesture. Dart edged round the desk, looking warily at Keith, who still held my jacket.

I followed Dart, limping slowly, the walking stick both a prop and a defense.

Conrad said mordantly, "I don't want to see you again, Mr. Morris."

I ducked my head, acknowledging fault.

Keith clung onto my jacket.

I was not going to ask for it back. Don't push your luck, I thought: the slightest quiver could erupt the volcano. I was glad simply to reach the door unmolested and to creep through into the hall, and scuttle across it ignominiously, as low in Conrad's esteem as a cockroach.

I held my breath until we were out of the house, but no angry yells stopped us. Dart scurried into his car, now flanked by Keith's Jaguar, and waited impatiently during my slower progress.

He let out an agonized "Whew" of relief as his engine fired and we sped to the road. "My God, he was angry."

"You're a bloody lousy lookout," I said bitterly. "Where was my warning?"

"Yes, well, look, *sorry.*"

"Were you asleep?"

"No . . . no . . . I was reading."

Comprehension arrived. "You were reading that damned magazine about hair loss!"

"Well . . . I . . ." He grinned, shamefacedly, admitting it.

There was nothing to be done about it. The toots on the horn would have given me time to transfer from Conrad's sanctum to the innocence of the bathroom near the rear entrance. Being caught with my hand in the till, so to speak, had not only been a rotten experience but might set Conrad checking the contents of the boxes. The consequences could be utterly disastrous.

"You took such a long time," Dart complained. "What kept you so long?"

"Just looking around."

"And it was *Keith's* car they came back in," Dart said, excusing himself. "I was on the lookout for Father's."

"Not much of a lookout."

"You looked terribly guilty," Dart said accusingly, shifting the blame.

"Yes, I felt it."

"But as for Keith thinking you'd steal . . ." He paused. "When you took your shirt off . . . I mean, I knew parts of the stands fell on you, but all those stitches and bruises . . . they must *hurt.*"

"Not any more," I sighed. I'd forgotten, in the urgency of the moment, that he'd been standing behind me. "It's the cuts on my legs that have made walking difficult, but they're all getting better."

"You gave Keith a shock, catching that walking stick."

I had made him more careful, I thought ruefully, which might not be a good thing, from my point of view.

"Where are we going?" Dart asked. He'd turned out of the gates in the direction of the racecourse, automatically. "Back to the Gardners'?"

I tried to think, to pull together a few scattered wits.

I asked, "Is Rebecca racing today, do you know?"

He answered as if bewildered, "No, I don't think so. She was at the meeting, of course."

"I need to talk to Marjorie," I said. "And to go to Stratton Hays."

"I don't follow you."

"No, but will you *take* me?"

He laughed. "I'm your chauffeur, now?"

"You're a better chauffeur than lookout."

"Thanks very much."

"Or lend me your car," I suggested.

"No," he said. "I'll drive you. Life's never boring, with you around."

"The Gardners' first, then."

"Yes, *sir.*"

In the Gardners' kitchen Mrs. Gardner greeted my return with friendly dismay, saying I'd lent her the five cooks for less than an hour, not long enough. I offered their services for another few hours. Accepted, she said.

"Tell me if I'm leaving them with you too much," I begged her.

"Don't be silly. I love it. And besides, Roger says that but for you he'd be half-way out of his job and we'd be sick with worry."

"Does he think so?"

"He knows it."

Grateful and partially comforted, I left Dart in the kitchen and went over to the bus, and there in the privacy of the cab fed the tape I'd stolen into the tape-playing slot of the radio.

It proved to be a recording of a telephone call made on a cellular phone: the sort of spying that was diabolically easy if one listened on a scanner close to the transmitting and receiving cell.

I'd always had misgivings about the randomness of overheard conversations that had come to public light: what sort of person listened in to other people's privacy day in and day out *and taped it all,* hoping to overhear marketable secrets? Someone apparently had, in this case.

The conversation was between a voice provisionally identifiable as Rebecca's and a man speaking in a southeast accent, not cockney, but all glottal stops where d's, t's or c's occurred in the center of words. Stratton came out as "Stra-on." Rebecca as "Rebe-ah."

"Rebe-ah Stra-on?" said the man's voice.

"Yes."

"What have you got for me, darlin'?"

"How much is it worth?"

"Same as usual."

After a short pause, speaking quietly, she said, "I'm riding Soapstone in the fifth, it's got no chance, it's only half fit. Lay off all you can on Catch-as-Catch, it's jumping out of its skin and they're putting a bundle on it."

"That's the lot?"

"Yes."

"Thanks, darlin'."

"I'll see you at the races."

"Same place," the man agreed. "Before the first."

The tape clicked and fell silent. I ejected it grimly and returned it to my pocket, and, climbing back into the body of the bus, unzipped my trousers and retrieved the glossy photograph and also the packet of dangerous knowledge.

From that I took out the interior, fatter brown envelope and slit it open with a knife. Inside were yet another envelope, white this time, and another short letter from William Stratton, third baron, to his son Conrad, fourth.

It read:

Conrad,

This grieves me beyond measure. Remember always that Keith, to my despair, tells lies. I sought out knowledge, and now I don't know how to use it. You must decide. But take care.

S.

Apprehensively, I slit open the white envelope and read its lengthier contents and by the end found my hands trembling.

My non-grandfather had shown me a way, once and for all, of dealing with Keith.

I reassembled the packet in its original order and, finding some sticky-tape, sealed the outside brown envelope so that no one could open it by chance. Then I sat for a while with my head in my hands, realizing that if Keith knew what I'd got he would kill me immediately, and also that saving myself from him posed a dilemma I'd never imagined.

Dangerous knowledge. Not dangerous: deadly.

15

D ART DROVE me to Stratton Hays. On the way, using my own mobile phone (anyone listening?), I got through to Marjorie's house and found her at home, forthrightly displeased.

"You didn't come to the meeting!"

"No. Very sorry."

"It was a shambles," she said crossly. "Waste of time. Keith shouted continually and nothing got done. He couldn't ignore the gate receipts, which were *excellent,* but he's fanatical about selling. Are you *sure* you cannot uncover his debts?"

"Does Imogen know them?" I asked.

"Imogen?"

"If I got her paralytically drunk, would she know anything at all of her husband's affairs?"

"You're disgraceful!"

"I'm afraid so."

"I wish she did. But don't try it, because if Keith caught

you at it . . ." She paused, then said without pressure, "Do you take his threats seriously?"

"I have to."

"Have you thought of . . . retreat?"

"Yes, I have. Are you busy? I need to tell you a few things."

She said if I gave her an hour I could come to her house, to which I agreed. Dart and I continued to Stratton Hays, where he parked in the same place as on my first visit and as usual left the key in the ignition.

The great graceful pile, full of forgotten lives and quiet ghosts, stood peacefully in the mottled sunlight, a house built for hundreds, lived in by one.

"What now?" the one said; Darlington Stratton, fifth baron to be.

"We've got almost an hour. Can we look at the north wing?"

"But it's a ruin. I told you."

"Ruins are my business."

"I forgot. Well, OK." He unlocked the rear door and took me again across the vast unfurnished, uncurtained front hall and along a wide windowed passage proportioned like a picture gallery, but with bare walls.

At the end of it we came to a heavy door, unpaneled, unpolished and modern, fastened by bolts. Dart wrestled with the bolts and creaked open the door, and we walked into the sort of desolation I went looking for: rotting wood, heaps of debris, saplings growing.

"They took the roof off sixty or more years ago," Dart said glumly, looking upwards to the sky. "All those years of rain and snow . . . the upper floor just rotted and fell in. Grandfather asked the National Trust and the Heritage people . . . I think they said the only thing to do was to demolish this wing and save the rest." He sighed.

"Grandfather didn't like change. He just let time run on and nothing got done."

I clambered with difficulty over a hillock of weathered gray beams and looked along a wide storm-struck landscape flanked by high, still-standing but unbuttressed stone walls.

"Do be careful," Dart warned. "No one's supposed to come in here without hard hats."

The space gave me no creative excitement, no desire to restore it. All it did give me, in its majestic proportions, and its undignified death, was an interval of respite, of nerve-calming patience, a deep breathtaking perception of life passing, a drawing-in of the faith and industry that had designed and built here four hundred years earlier.

"OK." I said, stirring and rejoining Dart in the open doorway. "Thanks."

"What do you think?"

"Your grandfather was given good advice."

"I was afraid so."

He rebolted the heavy door and we returned across the great hall to the rear entrance.

"Can I borrow your bathroom?" I asked.

"Sure."

He continued on past the door, heading towards his own personal quarters, the ground floor of the south wing.

Here, present life went on very comfortably with carpets, curtains, antique furniture and a fresh polished smell. He led me to the door of his bathroom, a mixture of ancient and modern, a room converted from perhaps a sitting room, with a large free-standing Victorian bath and two new-looking washbasins built into a marble-topped fitment. The surface of the fitment was covered with bottles of shampoo and conditioner, and every variety of snake oil.

Sympathetically I went over to the window, which was curtained in lace, and looked out. Away to the left, Dart's car stood in the driveway. Ahead, lawns and trees. To the right, open gardens.

"What is it?" he said, as I stood there. After a moment, when I didn't move, he came over to stand beside me, to see what I was looking at.

He came, and he saw. He switched his gaze to my face, searching, and without trouble read my thoughts.

"*Shit,*" he said.

An appropriate word for a bathroom. I said nothing, however, but walked back the way we had come.

"How did you know?" Dart asked, following.

"Guessed."

"So what now?"

"Go to Marjorie's house."

"I mean . . . what about *me?*"

"Oh, nothing," I said. "It's not up to me."

"But . . ."

"You were in the bathroom seeing to your hair," I said. "And through the window you saw who took your car on Good Friday morning. No one's going to put you to the torture to find out who it was. Just pretend you saw nothing, as you've been doing so far."

"Do you know . . . who?"

I half smiled. "Let's go and see Marjorie."

"*Lee.*"

"Come and listen."

Dart drove us to Marjorie's house, which proved to be unadulterated early Georgian, as well-bred and trim as she was herself. Set four-square in weedless grounds at one end of Stratton village, it had sash windows in disciplined rows, a central front door and a circular driveway reached past gateposts with urns on.

Dart parked near the front door and as usual left the key in the ignition.

"Don't you *ever* lock it?" I asked.

"Why bother? I wouldn't mind an excuse to get a new car."

"Why not just buy one?"

"One day," he said.

"Like your grandfather."

"What? Oh, yes. I suppose I'm like him, a bit. One day. Maybe."

Marjorie's front door was opened to us by a manservant ("She lives in the past," murmured Dart), who pleasantly guided us across a hall to her drawing room. As expected, faultless taste there in time-stands-still land, gentle colors overall in dim pinks, green and gold. The window embrasures still held the original shutters, but there were floor-length curtains as well, and swagged valances, and a view of sunlit spring gardens beyond.

Marjorie sat in a wide armchair that commanded the room, very much and always the person in charge. She wore, as often, dark blue with white at the neck, looking doll-like and exquisite and temporarily hiding the tough cookie.

"Sit down," she commanded, and Dart and I sat near her, I on a small sofa, Dart on a spindly chair—Hepplewhite, probably.

"Things to tell me," she began. "That's what you said, Lee."

"Mm," I said. "Well, you asked me to find out two things."

"And on the subject of Keith's finances, you've failed." She nodded decisively. "You've already told me."

"Yes. But . . . as regards your other assignment . . ."

"Go *on,*" she said, as I stopped. "I remember exactly. I asked you to find out what pressure that wretched architect was putting on Conrad to get his new stands built."

Dart looked surprised. *"Assignment?"* he asked.

"Yes, yes." His great-aunt was impatient. "Lee and I had an agreement. We shook hands on it. Didn't we?" She turned her head to me. "An agreement you did not want to break."

"That's right," I said.

"Aunt Marjorie!" Dart looked flummoxed. "You've had Lee working for *you?"*

"And what's wrong with that? It was for the ultimate good of the family. How can we proceed, if we don't know the facts?"

The world's politicians could learn from her, I thought with admiration. The clearest of brains under the waved white hair.

"Along the way," I said, "I learned about Forsyth and the lawn mowers."

Dart gasped. Marjorie's eyes widened.

"Also," I went on, "I heard about Hannah's bit of rough trade, and its results."

"What are you talking about?" Dart asked me, lost.

Marjorie enlightened him. "Hannah went off into the bushes with a gypsy and got herself pregnant, the silly ninny. Keith assaulted the gypsy, who demanded money, of course. My brother paid him off."

"Do you mean . . ." Dart worked it out, "that Jack's father was a *gypsy?"*

"Near enough. Not even a Romany. A good-for-nothing tramp," Marjorie said.

"Oh, my God," Dart said, weakly.

"And don't speak of it again," Marjorie commanded severely. "Hannah tells Jack his father was a foreign aristocrat who would have been ruined by the scandal."

"Yes." Dart's voice sounded faint. "Jack told me that himself."

"And let him believe it. I hope, Lee," she said to me, "that that's all."

The telephone rang on the small table beside her chair. She picked up the receiver and listened.

"Yes . . . when? Dart is here. So is Lee. Yes." She put the receiver down and said to Dart, "That was your father. He says he is coming here. He sounds incredibly angry. What have you done?"

"Is Keith with him?" My words came out with a jerk, which she pounced on.

"You're afraid of Keith!"

"Not unreasonably."

"Conrad said Keith told him to come here but didn't say if Keith were with him. Do you wish to leave now, at once?"

Yes, I did, and no, I didn't. I thought of murder in her quiet drawing room and hoped she wouldn't allow it.

I said, "I brought a photograph to show you. It's in Dart's car. I'll just fetch it."

I stood up and walked to the door.

"Don't drive off and leave me here," Dart said, only half joking.

The temptation bit deep, but where would I go? I picked the photograph, in an envelope, out of the door pocket, where I'd placed it, and returned to the drawing room.

Marjorie took out the photograph and looked at it uncomprehendingly. "What does it mean?"

"I'll explain," I said, "but if Conrad's coming, I'll wait until he gets here."

The distance from Conrad's house to Marjorie's was

short. He came very soon, and, to my relief, without Keith. He came armed, though, carrying a shotgun, the landowner's friend. He carried it not broken open, over his arm, as one should, but straightened, and ready.

He brushed past the manservant, who had opened the door for him and was saying, "Lord Stratton, madam," punctiliously, and strode across Marjorie's pale Chinese carpet, coming to a halt in front of me with the twin barrels pointing my way.

I rose to my feet. Barely three paces lay between us.

He held the gun not as if aiming at flying birds but down at his waist, easily familiar with shots from the hip. At that distance he couldn't miss a mosquito.

"You're a liar and a thief." He was growling with fury, his fingers frighteningly unsteady in the region of the trigger.

I didn't deny the charge. I looked past him and his gun to the photograph Marjorie held, and he followed my gaze. He recognized the picture, and the look he gave me was as murderous as any of Keith's. The barrels aimed straight at my chest.

"Conrad," Marjorie said sharply, "calm down."

"Calm down? *Calm down!* This *despicable* person broke into my private cupboard and stole from me."

"However, you may *not* shoot him in my house."

In a way it was funny, but farce was too close to tragedy always. Even Dart didn't laugh.

I said to Conrad, "I'll free you from blackmail."

"What?"

"What are you talking about?" Marjorie demanded.

"I'm talking about Wilson Yarrow blackmailing Conrad into giving him the go-ahead for the new grandstand."

Marjorie exclaimed, "So you did find out!"

"Is that gun loaded?" I asked Conrad.

"Yes, of course."

"Would you mind . . . uh . . . pointing it somewhere else?"

He stood four-square, bullish, unwavering: unmoving.

"Father," Dart protested.

"You shut up," his father said grittily. "You abetted him."

I said, risking things, "Wilson Yarrow told you that if he didn't get the commission for the stands, he would see that Rebecca was warned off as a jockey."

Dart goggled. Marjorie said, "That's ridiculous."

"No. Not ridiculous. That photograph is a picture of Rebecca receiving a wad of money on a racecourse from a man who might be a bookmaker."

I tried to work saliva into my mouth. I'd never before had a loaded gun pointed at me in anger. Even though I clung to the belief that Conrad's inner restraints existed where Keith's didn't, I could feel my scalp sweating.

"I listened to the tape," I said.

"You *stole* it."

"Yes," I agreed. "I stole it. It's damning."

"So now it's *you* who'll blackmail me." His trigger hand tightened.

"Oh for Christ's sake, Conrad," I said, almost exasperated. "Use some sense. I'll not blackmail you. I'll see that Yarrow doesn't."

"How?"

"If you'll put that bloody gun down, I'll tell you."

"What tape?" Dart asked.

"The tape you helped him steal from my cupboard."

Dart looked blank.

"Dart didn't know," I said. "He was outside in his car."

"But Keith searched your jacket," Dart protested.

I put my hand into my trousers pocket and brought out the tape. Conrad flicked a glance at it and went on scaring me silly.

"This tape," I told Marjorie, "is a recording of a telephone call of Rebecca selling information about the horses she would be riding. It's the worst of racing crimes. Sending it and that photograph to the racing authorities would end her career. She'd be warned off. The Stratton name would be mud."

"But she *wouldn't* do that," Dart wailed.

Conrad said, as if the words hurt his tongue, "She admitted it."

"No!" Dart moaned.

"I challenged her," Conrad said. "I played her the tape. She can be so hard. She listened like stone. She said I wouldn't let Yarrow use it." Conrad swallowed. "And . . . she was right."

"Put the gun down," I said.

He didn't.

I threw the tape to Dart, who fumbled it, dropped it and picked it up again.

"Give it to Marjorie," I said and, blinking, he obeyed.

"If you'll unload the gun and put it against the wall," I said to Conrad, "I'll tell you how to get rid of Yarrow, but I'm not doing it with your hand on the trigger."

"Conrad," Marjorie said crisply, "you're not going to shoot him. So put the gun down in case you do it by accident."

Blessed bodyguard. Conrad woke to realities as if in a cold shower, looking down indecisively at his hands. He undoubtedly would have laid down his firepower were it not that Rebecca, at that moment, swept in like a whirlwind, having outrun the manservant altogether.

"What's going on here?" she demanded. "I've a right to know!"

Marjorie stared at her with her customary disfavor. "Considering what you've done, you've no right to *anything.*"

Rebecca looked at the photograph of herself and the tape in Marjorie's hand, and at the shotgun in her father's, and at me, threatened.

"Keith told me that this . . . this . . ." she pointed at me, not finding words bad enough, "stole enough to get me warned off . . ."

I said fiercely to Conrad, "That tape is a *fake.*"

The effect on Rebecca was an increase in fury. While the rest of the family tried to understand what I'd said, she snatched the gun from her father, swung it round at shoulder height, took a quick aim at me and without pause pulled the trigger.

I saw the intention in her eyes and flung myself sideways full length onto the carpet, rolling onto my stomach, missing the ball of fizzing pellets by fractions, conscious of *two* barrels, two cartridges, and no way of escaping a shot in the back.

The room had filled with a thunderous cracking noise, with flame and smoke, with the acrid smell of cordite at close quarters. *Jesus,* I thought. God almighty. Not Keith, but Rebecca.

The second shot didn't come. I cringed on the floor— no other word for it. There was the smell, the ringing echo, and beyond that . . . silence.

I stirred, turned my head, saw her shoes, crawled my gaze upwards as far as her hands.

She was *not* pointing the second of the barrel holes at me.

Her hands were empty.

Eyes slowly right . . . Conrad himself held his gun.

Dart came down on his knees by my head, saying, "Lee," helplessly.

I said thickly, "She missed me."

"God, Lee."

I felt breathless, but I couldn't stay there forever. I rolled into a sitting position; felt too shaken to stand.

The shot had shocked them all, even Rebecca.

Marjorie, straight-backed, looked over-white, her mouth open, fixed, animation suspended. Conrad's eyes stared darkly at a bloody mess too narrowly averted. I couldn't . . . yet . . . look straight at Rebecca.

"She didn't mean to," Conrad said.

But she had indeed meant it; an act beyond caution.

I coughed once, convulsively. I said again, "The tape is a fake." And this time, no one tried to kill me for it.

Conrad said, "I don't understand."

I breathed deeply, slowly, trying to steady the racket of my pulse.

"She *couldn't* have done it," I said. "Wouldn't have. She wouldn't put in jeopardy the . . . the *citadel* of her most inner self."

Conrad said, in perplexity, "I don't really follow."

I looked at last at Rebecca. She stared back, her face hard and expressionless.

"I saw you race," I said. "You exult in it. And the other day, I listened to you say you would be in the top five this year on the jockeys' list. You were passionate about it. You're a Stratton, you're infinitely proud, and you're rich and don't need the money. There's no way you're ever going to sell sleazy information that could bring you unbearable disgrace."

Rebecca's eyes slitted narrowly under lowered eyelids, her face rigid.

"But she confirmed it was true!" Conrad said again.

I said regretfully, "She made the tape herself to put pressure on you to get new stands built, and she tried to shoot me to stop me telling you."

"Rebecca!" Conrad couldn't believe it. "This man's lying. Tell me he's lying."

Rebecca said nothing.

"You've been showing all the signs of intolerable strain," I said to her. "I would think it seemed a good idea to you to begin with, to let your father believe he was being blackmailed to save you from being warned off, but once you'd done it, and he had in fact allowed himself to be blackmailed, I'd guess you regretted it sorely. But you didn't confess *that* to him. You went straight on with your obsessive and drastic plan to modernize Stratton Park radically, and it's been tearing you apart for weeks and making you . . . lose balance."

"The hangers!" Dart said.

"But *why*, Rebecca?" Conrad begged, intensely disturbed. "I'd have done anything for you . . ."

"You might not have agreed," I said, "to build new stands at all, let alone have Wilson Yarrow design them. And it was he, wasn't it, who came to you and said, 'I have the dirt on your daughter, and all you have to do to save her honor is give me this commission'?"

Conrad didn't answer directly, but he broke open his shotgun and with unsteady fingers pulled out both cartridges, the spent one, blackened and empty, and the unfired one, orange and bright. He put them both in his pocket and stood the gun by the wall.

As he did so there was a quiet tap on the door. Conrad went to open it and found Marjorie's manservant there, worried. "Nothing wrong," Conrad assured him fruitily.

"Gun went off by accident. Bit of a nuisance to clear up, I'm afraid. We'll see to it later."

"Yes, my lord."

The door closed. I noticed for the first time that the spreading shot had smashed a mirror on the wall and torn pieces of gold silk upholstery from chairs. Much too damned close.

I reached for the walking stick I'd laid beside the small sofa where I'd been sitting and, with its help, returned to my feet.

"You must have said something to Keith about blackmail," I told Conrad. "He used that word in connection with Yarrow. You all heard him."

Conrad made a helpless gesture. "Keith went on and on at me to abandon the idea of new stands and I said I *couldn't.*" He paused. "But *how* did you find all this out?"

"A lot of small things," I said. "For example, I went to the same school of architecture as Wilson Yarrow."

"Architecture!" Marjorie interrupted.

"Yes. When I saw him . . . heard his name . . . I knew there was something wrong about him. I only vaguely remembered, so I looked up a man I was at architectural school with, that I hadn't heard from for ten years, and asked him. He kept a diary all those years ago and he'd written down a rumor he'd heard, that Wilson Yarrow had won a prestigious prize with an architectural design he'd sent in, while knowing that it wasn't his own. The college took the prize away and hushed it all up a bit, but the stigma of cheating remained, and there must be several hundred architects, like me, who associate that name of Yarrow with something not right. The word goes around in professional circles, and memories are long—and better than mine—and the brilliant career once expected of

Yarrow has not come to pass. There was his name alone on the plans he drew for you, which means he's probably not employed in a firm. He may very well be unemployed altogether, and there's a glut of architects now, with the schools every year training more than the market can absorb. I'd guess he saw the prestige of building new stands at Stratton Park as a way back into esteem. I think he was *desperate* to get that commission."

They listened, even Rebecca, as if spellbound.

I said, "Before I ever came to Stratton Park, Roger Gardner told me there was an architect designing new stands who knew nothing about racing and didn't understand crowd behavior, and that as he wouldn't listen to advice he would be the death of the racecourse, but that you, Conrad, wouldn't be deflected from him."

I paused. No one said anything.

"So," I went on, "I came to your shareholders' meeting last Wednesday, and met you all, and listened. I learned what you all wanted for the racecourse. Marjorie wanted things to remain as they were. You, Conrad, wanted new stands, actually to save Rebecca from ruin, though I didn't know that then. Keith wanted to sell, for the money. Rebecca, of course, wanted a clean sweep, as she said; new stands, new manager, new Clerk of the Course, a new image for old-fashioned Stratton Park. Marjorie managed that meeting in a way that would have had superpowers kneeling in admiration, and she manipulated you all so that she got *her* way, which was for Stratton Park to continue in its old manner for the foreseeable future."

Dart cast an admiring glance at his great-aunt, the grin very nearly appearing.

I said, "That was not good enough for Rebecca, nor for Keith. Keith had already enlisted the actor, Harold Quest, to make a nuisance of himself demonstrating against steeplechasing outside the main gates, so that people would be put off going to the races at Stratton Park and the course would lose its attraction and its income, and go bankrupt as a business so that you would have to sell its big asset, the land. He also got Harold Quest to burn a fence—the open ditch; symbolically the open ditch, as it was there that a horse had been killed at the last meeting—but that ploy was a dud, as you know. Keith isn't bright. But Rebecca . . ."

I hesitated. There were things that had to be said: I wished there were someone else . . . anyone else . . . to say them.

"In the Stratton family, as it is now," I resumed, approaching things sideways, "there are two good-natured harmless fellows, Ivan and Dart. There's one very clever person, Marjorie. There's Conrad, more powerful in appearance than fact. There's a strain of ruthlessness and violence in everyone else of Stratton blood, which has cost you all fortunes. When you ally those traits with stupidity and arrogance, you get Forsyth and his mowers. There is in many of the Strattons, as in him, a belief that you'll never be found out, and if you should be, you believe the family will use its money and muscle to save you, as it always has done in the past."

"And will again," Marjorie said firmly.

"And will again," I acknowledged, "if you can. You'll need all your skills soon, though, in damage control."

Surprisingly, they went on listening, not trying to make me stop.

I said carefully, "In Rebecca, that violence is chiefly controlled and comes out as a consuming competitiveness in a testing sport. In her, there's splendid courage and will-to-win. There's also a tremendous overpowering urge to get her own way. When Marjorie blocked her first plan

for achieving new stands, she hit on a simple solution—
get rid of the old ones."

This time, Conrad protested incredulously, and Marjorie
also, but not Rebecca nor Dart.

"I'd guess," I said to Rebecca, "that you told Wilson
Yarrow to do it, as, if he didn't, he could kiss the commission goodbye."

She glared at me unblinkingly, a tigress untamed.

I said, "Wilson Yarrow was in deep already with that
blackmailing attempt. He saw, as you did, that destroying
a part of the main grandstand would mean new ones had to
be built. He knew those old grandstands and, as an architect, he saw how maximum damage could be achieved for
minimum effort. The staircase in the center was the main
artery of the building. Collapse that core, and the rooms
round it would cave in."

"I had nothing to do with it," Rebecca yelled suddenly.

Conrad jumped. Conrad . . . aghast.

"I saw those charges before they exploded," I said to
Rebecca. "I saw how they were laid. Very professional.
I could have done it myself. And I know other dealers,
not as responsible as my giant friend Henry, who'll sell
you anything, few questions asked. But it's difficult, even
for people whose whole job is demolition, to get right
the amount of explosive needed. Every structure has its
own strengths and weaknesses. There's pressure to use
too much rather than too little. The amount Yarrow used
tore half the building apart."

"No," Rebecca said.

"Yes," I contradicted her. "Between you, you decided
it should be done early on Good Friday morning, when
there would be no one about."

"No."

"Wilson Yarrow drilled the holes and set the charges, with you acting as lookout."

"No!"

"He couldn't do it without a lookout. If you go in for crime, it's much best to post a lookout you can trust."

Dart squirmed. Then he grinned. Irrepressible.

"You sat on watch in Dart's car," I said.

Rebecca's eyes opened wide, abruptly. The "no" she produced lacked the fire of the other denials.

"You thought," I said, "that if you went in your own bright scarlet Ferrari, and any stray groundsman, perhaps, saw it on the racecourse on that non-racing day, he would remember it and report it after the stands had exploded. So you drove to Stratton Hays, and parked your car there, and took Dart's, which always has the keys left in, and you drove that car into the racecourse, because Dart's car is so familiar there as to be practically invisible. But you didn't reckon with Harold Quest, actor and busybody, who wouldn't have been at the gates there anyway on that day if he'd been a genuine protester, and you must have been shattered when he said Dart's car had been there, and described it to the police. But not as shattered as you would have been if Harold Quest had reported your Ferrari."

"I don't believe all this," Conrad said faintly; but he did.

"I imagine," I said to Rebecca, "that somewhere you picked up Yarrow and took him and the explosive to the racecourse, because the police tested the car and found traces of nitrates."

Rebecca said nothing.

I said, "Dart has known all along that it was you—or you and Yarrow—who blew up the stands."

"Dart told you!" Rebecca shouted, furiously turning to

Dart, who looked staggered and hurt. "You gave me away to this . . . this . . ."

"No, he didn't," I said fiercely. "Dart was unswervingly loyal to you. He went through a considerable grilling from the police yesterday and didn't say a word. They accused him of setting the explosives himself, and he's still their chief suspect, and they'll question him again. But he won't tell them about you. He's proud of you, he has mixed feelings, he thinks you're crack-brained, but he's a Stratton and he won't give you away."

"How do you *know?*" Dart wailed, agonized.

"I stood next to you when she won on Tempestexi."

"But . . . you couldn't tell from *that.*"

"I've lived and breathed Strattons for a week."

"How did you know?" Rebecca demanded of her brother.

"I saw your Ferrari from my bathroom, parked where my old car was supposed to be."

She said helplessly, "It was there for less than an hour."

Conrad's shoulders sagged.

"I was back in Lambourn long before the explosion," Rebecca said crossly. "And Yarrow was putting himself about in London by then."

"I want to know," Marjorie said to me, after a silence, "what made you first suspect Rebecca?"

"Such small things."

"Tell them."

"Well," I said, "she fanatically wanted things changed."

"And?" Marjorie prompted, when I stopped.

"She mentioned new stands made of glass. There are stands in Britain with glassed-in sections, aren't there, but not sheeted altogether in glass, as Yarrow's plans are, and I wondered if she had *seen* the plans, which Conrad had locked away so secretively. And then . . ."

"Then what?"

"Rebecca said she was the only one in the family who knew a rabbet from a raceway."

They all, except Rebecca, looked uncomprehending.

"I don't follow," Marjorie said.

"It's not a racing term," I explained. "It meant nothing to Roger Gardner."

"Nor to me," Conrad interposed, "and I've owned and ridden horses all my life."

"It's clear to an architect," I said, "and to a builder, to a carpenter, to an engineer. Not, I wouldn't have expected, to a jockey. So I wondered, but not very conclusively at that point, if she'd been talking a good deal to an architect, and if that architect might not be Yarrow. Just a vague passing speculation, but that sort of thing sticks in your brain."

"So what *are* a rabbit and a raceway?" Dart asked.

"A rabbet, with an 'e,' is a tongue and groove joint, mostly in wood, to enable you to slot boards, say, together, as in a fence, or floorboards, without using nails. Like the floor in the big top, in fact."

Marjorie looked bewildered, Conrad not.

"And a raceway?" she asked. "Not a racecourse?"

"I suppose it could be. But otherwise it's either a sort of gully for draining fast-flowing fluids, or it could be a sort of collar that houses ball bearings. In either case, it's not common racecourse parlance."

"A rabbet from a raceway," Dart said thoughtfully. "Wasn't your youngest son chanting that?"

"Quite likely."

"I should have killed you when I had the chance," Rebecca said to me bitterly.

"I thought you were going to," I agreed.

"She was aiming straight at you," Dart said. "Father

snatched the gun away from her. If you ask him, he'll probably say that shooting you once in the chest might have been passed off as an accident, but putting a second shot into your back couldn't be anything but murder."

"Dart!" Marjorie remonstrated severely; but there was no doubt he'd got it right. Dart was one of them. He knew.

Conrad had a question for his daughter. "Where did you meet Yarrow in the first place? How did you get to know him?"

She shrugged. "At a party. He was doing stupid imitations in the accent you heard on the tape. Rebe-ah Stra-on, darlin'. Someone told me he was an exceptionally good architect, but flat broke. I wanted new stands. He wanted a job badly and he wasn't fussy how he got it. We did a deal."

"But you don't usually like men."

"I didn't like him," she said brutally. "I *used* him. I despise him, as a matter of fact. He's in a blue funk now, predictably."

"So . . . what next?" Conrad asked me wretchedly. "The police?"

I looked at Marjorie. "You," I said, "are the one who pulls the levers in the family. You've ruled them all for forty years. You ruled even your own brother, in the gentlest of ways."

"How?" Dart said, avid.

Marjorie beseeched me with wide-open eyes, but it was for Perdita Faulds's sake that I said to Dart, "Your grandfather's secret was his alone, and died with him. I can't tell you it."

"Won't," Dart said.

"Won't," I agreed. "Anyway, to go to the police or not must be Marjorie's decision, not mine. My brief was to give her a lever against Yarrow, and she has it. That's where I finish." I paused. "I'm sure," I said, "for what it's worth, that the police haven't got, and won't find, enough for a prosecution against you, Dart. Just go on knowing nothing, and you'll be all right."

"What about Yarrow, though?" Dart asked.

"Marjorie must decide," I said. "But if you prosecute Yarrow you give away Rebecca's schemes and your own involvement. I can't see her doing it."

"But Keith?" Marjorie said, not dodging the burden I'd placed on her. "What about *him?*"

Keith.

I turned to Conrad. "Did you tell Marjorie that *Keith* sent you here?"

"I did, yes."

"Sent you . . . with a gun?"

He looked faintly shamefaced. "You can't really blame me. I mean, after you and Dart had gone, Keith and I were standing in my room talking about you breaking into my cupboard, and we found that key sort of thing of yours in the lock and I was saying what a risk you'd taken just for a look at some plans . . . and it simply flashed into my mind that you'd been so *involved* in things, and although I couldn't believe you'd been searching for anything else, or that you knew *enough,* I went into the cupboard and looked into the box where I'd put the photograph and the tape, and I was so devastated that Keith asked what was the matter, and I told him. He said—we both thought—you would of course blackmail me."

"Oh, of course."

"Yes, but . . ."

"You all do it to each other; you think no one's capable of anything else."

Conrad shrugged his heavy shoulders as if he believed that to be self-evident. "Anyway," he said, "Keith asked me to give him the envelope our father had entrusted to me shortly before he died. I told Keith I couldn't do that. We had a bit of an argument, but Father had given me very explicit instructions about not letting anyone else see it. Keith asked me if I knew what was in it, but I don't, and I said so. He said he had to have it. He began opening the boxes and tipping everything out. I tried to stop him, but you know what he's like. Then he came to the box where I thought I'd put that letter but when he tipped everything out it didn't seem to be there . . . but how could you have taken it when you couldn't have known it existed? In the end, I helped him look for it. Everything's out on the floor, it's a terrible mess and I'll never put it straight . . ."

"But you did find the envelope?" Marjorie asked anxiously.

"No, we didn't." He turned to me, insisting, "I *know* it was in there, in one special box, under a pile of out-of-date *insurance policies*. Keith told me to bring the gun and kill you . . ."

"But he knew you wouldn't," I said positively.

Dart asked, "Why are you so sure?"

"One twin," I said, "would kill the pilgrim. The other wouldn't. They can't change their natures."

"The fork in the road! You . . . you *subtle* bastard."

Marjorie looked at me forthrightly, not understanding or caring what Dart had said. "Did you take that envelope?"

"Yes, I did," I said.

"Did you open it? Did you see what was inside?"

"Yes."

"Then give it to me."

"No." I shook my head. "This one . . ." I took a breath, "this one I have to do alone."

The telephone shrilled beside Marjorie. Mouth tightening with annoyance at the interruption, she lifted the receiver.

"Yes," she said, her face going blank. "Yes, he's here."

She held out the receiver to me. "It's Keith," she said, "He wants to talk to you."

He knows, I thought, that I must have taken that letter; and he knows what is in it.

With foreboding, I said, "Yes?"

He didn't speak at once, but he was there: I could hear him breathing.

Long seconds passed.

He said five words only before the line went dead. The worst five words in the language.

"Say goodbye to your children."

16

M Y BRAIN went numb.

    A flush of fear zipped from my heels to my scalp in one of those dreadful physical disturbances that come with perceived irretrievable disaster.

I stood immobile, trying to remember the Gardners' telephone number. Couldn't do it. Squeezed my eyes shut and let it come without struggling, let it come subliminally, known as a rhythm, not by sight. Pressed buttons and sweated.

Roger's wife answered.

"Where are the boys?" I asked her abruptly.

"They should be with you at any minute," she said comfortingly. "They set off . . . oh . . . say, fifteen minutes ago. They'll be with you directly."

"With me . . . where?"

"Along at the big top, of course." She was puzzled. "Christopher got your message and they set off at once."

"Did Roger drive them?"

"No. He's around the course somewhere, I'm not sure

where. The boys set off on foot, Lee . . . is something wrong?"

"What message?" I said.

"A phone call, for Christopher . . ."

I threw the receiver to Marjorie and sprinted out of her drawing room, across her calm hallway, and out of her front door and into Dart's car. Never mind that the sprint was a hobble, I'd never moved faster. Never mind that I knew I was heading for an ambush, for some thought-out fate. There was nothing to do but rush to it, hoping beyond hope that he'd be satisfied with me, that he would let the boys live . . .

I drove Dart's car like a madman through the village, but just when I could have done with a whole police posse, there was no police car to chase me for speeding.

In through the racecourse gates. Round onto the tarmac outside Roger's office. Keith's silver Jaguar was there. Nobody in sight. . . *Yes* . . . Christopher . . . and Edward . . . and Alan. All of them frightened to eye-staring terror. I scrambled out of the car, driven by demons.

"Dad!" Christopher's bottomless relief was not reassuring. "Dad, hurry."

"What's happening?"

"That man . . . in the big top."

I turned that way.

"He's lit fires in there . . . and Neil . . . and Toby . . . and Neil's screaming."

"Find Colonel Gardner," I shouted to him, running. "Tell him to turn on the sprinkler."

"But . . ." Despair in Christopher's voice, "we don't know where he is."

"Find him."

I could *hear* Neil screaming. Not words, nothing intelligible. High-pitched shrieks. *Screaming.*

How does one face such a thing?

I ran into the big top, into the center aisle, looking for the fire extinguisher that ought to have been there at the entrance, and not seeing it, running on and finding Alan running beside me.

"Go back," I yelled at him. "Alan, go *back*."

There was smoke in the tent and small bright fires here and there on the floor; scarlet, orange and gold flames leaping in rivers and pools. And beyond, standing like a colossus with his legs apart, his weight braced and his mouth stretched wide in gleeful enjoyment . . . *Keith*.

He held Neil by the wrist, easily clamping the small bones in a vise-grip, and lifting him half-way into the air, holding my son at almost arm's length, the small body writhing and fighting to get free, but with only his toes touching the ground, giving no purchase.

"Let him go," I yelled, beyond pride, into begging, into any craven groveling needed.

"Come and get him, or I'll burn him."

Beside Keith, in a tall decorative wrought-iron container, stood a long-handled torch flaring with a live naked flame, the sort designed for garden barbecues, for torchlight processions, for the evil firing of houses in raids; Neil on one side, torch on the other. In the center Keith held a plastic jerry can missing its cap.

"It's gasoline, Dad," Alan yelled beside me. "He was pouring it on the floor and lighting it. We thought he might burn us . . . and we ran, but he caught Neil . . . don't let him burn Neil, Dad."

"Go back," I screamed at him, frantic, and he wavered and stopped in his tracks, tears on his cheeks.

I ran towards Keith, towards his terrible grin, towards my terrified son. I ran towards certain fire, ran as fast as I could, ran from instinct.

If Keith wants to get rid of something, he burns it . . .

I would overrun him, I thought. I would crash down with him. He would go with me . . . wherever I went.

He hadn't expected an onrush. He stepped back, looking less certain, and Neil went on screaming. One will do, I realized later, almost insane things in defense of one's children.

I was conscious then only of flames, of anger, of the raw smell of gasoline, of a clear view of the outcome.

He would fling the gas can at me and swing the torch, and to do that he would have to . . . *have* to let go of Neil. I would push him away beyond Neil, who would live and be safe.

Six paces away, running towards him, I gave up all hope of not burning. But Keith would burn too . . . and die . . . I would make sure of it.

A small dark figure launched itself in the shortening distance between us like a goblin from nowhere, all arms and legs, ungainly but fast. He banged into Keith and knocked him off balance, setting him reeling and windmilling backwards.

Toby . . . *Toby*.

Keith let go of Neil. I shoved my small son away from him in a frenzy. The gasoline spilled out of the can and over Keith's legs in a glittering stream. Staggering, trying to evade the fuel, Keith knocked into the stand containing the torch. It rocked; rocked back and forwards and then overbalanced; started the flame falling in a deadly arc downwards.

I lunged forwards, snatched up Toby with my right arm, scooped Neil into my left, lifted them both off their feet and turned in the same movement to escape.

There was a great whoosh at our backs and a blast of heat and sizzling fire as if the whole air were burning. I caught a split-second glimpse, looking over my shoulder, of Keith with his mouth open as if he, this time, would scream. He seemed to take a deep breath to yell and fire rushed into his open mouth as if drawn by bellows into his lungs, and he made no sound at all, but clutched at his chest, his eyes wide, with white showing all round, and he fell face down in an accelerating fireball.

The back of my own shirt was scorching from neck to waist, and Toby's hair was on fire. I ran with the boys in my arms, ran far enough down the aisle and tripped and fell over, dropping Neil, rolling onto my back and rubbing Toby's hair with my hands.

Desperate moments. Neil smelled of gasoline, Toby also, and there were fires, a maze of fires, to traverse on the way out.

I lay momentarily panting for breath, collecting some strength, my left arm curving round Neil who was crying. I struggled to reassure Toby; and then from far above fell a blessed mist of drizzling drops of water, cooling, life-giving, spitting and sizzling on all the small fires around us, blackening the flames to extinction and turning to a smoking ruin the humped shape of Keith.

Toby leaned on my chest, staring into my face as if he couldn't bear to look anywhere else.

He said, "He was going to set fire to you, wasn't he, Dad?"

"Yes, he was."

"I thought so."

"Where did you come from?" I asked.

"Out of the dining room, where we had lunch. I was hiding . . ." His eyes were stretched. "I was *scared,* Dad." Water ran through his singed hair and into his eyes.

"Anyone would be." I rubbed my fist over his back, loving him. "You have the courage of ten thousand heroes."

I fought for words. "It isn't every boy who knows he saved his father's life."

I could see it wasn't enough for him. There had to be more, something to give him a permanent feeling of self-worth, to steady him, keep him always in command of himself.

I thought of his little figure launching itself at an impossibly threatening target, arms and legs flying everywhere, but achieving the aim.

I said, "Would you like to learn karate, when we get home?"

His strained face split into a blazing smile. He wiped the trickling water away from his mouth. "Oh *yes,* Dad," he said.

I sat up, still hugging both of them, and Christopher came running, and the other two also, all of them staring beyond me to the blackened and unimaginable horror.

"Don't go down there," I said, pushing myself to my feet. "Where's Colonel Gardner?"

"We couldn't find him," Christopher said.

"But . . . the sprinkler?"

"I turned it on, Dad," Christopher said. "I saw Henry sticking all those labels on, the day you went on the train. I knew where the tap was."

"Brilliant," I said; but there weren't any words good enough. "Well, let's get out of here, out of the rain."

Neil wanted to be carried. I picked him up and he wound his arms round my neck, clinging tightly, and all six of us, soaking wet, made our slowish way out to the tarmac.

Roger drove up in his jeep, got out, and stared at us.

We must, I supposed, have looked odd. One tall boy, one little boy, clinging, the three others close, all dripping.

I said to Christopher, "Run and turn off the tap," and to Roger, "We had a fire in the big top. Bits of gasoline-soaked matting and floorboards burned, but Henry was right, the canvas didn't."

"A *fire!*" He turned towards the entrance, to go and see for himself.

"Better warn you," I said. "Keith's in there. He's dead."

Roger paused for one stride and then went on. Christopher came back from the errand, and all of the boys and I began shivering, as much, I supposed, from shock and anxiety as from standing wet in the light April breeze, in air too cold for comfort.

"Get into the car," I said, pointing at Dart's beaten-up wheels. "You need to get dry."

"But Dad . . ."

"I'm coming with you."

They piled in as Roger came out of the tent looking worried.

"Whatever's happened?" he said urgently. "I'll have to get the police. Come into the office."

I shook my head. "First, I get the boys into dry clothes. I'll not have them catching pneumonia. I'll come back."

"But Lee . . ."

"Keith tried to burn the big top," I said. "But . . ."

"But," Roger finished, "people who try to start fires with gasoline can end up by burning themselves."

I smiled faintly. "Right."

I walked over to Dart's car and drove the boys down to the bus, where everyone, myself emphatically included, showered and changed into dry clothes down to the skin. My checked shirt, its back blackened as if pressed by a too-hot iron, went into the rubbish bin, not into a laundry bag. Underneath I felt as if sunburnt: a first-degree sore-

ness, nothing worse. Dead lucky, I thought, that the shirt
had been thick pure wool, not melting nylon.

When the boys were ready I marched them over to Mrs.
Gardner and begged her to give them hot sweet drinks and
cake, if she had any.

"My *dears,*" she said, embracing them, "come on in."

"Don't leave us, Dad," Edward said.

"I have to talk to the Colonel, but I won't be long."

"Can I come with you?" Christopher asked.

I looked at his height, listened to the already deepening
voice, saw the emerging man in the boy and his wish to
leave childhood behind.

"Hop in the car," I said and, deeply pleased, he sat
beside me on the short return journey.

"When you went up to the big top," I asked him, "what
did Keith Stratton say to you?"

"That man!" Christopher shuddered. "It seemed all right
at first. He told us to go into the big top. He said you
would be coming."

"So then?" I prompted, as he stopped.

"So we went in, and he came in behind us. He told us
to go on ahead, and we did."

"Yes."

"Then . . ." he hesitated, "it got *weird,* Dad. I mean, he
picked up a can that was lying there and took the cap off,
and we could *smell* it was gasoline. Then he put the can
down again and picked up that rod thing, and flicked his
lighter, and the end of the rod lit up like those torches in
Ku Klux Klan films."

"Yeah."

"Then he poured gasoline onto the floor and trailed
the torch into it and of course it went on fire, but just
in one place." He paused, remembering. "We began to
be scared, Dad. You've always told us never to put fire

near gasoline, and he had a big can of it in one hand and the torch in the other. He told us to go up further into the big top and he came along behind us and started another fire, and then another, and lots of them and we got really frightened, but all he said was that you would come soon. 'Your father will come.' He gave us the creeps, Dad. He didn't behave like a grown-up. He wasn't *sensible,* Dad."

"No."

"He told us to go on further in, past that sort of stand thing that was there, and he put the torch into it so that it just burned *there,* and wasn't swinging about, and that was better, but we still didn't *like* it. But he put the gasoline can down too, and then he just looked at us and *smiled,* and it was *awful,* I mean, I can't describe it."

"You're doing well."

"He frightened me rigid, Dad. We all wanted to be out of there. Then Alan darted past him suddenly and then Edward, and I did too, and he yelled at us and ran about to stop us and we dodged him and ran, I mean, *pelted,* Dad . . . and then Toby didn't come out after us, and Neil started screaming . . . and that's when you came."

I stopped the car beside Roger's jeep. Keith's Jaguar stood beyond, and beyond that, a police car.

"And he didn't say anything else?" I asked.

"No, only something about not being blackmailed by *you.* I mean, it was silly, you wouldn't blackmail anyone."

I smiled inwardly at his faith. Blackmail wasn't necessarily for money.

"No," I said. "All the same, don't repeat that bit, OK?"

"No, Dad, OK."

Feeling curiously lightheaded, I walked across to the

office with Christopher and told the police, when they asked, that I had no idea why Keith Stratton had behaved as irrationally as he had.

IT WAS FRIDAY before I left Stratton Park.

All Wednesday afternoon I replied "I don't know" to relays of police questions, and agreed that I would return dutifully for an inquest.

I said nothing about rushing at Keith to overbalance him. It didn't sound sensible. I said nothing about Neil.

When asked, I said I hadn't used a fire extinguisher to try to save Keith's life, because I couldn't find one.

"Four of them were lying out of sight in the bar area," Roger told me.

"Who put them there?" the police asked.

"I don't know," I said.

Christopher told the law that Keith was a "nutter." They listened politely enough and decided he was too young to be called as an inquest witness, as he had anyway not himself been present at the moment of the accident.

The press came; took photographs; asked questions, got the same answers.

A policewoman, in my presence, asked the younger boys later, down at the Gardners', what they'd seen, but in the manner of children with questioning strangers they clammed up into big-eyed silence, volunteering nothing and answering mainly in nods. Yes—nod—there had been fires in the tent. Yes—nod—Keith Stratton had lit them. Yes—nod—Toby's hair had got singed. Yes—nod—Christopher had turned on the sprinkler, and yes—nod—their father had looked after them.

The Strattons, I thought ironically at one point, had

nothing on the Morris family when it came to keeping things quiet.

On Thursday the staples came out of my mostly healed cuts and, with Dart chauffeuring, I took Toby to Swindon to see what Penelope could do with his unevenly burned hair.

I watched her laugh with him and tease him. Watched her wash the still lingering singe smell out, and cut and brush and blow-dry the very short remaining brown curls. Watched her give him confidence in his new appearance and light up his smile.

I spent the whole time wondering where and how I could get her into bed.

Perdita came downstairs behaving like a mother hen defending her chick against predators, as if reading my mind.

"I told you too much, dear, on Tuesday," she said a shade anxiously.

"I won't give you away."

"And Keith Stratton is dead!"

"So sad," I agreed.

She laughed. "You're a rogue. Did you kill him?"

"In a way." With help from my twelve-year-old, I thought, whether he realized it or not. "Self-defense, you might say."

Her eyes smiled, but her voice was sober. She used only one word for an opinion. *"Good."*

Penelope finished the twelve-year-old's hair. I paid her. She thanked me. She had no idea what I felt for her, nor gave any flicker of response. I was six boys' father, almost double her age. Perdita, seeing all, patted my shoulder. I kissed the cheek of the mother and still lusted for the daughter, and walked away, with Toby, feeling empty and old.

Dart returned Toby to his brothers at the Gardners' and willingly took me on to see Marjorie.

The manservant, aplomb in place, let us in and announced us. Marjorie sat, as before, in her commanding armchair. The smashed looking-glass had been removed, the torn chairs were missing. Rebecca's shot at me had left no permanent traces.

"I came to say goodbye," I said.

"But you'll come back to Stratton Park."

"Probably not."

"But we need you!"

I shook my head. "You have a great racecourse manager in Colonel Gardner. You'll have record crowds at the next meeting, with Oliver Wells's flair for publicity. You'll commission superb new stands—and what I will do, if you like, is make sure any firms submitting proposals to you are substantial and trustworthy. And beyond that, as regards your family, you have more power than ever to hold things together. You don't have Keith, so you don't need any way of restraining him. You have control of Rebecca, who aimed—probably still aims—to run the racecourse herself. She has probably done herself in there, as, even after you're gone, Conrad and Dart can both hold blackmail and attempted murder over her head, enough to out-vote her at Board meetings."

Marjorie listened and came up with her own sort of solution.

"I want you," she said, "to be a director. Conrad and Ivan and I will vote for it. Unanimous decision of the Board."

"Hear, hear," Dart said, delighted.

"You don't need me," I protested.

"Yes, we do."

I wanted to disentangle myself from the Strattons. I did not want to step in any way into my non-grandfather's shoes. From beyond the grave his influence and way of doing things had sucked me into a web of duplicity, and three times in a week his family had nearly cost me my life. I'd paid my debt to him, I thought. I needed now to be free.

And yet . . .

"I'll think about it," I said.

Marjorie nodded, satisfied. "With you in charge," she said, "the racecourse will prosper."

"I have to talk to Conrad," I said.

HE WAS ALONE in his holy of holies, sitting behind his desk.

I'd left Dart again outside in his car, reading about hair loss, though not acting as lookout this time.

"With this American system," he said, deep in before-and-after photographs, "I would never worry again. You can go swimming—diving—your new hair is part of you. But I'd have to go to America every six weeks to two months to keep it right."

"You can afford it," I said.

"Yes, but . . ."

"Go for it," I said.

He needed encouragement. "Do you really think I should?"

"I think you should book your first ticket at once."

"Yes. *Yes.* Well, yes, I *will.*"

Conrad stood up when I went in. His cupboard door was closed, but boxes stood higgledy-piggledy on his carpet, their contents stirred up.

He didn't offer his hand. He seemed to feel awkward, as I did myself.

"Marjorie telephoned," he said. "She says she wants you on the Board. She says I'm to persuade you."

"It's your own wishes that matter."

"I don't know . . ."

"No. Well, I didn't come to talk about that. I came to return what I stole from you yesterday."

"Only yesterday! So much has happened."

I put on his desk the outer brown envelope marked "Conrad." He picked it up, looking at the sticky-tape closure.

"Like I told you," I said, "I did look inside. Keith knew I would look. I don't think he could bear the thought of my using what I learned. I confess that I'm glad I don't have to, as he's dead, but I would have done, and you'd better know that. But I'll not tell Marjorie what's in there—it's evident she doesn't know—and I'll never tell anyone else."

"I don't want to open it," Conrad said, putting the envelope down.

"I can't say that you should."

"But you think so."

"Keith would have burned it," I said.

"Burned." He shuddered. "What a death!"

"Anyway," I said, "the knowledge belongs here, whatever you do with it. Your father meant you to have it. So," I sighed, "read it or burn it, but don't leave it lying about." I paused. "I apologize again for breaking in here. I'll be leaving Stratton Park in the morning. I'm sorry," I made a vague gesture, "for everything."

I turned regretfully and made for the door.

"Wait," Conrad said.

I paused, half in, half out.

"I have to know what you know." He looked wretched. "He was my twin. I know he envied me . . . I know it wasn't fair that I had so much just for being twenty-five minutes older, I know he was violent and cruel and often dangerous, I know he beat your mother and all his wives. I know he nearly killed Hannah's gypsy. I saw him kick you abominably . . . I know all that and more, but he was my brother, my *twin.*"

"Yes."

The Strattons, whatever their faults, had their own tight indestructible loyalty; a family, whatever their internal fights, that closed ranks against the ordinary world.

Conrad picked up the envelope and ripped off the tape.

He reread the first letter, then drew out the second letter and the white inner envelope.

"Remember," he murmured, reading, "that Keith always tells lies . . ."

He removed the five folded sheets of paper from the white envelope and read the top one, yet another short note from his father.

It said:

> This lie of Keith's cost me a great deal of money, which I gave to Keith himself, too trustingly. It took me many years to suspect that he'd robbed me. A small matter, compared with the truth.

Conrad put the note down and looked at the next sheet, another letter, but in typescript.

"Arne Verity Laboratories?" Conrad said. "Who are they?"

He read the letter, which was addressed to his father, and dated two years earlier.

In essence, it said that the laboratory had conducted the requested analyses. The detailed results of each separate analysis were appended but, summarizing, the results were as follows:

You sent us three hairs, labeled "A," "B," and "C."
The results of DNA analysis are:
"A" is almost certainly the parent of "B"
and
"A" and "B" are the parents of "C."

Conrad looked up. "What does it mean?"
"It means there was no gypsy. Keith invented him."
"But . . ."
"It means that Keith was the father of Jack."

CONRAD SAT DOWN and looked faint.

"I don't believe it," he breathed. "I can't. It's not true."

"Jack doesn't look like a gypsy," I said. "He looks like Keith."

"Oh dear God . . ."

"Hannah doesn't like the gypsy story. She tells Jack his father was a foreign aristocrat who would have been ruined by the scandal. Apart from the foreign bit, that's more or less true."

"Hannah!" He looked even more distressed. "What are you going to do about *her?*"

"Nothing," I said, surprised he should ask. "With Keith dead, I don't need to use what I know. Hannah is safe from it ever leaking out through me."

"But she attacked you!"

I sighed. "She never had a chance, did she? She was conceived in rape, abandoned by her mother and impregnated by her father. She was rejected by young men and not loved by her grandfather but, whatever he may be, she has Jack, her son. I'll not spoil that for her. In the same way that Keith was your twin, Hannah, whether I like it or not, is my half-sister. Let her alone."

Conrad sat without moving for a long minute, then he shoveled his father's letters and the laboratory reports into the outer brown envelope and held out the whole package in my direction.

"Take it," he said succinctly, "and burn it."

"Yes, OK."

I went back to the desk and, taking the envelope, set out again for the door.

"Come on the Board," Conrad said. "As usual, Marjorie has it right. We're going to need you."

THE BOYS AND Mrs. Gardner said farewells as lengthily as Romeo and Juliet, with many promises of meeting again. Roger and I, less effusively, were nonetheless pleased at the prospect of working together in the future. "Such a lot to see to," Roger said.

Dart produced a diary. He would come to stay, he said, *after* he had been to America. He had, he said, made bookings.

The boys piled into the bus and waved like maniacs through the windows, and I drove us all away, back home to the peaceful Surrey-Sussex border.

"Did you have a good time, my darlings?" Amanda asked, embracing the children. "What did you find to do while your father was busy getting himself into the newspapers?"

They gazed at her. Bit by bit they would no doubt tell her, but at that moment the question struck them dumb.

Neil finally said, earnestly, "We made brilliant fruit-cakes."

Amanda told me reproachfully, "The phone here has been ringing non-stop." She looked me over without much concern. "I suppose you're all right?"

"Yes," I said. "Fine."

"Good."

She took the children indoors. I stood by the bus, its

engine cooling, and after a while I went and climbed into the oak.

Other trees might be flushing into leaf, but the oak as always hung back, vying with the ash to be the last turning green. I sat in the cradle of the fuzzy boughs, feeling the residual aches and soreness in my body, stretching for quiet in my mind.

After a while Amanda came out of the house and crossed to the tree.

"What are you doing up there?" she asked.

"Considering things."

"Come down. I want to talk to you."

I climbed down, not wanting to hear.

I said, "I was afraid I would return to an empty house. Afraid you and Jamie might have gone."

Her eyes widened. "You always know too damned much."

"I was afraid you'd met someone else."

"Yes, I have."

She wasn't exactly defiant, but she had already thought out what she wanted to say. She still looked lovely. I wished things were different.

"I've decided," she said, "that a formal separation from you wouldn't be good for the children. Also . . ." she slightly hesitated and then screwed up the courage, ". . . he is married, and feels the same about his own family. So we will see each other often. Take it or leave it, Lee."

She waited.

Christopher, Toby, Edward, Alan, Neil and Jamie. Six reasons.

"I'll take it," I said.

She nodded, making a pact of it, and returned to the house.

At bedtime she went up to our room an hour earlier than I, as always, but when I went up she was for once wide awake.

"Did you find a ruin?" she asked, as I undressed.

"No. I'll go looking once the boys are back at school. I'll go off for a while."

"Good."

It wasn't good. It was terrible.

Instead of lying the customary five feet away from her I went round to her side of the huge bed and climbed in beside her: and I made love to Penelope in Amanda, in a turmoil of lust, deprivation, hunger, passion and penetration. A wild, rough sexual action unlike anything before in our marriage.

She responded, after the briefest of protestations and withdrawal, with some of her original ardor, and lay afterwards apart from me, separate again, not full of recriminations but with her mouth curving in a secretive, cat-with-cream smile.

Two months later she said, "I'm pregnant. Did you know?"

"I wondered," I said. I screwed myself to the question. "Is it mine . . . or *his?*"

"Oh, yours," she said positively. "He can't give me a child. He had a vasectomy too long ago."

"Oh."

"It might be a girl," Amanda said coolly. "You always wanted a daughter."

In the fullness of time she gave rapturous birth to her seventh child.

A boy.

Fine by me.

Turn the page for a revealing look at
Dick Francis's
newest bestselling suspense novel,

WILD HORSES

Ride back into the volatile world of
thoroughbred racing with film director Thomas Lyon,
who uncovers a long-unsolved mystery first revealed
by a dying friend. Although he needs to know more,
he soon finds out he already knows too much—
and must use all his imagination and cunning
simply to stay alive.

Look for *Wild Horses* in hardcover
from G. P. Putnam's Sons

D YING SLOWLY of bone cancer the old man, shriveled now, sat as ever in his great armchair, tears of lonely pain sliding down crepuscular cheeks.

That Tuesday, his last, his stringy grip on my wrist tightened convulsively in a long silence while I watched his mouth tremble and move in abortive struggles to speak.

"Father." The words finally wavered out; a whisper, desperate, driven by ultimate need. "Father, I must make my confession. I must ask . . . absolution."

In great surprise and with compassion I said, "But . . . I'm not a priest."

He paid no attention. The feeble voice, a truer measure of affairs than the fiercely clutching hand, simply repeated, "Father . . . forgive me."

"Valentine," I said reasonably, "I'm Thomas. Thomas Lyon. Don't you remember? I come to read to you."

He could no longer see newsprint or anything straight ahead, though peripheral vision partly remained. I called in more or less every week, both to keep him up to date with the racing columns in the newspapers and also to let his beleaguered and chronically tired old sister go out for shopping and gossip.

I hadn't actually read to him on that day. When I arrived he'd been suffering badly from one of his intermittent bouts of agony, with Dorothea, his sister, feeding him a teaspoon of liquid morphine and giving him whiskey and water to help the numbness work faster.

He hadn't felt well enough for the racing papers.

"Just sit with him," Dorothea begged. "How long can you stay?"

"Two hours."

She'd kissed me gratefully on the cheek, stretching on tiptoes, and had hurried away, plump in her late seventies, forthright in mind.

I sat as usual on a tapestry stool right beside the old man, as he liked the physical contact, as if to make up for sight.

The fluttery voice persisted, creeping effortlessly into the quiet room, determined and intimate. "I confess to God Almighty and to Thee, my Father, that I have sinned exceedingly . . . and I must confess . . . before . . . before . . ."

"Valentine," I repeated more sharply, "I'm not a priest."

It was as if he hadn't heard. He seemed to be focusing all the energy left in him into one extraordinary spiritual gamble, a last throw of hell-defeating dice on the brink of the abyss.

"I ask pardon for my mortal sin . . . I ask peace with God . . ."

I protested no more. The old man knew he was dying; knew death was near. In earlier weeks he had discussed with equanimity, and even with humor, his lack of a future. He had reminisced about his long life. He'd told me he had left me all his books in his will. Never had he made any mention of even the most rudimentary religious belief, except to remark once that the idea of life after death was a load of superstitious twaddle.

I hadn't known he was a Roman Catholic.

"I confess," he said, " . . . that I killed him . . . God, forgive me. I humbly ask pardon . . . I pray to God Almighty to have mercy on me . . ."

"Valentine . . ."

"I left the knife with Derry and I killed the Cornish boy and I've never said a word about that week and I accuse myself . . . and I lied about everything . . . mea culpa . . . I've done such harm . . . I destroyed their lives . . . and they didn't know, they went on liking me . . . I despise myself . . . all this time. Father, give me a penance . . . and say the words . . . say them . . . *Ego te absolvo* . . . I forgive your sins in the name of the Father . . . I beg you . . . I beg you . . ."

I had never heard of the sins he was talking about. His words tumbled out as if on the edge of delirium, making no cohesive sense. I thought it most likely that his sins were dreams; that he was confused, imagining great guilt where none lay.

There was no mistaking, however, the frantic nature of his repeated plea.

"Father, absolve me. Father, say the words . . . say them, I beg you."

I couldn't see what harm it would do. He was desperate to die in peace. Any priest would have given him absolution: who was I cruelly to withhold it? I was not of his faith. I would square it later, I thought, with my own immortal soul.

So I said what he wanted. Said the words, dredging them from memory. Said them in Latin, as he would clearly understand them, because they seemed less of a lie that way than in bald English.

"*Ego te absolvo*," I said.

I felt a shiver through my body. Superstition, I thought.

I remembered more words. They floated on my tongue. "*Ego te absolvo a peccatis tuis in nomine Patris et Filii et Spiritus Sancti. Amen.*"

I absolve you from your sins in the name of the Father and of the Son and of the Holy Ghost. Amen.

The greatest blasphemy of my life to date. God forgive me my sin, I thought.

MUCH LATER IN the day, I drove back to my job, although I was a good hour late for the script conference I'd called for five-thirty. I did not apologize, having found that the bunch I was working with took regrets for weakness, chiefly because of their own personal insecurities. It was essential, I understood, for them to regard me as rock, even if to myself sometimes the rock was no more durable than compressed sand.

It was disastrously easy to make bad horseracing pictures and only possible to do it at bankable level, in my view, if racing became the framing background to human drama. I'd been given the present job for three reasons that I knew of, the third being that I'd previously stood two animal stories on their heads with profitable results, the second being that I'd been trained in my work in Hollywood, the source of finance for the present epic, and—firstly—that I'd spent my childhood and teens in racing stables and might be considered to know the industrial terrain.

We were ten days into production: that is to say that we had shot about one sixth of the picture, or, putting it another way, roughly twenty minutes a day of usable footage, whole cloth from which the final film would be cut. We'd been scheduled to finish in sixty working days; a span of under ten weeks, as rest days were precious and rare. I, as director, decided which scenes would actually be shot on which days, though I'd made and distributed in advance a shooting schedule to which we mostly adhered.

"As you've seen," I said generally, "these changes mean that tomorrow we'll be shooting on the railed forecourt in front of the Jockey Club's headquarters in the High Street. Cars arrive and leave through the gates. The local police will help with the town's regular traffic from eleven to twelve only, so all of our arrivals and departures will be condensed into that time. The Jockey Club has agreed to our using their front door for entering and leaving shots. The internal sets have, of course, been built here in this house. You three," I said to the actors, "can put some useful poison into your various encounters. George, be sly. Iago stuff. You are now secretly engineering Cibber's downfall."

The scriptwriter moaned, "That's not the right interpretation. I don't like what you've made me do. Those two are very good friends."

"Only up to the point of opportunist betrayal," I said.

Howard Tyler, the writer, had already complained about small earlier changes to the producer, to the accountant, and to the film company's top brass, all without getting me fired. I could put up with his animosity in the same way as I stifled irritation at his round granny glasses, his relentlessly prim little mouth, and his determination to insert long, pointless silences where only movement and action would fill theater seats. He adored convoluted unspoken subtleties that were beyond most actors' powers. He should have stuck to the voluminous moody novels from whence he came.

His book that he'd adapted for the present film was loosely based on a real-life story, a twenty-six-year-old Newmarket racing scandal very successfully hushed up. Howard's fictional version purported to be the truth, but almost certainly wasn't, as none of the still living real participants had shown the slightest sign of indignant rebuttal.

"You'll find you each have a plan of the Jockey Club forecourt," I said to the meeting. They nodded, flicking over pages. "Also," I went on, "you've made a list of the order of shooting, with approximate times. The three cars involved will be driven to the forecourt first thing in the morning. Get all the crews alerted so that lights and cameras can be set up where shown on the plan. If everyone's willing and ready, we should finish well before the daylight yellows. Any questions?"

There were always questions. To ask a question meant attention had been paid and, as often happened, it was actors with the smallest parts who asked most. George, in this case, wanted to know how his character would develop from the extra scene. Only, I enlightened him, as just one more factor in Cibber's troubles. Cibber, eventually, would crack. Bang. Fireworks. Cibber said, "Hallelujah," gratefully. George compressed his mouth.

"But they were friends," Howard repeated stubbornly.

"As we discussed," I said mildly, "if Cibber cracks, your motivation makes better sense."

He opened his little mouth, saw everyone else nodding, folded his lips, and began to act as if Cibber's cracking was all his own idea.

"If it rains tomorrow," I said, "we'll shoot the internal Jockey Club scenes instead and trust it will be fine on Thursday. We are due to complete the first Newmarket segment on Saturday. On Sunday, as I think you know, we're shifting the horses forty miles west to Huntingdon racecourse; to the stable block there. Actors and technicians will travel early on Monday morning. Rehearsals, Monday, from noon onward. Shooting Tuesday to Friday, return here the following weekend. Ed will distribute times and running order to everyone concerned. OK? Oh, and by the way, the rushes from yesterday are fine. Thought you'd like to know. It was a lot of hard work, but worth it."

The resulting sighs round the table came from relief. We'd spent the whole day in the stable yard, the human action in the foreground taking place against a background of routine equine life. Never could rows of horses have been mucked out, fed, watered, and groomed more times in any twelve hours before: but we had enough shots in the can to give the fictional stable unending life.

The script meeting over, everyone dispersed except a tall, thin, disjointed-looking man in an untidy beard and unkempt clothes whose unimpressive appearance hid an artistic confidence as unassailable as granite. He raised his eyebrows. I nodded. He slouched in his seat and waited until all backs but our own had passed through the door.

"You wanted me to stay?" he asked. "Ed said."

"Yes."

Every film with any hope of acclaimed success needed an eye that saw all life as through a camera lens. Someone to whom focus and light intensities were extrasensory dimensions taken for granted. His title on the credits might variously be "cinematographer" or "director of photography." I'd had a mathematical friend once who said he thought in algebra; Moncrieff, director of photography, thought in moving light and shadows.

We were used to each other. This was our third film together. I'd been disconcerted the first time by his surrealist sense of humor, then seen that it was the aquifer of

his geysers of visual genius, then felt that to work without
him would leave me nakedly exposed in the realm of
translating my own perceptions into revelations on the
screen. When I told Moncrieff what I wanted an audience to understand, he could instinctively slant a lens to
achieve it.

We had once staged a "last rites" scene for a man about
to be murdered by terrorists; the ultimate cruelty of that
wicked blasphemy had been underscored by Moncrieff's
lighting of the faces: the petrified victim, the sweating
priest, and the hard men's absence of mercy. *Ego te
absolvo* . . . it had brought me death threats by post.

On that Tuesday in Newmarket I asked Moncrieff, "Have
you seen the railings outside the Jockey Club? The ones
enclosing the private parking forecourt?"

"Tall and black? Yes."

"I want a shot that emphasizes the barrier qualities. I
want to establish the way the railings shut out everyone
but the elite. Inside can be mandarins of racing. Outside,
hoi polloi."

Moncrieff nodded.

I said, "I also want to give an impression that the people
inside, Cibber and George, the Jockey Club members, are
themselves prisoners in their own conventions. Behind
bars, one might say."

Moncrieff nodded.

"And," I said, "take a five-second shot of the hinges of
the gates as they open, also as they close."

"Right."

"The scene between Cibber and George is shot to begin
with from outside the bars. I'd like the zoo aspect made
clear. Then track the lens forward between the railings to
establish where they're standing. The rest of that conversation is in close-ups."

Moncrieff nodded. He seldom made notes while we talked, but he would write a meticulous worksheet before bedtime.

"We're not being judgmental," I said. "Not heavy-handed. No great social stance. Just a fleeting impression."

"A feather touch," Moncrieff said. "Got you."

"Contributing to Cibber's crack-up," I said.

He nodded.

"I'll get Howard to write that crack-up tomorrow," I said. "It's mainly a matter of a shift in intensity from the calm scene already in the script. Howard just needs to put some juice into it."

"Howard's juice is watered cranberry." Moncrieff picked up a vodka bottle from among the drinks clutter and squinted at it against the light. "Empty," he commented morosely. "Have you tried vodka and cranberry juice? It's disgusting."

Howard drank it all the time.

"Howard," Moncrieff said, "is radioactive waste. You can't get rid of it safely."

He knew as well as I did that Howard Tyler's name on the billboards would bring to the film both the lending library audience and attention from upmarket critics. Howard Tyler won prestigious prizes and had received honorary doctorates on both sides of the Atlantic. Moncrieff and I were considered lucky to be working with such a luminous figure.

Few authors could, or even wanted to, write screenplays of their own novels; Howard Tyler had been nominated for an Oscar at his first attempt and subsequently refused to sell his film rights unless the package included himself. Moncrieff and I were stuck with Howard, to put it briefly, as fast as it seemed he was stuck with me.

Our producer, bald, sixty, a heavily framed American, had put a canny deal together for the company. Big name author (Howard), proven camera wizard (Moncrieff), vastly successful producer (himself), and young-but-experienced director (T. Lyon), all allied to one mega-star (male) and one deliciously pretty new actress; money spent on the big names and saved on the actress and me. He, producer O'Hara, had told me once that in the matter of acting talent it was a waste of resources employing five big stars in any one picture. One great star would bring in the customers and maybe two could be afforded. Get more and the costs would run away with the gross.

O'Hara had taught me a lot about finance and Moncrieff a lot about illusion. I'd begun to feel recently that I finally understood my trade—but was realistic enough to know that at any minute I could judge everything wrong and become an artistic cropper. If public reaction could be reliably foretold, there would be no flops. No one could ever be sure about public taste: it was as fickle as horseracing luck.

O'Hara, that Tuesday, was already in the Bedford Lodge hotel dining room when I joined him for dinner. The studio bosses liked him to keep an eye on what I was doing and report back. He marched into operations accordingly week by week, sometimes from London, sometimes from California, spending a couple of days watching the shooting and an evening with me going over the state of the budget and the time schedule. Owing to his sensible planning in the first place, I hoped we would come in under budget and with a couple of days to spare, which would encourage any future employers to believe I had organizational talents.

"Yesterday's rushes were good, and this morning went well," O'Hara said objectively. "Where did you get to this afternoon? Ed couldn't find you."

I paused with a glass of studio-impressing Perrier halfway to my mouth, remembering vividly the rasping of Valentine's breath.

"I was here in Newmarket," I said, putting down the water. "I've a friend who's dying. I called to see him."

"Oh." O'Hara showed no censure, registering the explanation as a reason, not an excuse. He knew anyway—and took it for granted—that I'd started work at six that morning and would put in eighteen hours most days until we'd completed the shooting.

"Is he a film man?" O'Hara asked.

"No. Racing . . . a racing writer."

"Oh. Nothing to do with us, then."

"No," I said.

Ah well. One can get things wrong.